THE ARTISAN

Elser glanced at the callous faces, the grinning
SS officer, the dead eyes of the other guards
who had accompanied them into the
mortuary, then looked back to the charring
flesh and powdering bone as slowly the body
sank back into the flames. Tears of compassion
appeared in Elser's eyes. The man may have
been nothing to these functionaries of the
Third Reich, but once he must have had hopes
and dreams and a belief in the future. That,
no matter in which country they were born,
was the birthright of any man. The prisoners
in charge of the mortuary slammed the oven's
iron doors shut as Elser continued to stare. He
had come home to Hitler's Germany.

Also in Arrow by Stephen Sheppard

MONTE CARLO

The Artisan

STEPHEN SHEPPARD

ARROW BOOKS

Arrow Books Limited
62-65 Chandos Place, London WC2N 4NW

An imprint of Century Hutchinson Ltd

London Melbourne Sydney Auckland
Johannesburg and agencies throughout
the world

First published by Century Hutchinson 1986
Arrow edition 1986

Printed and bound in Great Britain by
Anchor Brendon Limited, Tiptree, Essex

ISBN 0 09 945260 X

Prologue

The ticking of the clock stopped. For a split second there was silence then four strikers hit the bell and chimed the hour. Georg Elser smiled with satisfaction, rewound the mechanism and carefully slid it into the cabinet he had created as a housing. More than a box and less than a work of art, the clock would be a proud possession of a middle-class burger somewhere in Switzerland or what had once been the Habsburg Empire.

Elser had worked in the small factory outside Zurich for several years, and although he was surrounded by other workers at their own benches, in the main he kept much to himself. He looked up at the 'official' wall clock, which showed almost midday, and was saddened at the implications – what a way for it all to end, just as he was becoming proficient and, indeed, proud of his abilities. He looked around the workshop. Some of the benches were already empty. Those that were occupied contained concentrated workers examining seemingly complicated mechanisms. At the back of the workroom was the glass-panelled door behind which the old proprietor was slumped in his seat at the desk he had inherited not only from his father, but his grandfather before him.

At twelve o'clock, chimes pealed, bells rang and cuckoo clocks plaintively declared the end of the morning and unknowingly, that day, the end of the family business. Elser heard the three cars draw up outside. The entrance doors were flung open, and suddenly the place resounded with the feet of strangers, bureaucrats and uniformed officials. Business had not been good for some time, they all knew; that it should come to this had been unthinkable, until unknown influences had brought pressure to bear on two banks to call in their loans.

The officials pasted a document on the glass door, before allowing the proprietor out. The old man with the grey moustache was in tears. He shrugged, a futile gesture and a substitute for words of thanks to his workers, who had been told, but disbelieved that this could happen. They began to pack their belongings and, one by one, shook hands with the old man as the heartless strangers bustled about, measuring the rooms and checking goods against an inventory.

Georg Elser shook hands with the old man. 'You have your last wages in the envelope?' Elser nodded. 'You have taken something to remember us by?'

A voice behind the inventory list, overhearing, said, 'He takes nothing, everything stays.'

Elser smiled at the old man and nodded. In his case were two Westminster clock mechanisms, wrapped carefully in an old cardigan.

The old man escorted Elser to the front door, his eyes still wet with tears, ineffectually angry at the ostentatious efficiency of these bustling bureaucrats around him. 'Did you keep your tools?' he whispered. Elser nodded. 'They are very valuable to a man with skill.' Elser smiled. 'Thank you,' said the old man, his voice breaking. 'It's the times we live in, I suppose. Things are changing so fast and I suppose I'm just too old. I never thought this would happen. Two centuries of tradition – gone.' He sniffed and wiped his nose on the sleeve of his worn shirt. 'And where will you go now, young man?' Elser shrugged. The two men were now standing outside the entrance where Elser's bicycle lay against the wall.

'Go home,' advised the old man, giving counsel from the heart. Georg Elser sighed deeply and looked to the north-east. Winter was over, the sky was clear and a light breeze ruffled his hair.

'It's been a long time, hasn't it?' stated the old man. Elser nodded. 'You'll find something,' he murmured. Elser took the handlebars of his bicycle and began to wheel it across the courtyard.

'Remember us!' waved the old man. Elser waved back, taking a last look at the stocky figure with the bald head, grey moustache and good heart.

'Write!' he shouted. Elser smiled. 'And do something big!' laughed the old man through his tears, making a huge gesture. 'I want to be proud of you!'

Elser climbed on his bicycle and began to pedal towards Germany.

1

A solitary figure strode ahead of his entourage along the narrow, red-carpeted corridor then halted before a small door. An aide, in uniform, opened the entrance to what had once been a royal box, and the several generals followed their leader to seats overlooking the entire opera house.

For a moment, the group remained on their feet, looking below at the serried ranks standing in evening dress, responding to the arrival with loud applause. A small gesture curtailed the ovation and, as the lights slowly dimmed, the audience re-seated themselves in anticipation of the overture, which began a beat after complete silence was restored.

Quietly at first, the notes of inspiration built to a melody, created an impetus, then hit a crescendo which was maintained by the sheer genius of composition.

The eyes of Adolf Hitler half closed as memory traced his path to power. The music was stimulating and seductively gilded the raw facts of the history of a man who had become Führer of Greater Germany. He began to cast his mind into the future beyond the early spring of 1938, into the summer of the year that would follow and the prospects for his people, his country, his ambitions.

The overture swelled to a finale, having outlined the story of a young man with a will and a purpose to fulfil – a revolutionary who had wished to change his world. Based on a real fourteenth century Roman dictator who had emerged from the masses, the opera described how he had rallied the people and led a successful revolt to be proclaimed leader, even by the nobility.

More than thirty years had passed since Hitler had first seen the story in the Austrian town of Linz. Walking back under a night sky with a school companion, something had remained in him and grown. An empathy with the character rapidly crystallized to an unshakeable belief that, like Rienzi, he would dedicate himself to the people and establish for the German nation a freedom, the like of which they had never dreamed. He remembered the moment well when Kubizek had gone home and he had spent the rest of the night alone under the stars. Destiny had brought him from that point in time when it had all begun and must take him onwards to the reality he had conceived for a glorious future.

The beginning of the opera, as he knew, was full of expectation, the struggle, the fight, the vanquishing of all opposition so far different from the end, which, hours later, would describe how, deserted and betrayed, the acclaimed young tribune of the people is struck down. Hitler watched the lights come up on the stage as the overture finished, and in the sudden silence, the dark curtain within the proscenium arch began to rise on the first act. He contented himself with thoughts of the drama to come, ignoring the fact that the opera had been created from history as a tragedy. Voices rose from the stage to the very back of the great auditorium – Wagner's *Rienzi* had begun . . .

Spring had arrived on Lake Constance. Although the weather remained crisp, flowers began to emerge amidst the grassy banks of the shoreline, and the glass-smooth water beyond only shimmered as vespers played upon its surface, disturbing the huge cumulus reflections which spread into the distance, where a small town sprawled on the border of Switzerland. The railway line that appeared beside the road and skirted the shore came out of a black tunnel as if from another world.

Hesitant birds in the peace of late morning conveyed messages of anticipation as a cyclist appeared, pushing on his pedals with the tiredness of a man who has travelled far. Bags over the rear wheel of his bicycle were the only possessions he carried. The man, in his early thirties, had a shock of dark hair, cropped above the ears, worn jacket and trousers, and a soiled shirt, open at the collar. He wiped sweat from his face and glanced ahead: he was almost there. For Georg Elser, the view was more than compensation for his efforts.

The train from Zurich roared out of the tunnel, disturbing the peace with the noise of wheels on steel, blasting steam and smoke as it moved towards the frontier, ever nearer its destination of Munich.

On the footplate, the engine driver signalled to the stoker to come to the cabin side. He leaned on an elbow as his other arm expertly adjusted the long accelerator lever, and looked out at the lakeshore. The stoker grinned, seeing the narrow road and, up ahead, the solitary cyclist just below the steel rail and shallow gravel embankment, slowly meandering towards the customs and police control station ahead. The driver indicated the steam valve and the stoker's grin widened. Only now did the cyclist register the fast-approaching train and glance over his shoulder at the huge engine bearing down towards him. He noted on the boiler above the wide lamp set like a single eye in a dark face, twin flags, both predominantly red, their short poles straining against the rush of air. One bore an emblem of a white cross, the other a white circle containing a black swastika. Switzerland and Germany – side by side.

Curiosity satisfied, the cyclist turned back to estimate the final distance to the border. Parallel to the bicycle for a moment, the engine suddenly exhaled loudly like a great beast, enveloping the cyclist in a blast of steam so that even the early buds appeared to shrink back from their branches as the hot mist rolled across the roadway. The cyclist wobbled, looking up with alarm at wheels and pistons thundering past. The engine driver waved, mouthing that it was only a joke. The cyclist put both feet on the ground as the full passenger coaches passed quickly, with faces at the windows laughing down at his limp figure. Georg Elser gritted his teeth and shivered as the warm moisture clinging to him cooled rapidly

11

despite the sunlight. He began pedalling again, with renewed purpose – to cross into what had been the Weimar Republic and was now the dictatorship of the Third Reich.

The guard at the border station gestured for identification. Georg Elser produced papers proving him to be dark-haired, blue-eyed, not tall but with firm features and born in Württemberg.

The guard looked up. 'Artisan?'

Elser nodded. From the border office, a wireless played a loud speech, apparently being broadcast live, exhorting what sounded like a huge audience to further solidarity of party spirit. Applause burst out together with a disturbing, crackling noise. Someone turned off the programme. The guard indicated Elser could pass, so he remounted his bicycle and, with a push, freewheeled his way across the small cobbled square to a café serving what smelled, even amidst the lingering smoke and steam of the now departed train, like real coffee. Elser propped his bicycle amongst others on a stand outside the café, took off the clips from his ankles and opened his first door in Germany for six years.

Immediately, he was almost deafened as the same voice continued the speech on a radio. Then cheering became martial music and a waitress arrived giggling as Elser put his hands over his ears and looked directly into the young girl's eyes. She blushed.

'Coffee?' The word was lost but Elser nodded. The waitress paused a moment, assessing possibilities, recognizing attractions, thinking them hers but revealing them to be the stranger's. Vulnerable but with a certain assurance, the man she had seen cross the square on a bicycle was certainly her type. She could feel the colour in her cheeks heightening as he smiled, a generous, wide-mouthed, giving smile of promise.

'With cream?' She heard herself ask. The man nodded. She sighed and turned away. So many strangers, all passing through; only she stayed on, at the insistence of her father, whose eye admonished even as she returned to the counter to operate the machine, squeezing hot water through grounds as

12

if making metal plates in a factory. While she waited for the coffee to drip, she glanced into the mirror, ignoring her father, who was already pouring beer for several of the local farmers. The stranger was in his thirties, she decided, and didn't look much from a distance, but those eyes and teeth – his smile had touched something inside her. She smoothed the skirt of her dirndl and saw, in the reflection, her cleavage emphasized by the tight corset. Perhaps he would be staying, or at least come back. He looked pale and – she sighed – interesting. Large fingers took her hands from playing with loose strands of hair, and she turned to see her father's face beside her. His beer breath bore down upon her delicate blushing features as he lifted the overfilled cup of coffee directly beneath her nose. The unshaven proprietor grunted. 'Serve,' he said.

She returned to Elser's table, where he was staring out of the window, oblivious of all but the uniforms stepping down from an armoured car that had stopped beside the guard post across the square. In his hand was a carefully broken half of a cigarette, the other half neatly placed on a packet. The waitress put down the coffee and took out some matches, lit one and offered it. Elser turned, took the light, thanked her and looked back to the border post, no longer concerned with anything other than the large poster the several uniformed men were pasting to the wall. The waitress coughed and wiped the table, bending low deliberately, but received no reaction from the stranger. The martial music stopped and again the harsh radio voice began to harangue its audience.

The young waitress sighed heavily and returned to the counter. 'A small world,' she admitted to herself. How she wished her life would change – being almost twenty and knowing only chairs and tables in a little café whilst everyone passed through and on to other destinies . . .

The portrait of the Führer of the German people was strong and imposing, made to impress, as it did, even Georg Elser. He inhaled tobacco smoke and blew it out slowly, then lifted his cup and sipped the hot coffee gingerly. The national anthem began to play through wireless static, and several other customers stood quickly as the words *Deutschland Über Alles* filled the border café. Outside, the uniformed men, back in their armoured car, drove off across the cobbles. Eyes were on the stranger as he looked from the window towards the counter and the fat proprietor, who motioned him to his feet. Georg Elser merely stared at the man then coughed and waited for the music to finish. Things had changed since he'd been away, he reflected. The Chancellor had now become Dictator, which meant it had been declared there was now one voice which spoke for the people. For all Germans.

Georg Elser inhaled deeply on the cigarette and coughed again. The music finished. As the others in the café sat down, the fat proprietor crossed slowly to the dark-haired stranger. Elser looked up.

'Pay and go,' said the fat man, wiping his hands on his dirty apron. Elser put money on the table, finished his cigarette, stubbed it out and blew smoke into the air. 'Where do you think you are?' grunted the man, referring first to the artisan and then to other customers gazing across at them both. Elser paid the pfennigs, pushed back his chair, stood up and stared. Shorter than the proprietor, he appraised him silently a moment, then smiled.

'Home,' he said.

The last half kilometre had always been the worst. The incline to the small farm had been a challenge to the boy, and now to the man it was just sheer effort. Georg Elser stepped off his bicycle and wearily began to push. There had never been a sign. There should have been, but no one had ever bothered. It was only rented property, so the care and love of a house bought and paid for had always been lacking. Now the board, nailed to the gate, declared clearly not the farm of Herr Elser and his family but *No Trespassing*. Georg Elser leaned his bicycle against the fence and stared at the dilapidated building where he had been brought up. It was

14

empty and felt dead, only the breeze played in the long grass outside the shuttered and bolted downstairs windows. Georg climbed over the chained gate, walked to the front door and pulled at the padlocks. He examined them a moment, with a professional eye and decided they were not difficult to open; but easier, he remembered, was the basement window at the back. He wandered around the house and dropped into the mud-filled brick trench, where he prised open the faulty shutter which had never had a bolt at the bottom. A small knife inserted between the windows lifted the casement catch, and in a moment he had squeezed through and was inside.

Evening sunlight from cracks and holes in other shutters penetrated the basement as Elser made his way across the familiar area to a mattress in the corner. He slumped down and lay against the damp wood panelling, surveying what had once been his room – the place of all his dreams. There were still some tools at a workbench, boxes, a cabinet, several other pieces of furniture and faded photographs; together with a painting of mountains which hung, lop-sided, in a frame on the wall. In the centre of the basement room was a panelled pillar, a support for the building but something more for Georg Elser still, as it had been for the young boy who had carved a secret place out of the brickwork.

Elser pressed hard, low, in one corner of the small beaded square, and, the panel opened to reveal a compartment. He reached in and felt with gentle fingers the instrument he had made during one long hard winter. He took out the beautifully crafted zither and held it up in the shafting pinpoints of sunlight. As he touched the strings, he heard the noise of keys turned roughly in the locks outside. Elser moved to lean against the pillar and pressed himself to the panelling as he heard the chains fall. The door was dragged open and, after a pause, a voice bellowed, 'Who's there?'

Elser held his breath. Torchlights snapped on and probed the gloom. The beams stopped on the pillar. At its base, wet mud from Elser's feet showed clearly. 'Come out!' came a guttural command. Elser slowly emerged and, for a moment, was blinded by the torches. Hands reached for him and dragged him outside, slamming him against the stucco wall. The zither fell from his grasp and one of the two men lifted his foot to stamp on it.

'Don't!' shouted Elser. The two men froze. Large-girthed and dark-uniformed, they represented the local police but looked more like militia than smartly turned out professionals.

'Well, well,' said one of them, 'so it's you!'

'Back again,' said the other. 'Papers.'

Elser fumbled for his documents of identity, presented them, then stooped quickly to retrieve the zither. 'Your mother was evicted six months ago,' said the first policeman absently as he surveyed Elser's papers. The second man's florid face grinned hugely at Elser's consternation.

'No credit, no home. She's gone north to your sister's, and now you're trespassing.' The second policeman looked up from the papers. 'Switzerland *and* a work pass! Well, well – a skilled craftsman, eh? So why did you leave?'

'To come home,' said Elser, quietly. The policemen nodded.

'Well, you'll find plenty of work here now. Times have changed. When the Führer came to power there were six million unemployed – now there are none . . . '

'You'll find something,' said the second man; then, 'Craftsman!' he added superciliously. Eyes stared in the bright twilight.

'Always were the clever one, weren't you?' said the first policeman resentfully, handing back Elser's papers.

'Why are you wearing a uniform, Herr Stadt? And you, Herr Beck . . . you were – farmers.'

Herr Stadt seemed to fill his dark jacket to bursting. 'We all wear uniforms in Germany now.'

'You've been away too long,' said Herr Beck, then grinned. 'Why are *you* not wearing one?' The two men laughed. Elser examined the two familiar faces. Never friends to the family, they were merely locals who were, as they all had been, altogether too inquisitive. Georg Elser prepared an answer, censored it, then began again.

'I am not political. I don't believe in . . . '

Herr Stadt stopped Elser short. 'That's dangerous talk.'

Herr Beck nodded and reached out to the zither. He touched the strings lightly.

'Little man,' he whispered, and gestured Elser to go. The two militia policemen watched Elser walk through the long grass of the overgrown lawn to the gate and his bicycle. Georg Elser didn't look back. His father dead, his mother gone, a sister in Hamburg and a home barred and bolted – an era was over. Only memories and now the small zither remained. Elser mounted his bicycle and began to pedal slowly, gaining momentum on the road towards Königsbron. At least it would be downhill all the way.

The pretty Swabian village was shrouded in rain. Night and the comforting sound of a storm moving away made the warm atmosphere within the small Brauhaus almost cosy. The large fire was stoked again by the landlord as the assembled audience of farmers and village merchants, their wives and several older children, with obvious anticipation, awaited the next song from the new entertainer. Many of them knew him, had known his parents, and been told stories of his family, which – like them – were part of the region of Württemberg. Georg Elser's audience appreciated music that was familiar and words they understood.

He began again – his voice hesitant at first as the lyrics described a story, together with notes on the zither which trembled as the mood dictated. The folk melody evoked great spaces, indicating yearning, longing for love. Sentiment created tears, stirred memories, forced reflections among those gathered in the Brauhaus. Notes and words plunged deep into the minds of people untroubled by conscience for actions with hidden motives. Simple and clear, their thoughts responded to the song on the zither; emotions were caressed, listening to the girl as she reached for the boy and he in turn bent to soft lips, given only by the moon and stars, denied until that moment but enchanted by the stolen evening in spring. Youth caught and entrapped. Applause sounded loudly as Elser finished, almost drowning the first noises from outside of an approaching convoy of lorries.

The landlord heard it but only glanced at his wife, who merely shrugged. He crossed the room to his newly employed zither player, carrying a stein of bouillon.

'You are an artist,' he said. Elser lowered his eyes. Compliments troubled him, even from old friends of his father who had spent many nights in this atmosphere – too many. Elser took the stein, placed the zither on a table and put his lips to the hot soup.

'Careful,' warned the landlord with a smile.

The first of six lorries pulled sharply into the forecourt of Königsbron's best-known Brauhaus, stopped, parked and switched off. The SA men crowded beneath the wet canvas dropped rear flaps, leapt down and ran across the slippery cobbles to steps up to the entrance.

'Beer!' shouted the first Brownshirt who thrust open the door. The young, muscular men began to fill the inn as each lorry unloaded. Minutes later, the convoy stood empty in the darkness and rain, as within the Königsbron's favourite Brauhaus more than fifty SA Nazi Brownshirts were being served Löwenbrau by the harassed innkeeper, his wife and two local waitresses.

Georg Elser continued to sip his bouillon and wished he were back in Switzerland. He sat beneath numerous coats in a corner and was hoping he might leave quietly, when curious eyes caught his and belligerent voices shouted, 'Play!' George Elser surveyed the new array of faces, all turned towards him, and waited for comparative quiet. Someone shouted loudly and there was a moment's silence; Elser began to play, then sing.

Had he been Caruso, no one would have listened. He had become sport. Tonight he was the presented victim. And it was already too late to think otherwise, and go. So he

18

continued to play and sing. He expected nothing and received nothing. Slowly the noise of the young men grew – the abuse developed into invective, insults, and criticism – then, as more beer arrived, finally was hurled directly at him; but still Georg Elser played and sang quiet folksongs, delicate melodies. After all, it was his job, he had agreed the hours and no one had ever altered the course of his actions once he had accepted and decided that a challenge would be met.

He had taught himself to play as he had learnt how to make and mend with his hands. He had honed his skill with natural ability and tenacity, until it had become of paramount importance to him. His pride in his work required fulfilment in whatever he did, and above all things quietly demanded respect. Arrogance, never a part of his life, was so obviously an expression of the unproven, uncertain, inadequate. Strange, he thought, as he looked at the many young men in brown shirts, red armbands, white circles and black swastikas, that the common factor of the new Germany seemed to be this arrogance. If the Führer must answer for anything, it must be for that. He had replaced the hopeless years after the Great War with images and posturing and called it confidence.

Did the people really believe they still controlled their own political destiny? Could they not see that they had merely been manipulated by the beguiling promises of the National Socialist Party and Adolf Hitler? Georg Elser finished his song, stopped playing and looked at his audience. He could hear the rain outside, see the fire burning in the grate, but now heard little else, even from the locals cowed by the many uniforms. It was ominously quiet.

A large man in his brown shirt with a red armband spoke up loudly, slamming his beer stein for emphasis.

'Play the "Horst Wessel"!' he commanded. The Nazi party anthem was known throughout Germany. Georg Elser looked across at the man.

'I can't,' he said quietly. Roars of laughter exploded in the small inn. Best hopes had been surpassed – here was the cabaret. The Brownshirt who had spoken finished his beer in one, hushed his companions and stood up.

'I said,' he began, 'play the "Horst Wessel".'

'I don't know it . . . ' Elser hesitated. ' . . . well enough, mein Herr.'

The Brownshirt stepped out from behind the crowded table, skirted several benches, crossed to Georg Elser and knelt down so he was eye to eye with the zither player.

'Play it.' His voice was soft and ominous.

'I only like to play what I do well,' said Elser. Expectant murmuring came from the curious audience.

'Are you a communist?' asked the kneeling Brownshirt.

'No.' Elser's eyes dulled with suppressed fear.

'A Jew?'

'Not a Jew,' whispered Elser.

The Brownshirt reached out slowly and touched Elser's cheek.

'What are you?' Tension in the room increased, and someone giggled.

'I am a German, like you. I only wish to work, that's all. I want no trouble.' Fair statements to a bully serve no purpose – public commitment means all the way or loss of face.

'So, play the "Horst Wessel".'

Elser coughed lightly and assumed an expression of conciliation.

'I have explained, mein Herr . . . ' The Brownshirt's fist dropped fast to Elser's fingers, tore them from the zither, seized the little finger of Elser's right hand and bent it – slightly.

'Play it.' The SA men began shouting encouragement.

'Please!' hissed Elser, trying to pull away.

'Play,' said the Brownshirt, thrusting his coarse features into Elser's face. Both men had begun to sweat, and although the Nazi could see the fear in Elser's eyes, there was something else he detected, something disconcerting . . .

The SA men, as one, began banging their steins of beer and

chanting raucously. '"Horst Wessel", "Horst Wessel" . . .'
The Brownshirt bent the little finger, more.

'Mein Herr!' mouthed Elser, his words lost to the noises.

'Play.' The Brownshirt grinned and bent the little finger –
further. Tears leapt into Elser's eyes.

'I . . . can't . . .' He suddenly shook his head; mostly from
pain, but it was seen as defiance. A roar went up from the
crowd of Nazis, and the kneeling Brownshirt bent the little
finger even further. Too far. The bone snapped. Elser's
scream of agony cut like a knife into the dense atmosphere.

'Play!' roared the Brownshirt. 'For the Führer!'

Elser fixed the Brownshirt with staring eyes and bellowed,
'Nooooo!'

The Brownshirt snarled and twisted the shattered finger.
Bone penetrated tissue, and blood spurted across the zither.
With a wild cry, Elser reached out his left arm, his hand
grasping for the thick glass stein, now empty of the bouillon.
He gripped the handle firmly then swung the stein in an arc,
with all his strength, cracking it against the Nazi's head. The
man sagged, his eyes glazing over as Elser swung the stein a
second time, now against the man's face. On contact, the
glass shattered and Elser dragged the jagged stein across the
coarse features, ripping at flesh, tearing into muscle and
sinew, gouging at bone, scouring channels of blood as the
Nazi shrieked, his hands clawing towards Elser's neck.

For a single moment, the SA men were in shock, then they
leapt up and inundated the corner against the wall where the
dark-haired zither player sank beneath a sea of Brownshirts
in a welter of blows. A boot stamped on Elser's right hand
and, as his fingers extended, a steel-tipped heel ground into
the damaged little finger and severed the first two joints from
the knuckle. Only then did the angel of death step into the
room and stand motionless at the open door, rain glistening
on the shoulders of his dark leather coat, light glittering in the
pale eyes beneath a black peaked cap, commanding order,
silence and peace.

The SS officer moved not a muscle as the room froze. His

eyes absorbed the scene without excitement. Professional interest surveyed the Brownshirts and rested a moment on the unconscious, sprawled figure of a man cradling the shattered pieces of a zither. SS Obersturmbannführer Otto Meyer reached out a hand slowly to the telephone just inside the door. He grasped the receiver, lifted it and put it to his ear. The long buzzing noise he heard seemed to fill the room. Someone coughed, another spat. Meyer's eyes found the two men, and they were again silent and still. He stared through the crowd to the innkeeper at the bar, who shook his head. The telephone was out of service. Unhurriedly, Meyer replaced the receiver in its cradle in the wall.

'Sir,' whispered a voice. Meyer's driver hovered behind him outside, in the darkness. The word contained a warning. Meyer nodded almost imperceptibly, then turned slowly on his heels and, as the driver quickly closed the door behind him, stepped back into the cold wet night. The driver slammed the rear door of the Mercedes, then settled himself into his seat, starting the powerful engine, switching on the lights and releasing the handbrake. He looked into the mirror at his passenger in the rear.

'Another telephone, sir? Munich is several more hours.' There was no decision to contest. The passenger made it plain with his eyes.

'Munich it is, sir,' said the driver in a quiet voice, then reversed up and, snapping on the headlights, began to glide out of the forecourt to the main road.

'What was all that, sir?' he asked, glancing again in the mirror at the black peaked cap surmounting a gaunt face. The silver eagle above a swastika and the small emblem of a skull head beneath it glinted for a moment in the glow from the dashboard. Otto Meyer sank back in his seat, then in answer to the chauffeur's question murmured a word of contempt and dismissal.

'Nothing,' he said.

2

At first light all the guards had changed in each of the towers
surrounding the perimeter fence of the concentration camp at
Dachau. The SS men negotiated the ladders, which from the
high platforms had a commanding view of the entire area.
Standing orders forced them to check the large machine-
guns, which they did efficiently, re-threading the ammunition belts through the breech and releasing the safety catches.
A flare was fired and immediately harsh voices, commanding
obedience and instant action, echoed throughout the many
huts. In cramped darkness, Georg Elser slid quickly from his
upper bunk and jumped to the ground, feeling around him.
There were so many other inmates, some grumbling, others
afraid.

Suddenly the door was thrust open on to the dawn of
another day. Orders were screamed into the huts and the men,
packed like cattle, pushed against each other in their anxiety
not to be last out, and piled into the area immediately in front
of the hut, which was surrounded by camp guards pointing
loaded rifles. The men, their heads completely shaved or their
hair shorn, lined up, bullied by several of the black uniforms
who took pleasure in hitting those who could not find their
place at once. In a ragged line, the men stood to attention and
remained silent.

A thickset SS officer went through the motions of
inspecting them, his cruel face seeking the slightest expression
of contempt or defiance. This morning he had energy and
decided to use his crop. All he needed was a victim, and
slowly he wandered down the line. He stopped three times,
then slowly he reached out and with his crop touched the neck
of the man beside Georg Elser. He took a pace back, allowing

the man to step forward. He had caught the glint in the eye, and that was enough. The SS officer smiled. The man smiled back. The officer's face hardened, and as his lips curled he struck the man twice with his crop. Blood appeared from the welts on his cheek, and the initial shock on the man's face turned again to a smile. The officer struck the man twice more, his eyes now silently challenging the defiance he had discovered. The man, thin, tall and gaunt, merely raised his head once more and smiled again. The officer's face contorted and he hit the man about the neck and head six times. Now the prisoner swayed but he raised his head, looked the officer in the eye and with gritted teeth, and seemed for a moment as if he was going to strike back, then his jaw sagged and he tried to smile again.

Elser, beside the man, whom he had known only several weeks since his incarceration in the camp, was about to turn away but already he had learnt that it would make him the new focus of attention. His fellow inmate was still swaying and now managed, through the bruised flesh and blood dripping on to his chest, a full smile of open defiance. The crescent of guards around the ragged line of men at a murmured order, thrust bullets into the breeches of their rifles, slamming down the bolts, ready to shoot on command. The officer pursed his lips, attempting to control the burning hatred in his eyes, then lashed out now with his fists. The blows, with such force behind them, seemed to explode against the man's exposed sinews and bare flesh. A smile of triumph appeared in the expression of the SS officer, as working with relish he saw the tall, thin man bow down before him amidst the welter of his attack. He stopped, breathing heavily. Still the man remained on his feet. The officer spat on to the ground and sucking air, raised his crop yet again.

Georg Elser winced and, unable to control himself, shouted, 'Fall!'

The officer froze immediately and turned, looking at the shorn head and wide eyes of Georg Elser. He dropped his arms and stepped towards the smaller man, touching him on the cheek gently with the bloodied crop. He examined the prisoner's expression, then took a pace back, guiding the man to follow. Elser shuffled forward and stood to attention, locking his knees to stop himself shaking.

'You,' whispered the officer, and extended the crop. Elser took it and glanced at the man. The officer smiled and stepped back yet another pace, watching. The unspoken order was clear in the mind of every man lined up outside the hut at dawn that morning in Dachau. The tall, thin, gaunt man turned his swollen face towards Elser; his eyes were puffed up and his lips thickened and bloody. He tried to grin. Elser raised the crop slowly then hesitated. The man tried to speak, bowed his head and fell heavily on to the ground at the officer's feet.

The SS man made a grimace at Elser and took back the crop. He had other plans for this 'little man'. The morning assembly outside each of the huts always contained some incident, which was seldom threatening, and had yet to prove dangerous. The machine-gun guards in the towers had become bored and only longed for a time, perhaps in the near future, when they could expend some of the ammunition they had been trained to use. After all, the targets had already been designated by the hierarchy of the Third Reich, as the dross of society and therefore expendable in any circumstances. Gypsies, criminals, homosexuals, Jews, communists, misfits and outcasts – who would miss them? As the machine-gunners often joked, they certainly would not, given the opportunity and, of course, the order, to fire. If anything, it was a waste of bullets. Perhaps some day they would invent a more efficient method of dispatch.

The two men in the tower overlooking Elser's hut lit cigarettes as they watched three men in a line marched off towards a distant building within the large compound – the only one with a chimney.

Twenty marble slabs spread the length of the mortuary, and only half of them were empty. Elser saw, on the others,

25

bodies laid out as he was marched to the end wall of the building, where he came to attention and awaited orders. Two inmates of Dachau, who had elected to cooperate for what few privileges they could elicit from their guards, grinned at the new arrivals and stood in front of several pairs of iron doors, which were closed, but Elser could feel the heat even from where he stood.

The SS officer examined the three faces he had brought into the building and his gaze rested upon Georg Elser. He indicated the corpses on the slabs, and there was a challenge in his eyes when he said to Elser, 'They died.'

The two prisoners already in attendance opened the oven doors, and the heat seared into the room. With extended arms they presented thin metal sheets to the three men. As Elser could see, the idea was obviously to place the body on the metal, then slide it into the oven.

The SS officer leant against the wall and appraised the Swabian from Württemberg with the staring eyes that he had somehow managed to empty of expression. He noticed a black sheath over the stump of the man's little finger. He did not speak for a moment, allowing the prisoner to listen to the roaring flames. The officer was laconic when he again indicated the bodies. 'Burn them,' he said. Elser turned to the first marble slab and saw the limp corpse. The face was mutilated and the expression was unmistakably one of violent death. These men had not died, they had been killed. It was obvious to Elser, but he said nothing. His only duty to himself was to survive the six months he had been given for 'civil disobedience'. Then he might be one of the lucky few that would leave Dachau.

Whilst he supported the weight of the corpse, which was placed on the metal sheet between the two metal arms, his fellow prisoners grasped the handles either side and together they slid the body to the edge of the oven where the heat was already intense, and pushing what amounted to a large shovel, Elser thrust its contents into the oven's roaring flames. He felt some strange fascination, in place of horror, as if what

26

he had just done was familiar – part of his history, which was, as yet, incomplete. He said a short, silent prayer for this unknown victim consigned to the flames, and as he did so, watched the cadaver slowly sit up. The shock on his face, at the normal reaction of bone and tissue contracting, brought laughter from those around him that were old hands.

Elser glanced at the callous faces, the grinning SS officer, the dead eyes of the other guards who had accompanied them into the mortuary, then looked back to the charring flesh and powdering bone as slowly the body sank back into the flames. Tears of compassion appeared in Elser's eyes. The man may have been nothing to these functionaries of the Third Reich, but once he must have had hopes and dreams and a belief in the future. That, no matter in which country they were born, was the birthright of any man. The prisoners in charge of the mortuary slammed the oven's iron doors shut as Elser continued to stare. He had come home to Hitler's Germany.

3

The spacious lounge of a house in Berlin's fashionable
Dahlem district was crowded awkwardly with boxes and
packing cases, all stamped, labelled and addressed from
Munich. Outside, in the pleasant garden of mature trees,
autumn leaves caught in the morning sunlight provided
colour enough to compliment the large, plain grey windows,
walls and bare boards of the newly acquired residence. A
batman in a crisp white jacket crossed through a swing door
from the kitchen to the short corridor and a bedroom, where
he once again checked the black uniform laid out on the wide
bed, then knocked respectfully on the panelling beside the
closed curtain and arch that led to the en suite bathroom.
There was no reply.

'Baur, sir,' he said, and knocked louder. Still nothing.
Gently he pulled back the thick velvet and looked in. The
long enamel bath was filled almost to overflowing with ice-
cold water, its surface undisturbed. For almost half a minute
Baur waited patiently, then a naked figure appeared, sitting
up unhurriedly before inhaling deeply.

'Thirty minutes, sir,' stated the batman.

Otto Meyer stared then nodded. 'Good.'

'And may I offer my congratulations,' continued Baur as
the man stepped out of the bath and took a towel from his
bathroom. Meyer nodded again and began to rub down his
slim but solid frame.

Although in his late forties, the SS officer tried to maintain
a vigorous physical routine. He often argued that his many
years of sport, abstinence and discipline provided his mind
with a clarity and precision. Thirty minutes of exercise on
rising, a sweat, then a cold bath had always given him a sense of

well-being. As a cadet, then army officer, it had become part of his life to maintain a level of fitness in excess of his companions.

During the Great War, he had suffered, as had all his contemporaries, the discomforts then privations and finally horrors of the trenches. With the armistice, he, as all those who remained, had attempted to create another life amidst the chaos of defeat. Not all were successful. Like his father before him, he became a policeman and rose in the ranks, partly through his father's reputation, mostly through his own ability. On Hindenburg's death and the accession to power of the Nazi party, he had begun to harbour doubts about the new regime and totalitarian state, but the prosperity of Germany after the anarchy of the previous decade convinced him that his destiny lay beneath the swastika. Although not political, and recognizing merely a career opportunity, he had accepted the proposition put to him having been noticed by Himmler's SS and proudly become a serving member of the growing organization, first as a Hauptsturmführer in the Criminal Police. Promotion had followed quickly, and a transfer into the elite Gehieme Stats Police – the Gestapo. But it had cost him dear. Family, friends and society became secondary, even his home in the city of Munich had come to see him as a rare visitor. His career had become his life. His home now, Berlin.

Meyer stepped into the bedroom and dried himself.

'There's so much to do,' said Baur. 'I don't know where to begin.' Meyer glanced at him. 'I'll just try to make it into a home,' said the batman, and picked up a starched white shirt. 'I've never been to Berlin before. But I'm sure I'll learn to like it.'

Meyer thrust his arms into the proffered sleeves. 'We must both learn to like it,' he murmured. Outside, through the long windows, still without curtains, he saw a black Mercedes draw up by the gate. Instinctively he glanced down at his long boots, polished to a mirror shine. Standards, as he knew, must always be conveyed to those beneath a new commanding officer.

Baur checked his watch. 'It's six thirty-seven, sir. Shall I pour the coffee?' Meyer merely nodded, finished buttoning his shirt and knotted his black tie. 'Would you like it in the lounge?' Meyer took his sharply pressed black trousers and began to pull them on. 'I'm sorry, sir, but the boxes and the crates . . . It's . . . a mess.' Baur stopped and helped his officer slide into the long boots as Meyer reached for the jacket of his uniform. Baur then pointed, 'Perhaps coffee by the window, looking out?' The SS Obersturmbannführer buckled his belt, accepted his peaked cap, placed it carefully on his head and then turned and stared.

'Thank you, Baur.' The batman's face tightened. It had become a strange moment for him. The man for whom he worked, knew well and even liked, disappeared. He was replaced by this dangerous black apparition whose silver buttons, badges and emblems glinted like sharpened steel, casting an undisputed aura of power and authority which quietly demanded obedience.

Meyer drank his coffee then brusquely left his new quarters. He descended the flight of stone steps to the garden path, brushed through the fallen leaves and strode out to the waiting Mercedes. The chauffeur snapped his heels then carefully closed the door as Meyer settled back into the dark leather interior. In a moment the car was out in the traffic of Berlin's centre, negotiating its way confidently, two flapping pennants creating spaces as other drivers recognized the authority and gave way. Meyer peered out at the already crowded pavements. The world started early, he thought, perhaps earmarking the Third Reich's success at generating a spirit in the people which drove them harder, created ambition. The driver coughed. Meyer glanced towards the rear-view mirror, which framed questioning eyes.

'Do you miss Munich, sir?'

Meyer stared into the mirror. The driver coughed again and changed gear to coast around a street corner, narrowly avoiding a tram, which pulled up then slammed on brakes, creating sparks. The passengers, thrown against the safety bars, glared out at the pale face in the rear of the black Mercedes. Meyer smiled to himself. 'The people were different,' he thought, 'less dour, more aggressive.' There was a sense of elitism and self-confidence. A long way from 1918; and war; and defeat.

Guards sprang to attention as the Mercedes passed through an arched gateway into a wide courtyard fronting an imposing building; the black uniforms were so impressive to those easily beguiled, he reflected. But then Germany had always loved uniforms. It wasn't long before that Meyer himself had only worn civilian clothes as a police officer, so even he had to admit that the black and silver with the small skull head did create, if nothing else at least – respect.

Himmler had successfully combined all the police and security services beneath one overall authority. As head of the SS, the Schutzstaffel created originally years before to provide protection in all political assemblies, he had grown rapidly to become an awesome figure of power. Even Heydrich, in charge of the RSHA, the Reich Security head office, ranked beneath 'the boss'. Now the RSD, the security service whose chief was SS Standartenführer Rattenhuber, had created a special security section of which Meyer had now assumed command as a Gestapo officer instructed to oversee all aspects of the Führer's safety. He had accepted the post knowing it to be a great privilege but heavy responsibility.

The Mercedes ground to a halt on the gravel. Meyer stepped out and looked at his new command centre in the Wilhelmstrasse headquarters of the SS. An array of vehicles already parked, some still attended by chauffeurs, indicated a hierarchy already at work. Meyer checked his watch – seven fifteen. He entered the building; passes at the door, identification at the north side of the large marble hall and a special entry permit allowed him access to the long corridor of the old wing. Sixteen high windows let shafting sunlight on to the panelled walls as Meyer strode towards the large door marked *IV.E.* His heels clipped the stone floor, sounding a challenge which was never answered. He stopped and reached for a polished brass door handle, pausing before he stepped into the heart of the Third Reich.

Security was at the maximum in any dictatorship. Without the head there would be no system, which was the only flaw, the single weakness in the greatest governing strength the world had conceived. The swamps of Babylon for Alexander, knives for Caesar, Tannenburg for The Teutonic Order and a mere book for the Empire of the Czars. Absolute power, of which he was a part and now protector, had always failed – eventually. Only the when was in question. Meyer had learnt his history but trusted no soothsayer to predict the future. There were no guarantees to the ultimate security of any individual, but he had been seconded and elevated to provide at least the impression that they were possible.

The rebirth of Germany was a miracle and its rapid growth was abundantly obvious – and all owed to one Austrian visionary. This man's life was now Meyer's responsibility. 'Adolf Hitler,' he murmured, and opened the door of his office.

He surveyed his new surroundings, slowly taking off his gloves. A generously proportioned room, completely oak-panelled, with three tall sash windows. On the longest wall at the centre was a wide desk. To one side of it was a filing cabinet, above which were rows of shelves to the ceiling, filled with books.

A movement to his left drew his attention; a balding man in his mid-thirties, wearing a black uniform with RSD flashes, looked up from papers spread on the leather top of a side table. He glanced at the clock on the wall then spoke in a supercilious tone.

'Early?'

Without answering, Meyer closed the door.

'I am to be the adjutant of this section, Sturmbannführer, liaising the Reich security head office with those recruited and under your command from both RSD and Gestapo.'

32

'Obersturmbannführer,' stated Meyer flatly. The man adjusted a monocle and smiled.

'Oh yes. Of course.' The man crossed and extended a hand to Meyer, who recognized the lower rank before him and stiffened at the familiarity. The man licked his lips wetly and cocked his head. 'The Reichsführer will see you – immediately.' He stepped past Meyer and gestured. 'Follow me.'

Another corridor, more security protocol, and Meyer was ushered to a guarded door. Two SS guards snapped to attention as the adjutant knocked politely then indicated Meyer should go in – alone. Blinds were drawn in the room, and only a desk light illuminated a lowered face concentrating on papers held at a distance. Pale eyes glanced up at Meyer without expression. Seconds passed as they absorbed the new arrival, then a finger and thumb lifted rimless spectacles, and the tired voice of a man who had worked throughout the night interrupted the silence.

'Welcome.' Heinrich Himmler spoke the word softly.

By late morning the weather had turned sour. Meyer returned from his initial meeting and briefing with the head of the entire Nazi SS network and stared gloomily out of the tall centre window into the pouring rain. Fifteen years before, the very existence of such an organization would have been deemed the wild imaginings of a madman. Now it was no longer fiction, but the power behind the stability of the political party that had taken charge of Germany with strength and assurance. No longer were dissenting voices raised above stifled whispers; contradiction was anathema. One purpose had been presented to the people, one goal to be achieved: the greatness of a nation which had so recently sunk, seemingly beyond saving. Sure that those shared memories of everyone who had lived through the despair of times now almost inconceivably already past, cemented the masses to an ideal which they sought to uphold with a commitment and willingness that had astonished the world. The results continued to garner the admiration of so many other countries.

But this re-established strength, proven in a vast autobahn system, thriving industry, almost full employment, and proud nationalism, also provided a threat to others who were denied a part of the glory, excluded by decree. Jews, communists, the unconvinced intellectuals, staunch trade unionists, masons, liberals, right-wing capitalists who refused to accept the Nazi dogma – these had been declared the enemy within to be dealt with efficiently and ruthlessly. The reward for loyalty was clearly proposed: one thousand years of consolidated power. This was either the declaration of an exuberant dictator or a truly attainable goal. It seemed ridiculous, but then as far back as 1923, it had all sounded merely the ranting fantasies of an unacceptable voice.

Meyer watched the rivulets of rain pouring down the window for a moment longer then turned back to his desk. He gazed around the room and he enjoyed a private moment of sheer wonder. All this was undeniable fact, here and now – his Germany, this Reich, the Führer. Perhaps it really would be more than a career opportunity in a passing administration. Perhaps he actually would contribute even a small part to some kind of immortality. After all, the British Empire had lasted . . . He shook his head. The Third Reich for a thousand years!

A loud confident knock at the door interrupted his thoughts. The adjutant entered and registered a look of surprise.

'Oh.'

Meyer watched him approach the desk and see the upright photographs now in place as he put papers beside their small frames.

'Settling in?'

Meyer sat down and leaned back in his chair, his hands lightly grasping the arm rests. The adjutant adjusted his monocle to appreciate the two young children in the tortoiseshell ovals. 'Pretty,' he said. 'Yours?'

'I hope so,' answered Meyer.

The adjutant's eyes narrowed as he scanned the desk for another photograph.

'No wife?'

'No longer,' stated Meyer.

'Dead?'

'Divorced.'

'Oh yes, that's right.' The adjutant chanced a smile which was a smirk in the full knowledge of Meyer's previous history. He continued brusquely, 'Still, one marriage is enough, isn't it?' Meyer watched the man lean forward and confide, ' . . . to the SS.'

Meyer listened to the rain on the windows, watching the man realize he had been rejected and slowly regain his poise. Only then did he answer concisely.

'I am a policeman. My "marriage" is to the State. My loyalty is to its Leader.'

'Adolf Hitler,' said the adjutant.

'He is the Leader of the State,' said Meyer.

'Of the Third Reich,' corrected the adjutant.

'Of Germany,' added Meyer.

The adjutant's eyes glared. 'Excellent. I shall inform Reichsführer Himmler of your well-chosen words.' Meyer's expression remained cold. 'I am sure you will. Well-chosen or otherwise.'

The adjutant's lips curled into a sneer and he lowered his voice. 'Take care, policeman, there were others here before you.'

Meyer hardened instantly. 'Remember your rank, Hauptsturmführer.'

The adjutant stepped back a pace from the desk and spoke almost facetiously.

'Obersturmbannführer, it is not the rank here which is of importance . . . it is the ear into which you may whisper.' He shook his head and looked at Meyer sympathetically. 'You have much to learn.' Meyer was about to speak when a knock sounded at the door. 'Come!' commanded the adjutant. A tall, blond, well-built SS man stepped in, closed the door and snapped to attention. 'Ah, Wolf . . . ' started the adjutant. 'This is Otto Meyer.' He turned back to Meyer and introduced 'Hauptsturmführer Schneider.'

'Good morning,' said Meyer.

'Sir!' barked Schneider.

The adjutant looked the arrival up and down. 'So well presented, Wolf,' he said, then in a whisper, 'I shall tell "the boss".'

Meyer waited for silence. 'Get out,' he said ominously.

The adjutant turned back to face Meyer challengingly. 'Are you talking to me?'

Meyer's eyes answered the question. The adjutant coughed then crossed to the door. He shook his head.

'Pity,' he said. 'We could have been friends.'

Meyer was unmoved. The adjutant went quietly. Schneider remained locked to attention. Meyer sighed.

'Stand down, Schneider. You are not on a parade ground. I will make myself clear from the beginning; in this room I want your brain not muscles.'

Schneider relaxed awkwardly. 'Yes, sir,' he answered, and watched his commanding officer get up. Meyer slapped his thigh loudly, relieving the tension of the atmosphere. It was the first time Schneider saw Meyer smile.

'Show me our files,' he said.

The small lift was discreetly set back in an alcove off the central corridor. It was for higher ranking officers, and a guard allowed access only after identification. Schneider moved the lever to *basement* and the lift whined then began to descend into the depths. When Meyer stepped out into surprisingly bright artificial light, he detected the unmistakable hum of an independent generator. Two guards with the inquisitive eyes and high brows of librarians awaited Meyer's request. He surveyed the vast room that was divided only by several wide pillars leading up to the many interlaced steel and cement ceiling supports. The stacks of shelving, solid with books and files, were only two metres apart and almost reached the regularly placed hanging lights, ten metres above the polished wood floor. The temperature was maintained several degrees below the air-conditioning system in the main building. Meyer shivered.

'All of Germany,' said Schneider quietly.

Meyer walked forward, followed by the two guards, and all four men then began to stroll around the array of records as if the new officer, merely by observing them, could absorb their contents and details. He started speaking softly only after several minutes had passed, and although he seemed to address Schneider, it was as if Meyer was talking to another part of himself.

'Protecting the Führer is a task of honour, a privilege we are proud to accept. But it will never be easy. We must always be vigilant, our thoughts ubiquitous. We must *anticipate* the worst that *could* happen. Our goal is *complete preventive* security. Should a single incident take place, it will be a measure of our failure, whether it is merely an attempt to discredit or . . .' Meyer paused; even the word held new fear for him. Boots stopped abruptly on the polished wood floor. Only the sound of the generator humming in the background interrupted Meyer's audience of three. ' . . . assassination,' he said. Schneider coughed. Meyer looked into the man's face. There would come a time when he might have to rely upon this younger officer. Delegating authority had proved difficult to Meyer and he knew well that the ultimate responsibility lay always at the top. Trust would be a problem but finally it might be necessary.

'Do you have a good imagination, Schneider?'

'I think so, sir.'

Meyer nodded. 'Without it you are not a policeman. It is a prerequisite. We must be familiar with the attitudes of those who do not feel as we . . . about the Reich, its future . . . its

37

Leader.' Meyer stepped away from the three men, then stopped, and memory bowed his head. He turned quickly, stating the words with respect. 'My father could read the mind of a criminal by inhabiting that dark part of his own . . . ' Meyer paused, warning his small audience, 'of *all* our minds – with imagination.'

Schneider had done his private research into the background of his commanding officer and the reputation of his detective father. 'His fame is an example to us all, Obersturmbannführer.'

Meyer looked at Schneider. 'Was,' he corrected quietly. Schneider shuffled his feet; the moment was awkward. He glanced at the two SS librarians already storing information of Meyer senior in their minds as if adding to some greater filing system.

'How shall we begin?' asked Schneider with deference.

'With known undesirables,' said Meyer.

Schneider smiled. 'Who have imagination?'

Meyer nodded, appreciating his statement had been absorbed. His eyes wandered over the many stacks – files filling each shelf of the huge underground room. The fertile mind ranged over so many ideas, concepts and fears before words précised the thoughts.

'When,' he said, 'and where.' Meyer shook his head, knowing the almost insurmountable problems. Almost. 'Someone we will not know.' He looked at Schneider. 'But he will know us.' Meyer stared at his assistant a moment longer then reached out and touched him on the shoulder. 'As he knows Hitler.' Schneider was so surprised at the physical contact he snapped to attention on reflex. Meyer smiled a second time for Schneider's benefit. 'And he probably already has cause to hate him,' he said, then led the men back to the lift. With a whine, it ascended into the higher echelons of Nazi Germany.

4

Dachau was a name evoking many things to the numerous Germans who had either already experienced the dubious lessons of incarceration by November 1938 or knew from hearsay of the rigours to be endured – concentrated amongst others in a camp designed for re-education, submission or, if all else failed, for destruction and liquidation.

In the morning of 7 November at eleven o'clock, the main gates opened. The sign above clearly proclaimed *Freedom through work*. None of the fifteen men who trudged out into the pouring rain even stopped to look back. Each carried their meagre possessions in a bundle. All were undernourished, their cheeks and eyes sunken, hair shorn. They approached a German army lorry and followed as the guards slung their rifles and moved quickly towards the steaming urn of ersatz coffee, huddling together at the back where the flap hung down beneath the relative protection of the canvas cover. Several bicycles lay beside the rear wheels. A fat Wehrmacht sergeant accepted signatures on a clipboard from two men, then a third who, with some difficulty, completed his name, fingers pressing on a black sheath strapped around his right wrist.

Georg Elser took his rusting bicycle, pushed it away, knelt to check the tyres, pumped them to some tension, then mounted and slowly began to pedal from the harsh memories of imprisonment. After six gruelling months, he was leaving a part of himself behind in crowded longhouses where suffering had been ignored, replaced without sentiment by the will to survive. Others remained; some had died; several had been killed, which was the extreme penalty for disobeying the punishment inflicted by the master race upon the helpless to 'maintain order'.

Elser's legs, unaccustomed to the movement, pushed on the pedals without power. His prison diet of pea soup, black bread and rotten potatoes began to tell on his emaciated frame, clothed in a now sodden old suit. His breathing became shallow and his head bowed quickly with exhaustion, but determination drove him away from the camp. He seemed to gain energy as he smelt the late autumn air, realizing that the stench of confined bodies was gone, and he sucked greedily through the rain at that first taste of real freedom. Civil disruption had been Elser's declared and fully witnessed crime His conviction had swiftly followed a short hearing. His obstinate behaviour in the Königsbron Brauhaus had cost him not only half a year of his life, but the little finger of his right hand. He adjusted his grip on the handlebars of his bicycle and, despite the dismal day, found something in his heart to cheer dampened spirits. Sustained application and resilience were the hallmarks of his occupation as they were the core of his personality. He had endured and emerged from his incarceration unbroken; a smile appeared on his face. Quiet, unassuming and essentially shy, he now had something within him that as yet he did not acknowledge but he would discover as others had done in history before him. It was the seed of vengeance.

Four Reichsmarks and seven pfennigs were all that Georg Elser had in German money. Several hundred Swiss francs, saved from his time in Zurich, remained in his wallet. He had received exactly what he had consigned to the authorities: a ring of his father's, a medallion from his mother, a picture of his sister, and all personal effects, emptied from a brown envelope – a testament to the new Germany's bureaucratic efficiency. Now, as the sky cleared and the hours from Dachau brought him to a roadside hamlet outside the suburbs of Munich, he decided to stop and sit, at tables still wet from the rain.

The swastika flag flew limply above the shingled roof of the small inn as Elser dismounted wearily and propped his bicycle against a broken stucco wall. He crossed to one of the unoccupied tables and slumped on to the bench facing south with a view down a long valley. Good farming country, arable land and lush pastures, well tended and cared for by farmers with obvious pride, not afraid of early hours and hard work, he noticed. His eyes strayed to another table beside him, where numerous old men glanced at him suspiciously; local farmers, past their prime, come for the mutual company, their routine interrupted by this stranger. They nodded, and Elser responded, knowing the type from his own upbringing. Once, he had presumed he too might have been as they were now, beer sacks of memories, with burnt craggy faces illuminated in bursts of sunlight.

Elser glanced above, where towering dark clouds exchanged positions majestically in a predominantly grey sky. Only when patches of blue were revealed was there a chance of the shafting sun which warmed him, causing steam to rise from his wet clothes. The large proprietor of the dilapidated inn waddled over, looked at Elser distastefully, then ambled away and took his time bringing a generous plate of fresh bread, goat's cheese, pâté, bottle of wine and a glass. Elser's patience was rewarded when he bit slowly into the hastily made sandwich with a sensuality he had never before experienced. He chewed each morsel then swallowed the cold, white nectar with delicate appreciation. Only the murmuring old farmers and the distant radio within the inn disturbed his absolute concentration now taste had been given a new meaning. Then memories began to intrude, recalling the past six months, and instantly bile spoiled the food and soured the wine.

'Times are changing . . . ' one of the old men was saying.

He was interrupted by another, who corroborated, ' . . . and for the better, I say. Always improving.'

A third man nodded. 'The Führer has the welfare of the German people at heart – be sure of that!'

'You're right,' agreed the second farmer.

'Be sure of that,' nodded the speaker.

'Raise a glass,' suggested the first man.

'To the Führer!' toasted the second farmer.

'And the future,' added the third man. The three men turned with raised steins of beer and stared across at Georg Elser.

'Young man!' shouted the first farmer. Elser looked up and acknowledged the three men, but he was already listening to another sound. A deep rumbling noise fast approaching.

'We are raising our glasses to the Führer,' explained the second farmer, then he, too, with his companions registered loud rumbling and turned back to the road. Where the forest came down to a grassy bank, several camouflaged tanks appeared, travelling fast. They slewed round the corner, passed by with a deafening roar of diesel engines and were soon disappearing into the distance. The three old farmers remained transfixed. They had all been soldiers in the Great War.

'If we'd had those in 1914 . . . ' murmured one.

'We'd have been in Paris in a month,' whispered the second old man.

The third farmer sipped his beer. 'Drinking French champagne,' he said. The noise of the tanks faded. Elser coughed and immediately became, once again, the focus of attention.

'Young man,' said the first farmer again.

'Our Leader,' stated the second old man, and raised his glass, awaiting Elser's reaction. Elser hesitated a moment, then fumbled in his pocket, pulled out some coins, put them on the table and reached for his half-full glass of wine. His right hand seized the goblet, but the little finger placed to support the weight of wine was no longer there. The empty black sheath crumpled, the half-full glass slipped and fell to the ground, smashing to pieces as wine splashed on to the flagstones.

The three farmers turned away from him in disgust. One of them said 'The Führer,' they chinked beer steins and drank their toast privately. Elser was ignored as he mounted his bicycle and began to pedal towards the city of Munich. He was far down the road before the first farmer looked back to see the broken glass on the stone.

'Shouldn't we do something?'

'Leave it,' said the second old man.

The third man nodded sagely. 'Somebody will be along,' he began, and paused to lick beer from his moustache, ' . . . eventually.'

'Why should we worry,' agreed the second old man. 'It's nothing to do with us.' The three farmers finished their beer, staring out down the long valley into the distance at a landscape in Germany almost unchanged for ten centuries.

Turkenstrasse 94 was clearly marked on a small china plaque inset on the outer wall of the narrow courtyard. Georg Elser pushed his bicycle through the archway entrance, propped it outside the front door, took his small bag and rang the bell. With nightfall, the weather had again deteriorated; a steady drizzle was fast becoming heavy rain. Elser was cold and shivering in his wet clothes when the lights came on inside the hallway and someone peered through the thick glass of a round window before unlocking and unbolting the door. Georg Elser forced a smile at the woman in a cotton dressing gown, with too much rouge, over-made-up eyes, crimson lipstick and hair piled in curlers, as she swayed slightly, holding a full glass of schnapps in her hand. She pursed her lips, looking him up and down.

'So, you've come back. Again.' She squinted to improve her short sight. 'Thinner,' she said. Elser stepped back to indicate his bicycle, but she only made a face and, wafting a hand, reached out for his arm to pull him into the house. Elser followed her down a short hallway, re-establishing the familiar, looking for differences as a large room appeared to one side where a strange assortment of characters looked up from numerous chairs crowded about a roaring fire. They were much as Elser was – the residue of Weimar's lost republic, people on the edge; just above poverty, boarding as lodgers in a rooming house where they were barely able to pay the little rent demanded by the landlady. They had grown together over the months, some even years. They had occupied their rooms and become a tight-knit group, acceptable within the secure confines of their sanctuary. They were odd only to an outsider. No one recognized him; he was an intruder, and their eyes showed immediate hostility to the threat he presented. Elser stared longingly at the fire, craving its heat before continuing down the hallway behind the landlady. She stopped and opened a door, lit the single dull electric bulb and gestured with a sip of schnapps and a grin of expectation. She remembered Georg Elser very well.

'Nothing's changed,' she whispered huskily. Elser surveyed his room, where once before he had lived for almost a year. She was right; it was as small, drab and bleak as ever. He looked at the woman as his nose detected aromas from the kitchen. The landlady ran her tongue over her moist lips and asked tantalizingly, 'Hungry?'

Elser nodded and the woman bustled away. Alone, he took off his wet clothes, towelled himself down and changed into a pair of corduroy trousers and an old cotton shirt. He gathered up his wet suit and stepped out into the hallway. His nose could have found the kitchen even if memory had failed him. The few remaining possessions he had lay sprawled on the narrow bed in the room he had taken. He stepped into the large kitchen, gave the woman his damp clothes and sat down, slumped on a chair at the scrubbed table, as hot sausages and steaming sauerkraut were placed in front of him. The landlady watched him as he began slowly, then wolfed down the food. She smiled seductively as Elser finished the meal and poured herself yet another schnapps.

'Good?' she asked. Elser nodded. She looked at him, focusing on his sensitive fingers for the first time – remembering the past. 'You always had lovely hands, Georg,' she began, then seeing the black sheath, seized his wrist. 'What happened?' Elser stared at her a moment and then shrugged. Explanations were unnecessary and complicated. The woman

44

gently slipped her hand into his and leant closer. 'If you stay on longer this time, perhaps you might like to use the cellar below.' Elser's modest reaction brought triumph to the woman's eyes. 'The old man was taken away,' she explained, and looked knowingly at Elser before whispering, conspiratorially, 'A Jew.' Elser said nothing. 'So it is empty,' she went on, 'with a workbench. It's what you wanted, isn't it?' Elser nodded and wiped his mouth with the back of his hand. The woman cocked her head. 'A man like you could do a lot, down there.'

Elser reached into his trouser pocket for his cigarettes. He tipped one out of the packet and, as he broke it in half, watched the landlady take a box of matches from the dresser, strike one and offer it. Elser inhaled then blew out smoke.

'You're a strange one,' said the woman. Elser's eyes smiled. He knew what she wanted. 'Can we do it again?' she whispered. 'Like before?' Her lips were almost touching his when someone opened the door. A plump old man with a flat pale face and grey stubble grinned.

'I was just wondering . . . ' he began, but was cut off by a curt dismissal.

'These are private rooms, Herr Herzog, get out!' The man's face tensed and he left without a word. The landlady sighed and turned back to Elser, still clasping his hand. 'Oh, Georg, I do like you. Ever since we . . . ' She paused and sighed again, now for effect, then winked, befuddled but determined. 'I've got some more schnapps upstairs.' She kissed Elser's hand with wet lips. 'You want some?' she asked. Elser only inhaled his cigarette. 'You did before,' she said. 'Beer? I can send out for some.'

'I'll get it,' said Elser, and stood up.

The landlady followed him with her eyes as he stepped to the door. 'You don't have to go.'

'I want to.'

The landlady's face hardened. 'Two marks a week. In advance.'

Elser regarded the woman for a moment, without malice,

but seeing just what she was – a pathetic, ageing creature, living with an image of herself that had never been real; even the mirror now told her lies. She sought, with a growing desperation, someone to treat her according to her inflated expectations, and sometimes she did find a man who was prepared to step into her world for a while, for whatever he could get, but she never saw it that way. It was, after all, her fantasy, her life, her gain.

'I always paid you,' said Elser quietly, and shuffled out into the hallway. The landlady hesitated, finished her schnapps, stood up unsteadily and went after Elser, who was already halfway to the entrance.

'Where are you going?' Elser stopped as the woman approached, measuring her steps. 'You'll need a coat,' she said. 'My husband was a big man. Did I ever tell you . . . ?'

'Yes,' answered Elser. She opened a cupboard, rummaged for the overcoat and presented it to Elser.

'It won't fit but it'll do. Try it.' Elser put it on. 'We used to go out together,' she began whimsically, 'in the old days.' Elser belted the large overcoat, dry and warm. 'Watch yourself,' said the woman. 'Our great Führer is speaking at the Burgerbrau tonight across the square. The SS are everywhere and I don't want them back here!'

'Thank you,' said Elser. The landlady dropped her head and shook it sadly.

'You're all the same when a woman offers you . . . ' she stopped herself and looked into his face. 'I thought you were different from all the others.' Georg Elser turned, opened the front door and stepped out into the night.

The small Bierkeller was crowded and reverberated with the noise of Hitler's speech on the wireless as Elser pushed his way to the bar, waited patiently, then asked for a stein of Löwenbrau from the heavily built, aggressive barman. Frothing over, the stein was slammed in front of Elser, who paid quickly and squeezed across the room to a corner. There

46

he stood quietly watching the citizens of Munich and the new Germany taking their pleasure. Many of the crowd wore swastika badges; some uniformed insignia and armbands. All seemed coarse and loud – not unusual in such a place, but there was a swaggering cockiness about the majority of them that made him feel uneasy. Attitudes were exaggerated, gestures emphasized, laughter was noise without humour. Respect rippled over the collected groups as someone hushed them for a moment to catch the words of Hitler's speech.

Elser peered out of the window across the square, where he could see the heavily guarded entrance of the Burgerbrau-keller, from which the Führer, at that very moment, was giving forth to a packed hall and, through the microphone, to all the regions and provinces of the Fatherland. Elser listened a moment to the wireless voice, which carried conviction and passion with words designed to stimulate an audience willing to be patronized. The quality of life was indeed improved, chaos stabilized, a future assured, but the national ambitions were presented seductively as if all opposition would accede or crumble before the sheer power of will. A single mouth was speaking for so many who had prayed for more than a decade only to be fed and clothed, simple words igniting new confidence and presenting fears to be grappled with and overcome. A reunited people was pledging allegiance to a system led by one man; a political Messiah come to show the way, seeking only trust, obedience and loyalty to the death.

A great ovation sounded on the wireless, causing Georg Elser to turn back to the noise. He looked above the bar where the clock showed nine fifteen. Hitler had seized his audience and was feeling his power. Elser surveyed the small Bierkeller; even here the crowds were in awe of the articulate persuader. Elser sipped his beer, unmoved, as shouts of 'Heil Hitler' roared around him. He felt the isolation of a stranger and yet he had come home.

For a moment, he actually experienced envy that he too could not be part of this surge of collective emotion. But there was a momentum in the speed of events which had consolidated the Nazis' rise that he recognized as dangerous. Strength had replaced sense; brutality, sensitivity; righteousness, integrity. Military might had once more arrived in Germany to become its defender. But it always ultimately destroyed the very society it championed.

Georg Elser pushed his way across the room and stepped out into the cold, wet but fresh air of night. He remained in the shadow of the small Bierkeller, watching cars arriving outside the Burgerbraukeller across Rosenheimerplatz. Hitler's speech was coming to an end. Elser could hear roars of approval from the audience within, now punctuating every paragraph of oration. Then the noise became sustained and moments later Brownshirts and the black uniforms of the SS crowded at the distant entrance, surrounding the Führer as he made his way to the waiting car and was driven away.

Two hours, every year, to celebrate the old comrades of the party in early days, a speech was made to evoke the struggles of the past and illustrate the achievements of the modern Nazi Germany. The darker side was only for enemies of the Reich: opposition that was unacceptable would be crushed, eliminated, liquidated.

Elser ground out the remnants of his cigarette butt and began to walk back to Turkenstrasse. He smiled as he remembered Hitler's last words, blasting from the wireless. There were always two possibilities for any problem – a temporary postponement or a final solution. Interesting, he thought, and turned up his collar against the increasing rain.

The landlady was waiting when he walked through the archway into the small courtyard and knocked lightly on the door. She opened it and giggled, holding up a lantern and keys on a ring.

'Let me show you,' she said and stepped past him towards the two doors which lay flush with the cobbles, seeing her hand with difficulty, catching herself on the single remaining support of what was once a balustrade, Elser took the keys, undid the padlock and lifted both doors, revealing steps leading to a basement. She led the way into darkness, illuminated only by the lantern.

The basement was large and bare but for a workbench, numerous tools and broken, rejected furniture from the house. Rain dripped from above and the atmosphere was dank and cold. The woman turned to Elser.

'You could do anything here,' she whispered, stared a moment and then gestured. 'It's yours.' Elser stepped to the wooden bench, saw the vice and examined the rusting tools. The landlady put the lantern on the workbench and turned down the wick. Rain dripped, noises of the city were distant.

'It isn't much,' she said.

'It's something,' replied Elser quietly. The woman moved towards her new lodger, allowing her now unbuttoned cotton robe to open, revealing once elegant legs. Her full breasts pressed against Elser's chest. Her eyes looked into his and her lips moved silently with unmistakable invitation. Elser reached out slowly and touched the woman's shoulders through the thin material. She shivered.

'You're cold,' he said. She smiled. Her hair was down, her manner composed; drink had given her impetus and confidence.

'I remember you,' she whispered again.

Elser felt her warmth and the longing in her flesh as she moved her body, voluptuous, sensual and expectant, securely enclosed in his arms beneath the large, unbuttoned overcoat. He closed his eyes as her mouth melted upon his and a delicate experienced tongue sought response between his lips. Heady perfume and offered sexuality forced capitulation; six months' incarceration proved too long for any defence.

He thrust the woman against the bench as her excitement intensified. She began breathing heavily as he lifted her on to the scarred worktop and, leaning over, hoisted himself towards the opening thighs. The woman's hands were already tearing at his trousers, pushing them from his hips as he sank into the female body, kissing and biting with increasing lust. Penetration caused the woman to drag her

49

lips from his and suck air, neck arched, hands grasping Elser's clothes.

Only then did he reach beneath the thin cotton and begin to caress with sensitive fingers the full flesh, erect nipples and the long curves that led to a moist cleft, shaved of hair, where the small hardening mound of her clitoris firmed immediately as he lightly stroked first one side and then the other, quickening his movement in rhythm with his body. As if she was an instrument to be played upon with understanding and skill, Elser's lips, hands and penis became a single musician creating an ecstasy that built from sighs and moans to cries of fulfilment.

The woman screamed as Elser came, exploding within her, convulsed with the released repression from months of denial. She clasped him tightly and he clung to her gratefully, equally vulnerable, equally lost for that moment. Then they lay quietly together, as their breath slowed and reality returned. Instinct, emotion and passion faded until all that remained was the sound of dripping rain from the open doors above.

'Oh, Georg,' she murmured. 'You've come back.'

It was a long time before he responded, but when he did his eyes were open and he was staring at the tools on the workbench. 'Yes,' he said quietly.

5

The train that took Otto Meyer and Wolf Schneider back to Berlin that night was the ten thirty-one express from Munich. The Führer's coach had been attached, and soon after the end of the Burgerbraukeller speech, the immediate entourage had boarded, whistles were blown, and with steam and smoke and the grinding of wheels on steel, the security guard of Adolf Hitler were able to relax for the first time in sixteen hours.

Meyer sprawled opposite Schneider, and stared out through the half-open blind at the flickering suburbs of a city en route. Industry knew no hours as he could see. Factory chimneys belching smoke, refineries pouring waste into the sky, blazed with light and flame as if a door had opened on Dante's inferno. It reminded the officer of another time, when he had been a young soldier of the Kaiser's army, cowering in the trenches during the bombardment before a dawn assault. Meyer closed his eyes again, hoping for sleep, but feared the dreams that would come, stimulated by this vision of the new and vibrant Germany.

He sat up and undid several more buttons on his tunic. Now there was only darkness outside and six hours before the first glimmers of dawn where the outlying districts of the capital sprawled eastwards towards the frontier with Poland. Schneider slept. Younger, fit, innocent of so many things. Brought up amidst a defeated empire, he had learnt only to appreciate the growth, consolidation and political definition which had emerged without question. How could there be alternatives when the Nazi party had proven their promises? Allegiance was so easy for the majority of youth, who had come of age into a new world and survived, and now had

51

hope and expectation. Hitler had been as good as his word. Who could doubt him?

Meyer stood up quietly in the compartment, stepped out into the narrow corridor and gently slid the door closed. The train had begun to sway as the engine driver increased speed outside the city. Meyer reached for a cigarette from his pocket and lit it, leaning against the compartment wall as he bent towards the leaping flame. Here he was, a protector of the greatest leader to emerge in German history since – who? Bismarck? Frederick the Great? A man of innovation. A pragmatic, dogmatic, ruthless statesman, a seductive persuader of the rich and influential, a seducer of the middle class, a champion of the working man.

Meyer blew smoke towards the carriage window and watched it curl against the condensation on the glass. His father had been a chief of police, representing solid order in a world of supreme stability until August 1914. The Sarajevo incident had revealed long-repressed resentments and erupted into a war that, culminating in defeat and collapse, had brought only despair. Meyer had joined his father – the conscript become policeman – with a flair which quickly showed him to be worthy of promotion. He had basked in his father's pride, gleaning so many things from the older man's years of experience.

Marriage, children, a responsible life as a Bavarian father, had led to maturity and a suspicion of accepted truths and the recounted history as it was now taught in the schools. Germany had not lost the war, she had been betrayed; not fought to conquer, but merely defended herself against the foe. Meyer had suffered during the trench warfare in France for two years. It was difficult to be an idealist in mud, rain and a ten-hour bombardment from one thousand French and British guns. But now it was over. Finished. Nothing mattered more.

He had created a family which had been peremptorily denied him, taken away by a love that had faded. He had been rejected by his wife who had received the custody of both son and daughter. The divorce had been a scandal but his professional reputation and his father's influence proved sufficient to maintain his position. Meyer inhaled deeply, staring out into the darkness of the past as the carriage swayed wildly, roaring at high speed. Now he was past forty years of age, without everything he had given his life to – Marianne had taken the children, as death had removed his father and mother. Cynicism had soured Meyer's prospering career with the Munich police and, strangely, had improved his perceptions. Himmler himself, appreciating Meyer's pre-eminent reputation, had abducted, although the official word was assimilated, him into the SS as a Gestapo officer and special security chief to the Führer of the Nazi party. It had been presented as a privilege although it was called a career opportunity by jealous colleagues. But it was proving a responsibility to Meyer that had begun to age him before his time. He looked into his reflection in the carriage window, wiping the condensation to see a clear image, searching for grey hairs.

'Sir!' came a voice. Meyer turned to see Schneider at the compartment door.

'What is it?'

The young officer smiled reassuringly. 'You can stand down, sir. Nothing can happen, the route is protected all the way to Berlin *and* we've the best security aboard. Our own men.'

Meyer took the cigarette from his lips and appraised the young officer, appreciating his concern.

The train rattled over steel points and the senior Gestapo officer braced himself against the movement of the carriage before blowing smoke into the corridor.

'Do you know where the Archduke Franz Ferdinand was sitting when he was shot by an assassin?'

Schneider paled at the knowledge and answered reluctantly. 'In his carriage sir.'

'Drawn by horses,' said Meyer, 'surrounded by protection, security and "his" men. This,' he gestured in the direction they were going, 'is pulled by a steam engine.'

53

'I'm sorry, sir,' said Schneider. 'I don't understand.'

'Progress,' stated Meyer. The young officer dropped his head, feeling like a fool. 'I am merely suggesting, Schneider, that we live in a modern world and destruction has perhaps become more ingenious and inventive than a bullet from a pistol.'

'Yes, sir,' murmured Schneider.

'Imagine,' said Meyer quietly, 'if a single rail along this track were to be – loosened?' Schneider looked up quickly. Meyer smiled wearily. 'The consequences would affect us both, even if we lived.'

'I'm sorry, sir,' repeated Schneider.

'Don't be,' replied Meyer. 'Just sleep. If you can.'

There was movement in the chicken run as the cockerel stepped between his hens, went out of the small door, flapped his wings, stretched his neck and, craning at the sky, crowed the first of many calls heralding the morning. Dew still glistened on the outside tables in the rear garden of the Burgerbraukeller an hour after dawn, when the first waitresses arrived as the cleaners stumbled out of the staff entrance, disturbing the quiet with laughter and gossip about the night before. Several of the old women, still carrying their mops and buckets, peered into the chicken coop looking for fresh eggs, but the early frost had already driven even the cockerel back into his hut, and the wet straw behind offered nothing.

Soon after nine o'clock, Georg Elser wandered over to a table past several others already occupied and sat down alone, waiting for service. The day was clear and sunlight had begun to filter across the garden. A waitress emerged from the service door and crossed quickly to serve customers from a tray loaded with steaming coffee cups. Returning, she passed Elser without acknowledgement and returned to the Burgerbraukeller. Elser could smell the coffee from the other tables and saw the traditional dry Bavarian cake provided on request. He took out a cigarette, broke it in half, replaced one part in the packet and lit the other, inhaling deeply. His jacket had dried during the night and, waking early, he had removed it from the warm kitchen of his Turkenstrasse lodgings and walked across Rosenheimerplatz to have breakfast where it had been impossible the night before even to enter for supper. The waitress returned and began wiping the dew from the table.

'What do you want?' she asked curtly, then looked up. 'Coffee?'

Elser nodded.

'With milk?'

Elser nodded again.

The young woman looked at Elser and slowed her brisk actions. 'Sugar?' she asked, as if it would be a gift if she brought it.

Elser smiled and nodded yet again. The waitress stood up straight, playing with the damp cloth for a moment, then she too smiled. When she returned with the coffee, the cup and saucer was all alone in the centre of her tray. She placed it carefully in front of Elser, then stayed to watch him sip. 'More sugar?' she asked. Elser nodded.

She took out of her apron pocket a small 'cellar' of sugar and, leaning towards him, sprinkled it in the coffee. 'I shouldn't' she confided. 'There's a shortage.' He looked into her critical eyes, which suddenly changed to complement the warmth of a lovely smile. 'I've not seen you here before,' she said, 'have I?' Elser shook his head and sipped more coffee. Her gaze continued to play over the stranger. 'Where are you from?'

'Swabia – Württemberg,' said Elser and drank more coffee.

'Oh.' She smiled again. 'So am I. From Ravensburg.' They looked at each other as if that was sufficient to start a sparkling conversation. 'What's your name?' asked the waitress.

'Georg,' said Elser. In the distance by the service entrance, Anton Payerl, the proprietor, stepped out briefly, wiping his apron, surveying the tables to count numbers.

'Annalise!' he shouted. The young waitress flinched, waved quickly and picked up her tray, glancing back at Elser.

'You don't say much, do you, Georg?' She suddenly giggled, then turned away as he finished the coffee.

'Annalise,' said Elser, exploring the sound of her name.

She turned back to him. He pushed the cup towards her. 'Another?' she asked. He nodded, and the young waitress saw that her flirtation had drawn a response from her customer, who was attracted. She let her well-proportioned body do the rest and, standing erect to show her ample bosom effectively displayed above the nipped waist of her dirndl dress, she began to giggle again. 'Cake?'

Elser smiled and held up the cup and saucer. She reached for it and their fingers touched. Neither of them moved as their eyes met; their fingertips reluctant to part, as if electricity held them together. They looked at each other, now in an altogether different way with an instinctive understanding, fear, wonder, even shock. The empty cup and saucer hovered between them then fell and smashed on the table-top. Annalise, in her traditional costume, blushed from her chest to her cheeks. She quickly gathered up the broken pieces and hurried away.

Sunlight dappled through trees on to the damp grass, warming the table and benches where Georg Elser was sitting. He blinked, realizing that the sun had risen further above the distant rooftops and was creeping towards the Burgerbraukeller. He stood up and walked through long shadows to the rear double doors, which were now half open. When Annalise stepped out of the kitchen, she saw immediately that Elser was gone. For a moment her face fell, then she saw the footprints in the dew, smiled, turned back and went through the swing doors into the main hall of the building. The dark-haired man from Württemberg was lying back on a bench beside a long table, gazing across to the pillars and first-floor balustrade, which ran the length of the hall in a series of bowed balconies.

'There you are,' said the waitress, and placed steaming

coffee on the table beside Elser. He looked up at the young woman and again something between them created a silence. He touched her hand and, unbidden, she slowly sat down. Across the large room, two other waitresses appeared from the serving doors, then, seeing Annalise with a customer, burst into giggles and disappeared back into the kitchen. Elser coughed and lit another half-cigarette as Annalise made a face at his unwavering, perceptive eyes.

She had naturally dark-streaked long blonde hair, pulled back and secured loosely over her shoulders. Her smooth forehead curved towards finely shaped eyebrows above pale blue-green eyes protected by thick black lashes. Her symmetrical features and well-shaped, generous mouth complemented fine nostrils and a narrow nose. Her skin was delicate and almost translucent, stretched over a jawline that pulled against her slender neck, where Elser could see a pulse beating faster than normal. She blushed, realizing he was appraising her.

'Famous place,' he stated softly. Annalise cocked her head and made another face at him, screwing up her nose and lips.

'How long have you worked here?' he asked.

Annalise closed her eyes then, hearing a noise from the kitchen, spun around and glanced towards the swing doors. She turned back to him and whispered, 'One minute.'

'What?'

'I've only got one minute,' she explained. Elser picked up his coffee cup, blew on the hot liquid and sipped carefully, watching the young woman's features relax. He replaced his cup. 'I started two years ago,' she murmured. 'It seems longer.'

'Is there a job for me?'

'What do you do?'

'Make things,' said Elser. 'Mend things.'

'What things?' asked Annalise with a wide, pretty smile, shifting uncomfortably on the bench.

' . . . and play the zither,' said Elser, ignoring her question.

'Well?' The question was a deliberate challenge.

'What I do,' stated Elser quietly, 'I do – well.'

The waitress's eyes twinkled then darted again to the kitchen doors as the proprietor appeared, bellowing her name. She stood up hurriedly and the large man withdrew.

'Do you dance?' she asked quickly. Elser nodded.

'Sometimes.'

'Tonight we have one, will you come?' Elser smiled.

'Perhaps.'

Whirling around a cleared central area of the Burgerbraukeller, Annalise and Elser moved quickly together to the music of a fast zither and violins. They passed Herr Payerl twice. The proprietor made a grimace the second time, but the waitress knew her free time was her own and only replied with a smile. Finally, they collapsed on benches beside a table empty of people but full of half-drunk beer steins. They were both breathless and happy.

'I told you,' she laughed. 'But it's too loud.' The couples on the crowded dance floor were all shouting, singing to the tunes or inciting friends who were still seated to join them. Annalise leant towards Elser as his face turned to hers, and kissed him impulsively.

Elser smiled. 'Is it always like this?'

'Once a week,' answered Annalise.

'Even Sundays?' asked Elser.

'Are you religious?' The waitress giggled. 'Germany has changed. It is our duty to work *and* enjoy ourselves *any* day . . . or night! The Führer has said so!' She reached for a half-full stein of beer and slid it towards Elser, who caught it as the music reached a crescendo and stopped. Loud applause came from all parts of the Burgerbraukeller and Annalise was immediately on her feet. She bent towards Elser.

'I have to work.' She kissed him again, lightly.

'When will you be free?' he asked, and she smiled slowly.

'Soon,' she murmured, and disappeared into the milling

58

crowds. Elser leaned back against the table and began absorbing the architecture of the building: its structure, construction details, supports, cross-beams, the colonnade, archways and a single central pillar holding the weight of the entire roof.

Damp with perspiration, but smiling at the knowledge that it was past her official hours, Annalise returned to Georg Elser, who was still at the same table. The crowds around him had dispersed into the night. Only the zither player continued to pick softly at chords denied him during the noise of the evening's occasion. Several drunks remained, slumped over their beer, and as two other waitresses reluctantly cleared their neglected tables, Annalise slid along the bench next to her 'new man', giggling as he looked away to survey the large beerhall. She kicked off her shoes, leant back, then touched Elser delicately on the shoulder. He turned to her and saw that she had been sipping in the kitchen.

'Where does he speak?'

Annalise's lips parted over well-formed teeth as her tongue ran their length before a wide yawn, which she instantly covered. Her eyes were again on Elser, as if he were a stern, disapproving father. She removed her hand and wiped her brow. 'I'm sweating.'

Elser continued to stare, and only then did his question register.

'Who?' she asked.

'Hitler,' said Elser.

Annalise glanced across the Burgerbraukeller and pointed. 'The staff are always in the kitchen when he talks, but they put the podium there . . . Why?'

Elser's eyes examined her a moment longer, then followed her extended arm and pointing finger to the middle of the room and its main supporting pillar. Sporadic applause sounded as the zither player finished. The young waitress assumed a forlorn expression.

'Please,' she said. 'More? You know!' The old man nodded and with a weary smile began to strum a folk tune.

59

Immediately Annalise took up the words and spoke them softly.

'*Kom ziga . . . kom ziga.*' She looked at Elser. 'Do you know it?' she asked.

'I play it,' he replied, then closed his eyes. 'Better.'

'That's what you are,' whispered Annalise, 'a gypsy.'

Elser's eyes remained closed and he shook his head. 'An artisan,' he murmured.

Annalise leant towards him and put her lips to his ear. 'Then you had *better*,' she emphasized the word, 'find a job.'

Elser turned to her and looked directly into her face, so close to his. The moment lasted as the music faded. 'Where do you live?' he asked.

Annalise dropped her eyes. 'In a women's hostel.'

'Oh,' said Elser.

She seized his hand hopefully. 'You?'

Elser squeezed her fingers but his face carried a warning, already seeing in his mind the landlady waiting for him to come back alone. It was too early for anything but survival yet.

'Difficult,' he replied to the expectant eyes, and watched the beautiful young woman's expression change, so gently he kissed her moist lips. The zither music stopped, but the two of them were oblivious to the silence, exploring those first sensations that either come to nothing or lead on to heaven or hell.

Millions of years had created the huge stone face that dominated the small, curving quarry, throwing shadow across half the flat area carved from the rock. A single moment blew it to pieces and the entire edifice collapsed as the set dynamite charges undermined the support of so many tons of what would eventually be ground into fine grain cement. Dust rose in the air as once again the mind of man took from nature the substance to create what imagination had conceived; not merely for the architecture of cities but for the bastions of war.

Georg Elser watched the newly made shapes of stone fall and settle, then hesitantly fell in to step with the explosives expert who was confidently striding towards the still settling pile of rocks. All three charges had been correctrly ignited. A cursory glance told the expert what he needed to confirm, that it was now safe. He nodded to his new assistant, who, on his first day, had already proved to be as skilful as he had described himself, his deft fingers wrapping wire and detonators like a hardened professional. References from an armaments factory in Weidenheim, and the now proven assurance about his familiarity with dynamite from blowing rocks on his father's farm, made this small Swabian a catch. He was good and would quickly learn that this was not a watchmaker's or a farmer's task. The large explosives expert grinned and nudged Elser, who immediately took the whistle hanging on a cord around his neck, put it to his mouth as he had been instructed and blew loudly the first signal for 'all clear'.

Watching the quarrymen emerge slowly in the distance, Elser wiped the dust from his eyes. Grime had already collected on his skin, even though it was still early. He smiled to himself as the burly work-gang approached, each man pulling on thick gloves to dispose of the rocks, all of them taking pleasure in cursing the prospect. As they brushed roughly past him, Elser felt a great sense of satisfaction. He'd finally come home, and for the first time he knew he had found something he wanted to do. The unfamiliar sense of purpose gave him confidence. For a moment, every problem that might arise seemed surmountable and even his still questioning conscience was merely a challenge. One man, one job; that, in the end was all it would be – a commitment to a job.

He put the whistle back in his mouth and a second time blew long and hard, indicating to the entire workforce throughout the quarry that the blast had been successful and it was now completely safe.

6

Otto Meyer saluted both guards rigidly flanking the wide
entrance of the pillared portico as he completed the flight of
steps and briskly entered the large building. Boots echoing on
the marble, Meyer strode between several cleaners still
polishing the ornate floor. Automatically his eyes surveyed
and absorbed his surroundings, checking doors, windows,
entrances, exits . . . He stopped at the very centre of the huge
foyer and looked up at the frescoed dome high above, then
turned slowly on his heels.

Schneider crossed towards him and waited patiently for his
commanding officer's attention. Meyer checked his watch,
then regarded Schneider's face. The young man had been up
since before dawn, inspecting all parts of the opera building
and placing guards throughout. He smiled as Meyer nodded
his pleasure. 'Circumspect, Wolf.'

'Thank you, sir.' Schneider coughed and went on, 'May I
say, sir, that it is not necessary for *you* always to . . . ' He
stopped himself, seeking the correct phrasing. 'I mean sir,
that in future, I am capable . . . ' Meyer cut him off with a
gesture and began to remove his black gloves as he praised the
Aryan ideal, standing tall and arrogant before him. His hand
made a circling motion seeming to encompass the entire
building with a waft of fingers.

'Have you?'

'Everywhere, sir!' snapped Schneider. Meyer nodded
carefully, put his gloves together then slapped them against
the palm of his other hand.

'You are from Berlin, Wolf?'

'I am Prussian,' replied the young officer proudly, 'sir.'

'Makes all the difference, doesn't it?' smiled Meyer. His

pale and normally fathomless eyes now glittered with irony. 'I am only a German from Bavaria.'

A hint of colour appeared on Schneider's face, humanizing the prepossessing impression.

'I want to see – everywhere,' said Meyer softly and, noticing the young man's face harden, immediately reached out to touch him lightly on the shoulder with the pair of gloves. 'Prussian diligence.' Meyer then indicated himself. 'Provincial curiosity.'

Schneider accepted the remark without reaction. There was no room for humour where he was concerned; he had taken himself seriously from a very early age and, as a result, his bearing and attitude had been the source of admiration by everyone. Now this 'policeman' from Munich was implying a measure of incompetence . . .

Meyer read his thoughts. 'I have every confidence in you Wolf,' he stated, 'but – show me.' Otto Meyer, followed reluctantly by Schneider, began to retrace every step the young SS officer had taken since long before dawn. The two men had all day; Hitler was not due to arrive until darkness.

Schneider knocked lightly on the ornamental panelling. There was no answer. Cautiously he opened the heavy door and stepped into the room slowly, accustoming himself to the low light. He crossed to a chaise longue beneath a huge tapestry and saw his commanding officer sprawled, head turned from a baroque lamp which glowed dully. For a moment, he surveyed the man: tunic unbuttoned, boots carefully placed on the floor, feet resting on a cushion. The Gestapo officer, a member of the all powerful SS – asleep. Reaching forward to tap Meyer, Schneider was startled by a voice.

'Is he here?'

Schneider coughed and stood erect as Meyer turned to him staring up at the young officer.

'He is coming.'

63

Meyer sighed, sat up, swung from the chaise longue and began to slide into his boots. He glanced at his watch then stood up, stamped to secure his heels in the tight-fitting leather and buttoned his tunic before straightening his tie.

'Late,' he said. Schneider nodded and handed Meyer his peaked cap, and the two men strode across the large upstairs anteroom to the short corridor which led out on to a balcony high above the vast foyer. The whole area was crowded with invited guests, in formal dress and uniforms, who had waited patiently for the man who now ruled Germany. Quickly Meyer cast his eyes around, noting the guards in key positions, and only then did he relax as a longer roar went up from outside.

'Everyone in place?'

'Yes, sir,' replied Schneider.

Meyer smiled. 'Good,' he murmured.

Hitler slowly made his way up the steps outside the opera building then walked through the pillared portico into the foyer, where the sound of applause from the gathered throng sounded out immediately. With little acknowledgement, the Führer continued on between the divided ranks of people pressing forward against SS guards and paused only once at the very centre of the foyer to gaze upon the beautiful fresco high above him. Although he could not see it clearly, in the past he had memorized every detail, and to be actually beneath it gave him great pleasure.

Traversing the pillared corridor overlooking the growing tumult below, Meyer stopped exactly as Hitler had done and peered down at the Führer, who was staring up into the huge dome. As Meyer's sharp eyes strayed over the assembled audience his blood ran cold. Amongst the aristocratic clique grouped directly at the bottom of the shallow stairway leading up and into the auditorium, something flashed as it emerged from beneath the dark cloth of an evening jacket. Gun metal glinted for a fraction of a second as an arm extended above so many heads, pointing, with the crowd's gaze, at Adolf Hitler.

Otto Meyer stepped from the shadow to the balustrade for a clearer view, exactly as a voice bellowed, *'Heil Hitler, Sieg Heil,'* throughout the great space. It was immediately echoed by almost one thousand others stirred to repeat the accolade, accompanied by a forest of hands raised in salute. Meyer could no longer see the man and was already running.

'The stairs!' he shouted to Schneider, and in the next instant was at the head of one side of the stairway going down to the central red carpet below. Steadied by his hand sliding over the rail, Meyer leapt down the wide, marble slabs. He turned twice on the stairs' axis then took the last flight directly on to the red carpet and shallow stairway to the foyer, three at a time. He plunged into the group of aristocrats as a final cry of *'Heil Hitler'* echoed in the great dome. Meyer grasped the man he had seen point towards the Führer and flung him to the marble floor. Shouts of consternation came from the immediate group lowering their arms as Hitler passed by them and went into the theatre auditorium, seemingly oblivious of the incident. Many of the audience were following him, and those hesitant were hustled on quickly by Schneider and several SS guards who had come to help.

The man in Meyer's grip squirmed, but the ex-policeman held him tightly. When most of the crowd had gone, Meyer dragged the man to his feet and thrust him against the marble balustrade. Breathing heavily, the SS officer studied the man's features. A middle-aged aristocrat with medals upon the chest of his evening jacket, now in white-faced shock, attempted to splutter his innocence of any accusation. He raised an arm hesitantly, as if guessing the cause of his plight and offering an explanation.

'I . . . was . . . only . . . saluting . . . with . . . '

Meyer looked at the fingers of the metal arm protruding from a crisp white cuff. Part of the man's right arm had been amputated and this modern device obviously allowed him at least some dexterity. The metal was highly polished and of the type gunmakers might use. Meyer glanced at Schneider and slowly released the man, angry at himself, his zealousness exposed. Schneider turned away and coughed to control his amusement, exactly as the loud overture began from impatient musicians in the orchestra pit within. They had been signalled to start by the anxious conductor, confident that even if the complete audience were not, at least the Führer was now seated.

It was a long opera – *Die Meistersinger* – that night, especially for Otto Meyer. It was late before light again cut through the gloom in the upper anteroom of what had once been a place to retire at the opera intervals, reserved for nobility. Meyer slumped on to the now familiar chaise longue and turned on the baroque lamp. Guards snapped to attention outside and the door was closed behind Schneider, who lifted a heavy ornamented chair easily and placed it opposite his chief. At Schneider's request, schnapps had been served on a small table, and he poured carefully from a cut-glass decanter.

Unbuttoning his tunic, Meyer lay back against stretched silk brocade skilfully woven. A story of huntsmen and deer decorated the large tapestry above. The detail was merely a mix of colour in the dim light, but the impression was of splendour, as indeed the entire building presented a grandeur from the past. Meyer smiled for the first time that night as he looked at it. The opera was over, Hitler safely escorted to the Reich Chancellory and the building would soon be released back to the local authorities. These few hours were his – until dawn.

'When I was a boy, I never thought I should ever enter such a place. To me then, this was only as real as a Grimms' fairytale!'

'I came here often with my parents,' said Schneider. 'During the Great War.'

Meyer nodded and accepted schnapps. 'While I was in the trenches, no doubt.' Schneider smiled and toasted, *'Prost!'* Both men drank from the small glasses.

'Now we have our own fairy-tale.'

'What is that, sir?'

'The Führer,' answered Meyer softly. 'A once young corporal, now carrying a future for a great and very old country.'

Schneider poured again. '*Prost,*' he said. 'The Führer!' Meyer drank slowly. 'And it will be a great future,' said Schneider. 'Do you doubt it?'

Meyer chose his words carefully. 'So far, things are improving. There is no doubt of that.'

Schneider poured again for himself as Meyer shook his head, refusing a third glass. 'If,' began Schneider, 'you have any doubts at all about our . . . leadership.' He paused. 'Why, if you will pardon me asking, sir, be a part at all, and such an important part, of our system of government?'

Meyer's eyes narrowed. Caution controlled his immediate reaction, but in truth the question was fair and imprudence was a prerogative of younger men. Besides, he was growing to like Schneider and all the obvious hard work he put into his perceptions. Meyer pressed the bridge of his nose and closed his eyes, suddenly feeling the pressure of the day. He was tired.

'These are the times we live in,' he answered. 'How could I ignore, at my age, having built a career, the opportunity of such advancement? I would think many Germans will have the same answer. No individual can be expected to agree totally with any system, but merely to appreciate the positive aspects of it prompts a loyalty of service. Life can always be better; be improved. That is a part of the human condition. It is what makes us strive – even fight!' Meyer paused, and now accepted more schnapps. 'Only the means,' he continued, 'are questionable.'

'Philosophy,' stated Schneider.

'Realism,' answered Meyer, and both men drank the liqueur.

Schneider began to laugh. 'Excuse me, sir, but the look on Von Brauchnich's face this evening . . . ' Meyer frowned at the reference to the man he had earlier thought an assassin, and his expression immediately warned the young SS officer to silence.

'We cannot always be right, Schneider – any of us.'

'Circumspect, sir,' countered Schneider quickly.

'Yes, Wolf.'

Schneider responded to the Christian name and felt some pride as he remembered with admiration the curt apology to Von Brauchnich from his commanding officer as Meyer had personally escorted the man to his very seat in the opera's darkened auditorium.

'Tomorrow?' asked Meyer.

'At seven,' answered Schneider. 'The car will be waiting in Munich.'

'Be sure,' said Meyer. 'You can telephone from Nuremberg, where we stop for five minutes. The train is under guard tonight?'

'Yes, sir. I gave full instructions.'

Meyer closed his eyes again as the implications of the morrow grew in his mind.

'The Führer wants tea in Berchtesgaden.'

'It has always seemed to me, sir, the greatest risk. People know he goes there often . . . '

'Yes,' interrupted Meyer. There was silence for a moment.

'The women, sir,' began Schneider. 'What do we do about them? They will crowd around the car and . . . '

'Take their flowers,' said Meyer. 'Be gentle but firm. They love him.'

Schneider smiled. 'Yes, sir.'

Meyer looked across at the clean-cut features of his younger assistant. The low light was cruel, showing how the years to come would take flesh from bone and the hardness Meyer now saw for only a moment would age the face. Experience would deprive the eyes of natural enthusiasm, as it always did.

'Are you married, Schneider? I never asked.'

'No, sir.'

'Don't,' whispered Meyer.

'Why, sir?'

Meyer paused before answering. 'You might miss her one day,' he said softly, and felt the familiar, unwanted welling of emotion within. He stood up brusquely. 'Get what little sleep you can.'

Schneider immediately snapped to attention then crossed to the door and knocked twice. It was opened from outside by one of the guards. Meyer buttoned his tunic, turned out the lamp and walked slowly into the shaft of light coming from the corridor.

The noise of the two roaring locomotives and the many rattling carriages had made conversation difficult in the compartment where Meyer, now alone, peered out at the passing panorama of middle Germany. Schneider interrupted his thoughts, slamming back the sliding door, grinning at his commanding officer.

'The Führer's in good spirits!' he shouted, and re-seated himself opposite Meyer, who nodded approval, checked his watch, then again looked out at the sunlit countryside.

The year had turned and now, in February 1939, this was only one of many journeys already made south on the Führer's train to Munich. It was almost always the same, and the security procedure, although complicated, was at least less taxing on Meyer's mind; the weight of responsibility lightened with his growing experience of the intricate movement orders to his under-officers. He allowed himself moments of pleasure now, appreciating the beauty of farmed fields, bright with frost beneath the late winter sun.

Even within the heated compartment, he felt the cold through the large windows, and he had even opened one of them to allow the crisp air to flow over his face. It kept his body awake and his mind sharp. The SS credo of constant vigilance he had adopted as his own. During the past months, the strain of responsibility had begun to show on his features and he had lost weight, but he had become more confident of his position. The unexpected was no longer a threat but a challenge.

Meyer looked at Schneider staring out at the undulating land far south of Leipzig with assured eyes as if he would always have command of any situation. Meyer again checked his watch. They'd arrive in Nuremberg shortly, where the usual telephone call would be made, ensuring the cars were waiting in Munich. Efficiency and punctuality were his orders. What the Führer did to change that was not his concern, but when it happened Meyer's planned alternatives were immediately implemented. Any contingency – Meyer smiled, he had actually begun to attract the eyes of his superiors and been complimented on his growing abilities. Pleasant reward, but perhaps also dangerous exposure; one jealous officer in high command and . . . He cut off his thoughts.

'Be ready, Schneider.' He indicated the time.

The young officer nodded and mouthed his reply loudly as the train rattled over a points intersection. 'Don't worry, sir. Everything's in order.'

Otto Meyer searched Schneider's face for the remotest glimmer of concern and, finding none, began to laugh loudly. But the sound was lost as the fast train sped towards the only stop before its final destination, the southern capital amidst the Bavarian Alps.

After a brief appointment had been kept at the old party headquarters in the Brauhaus, the convoy of Hitler's entourage accelerated out of Munich, then turned off the autobahn to take the valley road through Bad Reichenhall and on to Berchtesgaden. The seven dark Mercedes came to a halt in the small village square, which soon filled with well-wishers cheering and singing impromptu folk songs.

Hitler, amidst such a show of warmth, made Meyer's job difficult by dismissing many of the black uniforms which had initially surrounded him and, despite the fading light, crisp

70

air and remaining patches of snow, he insisted on taking tea outside so those around could see him and present petitions. Many did, doffing caps or curtseying with the greatest respect. Throughout the 'audience' small bouquets of flowers were thrown in the Führer's direction, to Meyer's intense consternation, but the late afternoon passed without incident. With the early sunset and increasing cold, Hitler and his entourage retired inside the large tea-house and spread themselves around a roaring fire.

In the back of their open Mercedes, Schneider and Meyer each finished giving instructions to their men, who saluted and ran from the car to comply with orders. Shortly, as had been arranged, the seven Mercedes would make their way up to the Berghof, which was Hitler's private residence overlooking the village and mountains. Only there, with the Führer amidst so much additional security, could Meyer truly relax. He shivered, reached for his leather greatcoat over the front seat and put it around his shoulders. Above, the twilight sky was clear and first stars showed brightly.

'Responsibility for the duration,' murmured Meyer.

'Sir?'

'We have a very good position, Schneider. It lasts as long as all is well . . . you understand?'

'A long time, I hope,' mused Schneider.

'Hope.' Meyer repeated the word softly. Laughter came from within the tea-house, which adjoined the large bierkeller. The small windows, shutters open, glowed from inside. Crowds outside peered in, looking for the dignitaries who had so suddenly arrived within their midst. Meyer noted the black uniforms interspersed among them and again relaxed, looking at even more stars appearing in the night sky.

'Do you believe in God, Schneider?'

'Something,' answered the SS officer. 'Do you?'

Meyer smiled and nodded. 'Something.'

Schneider's gaze lingered on his commanding officer, again evaluating the man, learning more. 'Have you travelled, sir? Been abroad?'

71

Meyer nodded. 'I was in northern France for a while some years ago.'

Schneider coughed, embarassed at the reference to the Great War. 'Of course sir, but I meant . . . '

'Switzerland,' interrupted Meyer, 'for two summers, and Paris once, for three days.' He paused, remembering a café on the Ile St Louis and the smell of black tobacco during breakfast under an awning overhanging the street.

'England?' asked Schneider.

Meyer shook his head. 'No.' He glanced at the building containing the Führer of Germany, then looked back at Schneider his eyes hardened. 'Not yet.'

Schneider grinned at the inference before stating, 'I'd like to travel all over the world.' Noises came from the building, applause sounded, the crowds outside began murmuring loudly.

Meyer spoke quietly. 'You might – soon.'

Light burst from the entrance across patches of snow on the cobbles and, moments later, Hitler and his entourage were through the cheering villagers, into their cars and on the mountain road to the security of the Führer's residence at Obersalzberg. The Berghof was his sanctuary from any opposition and all threats, where fear existed only in the mind. It was a place of peace from which contemplation became easier – and the swift development of long established, corrupted ambitions that would soon affect the daily realities of millions.

Meyer was almost asleep when the Mercedes came to a halt halfway up the mountain outside the main building. He watched the entourage follow their Leader inside, and with the closing of the large carved oak door, his job was done. The other cars immediately backed up on the gravel and drove the guards off to their familiar quarters. But one car remained. Even the driver and Wolf Schneider were mesmerized by the view as Meyer lay back in the Mercedes, staring out at the myriad distant lights of Germany spread beneath chasms of forest shadows. And above these, seeming to float between man and the firmament, were ghost-like snow peaks etched clearly by the rising moon; a mountain ridge containing, as legend had it, the spirit of a great German hero who would rise up in time of danger and save her from extinction.

'Drive on,' commanded Meyer softly. His head lolled against the folded canvas hood as the driver carefully reversed the Mercedes from the gravel terrace and nosed towards the smooth concrete road. Meyer's thoughts turned to bed and sleep. His dreams always became a single nightmare that someone, somewhere, one day would . . . He stared up into the dark heavens, where the stars flickered their indecipherable secrets.

7

Georg Elser, urinating against a side of the wooden shed, squinted to be sure he was not splashing his shoes. He could just make out speckled marks on the white, dusty toecaps and swore, finished, buttoned up, then turned to survey the immediate darkness in case anyone else had remained behind at the quarry.

He was almost frozen, having been hunched, waiting in the thick undergrowth behind the double-padlocked storage shed, but he had patiently listened to all his fellow workers leave until the last – the foreman – had secured the gates and spoken briefly to the watchman, who had then stoked up and ensconced himself, with constant grumbling, behind a fire glowing in an empty oil drum. Soon the smell of chestnuts indicated to Elser that the accompanying schnapps was broached, but only after the old man began humming marching songs from the Great War did Elser stand up in the darkness to stretch his frozen and stiffening limbs.

Now, breath frosting into the cold night air, he listened still to the old man mumbling in the distance beyond the wire mesh gate, drinking himself into oblivion and the dawn. 'One night, if the fire went out,' thought Elser, 'he'd freeze to death.'

Elser's hands found the two padlocks and cradled them gently. Not difficult to open, he had already decided, but they would take time, of which he had enough if he was not disturbed. His foot sought, then found, the small case he had brought to work that morning, empty. Even at a touch it upturned and, being empty, dropped lightly to the ground. Elser listened for a reaction to the slightest noise. There was none.

When he left the quarry that night, if he could climb the fence without detection, he knew he must be more careful with what he would be carrying. Gelignite could be moulded, but old dynamite was unstable and, unless treated carefully, a case full of it would send him to kingdom come, even if he tripped and fell in the street.

He'd bought himself a small, used flashlight and, wrapping it in a blue cotton handkerchief, he snapped it on. The dull beam played on the first lock. He examined it, then, trying to control his cold, shaking hand, took a thin pencil of steel from his pocket and began to explore the metal teeth within the large keyhole.

'Shit!' bellowed the old man from the distance, and immediately the sound of smashing glass stilled Georg Elser. Cold fingers had let slip the schnapps bottle and the watchman's anger was obvious, and dangerous for Elser. Drunk, the old man was no threat; but alert, Elser could hardly chance slipping out through the narrow, meshed barbed wire.

Elser swore to himself at his bad luck. It had gone perfectly. Both padlocks opened, the door pulled ajar. He had entered the shed and filled his small case with ten sticks of dynamite, gingerly taken from beneath the straw at the bottom of one of the crates. He had been disturbed because of the stamp date on the wood – the explosive was old and time made the normally stable sticks potentially volatile. Worse, if they were damp, as he was pleased to see they appeared not to be, they might sweat nitro-glycerine, which could prove disastrous. But he had no alternative, and with some courage decided to take the chance.

He moved slowly around the building into the darkness, where even the faint light of the fire and sparks dancing up into the night did not penetrate. With the door closed and padlocks re-set, all would look well in the morning, but now he was trapped inside the quarry. He swore again and settled back into the familiar undergrowth. He was freezing, and it would be a long night.

Morning came, grey, with drizzle. Wet and stiff, Elser stretched his limbs cautiously amidst the dripping leaves and muddy roots of the small copse. Men were already being admitted to the quarry through the now open gates, as he could hear from their shouts and greetings, muffled by the light rain. It was the smell of coffee that brought Elser to his feet and, after a hurried glance about him, he went to the storage hut, then out to the other workers who were converging on the wooden building which provided a primitive canteen. Inside, having waited his turn in the queue, clutching a mug of steaming coffee, he slumped down at a trestle table, shivered and peered gloomily out of one of the narrow windows at the dank, cold day.

'Where the 'ell 'ave you been?' asked the old watchman, who surveyed Elser's muddied clothes, then plumped himself down beside the bedraggled figure and, with a grin, revealing more gaps than teeth, asked, 'Been up all night?'

Elser nodded. 'Like you.'

The watchman remembered the broken schnapps bottle and nodded ruefully. Elser thought of his small case, hidden in the copse, and hoped the sacking wrapped around the dynamite would protect the sticks from the rain even if it penetrated the old leather, until he could get it later. There would be no problem, as he knew, unless they started to sweat. Then the dynamite would become unstable and . . .

The watchman interrupted his thoughts with a nudge. ''Ow much did she cost you?'

Elser sipped his coffee – 'Only a night's sleep.'

The watchman began to guffaw loudly.

They blew one more section off the face of the quarry that day and only stopped work when the rain increased to a heavy downpour. By late afternoon Elser was thoroughly soaked and in need of dry warmth and some food and drink.

The workers' truck took those without other transport back into the city centre, where Elser decided to walk the rest of the way, directly to the Burgerbraukeller. He carefully protected his wet case from the bustling crowds pushing past him as they ran for trains and trams, rushing to get home out of the gloomy, wet evening twilight. He was almost refused admittance at the entrance of the Bierkeller, but his soulful expression softened the heart of the bruiser on the door, who recognized him from his numerous visits over the past months, and he was ushered into a dark corner, where Annalise finally found him.

Her face changed when she saw his condition. 'Georg, what have you been doing?' White chalk dust caked with grit and grime, cemented with the mud and rain, gave his unshaven face the appearance of a theatrical music-hall performer off stage. 'You can use the washroom upstairs,' whispered Annalise, and indicated the stairway leading to the balcony. 'It's along at the end.' Elser nodded and stood up. 'I'll bring you some . . .'

'The usual,' Elser interrupted, and went to kiss her. But she backed away now with dreaming eyes.

'Later,' she said.

'Perhaps,' murmured Elser. He went up to the balcony area and looked down at the already crowded area below, tables and trestles thronged with customers becoming louder with the beer and the increasingly more smoke-filled convivial atmosphere. For a moment, he lingered beside the main pillar, which reached from the ground floor to the ceiling. Tentatively, he tapped the panelling. The light noise revealed a disturbingly solid composition, bricks around a steel frame or, worse, concrete.

Elser walked the length of the balcony, past numerous rolled-up carpets, propped against peeling plaster, stored in the gloom. Where the last balustrade was secured into the end wall, Elser found the door to the small washroom. He stepped into the confined space where a cracked basin protruded over the toilet seat. Despite a half-window being open above a fixed plate of opaque glass, the smell of stale urine was almost unbearable. Elser relieved himself, attempting to hold his breath for as long as possible, then reached up to pull the short chain. The cistern almost came off the wall. Plaster flaked down to the floor as the two flimsy, metal arm supports actually moved. Water flushed as Elser turned to the basin and briskly stuck his fingers beneath the cold tap whilst trying to peer out of the window into the darkness. With nothing to dry his hands on, he emerged from the small toilet wiping them on his trousers.

He strolled back along the balcony, past the rolled and stacked carpets, and stopped again beside the main pillar. Below, Annalise arrived at his place on the long table and, seeing the small suitcase for the first time, she reached down, seized the handle and lifted it, curious at the weight and contents within.

'Leave it!' bellowed Elser from the balcony. People glanced up from the many tables below and Elser, suddenly feeling exposed, began to run. Reaching the stairs, he took them two at a time, crossed to Annalise quickly, gently took the case from her grasp and kissed her tenderly.

'What is it?' she murmured, as heads still turned towards them, murmuring at the public display of attention.

'A surprise,' answered Elser quietly.

'For me?' The young woman's eyes became excited.

'It will be,' said Elser.

'Are you going to make something?'

'Yes.' Elser sat down and replaced the suitcase carefully on the floor. Annalise's hand lingered on his shoulder.

'Tonight?'

Elser looked up from the steaming sauerkraut, sausages and potatoes, and nodded.

'Can I come to watch?' Annalise mouthed the words, almost without sound. Elser glanced around the large bierhall, seeing faces lose interest in the two of them and the now partly concealed suitcase. Germany, never short of prying eyes, had certainly not changed in this respect since Hitler's accession to power. There would always be someone, somewhere, watching and waiting to intrude on the smallest privacy. He looked up into the eyes of Annalise and knew immediately he must beware of himself above all. Her expression of trust and vulnerability, coupled with his desire, would prove the hardest trial. She was falling in love and, after so many years of isolation from any emotional involvement, he felt himself losing control of his increasing affection for this woman.

'Georg – can I?' Fingertips touched his cheek as the tone of her plea entered his heart. The snatched moments, in dark alleys or trudged wet streets on many nights when he had escorted her back to the grim women's hostel, which had caused them both frustration, flashed through his mind. She knew where he lived but he had not taken her there. The landlady and her Weimar residue of residents had proved too much of an obstacle for Elser. 'Please?' whispered Annalise urgently. 'I must go.'

Behind her in the distance, Elser saw the large figure of Payerl, which was why he smiled and, before putting a finger to his lips, said, 'Then come, tonight.'

Annalise laughed and ran off quickly as Elser slid a hand down to touch the suitcase full of dynamite once more. Just for reassurance.

When Elser left the Burgerbraukeller, it was no longer raining, and by the time he reached his lodgings on Turkenstrasse, he had walked off some of his dinner and a stein of beer that had proved more than sufficient. Cautiously he stepped into darkness, went through the archway and entered the small courtyard. He placed the suitcase carefully behind his bicycle propped against the wall and unlocked the door. Light showing through the oval window at the top, and a faint sound of music from the radio, confirmed that a group of the lodgers were still awake. Worse, when he closed the door quietly behind him and pocketed his key, the landlady sashayed from the firelit lounge into the corridor, wearing only a silk gown over a thin nightdress, and greeted him with open arms and a drunken smile. Only as he approached slowly did she remember that he had not returned the previous night. Her face soured.

79

'Where have you been?' Elser stopped, but said nothing as he glanced towards the roaring fire surrounded by the curious faces staring at him from dilapidated furniture. 'Some woman taken your fancy, no doubt.' The landlady made it a statement.

Old Herr Herzog, partially deaf, waved at Elser, who gestured a greeting in return. The landlady stepped back, sweeping an arm across her body and bowing in mock respect.

'You may pass.' Elser stared at her as she straightened up and leaned towards him, smelling of liquor, then focused, regarding him with distaste. 'Clean yourself up,' she slurred.

Elser went to the single bathroom, shared by the entire house, undressed, stood in the bath, and doused himself with water from the cold tap. Shivering, he dried his naked body on a small towel then, holding his clothes at his waist, slipped out into the corridor and along to his own room. Wearing a dry, thick wool shirt, corduroy trousers and his other pair of shoes, Elser made his way past the group around the fire, now giving their full attention to the strident music heralding an announcement from the radio.

Outside, remaining against the walls and beneath the protruding eaves of the roof, Elser reached his bicycle, took the hidden suitcase and continued on to the double doors, flush with the wet cobbles, which led to the cellar. Only whilst unlocking them, did he feel the rain for the first time spattering his back.

Stepping down into the darkness, Elser reached out for a lamp, found matches, raised the wick and carefully lit the paraffin-soaked lamp. Immediately, the leaping flame threw shadows around the cellar. Elser trimmed the wick, replaced the glass, put the lamp in the centre of his workbench, checked that his new, gleaming tools were exactly as he had left them, then slowly laid the suitcase on the worktop. He undid the catches, lifted the lid and paused for a moment looking at the wrapped dynamite and several detonators. Rain whipped on to the wooden stairs and Elser glanced up;

80

he had forgotten the doors. He hesitated, then quickly crossed to a trunk against the wall and opened it. Turning back to the suitcase, he carefully took out the sticks of dynamite and carried them to the trunk.

A second time he returned, now with the detonators, and placed them at the bottom in a corner before lowering the trunk lid. In the months since he had occupied the cellar, he had made it habitable, having scoured the floors, cleaned what tools he had inherited and added more as required. He had done odd jobs and repaired some furniture as a handyman might, just to stay in practice. All the while the challenge of the direction he had decided upon, the course of action, the deed, grew in his mind.

The danger would come later; now only safety was required, and that he had secured by being anonymous and solitary in a big city, confiding to no one even the vaguest dissatisfaction with the form of rule in Germany beyond the normal grumbles of a working man who was reluctant to become a political part of the country. Hitler's carefully projected charisma had not been universally accepted, as his rough treatment of the unions had proved, and while there was much public lip-service to National Socialist achievements, private pessimistic optimism, as it was called, was still abundant.

Elser secured the catch on the trunk, satisfied that at least the first stage had been accomplished safely, then he heard feet treading gingerly on the wet stairs. He spun around to see the landlady descending, with a lamp held high in one hand and a drink in the other. She grinned and, slopping liquid, gestured with the glass as if to an audience in the cellar.

'Night after night – all night sometimes. What are you doing down here, Georg?' Elser stepped away from the trunk and sat down at one end of the long bench beside the worktop. He merely smiled in return and began to light one half of a cigarette. The woman stepped towards him, put down the lamp and leaned against the bench. 'And all alone.' She sipped her drink. The downpour in the night outside became heavier. 'You left the doors open,' she said. 'An invitation, I thought.'

'I forgot them.'

'Well, don't. It's damp enough in here . . . and cold. I like them warm.' She reached out and at first touched, then took one of Elser's hands. 'Don't you, Georg, like . . . a fire?' He watched the silk gown over the nightdress slip open as she pushed a thigh against the material and put one knee on the bench. The smell of schnapps was stronger than the liberally applied perfume. 'I hope they don't ruin your hands at that - place. It's hard labour for the likes of you.' She caressed his hand with her fingers. 'You're too sensitive.'

'I have to work.'

'Couldn't you do something else?'

Elser shrugged. The landlady glanced around the cellar, watching leaping shadows making shapes against the walls. For a moment she was mesmerized, then she remembered the old man's request and reached into a pocket of the silk robe.

'Herr Herzog was wondering . . . ' She produced the heirloom pocket watch. ' . . . if you would be so kind as to . . . ?' Elser took it, opened the back and examined the working mechanism and smiled. The landlady sat down suddenly, whispering, 'You've no time to yourself. All day at the quarry and here . . . half the night . . . '

'It's money,' said Elser. The woman moved closer, breathing schnapps into his face.

'I could find you work here. There's more important things . . . ' She paused. ' . . . than money.'

Elser turned away. 'Then I'll leave.'

'Georg, I didn't mean . . . '

'The quarry,' he interrupted. He turned back and stared at her until she grinned slowly. As he drew on his cigarette, a delicate knock sounded from above. Elser and the landlady looked up.

'Georg?' came a voice softly. Elser looked at the woman beside him and saw her eyes harden before she thrust the glass against her lips and sipped more schnapps. 'Georg?' came the voice again; now insistent. The landlady stood up, straining towards the darkness of the open doors, where rain now poured through on to the wooden stairs.

'Yes,' said Elser.

'Work!' exclaimed the landlady.

Annalise began to descend the stairs into the lamplight and leaping shadows. She saw the other woman. 'Oh.'

The landlady absorbed the well-turned ankles, long legs, slim waist, ample bosom and memorable face appearing hesitantly in the flickering light of the cellar. Only when she saw the wet shoulders of an old trenchcoat, and the piled dark hair showing in wisps beneath a stretched woollen cap, and the wide and seeking pale blue eyes, did the older woman grit her teeth and look at Elser, replacing obvious admiration for the girl in her face, with perfect sarcasm in her voice. 'Work!' she repeated with venom. Seizing her lamp from the workbench, she pushed past Annalise, forcing her aside with an arm, holding her glass as if it were a weapon. In a moment she had ascended the slippery steps, reached the courtyard above and, slamming both doors shut, was gone into the rain, her home, private room and solitary bed.

Annalise stared at Elser for several seconds, then slowly sat down beside him.

'I wasn't sure . . .' she began. He touched her cheek and smiled.

'The only problem,' murmured Elser, 'is timing.' Then, appreciating the luxury of their privacy, they kissed each other's lips, tremoring with the passion of anticipation . . . Getting back to the small room inside the house was difficult but accomplished quietly without even disturbing old Herzog, who was alone and snoring by the dying fire.

With the door securely locked, Elser and Annalise sat on the low bed and tried to make out each other's face in the darkness. The girl giggled and Elser put a finger to her lips, then they fell into an embrace and it all became easy and natural. The months of fumbling passion, wherever they could find privacy off the night streets, was over; here at least were a mattress and sheets where they could at last explore each other with more than eyes, mouths and hands. Georg's fingers deftly found every catch and button, knot and bow of first the girl's dirndl then underwear, garters, stockings and shoes. Naked she lay, suddenly shivering in the darkness, arms extended, imploring in murmurs that he shed his clothes and come to her. As he did, his sensitive hands utilized the experience of delicate craftsmanship to lightly caress the contours of the girl's slim, pale body. Tracing a pattern of sensuality across the bare flesh, moulding breasts, following the imperceptible dome of her diaphragm to the hollow stomach before slowly approaching, deliberately hesitant, the mystery between the girl's thighs, Elser's fingertips slid into the moist cleft as Annalise, moaning, opened her legs wider. He moved against her as she grasped his hardening erection. Hissing with anticipation, Annalise convulsed several times as her body, with grateful reluctance, gave itself to the increasing sensations. Her heart and mind had already declared themselves willing victims. The quiet artisan's skill in things had always been a revelation to women when they discovered that he could apply it to making love. He had an unerring feel and touch for whatever became his focus of attention. Often he found women less complicated than machinery and craftsmanship, but occasionally more necessary. In Switzerland, he had become a perfectionist in placing precise mechanisms gently into small cabinets and fragile boxes. Familiarity had never tempted him to be quick. He always gave his respect to time spent, applying the old Bavarian saying 'He who does not honour the crumbs does not deserve the cake.' Suddenly, gripping him tightly, Annalise felt Elser deep within her begin to tense, and before his lips sealed hers she whispered, 'Now.' Elser closed his eyes and exploded inside the young woman. Their mouths, pressed tightly together, stifled cries of reaction as their bodies locked against each other, twisted between the sheets.

Hard knocking at the door caused the young woman to go rigid in Elser's arms.

'Herr Elser,' came the landlady's voice, pausing for a reply before knocking again firmly and repeating loudly, 'Herr Elser!' Once more she paused. Silence from within. She drew long on a cigarette between her fingers, coughed, then asked, 'Is someone in there with you?' Elser put a finger to Annalise's lips. Outside, the landlady tried the handle, found the door locked and bent unsteadily to look through the keyhole. She could see nothing because, although Elser had removed the key, he had stuffed the hole with a handkerchief. The landlady stood up and leaned against the door. 'Visitors are not allowed.' Nothing from the bedroom. The landlady lowered her head, pressing an ear to the wood panel. 'I have rules.' Inside, Elser, eyes wide, stared towards the door as if he could see the woman. Her voice softened as she said, 'You know . . . the rules.' A long pause lasted as she thought about each one of them, then she remembered the glass of schnapps she'd brought downstairs and placed on the mantlepiece above the embers of the fire in the lounge, and her voice became plaintive. 'Georg . . . rules must be obeyed.'

Elser lay back on the hard pillow, his head beside Annalise. If he was right she would go now. He listened as the landlady, grumbling with frustration, wandered away down the corridor. How had she guessed the girl had come inside? They'd made no noise . . . He closed his eyes. Wet footprints. She must have gone to check the door and seen both his and the girl's . . . He swore under his breath. He wouldn't be able to afford mistakes – later.

'Georg,' whispered Annalise.

'What?'

'I can't go back now.'

'You mean it's too late?'

'Yes.'

Elser gritted his teeth, then relaxed and smiled into the darkness. 'I agree.'

Chimes for two o'clock sounded distantly in the city and Elser stirred. He lay still for a moment, hearing only the sound of dripping rain. Annalise was asleep and the house was quiet. He slipped from the bed, dressed, went to the door, found the handkerchief and pulled it from the keyhole. Then, inserting the key, gently turned the lock. As he opened the door, Annalise whispered, 'Georg, where are you going?'

'Lock the door after me,' he said softly. 'I'll be back later.'

Outside, he waited until he heard the key turn, then with his eyes growing accustomed to the darkness, he moved quickly down the corridor and paused beside the lounge area, where the fire continued to glow dimly. He could just make out the landlady, slumped in the armchair; her breathing was heavy and with some luck she would remain where she was until the cold penetrated her bones. Then, if she had sense, she would go back to bed. At the front door, he felt for the bolts and, with a single creak which caused him to hold his breath, he was outside, across the courtyard and making his way below into the cellar. The padlock from outside, he resecured through the two handles above his head as he stepped down into the cold, damp workroom.

With the lamp lit, the atmosphere became less bleak and, taking a key-ring hidden behind the trunk, he unlocked a drawer in the workbench to remove two oiled rags. Placed on the worktop and unwrapped, they each revealed a clock mechanism. Both were Westminster movements which he had brought with him from Switzerland. He wound first one, then the other, then watched the springs unravel, counting the seconds. He speeded the process by turning the minute hand quickly. Regular revolutions at first, then he began to spin it faster and faster, watching the strikers intently. He inserted a piece of wood beneath them, just before the final revolution hit the hour. Each of the strikers smacked into the wood heavily. No bells, no chimes, just the noise of impact. Elser smiled, hearing the second mechanism as it continued to whirr. A piece of wire drawn taut, during a period of time which he would set, would release these hammers to hit a pin. They, in turn, would strike a detonator, which would set off however much explosive he attached to the final contraption.

He took out of the drawer some sketches he had made of the pillar. They were rough but gave an indication of his first ideas. He took a cigarette from his pocket, broke it in half, lit the flaking tobacco and blew smoke across the lamp, watching the shadows curl above the drawing. He could feel the excitement, as he always did at the beginning of anything he decided to attempt. Then it was only a question of application, discipline and expertise to guarantee accomplishment. He wafted away the smoke and waited patiently for the second spring to uncoil, again slipping in a piece of wood beneath the strikers. As the minute hand hit the hour, all six hammers slammed down, the last actually causing splinters. He nodded to himself. 'Perfect.'

When Elser returned to the house, just before six o'clock, it had stopped raining. He entered cautiously and made his way down the corridor quietly. In the lounge the fire was out and the landlady gone. Outside his door he stopped and listened a moment for noises in the house – already somewhere upstairs old Herzog was beginning to stir. He could hear him coughing. Elser knelt and inserted a pair of long fine tweezers into the lock, then turned the key and opened the door. He stood over Annalise, his eyes, accustomed to the gloom, examining the contours of her face. She was sleeping like a child. There was an innocence in her expression asleep as there was a vulnerability in her eyes awake which, by some miracle, she had retained despite her job and circumstances. Perhaps it was a hope yet to be dashed that there could be something better, as there was always something worse. He wondered at her experiences in coping with men and, for a moment, speculated on her destiny without him. He had always been alone, so even if it was not easy, it was at least familiar. But she was a woman and, in his experience of them, they had so much and needed to give. She opened her eyes and he smiled.

'Time,' he said.

Light was showing in the sky when the two of them slipped out of the front door, crossed the courtyard and, already walking briskly against the cold, stepped from beneath the archway into the street. People were hurrying to work but, pressing close on his arm, Annalise saw no one but Elser. Her eyes were bright and her face shone against the crisp morning air. It was corny, thought Elser, but he'd do it all the same; they stopped beside a flower stall where the man was setting up. The buds on their short stems looked as tired as he felt, and the bunch he bought was hardly worth the money he paid until she laughed, which changed everything. Perhaps if they were to have a history together, he would look back and say that was where it all began – not in bed, making love, but on the cold, dawn streets surrounded by everything that was bleak in Germany. She accepted the flowers and kissed him on the cheek.

'You haven't shaved,' she whispered. Elser looked into her eyes. 'Or slept,' she said, and made a face. He stared a moment longer, wondering what was happening to him.

'Or had breakfast,' he said.

The Burgerbraukeller was opened for the staff by the time they arrived. Some of the girls giggled when Annalise ushered Elser to one of the tables inside, and several stared out from the swing door of the kitchen. As she sat quickly beside him on one of the long benches and watched him wolf eggs and ham that she had persuaded one of the chefs to prepare, he saw her nose crinkle when he paused to chew; it was to encourage him to continue. Chin on closed fists, he could see she was already dreaming. He'd seen the look before and been protected by natural cynicism; now suddenly he felt exposed, unprotected from the delicate emotions she revealed.

'I wish . . .' she began. He knew what was coming. If it was 'we' he was done for, at least for the moment. ' . . . we,' she went on.

'Annalise!' bellowed a voice from the kitchen. The door

was swung open and the proprietor, Herr Payerl, tall and stout, tying on an apron, bustled across to them. 'I asked you . . . ' he stopped, seeing Elser. 'So, this is our best customer.'

Annalise was already on her feet, flustered. 'He has work too, Herr Payerl. He is only here for . . . '

'On a Sunday?' interrupted the large man.

Annalise glanced quickly at Elser. 'Well, no.'

Payerl now looked at Elser, who gazed back steadily into small bloodshot eyes which flicked to the table and saw the sad bunch of flowers. The big man began to wipe his hands on the filthy apron, absorbing the story immediately. His voice was supercilious and his face leering when he said to the girl, 'You do.'

Annalise nodded, curtsied, snatched the flowers as an afterthought and ran off to the kitchen. Elser continued to chew his mouthful of ham and eggs whilst reaching into his pocket. He put half a Reichsmark on the table, which Payerl took immediately.

'There is nothing free here,' he said. Elser swallowed his food and smiled. A look of disgust which concealed jealousy spread across Payerl's bloated features. 'You look as if you've been up half the night,' he muttered, gesturing towards the kitchen, where Annalise had rushed through the swing door.

Elser shook his head and, staring the man directly in the eye, said, 'All night.'

Payerl flushed to his collar and, snorting contempt, strode off, almost colliding with Annalise bringing a steaming cup of coffee to Elser.

'He's paying for it,' said Payerl. Annalise glanced across at Elser, who nodded. 'Nothing is free,' shouted the man, and pushed through the door into the kitchen. The waitress put down the cup beside her customer.

'Nothing is free,' mimicked Annalise, and kissed Elser quickly.

He blew on the surface of the coffee and sipped. 'He's right,' murmured the artisan.

8

Otto Meyer stepped out of his staff car and stood for a moment surveying the familiar street. He had returned to Munich, spent two days at Berchtesgaden, then, with the Führer ensconced at the Berghof for the rest of the week, was free until the planned departure date the following Sunday.

He saw the long line of trees in leaf and remembered that spring had always been beautiful during the years when this address had been his home. Both his children had been born in the large house they had always called a villa. Marianne's great dream had been a summer place on Lake Como. She'd been spoilt by her father, and her aspirations had quickly exceeded her passion in a marriage that began to flounder when she realized that Otto Meyer was prepared to waste his time – and she had frequently repeated it to him – as a common policeman.

Meyer readjusted his black SS uniform and, tucking several small packages beneath his arm – belated Christmas gifts – made his way towards the residence where once he had been master, husband and father. The gate, as ever, needed oil and the pathway to the steps remained uneven from the ravages of winter. Standing within the large porch, Meyer felt uncomfortable for the first time. He rang the bell, realizing that he no longer had a key to the wide oak door. It was opened by the manservant who stared at the uniform, for a moment not recognizing the man whom he had known more than ten years.

'I telephoned,' Meyer reminded him, and to his own astonishment, found himself hesitating on the doorstep.

'Yes, sir.'

'Anyone in?'

'Not yet, sir.'

'Well, Rupert.' Meyer looked the man up and down, noting greyer hair. But there was still the elegant presentation he had admired when first Marianne's father had insisted that they take a manservant. 'You look fit.'

'Thank you, sir.'

'Can I come in?'

Rupert hesitated only a moment. 'Of course, sir.'

Meyer entered the house and, giving the presents to Rupert, went directly along the corridor, up the wide, shallow stairs and into the spacious salon. There were perceptible differences everywhere. Objects missing, new furniture, even the high ornate ceiling had been redecorated to match a new, pale colour on the walls. The grand piano was still by the long windows, through which sunlight shone intermittently as the storm clouds moved slowly away high above the city. Meyer lifted the cover and played some notes. They were pitched perfectly and it pleased him that it was still in tune.

'She still practises?' he asked, referring to his daughter.

'Every day, sir.'

Meyer grunted satisfaction and glanced at several framed photographs on the polished mahogany. His was markedly absent, but his children and his wife remained together with a new addition, the portrait of a man not obviously Aryan and near to fifty. He turned to Rupert, questioning silently.

The man coughed. 'A friend, sir.'

Meyer began to unbutton his tunic. Rupert took it, with the belt, peaked cap and gloves. Meyer loosened his tie and now in only boots, dark trousers and white shirt, feeling more comfortable, he crossed to the drinks cabinet and poured himself a schnapps.

'Where are my cigars?' he asked when Rupert returned to the room. For the first time, the manservant observed some familiarity and smiled.

'I hid them sir, just in case . . . I thought perhaps one day you might . . . '

91

Meyer interrupted to stop the disturbing sentiment he had begun to feel. 'Find me one,' he said, and stepped back to the piano, closing his eyes as he felt warm sun on his face. He recalled other times when he had been exactly as he was now, but with voices in the house. Family. He downed his schnapps in one and went back to the cabinet to pour a second. He walked out of the salon and took the stairs two at a time to the landing. He entered the main bedroom and stood for a moment looking at his marriage bed, perfectly made, sheets severely tucked into the mattress, quilt exactly placed. Above the headboard four photographs were as always. He and Marianne separately, together and with the children during a high summer on the shore of Bodensee. He remembered the schnapps in his hand and drank it slowly. He heard the door slam below and footsteps in the hall. He'd come a long way, married well; according to jealous colleagues, Marianne had been a sought-after heiress and he merely the son of a famous policeman. But it had been love on both sides – once. Meyer closed the bedroom door, went down the curving stairs to the hall and wide corridor, where Rupert met him, proffering a cigar, which he lit.

'Miss Gabbie, sir,' whispered the manservant. Meyer nodded and entered the salon as the girl, seated at the piano, began to play. She heard him and smelt the once familiar cigar smoke, but continued playing, seemingly oblivious of anything but the keys and the music. At eleven she was already an obvious beauty. Blonde hair, pulled back from a finely framed face containing the same intense blue eyes as her mother, complemented a slim athletic figure seated straight-backed on the piano stool. Only her hands, trained to be relaxed, carried skilled fingers across the keyboard. She made a mistake and stopped, sighing in exasperation.

'Well, come and sit down,' she said, not even turning to her father. 'Show me how.'

Meyer sat beside his daughter on the wide stool, laid the cigar in an ashtray and regarded her, absorbing the youthful concentration. 'Schumann is difficult.'

'Forbidden,' she said. 'He was a Jew. But I think it is beautiful.'

Meyer nodded. 'And difficult.' He began to play a simpler part but she stopped him.

'I can do that – but not this.' She showed him, and she couldn't.

Meyer smiled patiently. 'Spread your fingers wider.' For the first time in two years he touched his daughter, taking her fingers gently, showing her. 'Exercise.'

'I do.'

'More.'

Gabbie looked at him, steadily examining her father's face. 'Have you come back?'

'For an hour.'

The girl's eyes began to cloud with tears. She turned back to the keys. 'I'll play you something,' she said, but her hands remained in her lap. Meyer kissed her cheek. She spun round and fell against him as he enfolded her in his arms. It was a difficult moment for them both. Eventually she pulled away and smiled. 'Can we play the duet you taught me, Papa?' Meyer nodded, not trusting himself to speak, and they started badly, which brought laughter, then they improved and each remembered the notes of a well-practised piece, which they played almost to the end.

'Gabbie!' came a voice. They stopped playing. In the sudden silence, Otto Meyer turned and saw Marianne at the entrance to the salon in an elegant dark blue costume, pulling off pale grey gloves that matched a hat placed rakishly across her long black hair. She looked at her ex-husband coldly. 'It is not convenient. I told you.'

'It was my only opportunity,' he answered quietly.

'I think the time is passed for those,' she said, and gathered her gloves firmly in one hand.

Meyer smiled. 'You haven't changed.'

'You have,' she replied, and stepped towards the piano.

'How?'

'You look older.'

'Responsibility.'

'And promotion?'

'Yes.'

'Congratulations.'

Meyer almost smiled at the obvious insincerity and wondered why he had ever loved this woman. The front door slammed down the corridor and a quick voice began to chatter to Rupert in the distance. Meyer took his cigar, drew on it and stood up. Marianne's face had a natural beauty that the strictures of the society she so respected had hardened. There was no longer open vulnerability in the pale eyes, the sensuous mouth had tightened and she was thinner, angular. Supposedly, Meyer thought, more attractive in the mirror, but the mischievous humour was gone from her expression. Although there was no apparent pain, he could detect a sense of loss, perhaps even a concealed bewilderment, that time had rushed on or that he was elsewhere – already in the past. He remembered his portrait which remained on the wall above their bed and knowing that she would always be in his heart, always his Marianne, hoped that she too retained feelings for him.

'Why have you come?' she asked quickly. Meyer could hear footsteps approaching from the hallway.

'To see you.'

'You mean the children.'

'You,' stated Meyer.

Marianne saw the truth of it in his eyes and lowered her own. She coughed, almost embarrassed at the quiet intensity in the man she had once loved so much.

'Would you like some coffee?'

'If I must,' said Meyer softly. She looked at him again. A quick voice, now accompanying the fast approaching feet, laughed loudly and said something to Rupert. The confident stride in the long corridor, resounded on the marble floor.

'You look tired,' murmured Marianne.

'You look beautiful,' answered Meyer.

Marianne suddenly smiled and he was unable to contain his reaction to it. How would he ever stop loving this woman, he thought.

'I'll make it,' she said.

'What?'

'The coffee.'

Meyer nodded as Marianne glanced behind her.

'Coffee, Michael?'

'Yes, please,' shouted a quick voice, and in a moment a tall, but rather plump, middle-aged man was standing in the salon. He was well-dressed, noted Meyer, and no doubt attractive in some way to women. The man extended a hand and spread his face in an acceptable grin.

'Rosenburg,' he said. 'Michael Rosenburg.'

Meyer shook the hand. 'Otto,' he said.

A boy in Hitler Youth uniform bounded up the smaller stairs into the salon and stopped dead, seeing his father.

'Hello, Peter.' The boy only nodded. 'Lost your tongue, boy?'

'Hello, Papa,' said the boy hesitantly, and glanced across at his sister seated at the piano. 'Where's Mama?'

'Making coffee,' said Gabbie and pulled a face at her brother.

In the kitchen, Marianne stared out the window, listening to the cook grumbling with minor complaints as she assembled the crockery on a tray; the coffee had already been made in anticipation of her mistress's return. Marianne was trying to compose herself. Outwardly she had mastered control, but within something unwanted had been disturbed.

'Two years,' she said aloud.

'Pardon, ma'am?'

She turned and looked at the old woman fussing still with the tray. Rupert stepped into the kitchen. 'Why did he come?' asked Marianne harshly.

'He telephoned again, madam, but you had gone out.'

An uncomfortable pause lasted between them, then Marianne seized the tray herself and stepped past Rupert, who looked at the perplexed old cook and indicated silence.

In the salon, Meyer, sitting opposite Rosenburg, listened to the man babble nervously about his position in Munich, in Germany, in life. Peter and Gabbie sat patiently, waiting for him to stop referring to 'the children', finish speaking and allow them to ask permission to leave. Then each of them in turn looked at their father and decided to watch with increasing curiosity the outcome of the confrontation. They had known Rosenburg for more than a year, and although Otto Meyer had become a stranger, he was still – Papa, patiently giving his attention to 'Uncle Michael'.

'I am a veteran of the Great War you know,' Rosenburg was saying, 'so the position is even more awkward, you understand?'

Meyer nodded as Marianne entered with the loaded tray. 'Yes,' he replied.

'Being Jewish has become a serious problem in Germany. But I am no different from anyone else. I have always been a patriot, and as a soldier I fought four years for victory.'

Peter interrupted. 'He has the Iron Cross too!'

Rosenburg regarded the boy. 'First Class,' he added.

'I know,' Peter told his father. 'He showed it to me!'

Rosenburg shrugged. 'You see, it is now so . . . '

'Awkward,' said Meyer, recalling the euphemism, and sipped his coffee. There was a moment's silence as Gabbie giggled, Peter smiled and Rosenburg cleared his throat to speak, but Marianne interposed.

'Michael has been very good to us.' She stared at her husband, who indicated his cigar and spoke pointedly to Rosenburg.

'I hope I am not offending?'

'Oh no.'

'My wife used to like the smell of a good cigar. She came

from a good family and said that it always reminded her of wealth.'

'Perhaps her father.' Marianne's face froze. 'I have only met him – once,' Rosenburg added.

'No doubt,' smiled Meyer.

'More coffee?' Marianne asked him harshly.

'No, thank you.'

'What is it all coming to, I ask myself,' began Rosenburg, trying to lighten a growing tension he could now feel between the ex-marriage partners.

'What?' asked Meyer.

'In Germany,' Rosenburg explained. 'Are we to be faced with another war . . . ?' Meyer said nothing. The question hung in the air.

'If we must fight, we will win!' said Peter.

Meyer turned to the Hitler Youth – his son. 'Peter, you are only fourteen years old . . . '

'Nearly fifteen!' interrupted the boy. 'That is the best age for true convictions!'

Meyer observed the pursed lips of his wife and the forced smile on Rosenburg's face. 'The boy speaks well,' he said.

'We are all born to die, if we must, for our country.'

'Is that what they teach you?'

Meyer's son stood up to address his father.

'Peter!' said Marianne. 'Take your sister into the other room.'

'But, Mama´ . . . !'

'Please.'

'Peter,' said Meyer quietly. 'Out.'

The boy, responding to the authority of his father's voice, took his sister's hand and led her reluctantly from the room. When the door had closed, Rosenburg raised his hands in a gesture of hopelessness.

'Is peace so difficult?'

'It's what everyone fights for . . . ' said Meyer quietly.

Rosenburg nodded. 'Quite so . . . and for prosperity. Do

you know, we used to have a chain of shops in Hamburg and Berlin before . . . ' he censored his words and went on quickly, ' . . . Very successful business . . . My father, indeed, his . . . ' He glanced at Marianne and, seeing the look in her eye, changed the conversation mid-flight. 'But then who will we fight, this time – if we fight?'

Meyer had seen his wife's admonishing stare and smiled. 'Each other, as always.'

Rosenburg sat forward on the hard sofa and assumed an earnest expression. 'Tell us, what do you really think, Herr Meyer? You are obviously an intelligent man and a policeman, I gather?'

Meyer suddenly became aware that he was out of uniform and stiffened. 'Yes.'

'It must be difficult, sometimes. When, for instance, your duty is not aligned to your own sense of justice.'

'Or emotions,' murmured Meyer.

'I'm sorry?'

'It is a job like any other, which a man must do according to his abilities. I obey orders, as does the lowest civil servant. I do not judge. As a policeman, it is not for me to apply personal emotion or, as you say, my own sense of justice to the facts as they are presented.'

'But . . .' Rosenburg hesitated, then went on, 'the policies of National Socialism . . . '

'Michael!' said Marianne quickly.

'No,' he continued, 'I have begun and will finish. The policies of the present party do not encompass everyone. Opposition exists.'

'Does it?' asked Meyer quietly.

'Yes! On humanitarian grounds it is logical to provide within any constitution an area for dissent, surely? Or there can be no argument, no contrary opinion. The temperament of the people dictates that there must be . . . '

Meyer cut him off. 'Democracy?' he questioned.

Rosenburg, in the full knowledge that the people had voted their Führer and his declared policies to supreme power,

98

flushed and bent forward to place his cup on the tray. 'Perhaps I should be leaving.'

'Germany?' asked Meyer.

'No,' countered Rosenburg. 'I am late for an appointment. You see, I am still in Banking. I am given certain privileges . . .' He stopped, seeing Marianne now on her feet.

'Otto, please,' she said. 'It is the wrong time.'

Meyer stood up and bowed slightly to Rosenburg, gesturing him to remain seated. 'It is I who should leave.' He waited as Rupert brough him the items of uniform he had taken off.

Rosenburg bent forward again and sipped the dregs of his coffee. 'I really should be going too, you know, Marianne.' Behind him, Meyer winced at the familiarity as he slid his arms into the black tunic held by Rupert.

'If you must, Michael,' she said.

'I will telephone you later if I have been given permission to come with you to Berlin.' Rosenburg tried to turn to see Meyer but found it difficult, so he continued to refer to him, speaking louder.

'I met your wife, ah, I mean Marianne, Herr Meyer, in that city and she has kindly invited me to . . .' He looked at her.

'Michael,' she warned. Meyer had completed his tunic buttons and buckled his belt.

'Yes, of course,' nodded Rosenburg. 'I was just going to say, the shop in Berlin was so much . . . bigger,' he finished lamely. Meyer put on his peaked cap, took his gloves from Rupert and stepped round the sofa to face Rosenburg, whose mouth fell open as he stood up slowly, his eyes fixed on the black SS uniform.

'Can I take you?' asked the Gestapo officer.

'Where?' whispered Rosenburg.

'Wherever you are going,' said Meyer patiently, and indicated the way to the hall and front door.

'You really shouldn't . . . I don't want to put you out, really . . .'

'I insist,' said Meyer quietly.

When Peter saw his father's uniform, he recognized it instantly and stood in awe as he shook hands. Gabbie's eyes were wide when she accepted and then gave a kiss. Goodbyes were exchanged and Rosenburg, brushing Marianne's cheeks with his lips, went on down the steps and along the pathway to the road, where the large dark saloon car, shining in the sunlight, was already pouring exhaust fumes into the cold air. Meyer lingered within the porch and, as Rupert ushered the children back to their rooms, put on his gloves and examined his wife's face. She was looking anxiously towards the gate as Rosenburg stepped hesitantly out on to the pavement.

'Otto,' she murmured. Her eyes conveyed obvious fears, which shocked Meyer, as he pressed his fingers into the fine black leather.

'Marianne,' he said softly, 'we are not all . . . mad – yet.'

'He lost so much on "Crystal Night" as they call it.'

'That was last November,' said Meyer curtly. 'I was . . . in the mountains and saw nothing.'

'But you know what they are doing.' For the first time Marianne realized that the man before her in his ominous uniform was perhaps now indeed more than a policeman. 'They,' she repeated, 'is that you now?'

'You know me, I am only a policeman.'

'Do you remember Dr Tauber?' Meyer nodded. 'When Peter was so sick we thought . . . '

'Yes, give him my regards.'

'He no longer practises.'

'Where is he?'

'I don't know.'

'You mean he has been – taken away?'

'Otto, I am not an intellectual, I am merely part of a very old society in Germany. We all thought it would turn out differently, but Hitler's party has stabilized our country. To abuse its obvious strength by persecuting and bullying those who are weaker must be despised. You always told Peter that . . . '

100

'You sound like your father.'

'Is that so bad? Do you condemn a man for the wealth he has achieved from industry? You enjoyed it, when he gave it to us.'

'The only thing he ever gave me of any value was you.'

Tears of confusion sprang into Marianne's eyes. 'It is over Otto. Please, it is over,' she whispered.

'I loved you.'

'As I . . . once loved you.'

Meyer reached out to touch her but she stepped back a pace. From the kerb outside the house he heard a brief conversation and a car door shut loudly.

'I will investigate . . . try to find Dr Tauber. He was good to us for many years,' said Meyer.

Marianne's cheeks were wet as she again looked beyond him. 'It will be too late,' she stated sadly. 'History, Otto. We are now only part of each other's history.'

'Marianne,' he said, and his voice broke.

Then she resolved to tell him, knowing the words would be cruel, but she felt it was the only way. 'Michael took me to another doctor. A friend of his – also Jewish.'

'Are you ill?'

'No,' she smiled. 'I'm going to have his child.'

Meyer's lips began to tremble. His throat tightened. 'That is an offence.'

'In God's eyes or Hitler's?' asked Marianne coldly.

'Mine,' answered Meyer hoarsely.

'My poor Otto,' she said with true sympathy.

He suddenly seized and dragged her towards him. 'You expect . . . too much . . . from me . . . !' he spat out.

She averted her face and murmured, 'I always did.'

Meyer grasped her hair with one hand and jerked her head until she was only inches from the hate he could feel surging through him. He held her tightly and stared into her eyes – then all the strength seemed to ebb from his limbs. He let her go, spun on his heel and strode away along the path without

101

looking back. The front door closed as he stepped out of the gate. He entered the car and slumped into the rear seat beside Rosenburg. Looking out of the side window he saw his children waving to him from one of the upstairs bedrooms. He waved back.

'Where are we going first, sir?' asked the chauffeur respect-fully. Meyer could feel Rosenburg's eyes on him and distincly smelt the odour of nervous sweat but was unable to look at the man.

'Gestapo headquarters,' he said.

The staff car slowly drove the length of the pretty tree-lined street then eased out into traffic on the main thoroughfare. Inside, no one spoke until Rosenburg broke the silence. 'This is very kind of you, Herr Meyer. '

'Obersturmbannführer.'

'I'm sorry.'

'So am I,' said Meyer, his voice hardening.

Rosenburg summoned inner strength. 'Are you a religious man?' he asked.

'Are you?'

'I believe.'

'In what?'

'The future,' said Rosenburg. 'As I try to understand the past.'

'A philosopher.'

'A Jew,' stated Rosenburg.

'Jesus was a Jew,' said Meyer. 'A renegade, as was the Führer once – and you crucified Christ.'

'The Romans . . . ' began Rosenburg.

'History is full of blame . . . and guilt. Who will ever know the truth?'

'We are the truth, in this car. My fear is the truth,' said Rosenburg softly.

Meyer appraised the man. 'Personally I have nothing against Jews, you must understand. I could only ever hate

102

ndividuals, irrespective of their race or creed,' he smiled, 'Herr Rosenburg.'

The dark Mercedes slowed, indicated a left turn and entered through a guarded archway, a large courtyard and the portals of Munich's Gestapo headquarters. The car came to a halt, its wheels grinding into the loose gravel. The engine continued to tick over as Meyer stepped out, saluting the black uniform which had appeared beside the open door, then he leaned down and looked back at his passenger. 'Give him your address.'

Rosenburg glanced at the driver, who was peering at him in the mirror. 'Thank you,' he said to Meyer. The Gestapo officer absorbed details of the man's heavy features for the last time. 'For nothing,' he said and slammed the door. The Mercedes pulled away. Meyer stared at the gravel whilst he collected his thoughts and began to count the pieces, but quickly gave up; there were far too many. When he looked up, the car was gone.

In his office on the second floor overlooking the courtyard, Meyer sank into the soft leather chair behind his desk and stared at the portrait of Adolf Hitler on the wall, thinking of his wife and then, eventually, the Jew. Schneider knocked, stepped in and saluted smartly.

'The express leaves at six thirty-one tonight, sir.'

'Good,' muttered Meyer absently. 'I am beginning to miss Berlin.'

The young SS man could see something was troubling his commanding officer. 'Anything I can do, sir?'

Meyer surveyed the strong Aryan face of his assistant, finally made his decision and nodded.

'Yes, Wolf, perhaps there is . . .' He gave no orders or even direct instructions, just information – which could be acted upon when his chauffeur-driven car returned. Schneider snapped to attention and went out.

Alone again in the office Meyer stood at the window looking down at the gravel courtyard. The car arrived, Schneider got in with two other officers, the chauffeur backed

up, then drove off into the streets of Munich, directly back the
way he had come. Meyer turned from the view of the now
gloomy city again to the obligatory picture of the Führer on
the panelled wall. The room was dark, the day already
fading. There might be excuses he would present, even a
reason; after all, he had committed no crime, merely made a
suggestion to an under officer. But deep in his heart he knew
he would find no forgiveness. He was no longer merely 'a
policeman' but a member of the SS who had been tempted
and now used the power of life and death invested in him.

He had joined Hitler's Third Reich, body and soul.

9

The sad, white-faced clown in Georg Elser's lodgings was manipulated with some skill. In the half-light of the cellar lamps it was almost possible to ignore the strings which jerked the limbs and believe that the mouth actually conveyed harsh words in falsetto voice without moving its painted rosebud lips.

'Who are you? What is your name? Where are you from? Why have you come here? What do you want? What is your business?' Annalise giggled and looked above the clown walking eighteen inches tall on the workbench, as Elser tugged at the strings.

'Look at me when I am speaking!'

'I am,' laughed Annalise.

Elser jerked the clown. 'You are not!' snapped the high voice.

'Oh – sorry, Harlequin.' She bent down to kiss the clown. 'Better!'

'You are so handsome.' The clown's hand reached out to her face and the voice stopped.

'You are gentle.' The clown dropped its head.

'And shy.' The clown looked up.

'And kind.' Annalise kissed the puppet again.

'And I love you.' No reply. Annalise looked up again. Elser was staring at her and letting go the strings so that the clown collapsed slowly. He squatted, then slid to the edge of the workbench, where he sat next to Annalise. The flickering wicks threw lamplight across their faces, dancing with the shadows.

'I am only an ordinary man,' said Elser quietly.

'To me you are very special.' She kissed him. They parted, and Elser made a face.

'I only make things.' He took up the puppet. 'Mend things.'

Annalise lifted his chin to look into his eyes. 'You can change things.'

Elser's confusion became obvious until the young woman took his hand and put it to her breast. She smiled. 'Feel my heart.'

At first only Elser's eyes responded, then the serious mouth relaxed, and with a grin, he burst out laughing, threw his arms around Annalise and hugged her tightly. They were oblivious to the many other eyes watching them, staring out from bodies hanging from hooks in the roof. They had forgotten the strong smell of glue and paint, ignored the cut cloth and chippings on the floor, pushed aside the many carving tools employed to create their audience of silent harlequins because they had discovered, even amidst the damp squalor of poverty and the bleak prospects offered without hope by a ruthless regime, something even more precious than the uncertain life to come. They shared, with unmistakable trust, the joy in each other's eyes and, without choice or regret, found themselves plunged into an exquisite isolation from the colourless world around them, separated by their ill-concealed secret of love.

Spring became early summer. Elser paid the rent by a variety of jobs. He found occasional work with a mechanic named Dreschler, for a carpenter called Borg, and when there was no need of his services he bought materials and continued to craft puppets, which he had made since his youth, and sold them either to flower shops or in the open markets where traditionally there was always a demand. He managed to keep his landlady at bay by repairing furniture and doing odd jobs around the house in Turkenstrasse, even dismantling and rebuilding the ancient grandfather clock she had

inherited which had never worked and now, as all his fellow
lodgers remarked, kept perfect time.

Alone, unmolested and usually late at night after he had
walked Annalise back to her hostel, he worked on his device,
modifying it from his frequent visits to the Bierkeller. Sitting
amongst so many others during the evening, waiting for the
waitresses to finish, new ideas came to him for installing
sufficient explosive to bring down what he estimated would
amount to more than four tons of steel and concrete directly on
to the podium, where Hitler and his hierarchy had been
grouped between eight and ten o'clock on 8 November every
year, since the Führer's accession to power.

By the end of July, Elser felt ready to begin. With little
variation, the Burgerbraukeller was finished by eleven and
cleared by midnight. Elser had become a familiar face late in
the evening, sitting patiently, observing the people around
him, saying nothing, avoiding conversation.

Occasionally, it was still possible to invite Annalise back to
his lodgings where, at some risk, they entered the house, crept
to the single room undetected and made love in furtive
silence. Most of the time Elser would escort her home through
the night streets, pushing his bicycle or riding with the young
waitress perched precariously on the crossbar. Then, having
gone as far as they dared, her conscience and fears being
keener than Elser's, Annalise would enter the drab confines of
a pungent, dismal world where the odours of vomit, steamed
fish and sweat combined with urine and rotting cabbage,
providing an instantly unique welcome to a barely habitable
house of dormitory rooms, each with a shared toilet, a single
washbasin and only two baths off the long dark corridor for
the use of the entire hostel.

Annalise took more chances with Elser, straying as the
months passed near to the fine line of destructive possessive-
ness, forming jealousies if he spoke to another waitress,
creating unfounded fears for their relationship when he
insisted on returning directly to his lodgings, leaving her to
trudge to the hostel, where invariably she burst into tears,

much to the enjoyment of the others in her dormitory, who mimicked voices and invented cruel conversations amongst themselves in the darkness after the lights had been turned off.

A hard mattress, damp sheets beneath the coarse blankets, freezing in winter, unbearable in the humid summer: it was a difficult place to make dreams or believe they might come true. What she had once endured for no particular end but sheer existence in the city, the country girl from Ravensburg now found increasingly torturous. As she had longed for something beyond her small expectations in Württemberg, she now knew that soon Munich, as indeed life without Georg Elser, would prove unendurable. The bed beside the window allowed her, when the others were asleep, to lift the curtain and peer beyond the bars, through the glass, up into the night sky where, at certain times of the month, she could see the moon beaming down on to the housetops of the old city, like something described in a Grimms' fairy-tale. And so she wished, how he wished, for something better – anything that would at least provide hope as Georg Elser gave her love.

Hitler's meteoric rise had certainly swept Germany once again into economic recovery; those fortunate to be a part of it reaped the benefits. But there were many who lived in the wake of that rapid advancement, who were the victims, as Georg described them, who wanted no part of a greater glory but merely the right to a life dictated not by the whims and ambitions of a single politician, but by their own feelings. It was the only time Georg ever really showed his emotions, Annalise recalled, as she sank into a troubled sleep. Her Georg talking about such great things was confusing, but she always listened and often smiled, or was serious, according to his mood. She knew life would not be so difficult for them if they were together – she would make sure it would work.

Throughout August, tension mounted in central Europe. War seemed imminent, but avoidable with delicate negotiations. No one appeared to want armed confrontation, least of all Germany, as Hitler seemed to have acquired everything he had stipulated necessary to maintain peace. The Rhineland, Czechoslovakia and Austria were now part of the Reich, and only the Danzig corridor – created by the Treaty of Versailles that was signed to end the Great War – which gave Poland access to the Baltic, remained as a bone of contention. Rumours that Poles were persecuting the German population had been blown up in the press, until every street corner throughout the Fatherland contained groups speculating on what should be done. The stubbornness of both nations escalated the fears of the rest of Europe as England made a treaty with Warsaw and Russia signed a pact of non-aggression with the Nazi Foreign Minister, von Ribbentrop.

The last days of official summer were fraught with expectations of imminent action and the hope that it would be diplomacy which solved the impasse. But Hitler was fifty, time was running out, the army was strong, Poland was weak and, despite the generals' protests, it was clear that the Führer was prepared to take the gamble that England and France would not fight in the event of a border clash, leading to a brief war in the East. As high summer faded, Europe held its breath.

An accordion, violin and guitar trio passed amongst the mid-morning tables outside the Burgerbraukeller off Marienplatz under a clear blue sky that shimmered with the promise of a hot day. Munich had become humid, and old people at the long benches had already begun to seek the shade of the main building.

Georg Elser passed between the various groups, selling the last of a batch of his crafted puppets. With only one remaining, he sat down, feeling the strong sun on his face, and waited until Annalise saw him. When she was free, she came over and asked what he would like with an expression that made several other customers jealous, merely by the implications in her smile. She lingered a moment, pretending to wipe the table clean.

109

'You've sold them all?'

Elser nodded. 'I can make more.'

Annalise brushed his hand with hers. 'Dark eyes are better than white dust,' she said, referring to the condition he used to arrive in from the quarry. Now, although late-night working had darkened the surrounding area, Elser's eyes remained clear and sharp.

'This one is for you.' He held up the last puppet.

'I have one,' she whispered, and was about to kiss him quickly when his face gave her a warning. She turned to see the proprietor, Herr Payerl, who had stepped out of the building and was looking up at the roof of the Burgerbrau-keller, where several men were unfurling a large flag. It caught the light breeze and flapped then sagged, but Elser's consternation at the black swastika was obvious to Annalise.

'Instructions,' she confided. 'Official. They told Herr Payerl that he must show his patriotism.' She glanced again at the proprietor, who was too busy shouting up to the men to give any attention to a mere waitress. 'When are we leaving, Georg, tell me again?!'

'Tomorrow.'

'Oh!' she exclaimed, 'I hope the weather is glorious!' She swirled around, the hem of her dirndl lifting to reveal more of her shapely legs. She staggered a moment, clutched at the table, then grasped Georg's hand and squeezed it, smiling away the dizziness as if it was nothing, before running across the grass and into the rear of the building. Elser continued to watch the men on the roof hoist the flag higher, where it cracked several times. The predominant blood-red was like a small stain in the blue sky. Elser broke a cigarette in half, lit it and began to think of the next few days. Between them he and Annalise had saved a small amount; enough, they hoped, to sustain a long weekend on Lake Constance. Elser knew several boarding houses, an isolated beach and numerous forest walks. It would be good to get away, he reflected. Besides there was another, private, reason for being far from the prying eyes of the city.

That night was the last of August. In Elser's workroom cellar, the atmosphere was heavy. The double doors above the steps were shut and locked. He had assembled a small device – a clock mechanism with attached wires, a place to insert the detonator and space for two sticks of dynamite. He set the clock and spun the minute hand, watching the strikers, withdrawn until, on the hour, both of them smacked heavily on to a piece of wood in place instead of the detonator. Elser nodded grimly. 'Better,' he murmured.

10

Elser and Annalise took the first morning train from the Bahnhof, made the several changes required, and arrived at Constance in the early afternoon as first reports of Hitler's pre-emptive strike on Poland were being distributed in the press and touted in the streets. Blaring radio broadcasts greeted them at the provincial station, disturbing the tranquillity of the lakeshore town. The army and air force of the Third Reich were carving their way towards Warsaw. As Elser noted, stepping out of the station, there was a combination of fear and jubilation amongst the people. Perhaps it was just like steam from a pressure cooker, a reaction to the fact that finally something had happened. Elser realized, as did those with any intelligence, that this would mean more than a brief Blitzkrieg. Hitler would not be contained or satisfied as the Western Powers had desperately hoped – now they would fight, and Hitler would have the full-scale war he had been leading Germany towards since he was declared dictator. Looking at the sparkling lake, the crisp cumulus floating in an infinite sky, it was difficult to believe that hundreds of men were being killed at that same moment because of territorial demands sold to a gullible public and enforced by brutal might.

'Oh, Georg,' sighed Annalise. 'Five whole days!'

Walking with their small cases, the two of them were strolling arm in arm past the small harbour to an address where an old couple, who remembered Elser, had agreed to take them in for a reasonable rate. They rounded a pavilion where a uniformed band played military marches with little talent but great enthusiasm. Avoiding the crowds which had swiftly gathered to listen appreciatively, Elser led Annalise,

112

her cheeks already glowing with both pleasure and the sun, to a side street which was a short cut to their small hotel. As they stepped into shadow, a group of SA men, in brown shirts, burst out of the narrow cobbled roadway, laughing raucously and jostling the young couple. Elser fell against the warm timbers of an old building and followed the group with his eyes. Annalise could see the anger and kissed him, then squeezed his arm.

'Ignore them,' she said.

'Everybody does,' he whispered to himself, and only then did he look up. Above, from the traditional Bavarian houses, seemingly everywhere swastika flags fluttered. 'Everywhere,' he murmured, but Annalise did not hear – she was singing to herself and dancing on the cobbles.

They had been given a room on the top floor of the small hotel and, without help, climbing the steep narrow stairs with anything resembling luggage would have been difficult, but they were both young enough and Annalise sufficiently excited to discount anything that might mar their short holiday.

By evening they had explored most of the town and fallen asleep in each other's arms, only to awake soon after midnight to a full moon, seemingly suspended directly outside their window. They sat on the edge of the bed staring out over the rooftops of the old town where, in the far distance across the lake, lights sparkled.

'Is that Switzerland, Georg?' whispered Annalise.

'Yes.'

'Is it very different?'

'From Germany?'

'Yes.'

Elser nodded. 'Different.'

Annalise put her head against Elser's shoulder. 'Do you think the rest of the world could be as beautiful as Germany, Georg?'

He smiled. 'Different,' he repeated.

'How?' she asked. He said nothing. They could both hear a

113

group of people running down in the streets shouting to each other. Young, confident, over-loud voices, reflected Elser, like the eyes he had seen throughout the day, conveying a cockiness that perfectly matched the swaggering and posturing. Only the old people had sat quietly and watched, as Elser had done, the men puffing meerschaums, the women knitting or making embroidery, patient, awaiting the outcome of the hourly radio bulletins describing victory and Poland's imminent collapse. Elser listened to shouts from the night streets, which turned to laughter as someone below suggested swimming in the lake. Feet ran on the cobbles and the voices receded towards the shoreline. Summer was almost over – and so was peace.

'The Führer,' murmured Elser.

'What?' Annalise's eyes had begun to close.

'I said we have Hitler, in Germany. That makes us different.'

Annalise yawned. 'Is that bad?'

'Dangerous.'

'Why?' she asked, and snuggled closer to him.

'He lies,' said Elser simply. Annalise opened her eyes wide and looked up at the serious expression on his face. Elser returned her gaze. 'Promises bring a man to power. The facts speak for themselves.'

'What facts?'

'War.'

Annalise sat up, enfolded Elser in her arms and tried to kiss away the frown on his brow, pushing him back into the bedcover. He tried to speak but she put a finger to his lips.

'It's peaceful *here*,' she said, and sighed. 'Wouldn't it be wonderful if it was always like this?' He sensed the yearning in the flesh of her naked body and felt the response in his own. She gasped as he pressed her down on him.

'Yes,' he answered, and pulled her mouth towards his lips. This was their world now, here in this room, he thought, as their tongues touched and his sensitive fingers caressed the length of her back, gently contouring her tensed buttocks

114

before resting lightly on her thighs . . . And here, now, in the small room beneath the eaves they were safe in the knowledge that only the moon was a silent witness.

Lake Constance – the 'Swabian Sea' – extends from Lindau past Meersburg and Überlingen to the town of Constance on the Swiss border. The lake was calm, barely diffusing the clouds' reflections until a paddle-steamer churned leisurely past, some distance from the shore where Elser and Annalise lay side by side on the sand and pebbles of a small cove surrounded by trees which climbed high above them, forming a forest beyond the crest of the hill. When the steamer had gone, the wake reached the shore and the waves splashed loudly, disturbing Elser. He sat up and stared towards the other country so near . . . Hours on the train to Friedrichshafen, then several more on the ferry connection across the lake, could bring them both, a second time, to this place and then freedom. Feeling his concentration, Annalise opened her eyes.

'Georg, do you think we could ever cross the border?'

'With passes.'

'Oh,' she said, following his gaze, and her face became disappointed.

'I can get them.'

'Oh, Georg, could you?' Annalise's eyes became excited as Elser nodded. She looked at the land across the water in a different way and sighed. 'Switzerland.'

Elser stood up, thrust his hands in his trouser pockets and became lost in thought. They'd bought cheese and bread with a bottle of local wine, and eaten early. By the beginning of the long afternoon to come, they had been drowsing, with only the birds and insects around them for company, until the paddle-steamer had passed between distant yachts with limp sails and stirred more than the lake's surface; its noise had focused Elser's mind. It was the ferry from Friedrichshafen, the connection from the Munich train to Constance, the border and freedom. He constantly reviewed the task ahead of him. Once he had started he must be sure how long it would take – be sure he could complete the job – estimate the difficulties, examine the potential problems, ensure there would be no trace of his work – then he – they – would be free to leave, escape undetected and find sanctuary in the neutral country before him, such a short distance away.

'What is the date?' asked Annalise quietly. Although he had kept his clothes on, she had changed into a bathing costume. The weather was hot, the lake warm. She stood beside him and put one foot towards a small wave.

'September,' replied Elser, 'the second.'

Annalise played with the lapping water, toes curled. 'Then the baby will be born in the middle of May next year.'

He responded slowly, eventually turning to her. He looked into her face but said nothing.

'Georg, did you know?'

He shook his head.

'Are you angry?'

'No,' he replied. 'It's just that I hadn't planned . . . '

'Planned what, Georg?'

'A baby.'

'I'm not a puppet, Georg,' she said softly. 'We . . . went to bed.' Her face became even more vulnerable and suddenly he saw her eyes misting.

'We made love,' he said.

Annalise burst into tears of happiness; she clasped Elser tightly, holding him for some time as they began thinking of the future, and for each of them it held a different prospect. He started to laugh.

'What is it?' she asked.

'I wrote a song – for the zither.'

'You didn't bring it with you,' she pouted.

'No.'

'Sing it.'

'I only play.'

'Tell me the words.'

116

Elser hesitated and then began, 'First there was you, then there was me, now there is us and our love which will be, always and ever, what more we cannot say – as time takes us on, as time takes away . . .'

'It's beautiful.'

'Appropriate,' he said quietly.

'Will it, Georg. . . . take us away?'

He smiled. 'No. It will take us on.'

It was many years since Annalise had felt as secure as she did at that moment. When they made love among the ferns beneath the low branches of the shoreline trees she opened herself to him with a trust she had never believed possible, and at the climax between them she experienced an orgasm which suffused her entire body. She lay trembling in his arms until, induced by the warm sun and sexual satisfaction, she slipped into a dream less exotic than her immediate reality.

Gently Elser rolled away, buttoned his trousers and stood up. He reached over to the bag he had brought with him, took the handles and carefully weighed the contents before stepping back to look high up, where tall trees grew thickly against the skyline.

By three o'clock he had made his way through the undergrowth and in another half an hour was far above the lake. He strode through the long grass and wild flowers of several meadows surrounded by dense woodland and was soon deep amongst pine and bracken. He had worked up a good sweat and gratefully sat down to listen to the sounds of the forest. He thought for a moment he heard distant laughter, then a flock of geese flew overhead, making for the lake, cackling with expectation.

Elser gritted his teeth at the thought of his frayed nerves, broke a cigarette and smoked half, looking at the large pine tree in front of him just off an overgrown pathway. Eventually, when even the birds and insects had accepted him, he stood up, walked over to the pine, put down the bag, took out a chisel and began to cut into the large tree trunk. It was twenty minutes before he had bitten deep enough into the living wood beneath the bark to stop work and take stock of his efforts. He wiped sweat from his forehead and knelt beside his bag. Carefully he slid out the device he had created and carried gingerly since leaving Munich, then placed the small prototype of the bomb against the wood where it fitted roughly into the section he had cut away. With strong cord and some dexterity he finished the job, made awkward by the diameter of the trunk, tying the device securely against the tree. He wound the clock, set the time for three minutes and watched the second hand begin its revolutions. He picked up his bag quickly and retired through the fern, staring at the device as though it might fall, or the tree even reject it . . . But it remained in place, ticking quietly towards the alarm when the strikers would declare the hour against the head of the detonator he had slotted into its allotted space beside the dynamite. Thirty metres away, almost obscured by the tall ferns but with a clear view of his handiwork, Elser sat down to wait impatiently, straining to hear the fast regular noise of the mechanism, alert for any failure and praying for success.

Like a predator in the jungle concentrating solely on his intended victim, Elser was no longer aware of the geese circling high above as they decided on another destination further down the lake. Nor did he detect the first sounds from a quiet meadow several hundred metres away as ten Hitler Youth boys, rucksacks firmly slung, paused to check their bearings and agreed with their leader that the overgrown pathway on the forest edge would take them out of the strong sunlight and into the cool shadows amidst the crowded pines and fern, and towards their objective many more miles along the lakeshore. Again, with some laughter at an ill-intended joke which was silenced at a single command, the group followed their leader, marched out of the long grass and abundant flowers, and plunged into the dark undergrowth. Alternately in the light and shade as sunbeams penetrated from the tree-tops, the boys, none less than twelve or more than fourteen, moved vigorously through the bracken and brambles, thrusting aside nettles, retreading the old path marked clearly on the out-of-date map their leader had borrowed from his father. Their sense of freedom and pride in the uniform they wore – brown shirts with swastika armbands and badges, belted shorts, hiking shoes and long socks – brought smiles to their tanned faces, conveying the sheer joy of being part of the group, healthy, active, striding towards their destination and into the great future the Führer was planning for each and all of them.

As Georg Elser coughed quietly voices suddenly rose in unison behind him, barely eighty metres away. He spun around, hearing now quite clearly the Horst Wessel song being chorused loudly to the very tree-tops. Peering above the ferns, he saw the fast-approaching Hitler Youth group, who were drowning out the delicate sound of fast ticking. He estimated that the mechanism against the tree had less than a minute to run and, controlling panic, sank back deeper into the ferns, swearing beneath his breath, knowing he was helpless and unable to alter the course of events.

Pressing himself flat, he squeezed his eyes closed, prayed he would not be seen and began counting the final seconds – now hoping that his device would malfunction. At thirty-seven seconds, the group were not more than twenty metres from him. At nineteen seconds, he held his breath, digging into the moist soil as the boys changed the pitch of their singing, started another chorus and passed by directly above him as he lay absolutely still in the undergrowth beneath the path. At seven seconds, the leader was only as many metres from the tree whose trunk had the cord strapped tightly against the bark. The sharp eyes of the older boy caused him to slow, seeing that the clean cord had been recently applied. The group checked their stride but continued, their curious gazes seeking the object of their leader's interest. They were on the pathway, parallel to the base of the tree, as Elser counted the last seconds. The ticking stopped exactly as the leader held up his hand. 'Halt.'

Elser opened his eyes and looked up. The bomb exploded. Slivers of wood torn out of the core of the trunk erupted from an ear-splitting crack as the tree's life was ripped away and a tremor passed into the earth. Those among the Hitler Youth group closest to the blast were thrown backwards. The others leaped aside as the huge tree crashed into its neighbours of so many years and, with a splintering of boughs and increasing speed, the great weight hurtled towards the ground. Then came a sound Elser could never after forget. It was like a scream of anguish, the mortal cry of death, as the pine thundered into the fern and bracken, rolled once and lay still. Broken twigs, shattered branches, a shower of pine needles rained down for several seconds, then there was a silence so complete Elser thought he had gone deaf. He panicked and stood up. Smoke hung eerily in the shafts of sunlight, nothing moved but him . . .

Clutching his empty bag he began to run wildly down the hillside, leaping fallen logs, thrusting through the undergrowth out into the steep meadows, plunging again into the forest, racing downwards to the lakeshore, until, lacerated by the brambles, stung by nettles, cut and bleeding, he emerged out of the trees directly on to the small beach. Seeing Annalise swimming sedately some yards from the shore, he ran straight into the water. With a scream of shock the young woman found her feet in the shallows and, now completely naked, stood up with some difficulty. Elser waded out to her, shaking but with a strange excitement in his eyes that Annalise found disturbing. He seized her face and kissed her lips hard. She broke away.

'What is it, Georg?'

'Dress quickly,' he snapped.

'Why?'

'Dress,' he said again now more calmly. She splashed past him then turned back, squinting against the sun.

'Georg?' There was no response. 'What have you done?'

When the Hitler Youth boys had examined first themselves, then each other and last the tree, they began to babble excitedly. Several attempted to follow the noises some had heard crashing down towards the lake, but eventually the leader assembled the group and they made good time to the nearest farmhouse, where they were directed to a Gasthaus. Whilst the younger ones drank apple juice, the leader, surrounded by the others, made a report in a breathless voice to the authorities in Constance. It was not until sunset that police dogs dragged their handlers out of the trees on to the small secluded beach, sniffing around, finding nothing but the fading scent of unknown persons. As the Alsatians lost interest and began lapping the calm water, the two policemen lit cigarettes, watched the sun go down and, as no one had been hurt, decided to keep their report of the mystery as short as possible.

Church bells woke Annalise on Sunday morning, so she stretched, yawned and reached out for Georg. Then, finding him gone, she opened her eyes and sat up. Already dressed, Elser stood beside the window staring out. Annalise slid from the bed, stepped over to him and slipped her arms about his waist.

'Couldn't sleep?'

'No,' he replied.

'Bad dreams?'

He nodded.

'What happened Georg? Please tell me.'

Elser smiled slowly. 'I fell. I panicked. I ran.'

'Nothing more?' asked Annalise softly. Elser shook his head.

'Perhaps we could just go . . . now,' he said quietly.

'We have to . . . ,' said the young woman sadly. 'It's our last day.'

'To Switzerland,' murmured Elser.

Annalise turned him around and kissed his cheeks gently. 'We can't. Soon, but not now – not yet. We can plan it first, but we must go back now. You know that, Georg.'

He looked at her for a long time, then nodded, which

brought a smile to her face until he whispered, 'I can't go back now.'

Annalise kissed him persuasively and murmured, 'You must.'

Georg Elser said nothing.

Pealing loudly, the bells of the old church off the main square in Constance heralded the second service of the morning. The congregation was unusually dense, noticed the Reverend Father, as he turned from the altar to survey his flock and more of the day's takings. No gaps amongst the pews meant that he had a full complement. His short-sightedness was an aid to concentration during the sermon but it prevented him identifying individual faces until they shook hands with him afterwards. He intoned the opening of the service, announced the prescribed hymns, then stepped up to the pulpit at almost eleven thirty. His lean face was accentuated by a high forehead and sparse close-cropped hair. He was lightly tanned, spare of flesh, square framed, and his eyes had a suitably penetrating quality that was often remarked upon by the local burgers' wives. He quoted Genesis, alluded to Matthew, then described Jesus throwing the moneylenders from the temple with a passion that almost matched the violence he was sure must have been used by the Lord.

At ten minutes to midday, he was in full flight, emphasizing the individuality of man and his social responsibilities, the collective efforts of a community and the loyalty demanded by the state being almost as important as the trust in God, whose will dictated all things. He finished several minutes before midday, held up a hand and caught his breath in the silence before announcing a final hymn and the Lord's Prayer to end the service. If the congregation had been allowed to applaud he would have received an ovation. He had often wondered why he had not gone into politics instead of the Church. The world of religion was so much smaller, ephemeral, delicate, than the cut and thrust of public life and its exhortations. He must always be content and concerned with the hereafter, he mused, as the congregation knelt waiting for him to lead them in the Lord's Prayer. As he said Amen, closely followed by more than a hundred voices, he snatched a look at his wrist watch and wondered what he would be eating for lunch. The organ began to play suitably pious music and the service was over.

Georg Elser and Annalise filed out of the church and shook hands with the Reverend Father, exactly as a voice in an island capital hundreds of miles away, with equal reverence and certainly more import, revealed to his people on the wireless that the deadline set and presented to Berlin by the British and French governments to cease hostilities and withdraw its military presence in Poland was now past. In London, where it was just gone eleven o'clock, Prime Minister Chamberlain finished by declaring that as of that moment, a state of war existed.

By the time Elser and Annalise entered the small restaurant in the station to eat a frugal meal before taking the afternoon train back to Munich, the news was out. Customers, even those sharing tables, stared beyond each other, chewing silently, lost in private fears for the future. Annalise was quiet merely because the holiday was over, but Elser, who had found himself trying desperately to find a reason not to go on with his plan to eliminate Adolf Hitler, now realized that the advent of war against the Western Powers confirmed his private verdict for which he, as judge, jury and executioner, must take responsibility.

Annalise put her hand on his across the table and with a child-like expression, moist-eyed and sad that it was so quickly over, said: 'It was a lovely holiday, Georg.'

He nodded absently, in his mind already in his cellar off Turkenstrasse. Outside, on the platform, there was a sudden bustle of people and he heard the distant shrill whistle of an approaching train. He paid the bill for their beer, bratwurst and sauerkraut, and as Annalise took her coat from the hook, he glanced up at the hall clock. It was time. He would be no martyr, he decided, as he watched the train for Munich pull in and take on passengers into the already crowded carriages. It was his full intention to get away. As he had planned in detail the mechanics of the task ahead, so he was determined to ensure that he, and now Annalise, would survive the immediate consequences of the assassination, which must obviously begin with a vast manhunt. If he remained undetected at all times and escaped before the explosion, how would the authorities ever trace any clues they may find – to a mere artisan?

That thought gave him a sudden urge of confidence and he grasped Annalise's arm as they sat down on the wooden seat of their compartment, with the sheer pleasure of no longer being alone. He had toyed with the idea of revealing his intentions to her, but he had always been an enigmatic man and secrecy had become a habit with him. He had never exposed more than was necessary to anyone. As he was a perfectionist in his skills, he was proud of the fact that he could evaluate information, conclude opinions and decide a course of action for himself. He had never followed or dictated to anyone. He was of a unique class in Germany – his own man with his own mind.

Contrary to popular and international belief, he knew that there had been no great social workers' revolution in Germany. The Führer had come to power on the backs of the wealthy families, and as they profited from the vast combines they had been allowed to form, so the workers' lot had become pitiful. Their earnings had fallen even below the 1933 standards which the great Leader had promised to improve. After six years of power, the truth was that Hitler had locked himself and the German ruling classes in the top storey of society and thrown the key out of the window. But it was not sufficient protection, as the Nazis should have realized, for they had already illustrated that if you couldn't get in the door, you demolished the building.

On the slow journey back through the small hamlets of southern Germany, as 3 September 1939 began to ebb away with the sun casting longer shadows across the beautiful countryside he loved so much, Elser could not get the last hymn of the church service out of his mind. He had known the words since he was a child but only now did they have meaning to him as he looked out of the carriage through the reflections on the glass at the passing woodland and green hills. The wheels of the train seemed to repeat 'where our dear Lord was crucified, who died to save us all . . . '

They arrived just before eleven o'clock. Munich's station was still busy but, strangely, despite the loud military music blaring from speakers throughout the large entrance hall, the crowds were obviously subdued. In groups, they spoke in hushed voices. Alone, scuttling across the marble floor beneath the huge roof and its many lights, they threw their shadows in all directions and seemed reluctant even to catch the eye of another traveller. This time there was no jubilation, flowers, exultant populace. Apprehension soured the mood of even the most extreme optimist.

The declaration of war in 1914 had produced a fervour of patriotism amongst the population, reflecting the attitudes of bombastic leaders, hiding beneath moustaches, beards and girths, as they expostulated the usual ethics of righteous aggression which had taken ten million young men to their graves. 'If only they'd known,' thought Elser, as he and Annalise stepped into a tram and bought tickets for their ride to the square near Marienplatz, 'perhaps they would never have fought.' But then there had never been one country, one government or one man behind the conflict. It had been created by fostered revenge. The French had hated the Germans, the English had borne a grudge against the Hohenzollerns and resented the power of Habsburg rule in central Europe. With dissolute politics and decrepit royalty as partners, the powder keg had ignited merely by a single bullet into the brain of the Archduke Ferdinand in Sarajevo. 'How simple,' thought Elser. 'One bullet, and as a result, a generation of young men disappears.' The tram rocked across an intersection, halted at the crossroads, whined with the effort of acceleration pulling a full load, and carried the young couple nearer to their destination, sparks cascading from the wires.

The Great War had been fought to end all others, reflected Elser, and now another had just begun. How? No bullet. No gun. Just a voice. A persuasive tongue. Promises and lies. Glory offered – for what? Blood, suffering and death.

Georg Elser stared out at the gloomy streets, where an ineffective black-out was supposed to bring home to most people that the conflict would be more than mere words. The threats and posturings were over. It had come at last – unwanted, but now accepted as a fact, without protest, as if no one chose, but were all inflicted with the dictates of a solitary leader. One people, one government, one man.

The tram stopped, and Elser and Annalise stepped off. Building up speed, it rumbled off into the growing darkness. As they began walking, Annalise clasping his arm, Elser realized that what had started in his mind as the seed of an idea and grown slowly into a conviction, now proved beyond doubt to be the only solution – above the law of any single country, beyond morality, answerable only to God.

He knew at that moment that, of all other nights in his life, he would remember this one, escorting his woman back to seedy accommodation in the poor district of Munich.

He could feel her warmth and sensed the love in her heart. A jeweller's shop was the last shop in the street before Annalise regularly turned the corner towards her lodgings. She had always lingered here and dreamed. Now, as the two of them passed, they saw the jeweller boarding up his windows, but both of them caught a glimpse of the last tray of rings he was removing, and Elser did not have to guess what was in her mind as she turned to look in his eyes. Gently he persuaded her on and they walked even closer together, finding the pathway which they were growing to know so well. Then Elser stopped outside the hostel and, reluctant to let her go, watched Annalise's slim figure vanish into the portals of poverty she had no choice but to call home.

He looked towards the heavens, where there were no stars, only darkness. Perhaps other men in other ages, he thought, had felt as he did now. To elect to become, from personal conviction, one of an exclusive brotherhood – an assassin – carried with it responsibilities beyond the act itself. Reason and excuse, he already understood instinctively, would be sufficient for his own private emotions afterwards. He had wandered through the years without a goal. He had found pride in his work, occasionally love of a kind, as he passed on. But God was a myth, faith a demand. Government was the instrument of order, politics the choice of the people. In Germany, there was no longer anything but Hitler. He was the politics and the order, had faith, and presented himself to the people before God as the myth of salvation.

Walking back to his lodgings on Turkenstrasse that night, Georg Elser quickened his step. He had done many things in his life as an artisan, but only now had he found his true vocation.

11

A Stuttgart Becker clock was ticking on the wall. It sounded
loudly in the sudden silence. Schneider had turned off the
wireless. The military music following continual reports
from the front had proved too much for Otto Meyer. With
a gesture he had indicated his disapproval and his aide
had reached for the switch. The clock's regular rhythm continued towards the hour. Meyer, gazing out over the rooftops of Berlin to the bloody afterglow of sunset, sighed and
turned back to the sombre room, slid into his leather chair
and reached out to turn on the desk lamp.

'So. Now we know who we are fighting.'

Schneider nodded and sat down opposite his chief. 'This
time we will beat them.'

'Who?' asked Meyer.

The young officer opposite hesitated. 'All of them.'

Meyer said nothing, merely remarking silently to himself
on the brash trust of these younger men in uniform.

'The Führer will *ensure* the outcome,' stated Schneider.

'You believe that?' asked Meyer.

'Of course,' answered the younger man.

Meyer shook his head. 'At heart you are a soldier. I
am . . . ' He paused, the words were familiar but the sentence
remained unfinished.

'A policeman?' prompted Schneider with a smile. The
ticking clock intruded on their thoughts and both men looked
at the wall.

'Yes, Wolf,' answered Meyer quietly. 'I was a good
policeman. Efficient, honest.'

'Of course, sir.'

Meyer stood up and returned to the window. The colours
were already fading and the first night of war had seized hold

of the city, cloaking it not with comfort and warmth but with humidity and heavy dark cloud. 'Did my wife ring again today?'

'Yes, sir.'

Meyer bit his lip then turned slowly, ostensibly relaxed, leaning back against the sill of the large window. He spread his arms for support and began to speak softly. His voice was directed at Schneider but seemed to fill the silence of the room as if more than the walls, even the furniture listened with curiosity. Only the clock continued to eat away time.

'I have nothing against Jews. I respect the industry of their race. They have a real concept of life and use it well. Germany has been for many years a haven for them; no matter what they think of us, we don't denigrate the teachings of the synagogue. But there is a threat in their success. Illustrated, it is enviable but something to be emulated. Flaunted, it incurs jealousy, suspicion and hate. Jews take pleasure in achievement, which is to be admired. They understand the rewards of life and seek them out with tenacity. It is only their ruthlessness which is rejected, by any people who encounter it – anywhere. And it can only be countered by a greater aggression.' Meyer paused, ensuring his audience. He had no worry, Schneider was fully attentive, so he went on: 'Why is there anti-Semitism? Why should it exist more than the vigorous dismissal of any religion or belief? Because Judaism is more than a religion, a belief, even a race of people – it embodies a commitment to an exceptional tradition denied to others who are born without a core to their lives and have not the ability to create that stabilizing influence offered to those within a faith which is ostentatiously exclusive. Loyalty to a country, a creed, the ethics of civilization, changes as progress confounds the contented mind, but the Jew is eternal – the reed in a swollen river, the sapling in a wind-storm. They survive and remain the same.' Schneider coughed, interrupting Meyer who moved back to the chair and lowered himself slowly into the soft leather. The desk light cast shadows across his face, which had hollowed and aged with his increasing responsibilities. 'They should take pride in the hate of others because it continues their historical cohesion and only emphasizes the chosen quality they profess to be given by God. That hate pulls them together and creates a strength – in itself – a problem – if they were accepted – integrated – easily, how would they claim to be different, apart, at risk? Even a single idea is bound tightly by conflict, feeding from opposition it is nurtured. Imagine how centuries of conflict binds a religion, a race, a people. If it does not exist – then it must be created for the sake of continuity, survival and prosperity.'

Meyer stared at Schneider: 'Do you understand?'

'Yes sir.'

'You agree?'

'Yes sir.'

'Have you nothing to say?'

Schneider became uncomfortable. 'Well – Rosenburg was a Jew and I do not see why you concern yourself with trivial . . .'

'Herr Rosenburg *is* a Jew.'

'Unfortunately not, sir.'

'You have a report?'

'Yes, sir. Influenza.'

Meyer's eyes flickered around the room as if he were looking for witnesses. He nodded to Schneider, continuing the charade. 'That is unfortunate. My wife will be . . . concerned.'

'She was taken to the clinic, sir, in Munich.'

'Oh,' said Meyer. 'How is she?'

'Her normal self, sir. Now.'

'Good,' murmured Meyer. 'No Jew. No offspring.' The clock struck eight and both men listened to each chime.

'Have you ever been to Poland, sir?'

Meyer shook his head. 'When *he* goes,' he said, indicating Hitler's portrait on the wall panelling, 'we will. Do not be impatient, because it will not be comfortable.'

'But stimulating,' smiled Schneider.

'War?' asked Meyer, looking at Schneider in sympathy. He

130

remembered his own experiences. 'It leaves chaos. Memories of many lost friends. And,' he tapped the iron cross on his tunic, 'men with medals. I know, Schneider, believe me, I know.'

'Yes, sir,' said the young officer soberly. 'I was just thinking that now, perhaps, another unit will be formed, leaving us . . .'

'Redundant?' finished Meyer. 'As an SS officer you will never be "put aside" whilst the Third Reich flourishes. Of that I am sure. Your future is safe, if we win.'

Pride actually brought Schneider to his feet before he spoke. 'We are the strongest military power the world has known, sir. It is not a question of failure, merely time.'

Meyer stood up and checked his wrist watch.

'"Victory has many fathers,"' he quoted, '"defeat is an orphan."'

'Sir?' questioned Schneider.

'Napoleon.'

A brisk knock on the door heralded the adjutant disliked by Meyer but foisted upon him from the higher echelons.

'Now, gentlemen, please. The Reichsführer is waiting.' Meyer nodded and the man went quickly, leaving the door ajar. As Schneider moved to follow, Meyer put a hand on the young officer's arm.

'Wolf. If you were a Jew and felt as they must, would you . . . make an attempt on the Führer's life?'

Schneider stiffened. 'I cannot answer that question, sir.'

Meyer looked at him, understanding the rigorous indoctrination that must have formed such a reply.

'As a German who, say, merely disliked the party . . . its leader . . . ?'

'Not a German, sir. Never.'

'Why?'

'He,' Schneider faltered, the word more difficult than the thought, ' . . . would be a traitor.'

Meyer smiled. Hitler had done his job well. Pride now went before sense. Outside, the sound of sirens began and swelled loudly. Instinctively both men looked towards the

131

window. Meyer crossed to the desk and switched off the lamp. In darkness he said, 'Come, Wolf, they're waiting.'

When the door had closed, the empty room flickered and glowed from searchlights that sought an invisible enemy above the clouds, as the Oberheimer clock on the wall in Berlin continued to tick away Hitler's time.

George Elser walked through the archway of Turkenstrasse 94, crossed the courtyard, only glancing at the double wooden flaps flush with the cobbles leading below to the cellar, reached for his keys, opened the door, then closed it quietly. He paused inside his lodgings, listening. Hearing only the soft ticking of the familiar grandfather clock, he walked gingerly along the corridor towards his room. Opposite the lounge area, separated from the corridor by two aspidistra plants in large china pots, he looked towards the empty grate. He noticed his repaired furniture; the new cabinet he had made; the frame he had hand-tooled and varnished, containing the dull picture of Daphnis and Chloe, against drab wallpaper; checked the accuracy of the old clock face, showing one entire minute after eight o'clock – then realized that the entire household of fellow lodgers occupied the lounge, seated, silent, some smiling, all waiting as the landlady moved towards Elser, who could not take his eyes from the large swastika flag draped over the mantelpiece.

'Well,' she said. 'Back.'

Elser observed her excessive make-up, and nodded.

'Everything is safe,' she went on. 'We have looked after it for you.' She giggled, as did some of the older women and old Herzog, who then began to cough.

'The Führer,' he said in his strained voice. He lit a cigarette, blew smoke across the room and pointed. Elser turned to see the other addition – a framed portrait of Hitler.

The landlady smiled. 'He is so wonderful.' She bent to pour more schnapps into her empty glass and then turned to the group. 'We think so, don't we?' Several of the still giggling women nodded. 'So clever,' she went on, and sipped her drink. 'Like you.' Elser's face hardened as he caught the glint in the woman's eyes. One of the old men, a veteran, stood up and attempted to salute with a 'Sieg Heil'. Another switched on the wireless. 'Herr Herzog, particularly, thinks that you are an exceptional young man.' The landlady indicated the old man, who grinned, revealing his few teeth. 'But we think your workroom is . . . too damp. It's cold,' she emphasized. 'Anti-social.'

Elser realized what they had done and controlled his anger. 'You've been down there?' he asked quietly.

'Of course,' answered the woman and readjusted her silk robe, revealing a long, thin nightdress. 'We all have.' She encompassed the group in a gesture. 'They were curious.'

'What did they find?' Elser asked in a whisper.

'Nothing,' said the woman, as her eyes strayed down his body. 'Except the mess you left behind.'

'I always clear up.'

'Do you?' challenged the woman.

Elser saw the argument she wanted in her eyes, nodded once, smiled, and went directly back down the corridor, into the courtyard and, opening the padlocked flap doors, stepped below into his private workroom. He lit a lamp and surveyed the cellar. It was neat, as he had left it – everything seemed to be precisely . . . Then his eyes caught the lock on the trunk, reflecting the flickering flame. He crossed and examined the scored metal. A blunt instrument had been used to try and penetrate the mechanism and release the bent arm. It had remained secure. With a sigh, Elser sat down on the trunk, broke a cigarette in half, lit it and inhaled deeply. Then, realizing just how much explosive he was sitting on, began to laugh, loud and long. Only when he stopped, actually wiping tears from his eyes, did he hear thunder and the falling rain. Autumn had come and it was time to begin.

The Burgerbraukeller was full when Elser entered soon after

nine o'clock. At the long tables, there were many SA men in their brown shirts and red swastika armbands. Elser slid on to a bench at one end of a crowded table, opposite the main pillar, across the smoke-filled room. The voices were loud, the laughter coarse and forced, coming from groups seemingly telling stories against each other. The atmosphere, aided by the copious amounts of beer being swilled, was deafening. Elser watched Annalise thread her way amongst the customers, then smiled as she curtsied quickly to him.

'What would you like, sir?'

'I didn't think you'd see me,' replied Elser. Annalise said nothing, but her eyes and mouth seemed to indicate that she would have found him anywhere. She glanced down to see a large Alsatian from one of the other tables sniffing at Elser's cheap battered case. Elser fondled the dog, ordered the basic meal with a beer, then watched Annalise retrace her steps through the crowds. He had two hours to kill.

The chef had sworn at her, two of the other girls had been supercilious and, beside the pantry door, Annalise had burst into tears as the kitchen bustled towards the end of the evening. She felt strangely vulnerable and was contented only in the knowledge that Georg was outside and waiting. She could already feel changes in her body, her attitudes to people – she was more protective, less humorous and the laugh, hitherto such an asset in public as she brushed aside innuendo at a glance, had become strained as her temper was now short. Months from its birth, the child was already making demands on its mother, whilst the father . . .

Annalise peered out of the kitchen swing door, just before eleven, at the half-empty Bierkeller and saw the vacant place against the wall where he had been sitting. Other girls pushed through the exit, laughing at her consternation. She just stared across at Georg's seat, begging him to be there; frantically she searched the large room with her eyes but saw only other familiar customers, familiarly drunk. She slid back

134

into the kitchen and pressed herself against the wall sobbing. Two of the waitresses pushed back into the kitchen loaded with handfuls of steins, expertly carried in both hands.

'Not tonight, Josie, eh?' giggled one.

'You're putting on weight,' winked the other.

A plump young man, the second under chef, dressed in dirty whites and drinking from a full Löwenbrau stein, approached and said conciliatorily, 'You'll be all right, young girl. There's plenty of fish in the sea.' He nudged her. 'And we all swim, eh?'

Annalise turned slowly with a lowered head; she reached for a cloth in her apron pocket to wipe her nose and the tears from her cheeks.

'He's gone,' chorused the two waitresses, and thrust their many glass steins into the large sink of steaming water, narrowly avoiding the filthy kitchen porters whose wet hands reached out longingly for their warm flesh. Their shrieks drowned the words that Annalise tried to form as a reply.

'Come with me,' murmured the plump young second chef. He belched and, never rejecting an opportunity, he tried to cuddle the girl he had found attractive for so many months. She pulled away and ran off toward the small, shared changing room with a single bare dull bulb illuminating the frayed coats hung against the exposed wall.

She stepped out into the night and, although the dark sky was clear, buttoned her jacket tightly. The first chill of autumn had set in and already she had visions of the approaching winter and the same pathway she had taken each night for the several years she had spent in the city. A bleak life, merely offering survival, whilst elsewhere the world turned with lights, hope and prospects for the future. Head bent, she trudged the beaten way back through the half-accepted black-out to her hostel.

Lamps in the corridor to save electricity and candles in the dormitories provided no welcome, merely a reminder of where she was and how fast her expectations and youthful excitement could be dissipated. She washed in the only unlocked bathroom and entered her dormitory, where the single remaining candle was immediately blown out by one of the girls already in bed, who laughed at the intentional inconvenience. So she changed silently amidst the first muffled comments coming out of the darkness. She slipped the few tips she had made that night beneath her pillow, climbed into bed wearing only a thin cotton nightdress and, pulling the sheet and blanket to her chin, awaited the usual invective. If she was naturally beautiful she was the last to realize it, and how much jealousy it caused. All she understood was the dislike in the sniping voices that now filled the dormitory, alternately outdoing each other in their attempts to humiliate the only one amongst them, perhaps, with a real chance of something better.

'She snores – wait for it.'

'She cries – listen.'

'She's getting fat . . . '

'And ugly . . . '

'Anny . . . lees . . . ahh! Oh Anny . . . lees . . . ahh! I love you . . . I want to do it to you . . . '

Giggles.

'He has!'

'Has he?'

'Haven't you noticed?'

Laughter.

'What?'

'She used to have a figure!'

'Breasts and waist and hips?'

'No waist – soon!'

Annalise clutched her stomach beneath the covers and tears formed in her eyes. Suddenly the door opened at the end of the dormitory and the wide shape of the female administrator was silhouetted against the corridor lamps. She said nothing but conveyed unmistakable authority. When there was absolute silence she went away, closing the door firmly.

Annalise thrust her face into the hard pillow to stifle her sobs and thought only of Georg and where he might be . . .

12

Hidden behind the rolled carpets on the upper balcony area
in the Burgerbraukeller, Georg Elser listened as, below, lights
were switched off, voices receded and keys rattled in the lock
of the outer door at the back of the building. It was evident
that conversation had come to an end outside as the last of the
staff said their goodbyes and dispersed. Elser switched on his
torch and, pushing the small case before him, crawled from
behind the stored carpets. He stood up and stretched, shaking
the cramp from his limbs, then held his breath, aware of all
sounds. He heard only the distant noises of the city.
Somewhere a clock struck midnight. The Burgerbraukeller
was his alone.

He stepped quietly across to the pillar, following the beam
– which seemed very bright in the complete darkness – so
when he reached the base he knelt down, took off his blue
cotton scarf and wrapped it around the end of the torch. He
opened his case, placed the torch on the floor and took out the
bundles he had prepared containing tools. Then cautiously
he pressed his fingers against the panelling. The square frame
formed by the beading motif was repeated throughout the
interior of the building. He unwrapped the cloth and
carefully extracted several long, fine saws he used for delicate
craftwork on cabinets. Selecting one of the blades, he inserted
it an an angle beneath the beading, and as it bit he began a
slow, regular rhythm which he continued for almost a
minute. He stopped and withdrew the blade, then bent to
examine the incision, which was barely three centimetres
long. His eyes had grown accustomed to the light dimmed by
the blue scarf, and he made out the narrow cut, barely
discernible, even to him. He grunted with satisfaction. It
would do.

He sat back on his heels, realizing how uncomfortable his knees felt already on the hard wooden floor, but his concern was for the boards themselves where a small amount of sawdust showed clearly to his sharp eyes. He had come prepared; spreading out a large folded newspaper against the pillar, he once more knelt close, placed his pocket watch beside the torch, inserted the blade again and set to with a will. Patiently, centimetre by centimetre, he cut beneath the beading, working from the top to the bottom corner. He would have to complete the first part of the job in one – he only had until dawn and he could not afford to hurry – a single nick in the panelling could be seen and might prove suspicious; care was essential. Slowly the blade moved downwards, sawdust now falling on to the paper. It was not easy, and he realized it would take longer than he had planned. But he was now committed.

Outside in the street, a dog howled, answered by others as creatures of the night emerged and the city slept. Elser bit into his lower lip with concentration, fingers of one hand spread on the panelling, the other grasping the blade, applying a firm pressure. To cut the full square he estimated would take almost four hours. His watch showed two eighteen. Sawdust powdered softly on to the paper, whose newsprint described the victories of the German armies in Poland. Sweat formed on the brow of the Swabian artisan, who was now the professional doing what he did best. People around him had always been a distraction when he was working. He was no longer tense, but had relaxed, taking pleasure in working alone.

Elser was right, just before four fifteen the blade was almost full square. His body was cramped and both knees were painful, even though he tried continually to adjust his weight, and the now loose panel was giving him problems. He put his shoulder against the wood as he finished the last centimetres to the corner. The blade found the space where he had started, the powdering sawdust stopped and Elser carefully withdrew the thin steel. He placed it on the newspaper, then

138

put his other hand on the panel and, with spread fingers, gently moved it until one side came completely free. He lifted the piece of wood from the pillar, leant it against the base, seized the torch and, with his breath held, cast the light on the space revealed.

It looked like solid concrete. Elser's throat tightened. Impossible. It must be brick, concrete would prove too difficult if it went the depth of the pillar. Time would have hardened it to the degree that only heavy tools could break it up. And heavy tools made too much noise. He selected a chisel and chipped at the grey surface, disloding some flakes from the scar in the concrete. He sighed with frustration, sat back on his heels, broke a cigarette and lit half, inhaling deeply. A dog outside began barking again, but Elser took little notice, concentrating on the pillar, evaluating altern-ative possibilities, knowing he was running out of time.

Keys turned in the locks of the back door and suddenly the barking dog was inside the building, its noise echoing in the large interior. Elser froze, listening to the night watchman grumbling and flashing his torch, first between the tables, then up and cursorily along the balcony areas. He dragged the dog towards the serving area, found a full bottle behind the counter, flicked off the top and kicked the dog hard before upending the beer and gulping it down.

Elser heard the whining dog, and the empty bottle being slammed down on the counter with a curse. He saw the play of light again traverse the room, then listened for the door and lock once more being secured, the keys being withdrawn outside. Only as the watchman dragged his hound off into the night did Elser realize that he was still holding a lit cigarette, illuminated in the dim blue torchlight. He swallowed and finished the cigarette, which he vowed would be the last one – if the old man had smelt it, as he knew the dog must have done . . . There would be other times for smoking.

He took up the chisel, placed it against the concrete, and tentatively tapped its head with a small hammer. He had beaten the wood soft to dull any noise, but still to his ears the impact seemed to resound throughout the quiet building. He held his breath and twice more hit the chisel, then saw the first red dust of brick appear. He closed his eyes and gave out a silent prayer. So it *would* work – if he finished the panel. It had to be perfect and it had to be done before the women cleaners arrived at first light. He checked the pocket watch on the floor. It was already four thirty-six. He swore under his breath and began quickly to gouge into the concrete surface close against one edge of the exposed wood. He removed two shallow sections to take the hinges on one side, and a third on the opposite side for the press catch. At four forty-eight he was satisfied that he had done enough to allow for a flush fitment. He reached for the panel, held it in place for a moment and marked it carefully.

Near the Bahnhof a night goods locomotive hooted intermittently as it made its way through the many points of the junction, pulling its long train of loaded waggons which rattled and squealed as they moved slowly over the steel rails. The noise disturbed Elser's concentration and he was suddenly alert, but not even the first cock crowed – yet. Elser unwrapped the two hinges, taken from his case, and placed them lightly on the panel, measured the six screw-heads individually then, with a fine bladed knife, cut six small circles from the wood, barely a millimetre deep. A seventh on the opposite side was larger and would eventually conceal the catch. He put each one carefully on the newspaper, took a screwdriver from the bundle of tools in his case and attached the hinges, pushing each of the narrow grooved screws into the panel, fastening one side of the metal securely. He thrust a longer screw through the panel at the centre on the opposite side, to provide one part of the catch mechanism. He took out of the case a lead tube of cabinet glue and placed it beside the small wooden circles.

He glanced at his pocket watch. It was already five eleven. Outside in the beer garden the sound of cackling began, then a tentative crowing from a single cock in the hen-run.

Elser again bit his tongue, concentrating even more as he

leant against the pillar, applying pressure on the hand drill, pulling the centre arm over and over as it bit into the concrete and brick. Three holes for each hinge, one deeper for the catch. Withdrawing the drill, he reached for a box of rawlplugs and pressed the fibre into each hole, softly hammering each one home.

He paused to wipe sweat from his forehead, and for only one second the picture of his discovery exactly as he was now, kneeling before perhaps ten Brownshirts or Gestapo, flashed into his mind. He gritted his teeth and shivered. Outside the biggest cock in the hen-run crowed loudly and with pride at its night's activity.

Elser placed the panel against the pillar until it almost fitted into the space, then prising open the hinges and supporting the weight of the wood awkwardly with his knee and shoulder, he turned the first of six screws, deep into the rawlplugs. Tightening the last one and cutting away excess fibre with the fine knife, he hesitated a moment before releasing the panel to take its own weight. It didn't fall – or even creak – but just hung there in its place at an angle away from the scarred concrete of the pillar. Elser examined his workmanship quickly and expertly. The panel was fastened close against the wood beading motif. He put a small, hollow metal tube, pointed at one end, against the single rawlplug pressed into the concrete beside the centre of the opposite beading and, holding his breath, hit the metal gently but firmly with his hammer.

The noise seemed to reverberate once more throughout the beerhall as the metal sank into the fibre. He stopped and felt the edge with his thumb, then cut away the fibre until it was smooth. He glanced at his pocket watch on the newspaper. It was five thirty-seven. The torch suddenly began to fade, and as Elser reached out he knocked it to the floor, where immediately the light went out as it began to roll. Elser scrabbled about in the darkness, seizing the torch between two slats of the balustrade a moment before it would have fallen into the main hall. Wasting no time, he unscrewed the back,

141

removed both large batteries, felt in his case for the spares he had brought, inserted them and again pressed the switch, and the light shone brightly beneath the blue cotton scarf.

Outside, the cock crowed. Having seen the first glimmer of morning, he sang out much louder and with a penetration designed to wake every slumbering soul in the vicinity.

Aware of the urgency, Elser, now with great care, took up the small circles of wood, pierced the lead tube of glue with a pin and touched the clear liquid into the indentations where the screw-heads glinted. Then, matching the grain exactly, he covered each hole, pressing the delicate piece of the panelling back into place. Under the scrutiny of the torchlight, Elser could just make out the incision he had cut with the fine knife, but from a distance, as he leant away, it was difficult to detect. When he had finished, the panel looked whole and untouched.

At three minutes to six he heard noises from the garden, then voices and laughter. Already a dim light was beginning to appear through several of the skylights. Dawn.

Elser sucked air deeply, held his breath and closed the door he had created in the panel. As the long screw bit against the hollow metal tube there was a slight sound - a click. It fitted flush, perfectly. Elser flashed the torch over the beading - full square, and he had trouble seeing even the smallest scratch on the wood. Someone began unlocking the rear door - from outside. Elser swiftly folded the newspaper containing the residue of his night's work, thrust it, together with his tools, into his case, locked the case and crawled painfully on all fours towards the carpets which would again conceal him. Below, the door was opened and the cleaners entered - four women, grumbling and laughing cynically, the sound of their metal buckets clattering and wet mops slopping on the floor almost drowning their mild invective against the world.

Elser lay back against the cold wall behind the stacked and rolled carpets. He switched off his torch and closed his eyes, exactly as one of the women turned on all the lights in the Burgerbraukeller for them to begin their work.

142

*   *   *

At eight o'clock Georg Elser was seated in the garden outside at one of the trestle tables with the sun on his face and a cup of hot coffee in his hands. The morning chill was seeping from his bones and, although he felt spent and weary, he also harboured a growing sense of elation. One of the waitresses, who had recognized him as he sat down, had taken his order. There were other early risers, some with inquisitive dogs who, having been exercised, conducted their own social rituals on the grass between the tables whilst their owners remained stolidly oblivious of anything but their hot coffee and dry cake. Now there was war, mused Elser, this might well be the last of the good stuff. He gratefully sipped the hot beverage; soon it would be ersatz, with its familiar bitterness, which had always conjured the taste of a suicide pill he'd read about as a boy before the Great War. His eyes narrowed as he saw Annalise hurrying over the grass towards the pathway and rear door of the Bierkeller, then, seeing him, pause, staring.

In the hiatus after the cleaners had gone and before the first staff arrived, Elser had found no difficulty descending the stairs into the main room of the Bierkeller, making his way to the back door, stepping out, and mingling with the first few customers. He had expected Annalise to be the first waitress he saw, so that he could quickly explain he had been working for Borg the carpenter or Dreschler of the machine shop during the night. He glanced about him. More patrons were arriving; two dogs had begun to bark, then fight. He didn't want a scene. That would be dangerous. She'd been crying, which he could see as she stopped in front of him then slumped on to the bench. She looked at him in disbelief, almost as if he were a ghost.

'Where did you go?' Elser did not reply, only sipped coffee. 'You said nothing, told me . . . ' she paused, eyes wet.

'I had to work.'

'You look terrible.'

143

Elser smiled ruefully and felt the stubble on his face. 'Compliments, and so early.'

'What did you do?'

'You're late.'

'Last night?' persisted Annalise.

'Herr Borg.'

'The carpenter?' She remembered Georg having mentioned him before.

He nodded. 'I borrowed some things.'

'And worked?'

Elser nodded again in reply and gulped the cooling coffee. He noticed that people had begun to cast an eye towards them, perhaps anticipating an emotional outburst. From the rear door across the lawn the proprietor, Payerl, stepped out and looked up to the flagpole, where a large red flag with its black swastika on a white circle was being raised to catch the freshening breeze.

Annalise was on her feet immediately. 'Tonight?' she asked softly.

Elser smiled and touched her fingers. 'I'll come.'

'You're late!' bellowed Payerl across the lawn. Arms akimbo, his girth thrust forward in lederhosen above thick legs spread firmly astride the gravel path, he would have been imposing but for the high colour of his face and the elaborate, luxuriant moustache which, Elser had confided to Annalise, probably was an attempt to compensate for the lack of hair on his balding head. Reluctantly Annalise left Elser and with an anxious face ran over to Payerl, curtsied, apologized, then entered the Bierkeller. The proprietor remained in his favourite pose a moment longer, surveying his regular early customers, some actually already drinking beer. He nodded to several, deliberately ignored Elser, turned on his heels and returned with conscious dignity to the kitchen of his beer-hall.

Elser finished his coffee, left coins on the table, slid from the bench and stood up, feeling his aching bones and the pain in his knees, which was something he had not foreseen. He

144

walked stiffly out on to the pavement and began to make his way to Turkenstrasse and bed.

'Herr Elser.' It came as a whisper intruding on his dreams as he turned his head and, only semi-conscious, peered through the half-light of his curtained room towards the door, where someone knocked again and repeated more urgently, 'Herr Elser.'

Elser opened his eyes and listened, identifying the voice as old Herzog, seeking some clue to why the old man should be so excited. He calmed himself, noting once again that he must find a way to bring his nerves under control. He looked at his pocket watch and made out that it was already late afternoon.

'Coming,' he said, swung his legs from the bed and, still fully dressed and unshaven, opened the door.

The old man standing before him grinned his almost toothless smile, appraised Elser's condition, then put a finger to his lips quickly. 'Herr Elser,' he hissed, 'the police!' Elser's eyes snapped open as the old man giggled. 'They are here,' whispered Herzog, and giggled again.

'What do they want?'

The old man smiled, 'You,' he said.

Elser followed Herzog into the lounge, where all the lodgers were assembled. The landlady was directly in front of an officer who was seated at the desk, which had been moved across the room to provide him with an instant office and emphasize his authority. Two other policemen remained behind him, against the wall, silently observing everything. The officer was examining papers, and without looking up addressed the landlady, who had put on a smart costume cut too tight for her spreading flesh, but of a quality complimented by a fine grey-and-pink coloured silk scarf, an excuse for lipstick and make-up, noticed Elser.

'A formality, you understand,' murmured the officer. Suddenly aware of his quiet attentive audience, he coughed self-consciously, which seemed strangely inconsistent with the presence his dark uniform created. 'Now we are at war, all "aliens" are to be identified.' He looked up and stared at the landlady, who smiled amiably.

'I have no aliens.'

'I will be judge of that,' stated the officer, and surveyed the group behind the woman.

'Would the Herr Officer like a schnapps?'

The policeman absorbed the woman's expression and began to estimate his chances. 'Perhaps,' he said, 'later. When we have finished.'

'Then you must start, Herr Officer.'

'Captain,' he said.

'Captain,' she repeated.

'Herzog!' he barked. The old man stepped forward, came to attention awkwardly and saluted. The policeman saw the face of an old veteran as the papers described him, existing on a small pension and the pittance he had saved. He dismissed the man with a gesture. Still at attention, Herzog spun round and nearly fell into the group. The officer took another paper, and looked at the attached photographs.

'Ilse Guber!'

The landlady approached and stood, as she thought, demurely.

The policeman smiled. 'A good likeness.'

'Terrible,' said the woman. 'There are no good photographers these days . . . '

'Why?' asked the officer quietly. Behind him, his men shifted on their feet and silence held the room.

'Well, because . . . ' the landlady suddenly felt uncomfortable under the man's gaze.

'Because we are at war?'

'Yes,' she answered, almost defiantly.

'I see,' murmured the man.

'We still have to live, Herr Officer, and war takes away from women such things as . . . we feel most strongly about. Perhaps – but then we are more delicate creatures, sensitive to deprivation.'

146

'You are deprived?' asked the officer ominously. 'Of what?'

'Shortages,' answered the woman hoarsely.

'Really,' said the man. 'Name one.'

Someone in the group behind the landlady sniggered, distracting the officer's attention. 'Well, you men . . .' began the woman, and now someone laughed openly.

The officer stood up and became dangerous. 'I am here,' he began slowly, 'with the authority vested in me by the state, and no matter what the age or condition physically or mentally of anyone in this room, if that authority is not treated with the respect it deserves I will arrest that person or . . . ' He paused. 'All of you. After which, you will be merely a part of the system of justice we have established in the Third Reich, firm with its own people and ruthless with those who are disloyal or need to be reminded of the power of our Führer.' The officer indicated the portrait of Hitler on the dull wall above the fireplace. 'You understand?' he finished, and waited for a reply. The lodgers murmured their agreement and watched the man reach for another paper, absorb its contents, then glance at the photograph and shout, 'Elser!'

Elser stiffened, then stepped forward for scrutiny.

'What work do you do?'

Elser could hardly speak. His pulse was racing. Only old Herzog saved him. 'He repairs furniture,' stammered the old man, and he pointed at several chairs, a table, even the desk. Then, remembering, he rummaged in his pocket. 'And my watch.' He showed it to the policeman. 'Very well, too.'

The officer cut him off. 'Where do you do this?'

'He has a workroom,' went on the old man, warming to his subject, 'but it is too damp . . . too . . . '

The policeman gestured Herzog to silence impatiently. 'Here?'

Elser nodded.

'Then let me see it.'

Followed by first the officer and his men, then the landlady and those lodgers mobile enough to descend the stairs, Elser

147

removed the padlocks and led the way below into the cellar, where he lit a lamp then leaned against his workbench, watching the three uniformed men exploring his private workroom. They touched a single hanging puppet, noted two broken chairs in a corner, an upended table, numerous tools laid out on the benchtop, chippings on the floor – then the trunk which the officer approached slowly. He stopped in front of it and smiled as he observed the padlock.

'Do you believe in Adolf Hitler, Herr Elser?' He glanced at the dark-haired artisan with strong features and pale skin. 'The glory of the Reich?' prompted the policeman. Elser seemed struck dumb, not even a muscle of his face moved.

'Of course he does,' interposed the landlady. 'We all do. And,' she gabbled, 'it is not so difficult. The Führer is so . . . so . . . clever . . . ' she finished lamely, appealing to her lodgers.

The policeman ignored her and remained transfixed, watching for a change in Elser's expression. He smiled, lifted the padlock with the toe of his polished boot and, without raising his voice, said, 'Open it.'

Elser said nothing, did not even move. The officer let the padlock fall. 'Open it!' he commanded.

The landlady pulled herself erect and folded her arms nervously, willing Elser to respond. The officer's face hardened.

'I said open it!' Then he exploded, 'Now!'

A murmur went amongst those gathered in the room as Elser went to a drawer in his workbench, took out some keys and selected one from the ring, which was snatched by one of the other policemen. He crossed to the trunk, bent down and released the padlock. As Elser watched with less apprehension than the others, the officer lifted the trunk lid, again with the toe of his polished boot. Feet shuffled and faces peered to see the contents.

The officer touched his thin moustache and referred to Elser without looking at him. 'What were you going to do with these?'

148

Elser said nothing.

'Sell them?' asked the officer.

Elser nodded.

'For a profit?'

The landlady stepped forward, speaking with exaspera-tion, but hoping to see the mystery in the trunk. 'Well, why else would he want to sell anything, whatever it was . . . ?' Then she saw them. The trunk was half full of books, most of them about Adolf Hitler, some second-hand photo albums of the Nazi party at play and playing at war, others cheap editions and obviously brand new – certainly unread – copies of *Mein Kampf*.

The landlady looked at Elser with wide eyes as if he was a magician who had changed a pistol into a rabbit, and although she had not the slightest idea of how near the truth that might have been, her sense of surprise was communicat-ed to the entire audience. 'Books?' she said.

'Are you surprised, Fräulein Guber?' asked the officer. The woman delicately put her hand in front of her mouth and coughed before touching her scarf then, with some allure, now that the tension seemed to be over, said, 'You flatter me. I was once married. I'm *Frau* Guber.'

The officer would not be distracted and sensed something wrong, but could not have known that Elser had learnt his lesson when he discovered the scored padlock on his return from Lake Constance. As a result, he had created a compartment under the floorboards beneath the workbench where he had carefully stored the dynamite sticks. The books he had been forced to accept in part payment for some work he had done at Dreschler's machine shop.

The officer stood in front of Elser and looked down at him. 'Do not hope to profit from the Führer, as if you were a gypsy, or a Jew. You are not a parasite. As a German you must expect to give to your country as *he* has given to us all – new hope for a great future.' Elser's gaze was disconcerting in the face of this superficial political nonsense. The officer con-tinued quickly, 'From Württemberg?' Elser nodded. 'My

149

sister is married to a man from – Württemberg.' The policeman repeated the name of the province as if it were a swear word. 'And I do not like the man.' And he did not like the look of Elser's eyes – it was not open defiance, but a quiet confidence, an inward belief that the policeman had only ever seen before in the eyes of a priest.

'Schnapps, Herr Officer?' asked the landlady.

For the first time thankful for the intrusion, the officer turned, clicked his heels, bowed with excessive politeness and said, 'Thank you kind lady. When we have finished the rest of the formalities, which will take us no time, I would be more than pleased to accept your invitation.' He led the way up the shallow stairs and everyone followed.

The landlady exchanged a single look with Elser, as if he were going to close the lid of the trunk and change the rabbit back into a pistol. For the first time, Elser, who had said nothing, smiled almost imperceptibly. The woman hitched up the skirt of her costume and, with a snort of disapproval that any form of suspicion should have fallen on a person in her house, she followed the group. She was already thinking of the special schnapps for this increasingly attractive officer. Such authority and so charming . . . Above, she actually slammed one of the door flaps against the cobbles, as an indication to her lodger that she was displeased and even, perhaps, that he should be more careful in future.

When Elser broke a cigarette in half, his hands were shaking and he could hardly light the match.

Georg Elser stepped out of his lodgings shortly after lights out was declared in the streets by over-enthusiastic air raid officials. The night sky was clear, and although it was chilly, the cold of approaching winter had not yet arrived. He carried no case, as he quickened his step towards the Burgerbraukeller. It was the single night of the week Annalise was free early, and they always went out together, often to the cinema, sometimes for a meal, seldom both. Elser had shaved and washed, sponging down his knees, which seemed unusually sensitive and puffed up until he applied cold water. Even now, he felt a disturbing sensation as he walked faster to be on time.

Annalise's consternation disappeared as Elser stepped into the large, crowded hall. She was seated just inside the entrance with a new coat over her shoulders. Her hair down, she had applied what little make-up she had to her cheeks and eyes, and her expression when Elser touched her was total vulnerability.

In the past, with other men, the few she had taken a fancy to, she had been curt if they were late, taken from the evening as much as she could extract, and outside her hostel, donated some kisses and as little else as possible. With Georg, her emotions ran the gamut from wretchedness to irritation in his absence, from pleasure to euphoria at his presence. Before he stepped into her life, she had certainly had several 'experiences' but had always been in control. Georg was different in that he seldom made demands and she had found herself in the disconcerting position of making whispered suggestions, wanting him, always seeking some tangible evidence that he cared. Even if he was a minute late, she felt that he had begun to feel less for her, and when he was not waiting for her when she had finished work late, a terrible anguish of suspicion enveloped her and remained to torture her during the night until she saw him, either at breakfast in the Bierkeller garden, or in the evening, as the small figure stepped in amongst the crowded tables amidst the loud, coarse behaviour and smoke-filled atmosphere. Then there were no doubts. She knew she loved him.

'New coat?' he said.

'Nearly new . . . I bought it from one of the girls . . . .'

Elser smiled and looked across the already packed hall, then at the stairs to his left, which led up to the balcony. He must be sure – he knew he would have to look. 'One minute more,' he murmured, and indicated the toilet and the end of the landing. Annalise pursed her lips, but Elser was already gone.

Pushing through the group waiting to be seated, Elser went up the stairs and walked along the balcony, where he paused beside the main pillar. He leant on the balustrade and looked down, feigning curiosity in case he was being watched, then he turned slowly and quickly examined his work. For a moment he could see nothing, then as he peered closer he just made out the fine line around the matched circles of wood covering the screws. He grunted in satisfaction, wandered on to the toilet, left the door open to provide light, glanced at himself in the filthy mirror and pulled the chain. The cistern moved on its mountings and some plaster fell from the wall. The small window was closed. He tapped the glass. It was opaque and too thinly composed to be of quality. Difficult to cut. Easy to smash. He exited gratefully, the stench of old urine almost unbearable.

At the bottom of the stairs, he took Annalise by the arm and led her through the incoming crowds, out into the cool night air.

'What would you like to do?'

In answer, she kissed him. Tears came only at the end of the evening, when Elser suggested it was unwise to go back to Turkenstrasse together. He explained what had happened and that it would probably be a topic of late-night conversation amongst the lodgers. They parted outside her hostel and Elser walked home in light rain from an unsympathetic night.

The only cinema not full had been showing documentaries of the Polish campaign, so they had eaten a meal in a cheap restaurant, where the plump proprietress gave the two lovers a discount. Their earnest silences and whispered conversations had touched her heart. She had long since ceased to be jealous – even her memories were only worth forgetting – but she would always recall the eyes of the young couple. She saw them exchange small tokens, which were more than they

152

could afford, of their feelings for each other. The girl had reached for her gift and presented what, even in the dim light, she could see, was a cheap gold ring. The man had obviously been touched, but smiled as he took from a pocket a similar ring of equally poor gold. The two of them had examined the inscriptions and spoken the names as if for the first time. To the old woman, they sounded like 'Georg' and 'Annalise' – no doubt scratched hurriedly and paid for in excess. But as the fingers of the two lovers met across the table, the expression in their eyes was worth more than diamonds.

She knew the girl from before, but as she said goodbye to the young couple, she saw the man's face in the harsh light of the hall lamp. Only as she closed the door and let fall the black-out curtain, did she murmur to herself, 'He's different.' She had belched to emphasize the fact and waddled over to the bar for a nightcap.

13

The following evening, Elser ate in the main hall as usual, and waited until the crowds were thinning out. When Annalise finally emerged from the kitchen just before eleven, he was gone. She contented herself with thoughts of the night before and the promises for the future they had exchanged over a simple meal on a stained tablecloth with a single candle between them. But she cherished the evening, imbued it with magic and remembered every minute of it all the way back to her only home in the city, where her private, grim reality waited patiently.

Jangling keys and increasing silence alerted Georg Elser, who had been dozing against the wall behind the stacked carpets on the balcony. Pinpoints of light, which had penetrated his concealment and fallen across his face, had now disappeared.

The Burgerbraukeller was dark and empty. He switched on his torch, dulled the beam with his blue cotton scarf, then checked his pocket watch. It was later than usual – twelve thirty-eight. He crawled out on to the floorboards of the balcony and, dragging his case, he slid across to the pillar. He knelt in front of the panel, reached out, and knowing exactly where the catch was located, carefully prised open the door he had created, using a fine blade wrapped in gauze to prevent a mark on the beading. With a click, the screw was released from the hollow metal and the panel swung open. He pushed it wide, put down newspaper, opened a bundle from the case, positioned the torch, and with hammer and chisel began cautiously to chip at the concrete surface, working patiently towards the brick beneath. He had tied oilcloth on to the chisel head to absorb as much sound as possible; it proved more efficient than the softened wood, which had quickly hardened with each blow.

He frequently checked the floor to be sure all the debris fell on to the spread newspaper, and as the night passed he saw the pile begin to build. The outer layer of concrete was almost gone by three thirty. An hour later, he had begun to attack the mortar holding the central bricks in place. At the first light of dawn, heralded by the familiar cock from his garden harem behind chicken wire, Elser had dislodged almost more than he could carry out. That was the next problem to solve, so he would have no worries about disposing of the evidence. He had decided he could not chance leaving it behind the carpets. Should the carpets be moved, he might find another hiding place, but the fresh debris would cause more than suspicion; he was sure it would initiate a search, which would be a disaster.

He had brought a small sack and, having broken up the larger pieces of brick and slivers of concrete, he poured the bits into the open neck from the half-folded newspaper. He pushed the panel closed, listening for the sound of metal biting metal, felt the firmness of the panel, examined the flush fit against the beading, then, folding the paper, bundling his tools into the case next to the full sack, he tried to stand up. He almost fell, and grasped the balustrade, gasping at the pain in his knees. In his concentration, he had forgotten that he had remained in the same position so long. He became aware of what seemed more than cramp, but he strengthened his legs, locking them, and the pain lessened. Then he heard the noise of cleaners entering at the back of the building. Lights went on, coarse voices rose towards the roof, and gratefully Elser slumped against the wall, concealed behind the carpets. He switched off his torch and closed his eyes just before six o'clock.

The next night, it proved difficult to escape Annalise, and when he finally climbed the stairs, being careful as always to stay against the wall in shadow, he could see even as he reached the balcony that the carpets had been moved. They were still stacked and rolled but had been added to by several folded trestle tables, one obviously broken. He slid behind, unobserved, and lay back in his usual position against the damp outer wall. When the beerhall had emptied, the lights were out, the doors locked and he was alone, he spent some minutes exploring his immediate area, then the base of the pillar, to be sure that not even a grain of brick remained on the floorboards to give him away under scrutiny.

Satisfied, he set to work once more, opening the panel and digging slowly into the pillar until dawn and the arrival of the cleaners. When the lights went on, he hazarded a look at his knees, extending his legs beyond the carpets and tables. Having pulled up his trousers, his flesh was exposed, and blood appeared above the bruised bone. He wiped his skin painfully then eased himself back into the dark hiding place.

Carrying the heavy case bound with thick cord, he mingled with the early risers gathered inside the great hall and stepped out into the garden, which was closed because of the increasing rain falling from a dull, overcast sky. He had only glimpsed Annalise, waved and gone after a quick coffee from one of the other girls.

Walking beside the River Isar, he stopped beside a break in the wall he had found. He was never able to remove more than he could carry, and even this had proved hard enough to hack from the pillar; he was always conscious of the noise. Once again he emptied his sack of debris from the night's work into the flowing water. He stared down for several minutes at the ebbing and swirling patterns on the surface, feeling the rain on his back and the throbbing pain in his knees. It would be so easy to give up, to stop now, he knew; the only reason he continued was because he had determined his course of action, and he never failed to complete a task he had begun.

He began walking again eventually, and as the distance

from the river increased, it became more difficult. He could not afford to leave his bicycle near the Bierkeller throughout the night and doubted that he could even ride it. Despair came in waves as he made his way back to Turkenstrasse, where he had promised to do more repairs. He would have to sleep, perhaps leave the pillar several days and ask Dreschler if he had more machine work. Even Borg could provide him with cabinet-finishing, but he always wanted his workers on a more permanent basis. Elser had explained that he was prepared to do the skilled craftwork once the basic cabinets were completed, but not as a full employee. Only his abilities, appreciated by the carpenter, allowed him his wish, and he had begun to establish a pattern, sometimes actually working at night for both men to show that his dedication matched his skill. More importantly, it created an alibi, should the worst happen and suspicion fall upon him if the lodgers discovered he was often out until morning.

Several of them saw him come in now, pass by the lounge with a nod and go directly to his room. Inside, having locked the door, he collapsed on the bed and was almost instantly asleep.

A week passed, and with another gone, it was suddenly early October. He had begun to bind his knees with cotton and lint, which at first proved effective, but the hours in the same position, painstakingly crumbling the brick and mortar, which time had bound harder than he had imagined, took its toll. Even through the bandages he could feel the very fibres of the wooden boards. His coat, acting as a cushion, was also a relief at first, but the taut skin over bone suppurated, staining the jacket sleeves. This was immediately commented upon by Annalise, whose sharp eyes had also seen the worn patches on his trouser legs.

A knock on Elser's door at the end of that first week in October opened his eyes; a second prompted him to slide from the bed and a third, more impatient, forced him to pull on his trousers and switch on the dull electric light and turn the key in the lock.

The landlady entered and noticed the numerous cigarette butts in a small ashtray by his bed. With a grimace of disapproval, she gathered her houserobe about her, an indication to Elser that she hadn't dressed all day, then snorted as her eyes flicked around the room, noticing every detail.

'So,' she said, and looked at Elser with assumed distaste. 'We don't see you.'

Elser reached for a half-cigarette from his pocket, lit it and sat back on the bed.

The woman looked closer at him. 'Are you well?'

He nodded, puffing smoke, which the landlady ostentatiously wafted away.

'You are working?'

Elser's eyes answered affirmatively.

'To pay the rent I hope?' she asked harshly.

'Yes.'

'You are behind.'

'I know.'

'You must make it up.'

'I will,' he said, and dropped his head.

The woman softened and sighed, as if finding patience and discovering a solution. 'Or . . .' she began, 'I have . . . other repairs, Georg.' He looked up. She smiled and sat close beside him on the bed. 'There's so much you can do here, you know. The house is old and needs . . .'

'I'll do anything,' he murmured.

The landlady kissed his cheek lightly. 'You never call me Ilse.'

'Ilse,' he whispered.

She appraised his profile and unkempt appearance. 'You look tired.'

He inhaled smoke, coughed and nodded. She put a hand on his thigh and leant her head against his, so that even through the smell of tobacco smoke and cheap perfume, he

158

could detect the schnapps of the day each time she opened her mouth.

'We had our first snow today.' The woman had assumed an intimate voice, as seduction moistened her lips. 'Snow before November means a cold winter. Cold blood; cold bodies.' She touched his face and turned it to hers, 'Cold beds.' She kissed him with a passion to which Elser was unable to respond. She drew away and bit her lips as her eyes hardened.

'I'm sorry,' muttered Elser.

Ilse Guber stood up. 'You're tired,' she hissed. 'I wonder why?' She turned and stepped to the window, opening the curtains a little to look out into the darkness where snow was falling lightly. 'Most of your days you never see – only sleeping,' she mocked. 'We know these things. People here talk. What else can they do?' She turned, looking back at Elser, lit dully by the single electric light bulb. 'What do you do?' she asked curiously.

Elser smiled wearily and spoke the familiar words, 'Make things, mend things.'

'With waitresses?' she asked sarcastically. 'If you make love, Georg, what do you mend?'

'Whatever is broken,' he answered quietly. The woman's eyes misted over and she put a hand to her puffy face and a finger to catch a falling tear. 'Oh, Georg,' she whispered plaintively, 'be kind.'

'I try.'

'With me.'

'Ilse . . . ' he said, and stood up slowly.

'I'm so alone,' she murmured and moved towards his arms of compassion.

'So am I,' he said.

She put her cheek against his, feeling with a shock of pleasure the stubble of his beard. 'Georg, there are people around me, I know, but I have not one to turn to since he . . . My husband, with all his faults, was at least . . . in my bed at night.'

Elser pressed his face against hers in sympathy. 'If each

of us could find someone to turn to, we would all be lucky.'

'Are you lucky, Georg?' She turned her head and looked into his eyes.

'I hope so,' he said softly.

She kissed him tenderly and felt his response, unaware it was from the sadness he felt for her lost dreams. Her lips strayed from his and she murmured, 'I have not many years left, Georg. I shall get old. I don't want to be old. Please . . .' She pulled him tightly into her embrace and their bodies bent towards the bed. ' . . . mend me.'

What Georg Elser did, he did well, and as most of his best work was done in private and presented as a *fait accompli*, there were seldom witnesses to corroborate that it must have taken a great deal of application and patient, even inspired, skill. He always felt that he became one with the material at hand, and his perfectionism always dictated a thoroughness and dedication that those who benefited from it never forgot.

Having taken Ilse Guber to her own bed, he did not get back into his until the early hours of the morning. If he had missed a night's work in the Burgerbraukeller, he had at least given his landlady's illusions some substance for several hours – and established a rent credit that might well last him until Hitler had been blown to hell.

By the early morning of 15 October, Elser had hollowed a deep hole in the pillar and dug out the bricks and mortar around the central support, made of reinforced concrete. He was sure sufficient explosive would sever it completely and collapse the roof on to the balcony, the combined weight taking the full tonnage of construction materials directly where he had estimated. He peered through the balustrade down to the area below, where the Führer's podium would be placed, then looked up, shining the light of his torch at the roof, and grunted in satisfaction. Enough weight to kill, even if the blast didn't do the job.

Suddenly he heard laughter, loud whispers and keys jingling in the locks of the rear door. He glanced at his pocket watch. It was only three sixteen. He sank back amongst the piled debris on the newspaper, wincing at the pain in his knees. He could do nothing – it was too late to clear so much . . . his case, the tools . . . He turned off his torch and pressed against the pillar, carefully pushing the panel door closed. Below, the door opened, two women entered, switched on only two side lights and stood giggling as two SA men in brown shirts entered, closed the door and drunkenly began to kiss and bite the two waitresses, whose voices Elser recognized. Sweat broke out on his forehead. 'Not now,' he thought, 'not like this, please God.'

Stifled shrieks, suppressed giggling, then unconvincing protests led to a moment's silence, after which Elser, holding his breath, heard heavy breathing and the sighs, moans and hissing of both couples exploring each other's bodies through obstructing clothes. One of the women screamed with pleasure; a sound that would fill a stadium, which drove Elser against the pillar as if he might actually penetrate the wood, as the SA man had certainly entered the waitress between her legs spread apart on the top of a trestle table. Laughter from the other couple on the floor, who were themselves panting with exertion, mingled with the cries of growing sexual fulfilment.

Exposed, everything he had brought with him around, the hollowed pillar above his bent head, Elser was panic-stricken. His breathing had become shallow and he squeezed his eyes tight in the half-darkness.

A key fell to the floor, cushioned by a pair of woman's underpants, as the waitress released her grasp and clung to the SA man, whose rhythmic thrusts prised her soft thighs wider. At climax, she shouted wildly, 'No!' and the table collapsed, carrying the couple to the floor, where they rolled over their friends, who were too busy to be interrupted, and only when they too had achieved a measure of drunken satisfaction did all four of them lie still. Then one of the girls

161

started crying and her partner coughed as they began to reassemble themselves, whilst the other couple disentangled, the palliative of lust now evaporated.

The barking dog and penetrating bellows of the watchman brought them all to their feet. The two SA men, ignoring his accusations, wandered over to the bar counter, found the bottled beer, poured full glasses and drank, whilst the old man ranted at the two girls, now both in tears, threatening as they pleaded until, to increased barking, one of the Brownshirts slammed the watchman against the wall beside his noisy but cowering dog and warned him, in language that was unmistakable, to remain silent. The argument was convincing and created a moment's quiet. The two men took the waitresses and went out of the open back door into the night. The watchman, mumbling to himself, drank a beer slowly, then deliberately smashed the bottle on the floor. It frightened the dog, which broke from its lead and ran across the beerhall. The watchman shouted and the dog paused at the bottom of the stairs.

'Come here!' shouted the old man, and flashed his torch. The dog had raised its nose towards the balcony and was sniffing, having discovered other curious smells. The watchman shuffled between the tables with the chairs and benches upended on their tops, reached for the dog, grasped his collar, hit him hard and resecured the lead. Swearing, he made his way to the rear exit, turned off the side lights, went out, locked the door and, with his barking dog marking his progress into the distance, was gone.

Elser sighed deeply and wiped his brow. He'd had enough. He began to gather the debris, emptied it from the newspaper into his sack, secured the neck, put it beside the tools in his case, which he closed, and pressed the catches shut. He examined the floor in the torchlight but found nothing that might indicate the pillar had been tampered with, so he pushed the panel into place and listened for the click. For a moment he looked up at his hidden handiwork, then tapped the panel for luck. The hollow sound was unmistakable. He tapped the panel below, and the difference was obvious. One was backed by solid materials, the other concealed the space he had carved. His face fell. There was nothing he could do until the following day. He had been confident that he had thought of almost everything, but he was learning continually as he increasingly explored the unknown. Dragging his case, he crawled towards the carpets, switched off his torch and fell asleep.

He awoke to the sound of rain. The noise of a steady downpour on the roof, mixed with murmuring and some laughter. Elser opened his eyes wide and stared at his pocket watch in disbelief – eight thirty! He quickly scrambled to his feet, gritted his teeth at the initial pain in both knees, then stumbled toward the toilet at the end of the balcony. Several faces below looked up with little interest as Elser passed behind the pillars and along the balustrade. He glimpsed Annalise serving at tables, and she acknowledged him with a wave. He could smell the coffee and felt the dry tongue in his mouth. Only as urine splashed against the enamel and into the water did he remember the hollowness of the pillar. He would have to back it, he decided, with metal behind the door, which would increase the weight and strain and therefore require another hinge. He pulled the flush and watched the cistern move as plaster flaked from the wall. He opened the small window and peered out into the rain. It was a long way down. He examined his face in the dirty mirror – his eyes were clear but his stubble made him look like the gypsy Annalise called him. Her *Ziga*.

Picking up the case, he wandered back to the stairs and descended into the hall, where he was greeted first by the watchman's Alsatian, which he fondled affectionately, then by Annalise, whose face brightened but could not conceal a curiosity that Elser detected immediately.

'I didn't see you come.'

'Can I have an egg?'

'And coffee?' smiled Annalise. Elser nodded and stretched out a hand to stroke the Alsatian, which sprawled beside him, growling with pleasure. 'You look as though you need it,' said the young woman.

Elser continued to gaze at her pretty face as he took out a cigarette, broke it, then lit the tobacco. She glanced around, saw only contented customers and hazarded a conversation.

'Is something wrong, Georg? In ten days we've hardly been out together. Once to see a war film, to old Irma's again . . .' she paused recalling the cheap restaurant where they were always at home, 'and,' she remembered, lowering her voice, 'to your lodgings one night . . .'

Elser reached out and touched her stomach with a quick smile. 'You are always working,' he murmured.

'Me?' She paused. 'I am not . . . always. *You* are always working!' she said with accusation.

'Yes.'

'Who with?' she asked.

Elser puffed on the half-cigarette. 'Dreschler, Borg. I told you.'

'During the day . . . and at night?'

'Sometimes.'

'Are you working late tonight?'

'Are you?' he asked.

Her face fell in answer. 'Two of the girls were sacked this morning – apparently they came in here . . . ' her eyes sparkled for a moment at the gossip from the kitchen. 'I'll tell you later, if you wait for me, but I'll be late . . . '

Payerl stepped out of the kitchen and Annalise hurried away. Elser slumped against the wall, smoking, and stroked the Alsatian, who sniffed curiously at the old case. Above, the noise of the rain began to lessen and there were, every few seconds, shafts of sunlight pouring into the Bierkeller through the skylights. In front of the artisan was the pillar and another unforeseen problem.

14

The black Mercedes stopped in traffic. The chauffeur glanced into the mirror at his passengers. 'More like Berlin every day, sir.'

Meyer nodded absently as Schneider checked his watch again. 'What time do we leave?' he asked.

'The next train is in one hour.'

Meyer looked out at the brightening streets of Munich. They had travelled far over the previous weeks. Autumn had fallen on Poland, together with the German army. Opposition had crumbled as mechanized units engaged cavalry formations and, despite the courage and tenacity of these inadequately equipped divisions, they were soundly beaten. At the Führer's headquarters in the field, increasing jubilation at the sweeping victories gave rise to a series of unkind jokes directed at the Polish nation, ignoring the unrelenting valour of the people. Meyer had been glad to leave the arrogant Wehrmacht officers to their celebrations. Towards the end of September the Russians, as had been secretly agreed, moved from the East and met German commandos at Brest-Litovsk. Poland was to be occupied and partitioned jointly by the two powers.

At the beginning of October it was all over. Returning with Hitler in his private railway carriage, Meyer had heard disquieting reports of atrocities which had been glossed over in further celebrations. Persecution was part of war, it was generally agreed, and examples of how Germans had suffered for twenty years submerged the gossip of unjustified killing. Pursuing the facts, Meyer was merely reminded that his job was altogether different and that he should concentrate on details relative to his important role.

Schneider was peering out of the rear window of the Mercedes. 'Where are we?'

'Preysing Strasse,' murmured Meyer.

'Near the river, sir,' answered the chauffeur.

'We've plenty of time, then,' said Schneider, and relaxed. 'We won't miss it.'

'I'm beginning to miss Berlin,' Meyer remarked, and tapped the glass with growing irritation at his thoughts. Unlike Schneider, for him Munich was full of ghosts: his father, a younger life, marriage, the children, Marianne, and now this Rosenburg. The campaign in the East had occupied his mind. Exploring the new logistical problems which had constantly arisen to safeguard the Führer in occupied territory, he had had little time for private examinations of his conscience and his attitudes to the changing fortunes of the Third Reich, or for speculation on his part in its future. Now, with Hitler in Berchtesgaden, to be flown back by the Luftwaffe to the capital later in the week, Meyer's freedom had allowed him to become disgruntled and introspective.

'We'll be back here again in three weeks,' said Schneider, 'for the old comrades' gathering.'

'If he comes this year,' muttered Meyer, remembering the regular meeting in the 'sanctified' beerhall. He stopped tapping on the glass as his mind focused on the event. 'Rosenheimer Platz,' he said.

'Sorry, sir?' Schneider was unsure at the command.

'The Burgerbraukeller, sir?' asked the driver.

Meyer nodded. 'Might as well take a look at it.'

'Have we time, sir?'

'Yes.'

'Isn't that SA security there, sir? Not our job, surely?'

Meyer pursed his lips, knowing the directive. 'SA inside. SS outside.'

The Mercedes moved slowly across a wide boulevard, and the driver indicated left then, crossing in front of a train, nosed ahead of several lorries and entered a side street, which

166

was the short cut he knew would take his passengers directly to the Burgerbraukeller.

'Provincial curiosity,' smiled Meyer, and glanced at Schneider. 'We're policemen, remember.'

Two boiled eggs, buttered bread and a steaming cup of coffee were placed in front of Georg Elser. He looked up to see Annalise's wet eyes and touched her hand as she sat down quickly beside him with lips pouting, badly concealing harboured suspicions.

'Georg, tell me please – is there someone else?'

He brushed the tears from her lashes, thought of the landlady and said nothing.

'Because if there is – please, just tell me. You don't know what it's like in the hostel. The girls make jokes. They know I'm going to have . . . a baby. I'm frightened. Please, Georg.' She gripped his hand tightly. 'Oh, what is going to happen to us? We have so little. Me, a waitress and you . . . a . . . ' She hesitated to finish, longing for him to interrupt, to offer her the security she was craving.

'A gypsy,' he said.

Annalise sniffed and wiped tears with a handkerchief.

'A Ziga,' she said. She blew her nose, then smiled at him. 'You need a shave.'

'I *want*,' he emphasized the word softly, 'you.'

Annalise stared at him. 'Are we in love, Georg?' she whispered. 'Really?'

Elser ran his fingers down her cheek before kissing the damp flesh tenderly. 'In three weeks . . . we will go . . . '

The young waitress was suddenly confused. 'Three . . . ?' She began counting days, calculating dates. 'Georg, I can't. You know the most important day here is the eighth, and after the Armistice night on the eleventh, I get a bonus . . . It must be more. In a month, perhaps, if you want to, I'll leave and we can go together . . . '

Elser interrupted. 'Where?' he asked.

'Anywhere,' she whispered.

'Three weeks,' he said.

'Georg, you know I can't . . . '

'You must.'

'I can't,' she repeated.

Elser became angry, and Annalise was astonished that, for the first time, he shouted – 'You will!'

She stood up slowly, staring at him as if suddenly he had become a stranger. Without a word she turned and went across the large hall towards the kitchen. The Alsatian at his feet began to growl as Elser watched Annalise push through the kitchen door. How could he tell her? He must convince her to leave, that was obvious, but how, without revealing something . . . ?

A movement at the entrance of the Burgerbraukeller distracted him and he turned from the distant kitchen doors as the Alsatian, called Schatzi, growled louder in warning. Silhouetted against the sunlight reflecting off the wet pavement outside, two uniformed figures had entered through the open doors into the shadows of the archway. Unable to control a last look at the pillar, Elser bent to his breakfast and cut the top off the first of his boiled eggs. He recognized the Gestapo silver insignia and involuntarily shivered.

The huge hall became silent. The few customers, accepting the authority of the severely tailored black cloth, said nothing, although several with some courage turned to stare in the direction of the two men who walked the length of the building with a measured tread, their boots reverberating on the wooden floor. They were almost beside Georg Elser when Schneider slowed and Meyer stopped. The two officers looked around, absorbing everything. Sunlight poured through the skylights and upper windows, throwing shafts of light across the tables, illuminating patches of the great hall.

'To think,' said Schneider in a hushed voice, 'this is where it all began.'

'How old were you in 1923?'

'Sixteen,' replied the young officer. 'And you, sir?'

'I was . . . ' began Meyer, then smiled, '*just* on the side of law and order.' Schneider acknowledged the evasion and watched his superior's gaze wander about the beerhall. 'They were turbulent times, but my father indicated the right way . . . he convinced me . . . '

'How, sir?' asked Schneider.

Meyer laughed.

'He told me I'd be in prison in a month if I didn't join him and become a policeman. So . . . '

'Prison, sir?' interrupted the younger officer, laughing.

Meyer nodded. 'Well, Schneider, I said they were turbulent times. We all did things that perhaps, in retrospect, we regretted. We were idealistic and thought we were above the law. Age and experience taught us otherwise. The stability of a nation depends upon its law and justice. No one is above it – or beyond it. No one.' He looked at one of the customers eating an egg, his head bent over his plate. An Alsatian beside the man leapt up and, tongue hanging, tail wagging, thrust its forepaws on Schneider's chest as Meyer stepped back a pace to watch the two play a moment.

'What's he called?' Schneider asked the customer eating the egg. The man froze. 'His name?' questioned Schneider, barely keeping the dog's tongue from his face.

Georg Elser, who had been praying to become invisible, looked up. His eyes met those of Meyer and for a second nothing was said, then Annalise shouted from across the hall, 'Schatzi!' and bustling over to the Alsatian, grasped his collar and firmly dragged him down to the floor. 'Sit!' she commanded. The dog obeyed. Annalise curtsied to the uniforms and mumbled an apology for the watchman's dog.

Schneider and Meyer exchanged an expression of mutual appreciation at the girl's obvious beauty. The younger officer bowed good-humouredly in response to the waitress's nervousness. She glanced quickly down at Elser, seated directly beside her, who seemed to be trying to sink his face into the steaming coffee in the large cup.

169

Schneider smiled at the girl's lowered eyes. 'Don't be shy, pretty one. What's your name?'

'Annalise.'

'How long have you worked here?' asked Meyer quietly.

'Two years and one half.'

Meyer nodded. Schneider's interest became more than professional. 'And where, pretty Annalise, does the Führer speak from?'

Georg Elser spilt his coffee into the saucer, ignored it and continued drinking with his head down as Annalise involuntarily looked at him as if seeking help. Finding none, she answered quickly.

'I'm not sure, sir. We are not allowed into the hall when he speaks and must stay in the kitchen. We listen, of course . . . but I think perhaps . . .' Her eyes began searching the room quickly, then she remembered, to her confusion, the podium and the main pillar, 'Oh, yes, of course . . .' she began.

'There, Schneider,' murmured Meyer who was already staring. He pointed.

'Yes, sir. There,' agreed Annalise.

The SS officers remained silent, their black uniforms a harsh contrast to the predominantly soft brown and grey colours of the Burgerbraukeller, heightened by the shafting sunlight. The two men were projecting their thoughts into the near future when the hall would be full and the Führer behind a lectern giving a speech to the party dignitaries.

'Bring us two coffees, Annalise,' said Schneider. 'Black.' He sat down on the long bench only several metres from Georg Elser and began to fondle the Alsatian.

Meyer walked slowly across to the main pillar. He touched it lightly, looked up, saw the balustrade either side on the balcony and, stepping behind the pillar, moved along the wall until he was at the foot of the stairs. Elser snatched a look at Meyer and, seeing him begin to climb the stairs, slowly dug his spoon deeply into the boiled egg.

Reaching the balcony, Meyer stepped to the balustrade

and surveyed the entire interior of the beerhall before walking unhurriedly towards the first pillar, his black-gloved hand trailing on the rail. He noted the curve of the balcony, stepped to the outer panelled support of the pillar and tapped the wood with his knuckles. He nodded absently, confirming to himself that the pillar was of solid construction. He looked below as Schneider accepted coffee from the pretty waitress, then he continued around the first pillar towards the main support at the middle of the beerhall. Across the expanse of tables, benches and chairs, a similar support balanced what Meyer had already privately dubbed 'Hitler's pillar', and together they held up the weight of the central section of the roof. Meyer grasped the rail of the curving balustrade and tried to shake it – but the construction was of high quality and it remained firm, solidly implanted into the wood. Meyer stopped still, gazing up at the skylights and roof, then focused on the upper panelling and the craftsmanship of the detailed work of the pillar.

Below, on the bench, Schneider signalled to his superior that the coffee had arrived. Schatzi barked and Elser, with his egg spoon between his lips, could only bite on the metal, hard – and pray.

Suddenly Meyer crouched and peered through the balustrade to see the great hall from a different angle. His mind evaluated the potential security problems, recalling the traditional scene from his memory. He looked down at the polished toecaps of his black boots, where the floorboards of the balcony were fitted tightly together and there, although only a speck, he saw the chip of red brick standing out against the dull, dirty wood. He picked it up between a gloved finger and thumb, stood up and held the chip to the light. He gazed above; where the pillar met the ceiling, cracks were showing. With a grunt of satisfaction he dropped the red chip, deciding to mention the fact that the place needed examination by an engineer at some point soon, and perhaps refurbishment. Reaching out he rapped the panelling with his knuckles. Again, it was solid. The lower panelling appeared to be equally crafted, obviously a fascia over concrete and brick covering a reinforced steel frame.

Below, lounging against the table, Schneider, seeing his commanding officer on his feet again, checked his watch and realized they were running out of time. On the balcony, Meyer raised his boot to tap the lower panel behind which was the cavity Elser had hollowed out over the weeks. Elser saw the flash of light on the polished leather and held his breath. The Alsatian, sensing fear around him, barked loudly. Schneider smiled and opened his mouth to shout, 'Obersturmbannführer!'

Meyer, distracted, turned to look down and stamped his boot on the floorboards.

'We have only thirty minutes, sir.'

Meyer nodded his understanding, stepped around the pillar and, as an afterthought, kicked the lower panelling on the opposite side of the hold Elser had dug deep against the steel support. The polished leather connected hard with the wood panel. Solid. Satisfied, Meyer wandered on towards the distant door leading to the toilet. He passed the stacked carpets and upended tables, stepped into the small room, noted the stench of urine, pulled the flush and watched plaster flake from the wall beneath the cistern. He turned briskly and walked back to the head of the stairs, descended quickly, arrived at the table and sipped his cooling coffee.

'He may not come this year,' he mused.

'It would be the first time,' said Schneider, surprised.

'War,' clarified Meyer. 'He might send Hess.'

'Who can predict . . . ' began the younger officer.

'You're learning,' smiled Meyer. '*That* is the best security of all.' He upended his cup and finished the coffee, appreciating that it had real flavour and was not ersatz.

Schneider stood up as Annalise arrived and hesitated. 'Annalise,' he pronounced. 'Pretty as a spring day. See, sir, how she blooms . . . '

Annalise blushed.

' . . . and blushes.' Schneider reached out and touched

her cheek. At the table, Elser put down his spoon quietly and snatched a look across at the black uniform beside the young waitress.

The older officer stood up, pulling his gloves tighter. 'Don't be cruel, Schneider,' smiled Meyer.

Annalise whispered, 'Would you like more coffee, sir?'

'Thank you, no,' he replied, staring at the attractive features, wondering where she came from and what would be her future. She'd probably have children, he speculated, get fat, slave over a stove in some village outside the city whilst her husband became more of a beer-swilling bully every day. She might marry a farmer, perhaps a restaurateur, more like an artisan or labourer, even a gypsy . . . A future that would become her history, which he'd never know. But now, here before him, there was something in her young eyes that shone – hope and expectation. Youth demanding something better.

'You are a pretty thing,' said Meyer softly. 'My wife looked like you – once. Have you a boyfriend?'

Annalise nodded and glanced at Elser, who put both hands around his cup almost completely concealing his face, but Meyer had eyes only for the girl.

'He is a lucky man. What does he do?'

'He makes . . . ' began the waitress, but was interrupted by Schneider, who laughed and winked.

'Babies,' he said.

'Schneider,' warned Meyer with humour.

Annalises's blushes deepened again as the young officer pressed the price of the coffees and a healthy tip into her hand.

'Goodbye, and thank you, Annalise,' he said. The Alsatian beside Elser growled as Meyer led the way between the long tables down the very centre of the great hall. The sun continued to stream from the skylights and upper windows, reminding the two men of the freshening day outside which remained crisp and cloudless.

'Well, it's not our problem,' said Meyer, speaking on the

move to Schneider, above the noise resounding from their polished boots.

'But we will come, sir?'

'Yes, Wolf – we have to be here, if only to watch the inefficiency of our Brownshirt brothers.'

'How many minutes to the station, sir – from here?'

'Eleven, twelve,' answered Meyer. 'At night!'

'We must remember that, sir.'

'Yes,' murmured Meyer. 'We will.'

The two men stepped through the arched entrance and out of the Burgerbraukeller on to the pavement. Their chauffeur opened the rear door of the dark Mercedes, whose engine murmured patiently as the exhaust fumes created patterns in the clear air.

It was several seconds after the Gestapo uniforms had gone before Georg Elser dared to look up, and he only relaxed when he heard the big limousine outside drive away.

Annalise touched his shoulder and, with persistence, returned to her interrupted conversation about her fears of another woman.

'You would tell me, Georg, wouldn't you?' she asked him quietly.

The Alsatian whined. Elser shook his head absently and could think only of the pillar as he spoke the lie quietly. 'Yes,' he said.

15

Georg Elser entered the church of St Stephen the Martyr hesitantly, but he relaxed once he had stepped through the long velvet curtains giving a clear view of the nave and distant altar, beneath a high roof supported by tall, fluted pillars and decorated capitals. He eased himself into a pew off the centre aisle and placed his case carefully on the floor, sat down and bowed his head.

At mid-morning it was too early for the church to be crowded, and only church wardens wandered distantly, preparing the altar and pulpit for the midday service. Elser had passed the church many times on his way to Dreschler's machine shop, but only today had sanctuary drawn him inside.

Somewhere an organ started up and Elser peered over clenched fists as he leant forward against the next pew, but the ethereal sound seemed to have no source. He remained in the same position fully five minutes, his mind wrestling still with conscience and conviction, morality, sin, guilt, truth – sacrifice. The last word lingered and he turned his head, pressing his unshaven cheek against his white knuckles. To one side of the nearest pillar was a typically Bavarian carving of Christ, illustrating the agony of being on the cross. No sublime revelation to assuage the physical trial here, but a dark varnished wood representation of pain and suffering. Elser stared long and hard at the depicted saviour, and only after he had become familiar with the artistry did he notice the shelf below, containing collection boxes. They were not all the same size or colour or material, but each one did have very clearly embossed on its side a Nazi Party swastika. Elser's eyes hardened. And exactly at the moment when his

175

resolve had begun to ebb, so something within declared itself committed.

Deliberately Elser slid from the pew, went down on his knees and, ignoring the initial sharp pain, waited until he felt only a dull throbbing ache, then bent his head and whispered the Lord's Prayer as best he knew. He crossed himself, levered his tired body to its feet and, taking his case, made his way back to the exit.

A large table lay between the two doors, where many leaflets were piled and more collection boxes were liberally distributed. Here swastikas were everywhere. One of the wardens, in a hushed voice, was discussing his duties with the Reverend Father, but the conversation stopped as Elser, instead of passing by, remained staring at the table, absorbing its contents with growing disgust.

'It shouldn't be allowed,' he murmured.

'What is that, my son?' asked the Reverend Father quietly.

'These are political,' answered Elser, referring to the leaflets. 'This is a church.'

'We have received instructions and obey them,' interposed the warden authoritatively.

Elser looked at the Reverend Father, seeing the man's well-tailored dark flowing robe, topped by a white collar. He had the face of a well-groomed business man and smiled with practised sympathy.

'We are all instruments of God, my son. I am merely his servant on earth. If it is his will, then it is allowed. If it is not, it would not be allowed to happen.'

Elser glanced over his shoulder and looked the length of the church to the altar and a golden crucifix catching the light from the stained-glass windows. He gestured before staring at the patronizing face of God's servant on earth.

'Do you think he believes you?' asked Elser. The man's eyes narrowed and he adjusted his robes.

'That is enough,' warned the warden, stepping forward.

Elser retreated to the table, dislodging a pile of Nazi Party tracts. 'They are here on Hitler's instructions – not God's.'

176

'My son, if you undermine the authority of God, then you blaspheme – is that your wish – in his own house?'

Elser's face set in an expression of Swabian stubbornness. 'Something should be done,' he muttered.

The warden spread his arms aggressively and thrust his hands on his hips. 'What?' he growled.

Elser saw quite clearly, through an opening in the man's long outer robe, that on his lapel was a Nazi Party badge. He bit his lip and said nothing.

The Reverend Father smiled again at what he regarded the confusion in the tired face before him. 'Bless you, my son. May God go with you.'

Elser backed away, then stepped out through the velvet curtains and the church door into the street.

'Poor man,' said the servant of God, shaking his head as he gathered his robes before striding purposefully towards the altar. 'Does he not realize that we are here to administer religious understanding, not create political opposition?'

The warden nodded agreement as, side by side, the two men moved briskly down the aisle. The Reverend Father cleared his throat. 'Imagine, if we were not to cooperate with the authorities controlling our country it would be but a short step before we were advocating insurrection!'

'Quite so,' said the warden. 'It is an attitude to beware of . . . I shall bring it up at the next party meeting.'

Both men stopped at the steps leading up to the ornate altar. They crossed themselves quickly and were about to move off in different directions, when the Reverend Father stayed the warden with a gesture and indicated the large crucifix caught in the sunlight. 'It's looking a little dull. Polish it up, would you, or people will talk. You know what they are.'

A military band was playing loudly in the square fronting the street which led down to Dreschler's machine shop. Elser skirted the gathered crowds and made his way to the familiar large open doors. Noise and showers of sparks from numerous men working at their benches obliterated the distant brass band and distracted Elser until he saw the owner supervising a welding job. Only then did he allow his introspection to dissipate, and concentrated on the exact requirements he had decided were necessary.

He knew that he would have to exchange favours. Sheet steel and cork were classified as war supplies, and he must barter work for materials as he had insufficient money to pay outright. It would have to be discussed discreetly. To be caught utilizing 'war materials' privately was an offence and could cause immediate trouble or, worse, suspicion of his intentions. He shook hands with Dreschler and quietly negotiated, explaining that he was doing some work for a special client.

The big man, thickset, with a shock of greying hair and dark, hooded eyes, liked the small artisan from Swabia, and after some hard bargaining agreed time for material. The steel was cut and rolled, secured with wire, then, together with strips of cork, given to Elser wrapped in brown paper. Dreschler winked, enfolded the smaller man with a strong arm around his shoulders and led him out through the workshop into the busy street.

Elser had hesitated to ask, but he knew it must be now. He put down his weighty load and case, reached into his pocket and drew out a stained envelope containing his Swiss work-pass, which had allowed him across the border without a passport. In the Constance area, skilled workmen, and sometimes even their wives, had a daily pass or a form of resident's visa issued at the discretion of the authorities. Elser had the best possible. It was open and could be reissued if lost.

Dreschler read it with raised eyebrows, understanding, perhaps for the first time, that Elser's abilities were more than locally appreciated. When the little man from Swabia made his request, Dreschler stared hard into his face, knowing the trouble he must take and the dangers, realizing at the same time the amount of work he could get from this Elser, with

178

hard bargaining. They went back inside his machine shop, took a pad and pencil and wrote down the name – Annalise Palin. He knew enough people, as Georg Elser had been told, and it would take money, which Georg Elser was prepared to repay with work-time, so Dreschler agreed. The pass could be issued to this woman, to join her 'husband to be' in Switzerland. The bargain was struck. Elser shook hands on the deal and, carrying his awkward parcel, made more so by the weighty case dragging at his wrist, he shuffled off, tiredness in every step.

Shadows leapt around the workroom under the cobbled courtyard of Turkenstrasse 94 as draughts from the badly fitting padlocked door flaps whisked about the cellar, disturbing the otherwise steady flame of the two lamps Elser pulled nearer to examine the framework he had constructed. He reached out and readjusted the wicks, then bent again to quickly tighten the nuts and bolts which held the metal arms together. He carefully slotted in one of two clocks, which fitted perfectly. He murmured with pleasure at the expertise of his measurements, then connected a wire to one of the strikers, extending it from the axis of the hour and minute hand. He set the clock, spun the minute hand until the wire pulled taut, then watched the arm and pin slam down on the wooden wedge he had placed beneath.

He nodded absently and lit the second half of a cigarette, inhaled deeply and checked his pocket watch. It was eight forty and he was later than usual. Normally he would already be on his way to the Burgerbraukeller. He swore under his breath then listened for a moment to the night air blustering outside. Rain on the wind. Winter fast approaching – and war.

He bent under the workbench, lifted the floor panel he had cut and carefully withdrew ten sticks of dynamite, which he had wrapped in an old cardigan stuffed into his case. Dismantling the frame, he put the metal bars and their nuts

179

and bolts beside the explosive, snapped shut the catches of his case and tied it with cord, then stubbed out his cigarette, blew out the lamps and stood up in the darkness.

It was at moments like this that he felt most isolated. The world of the Third Reich, outside his small workroom, seemed impregnable, formidable, invulnerable. For a second time he saw himself as presumptuous even to consider that he might have the slightest chance of success. Hitler was already a demi-god in the minds of so many of his followers, a man of destiny who already held the fate of a nation in his grasp.

Elser climbed the short flight of wooden steps and reached up for the padlock on the door flaps, where rain dripped through, driven by the gusting wind. He paused and listened to the noises of the night outside, and replaced fear with the encouraging thought that he was already well on his way to completion of the task he had set himself. It had taken five nights over the past ten days to smuggle into the beerhall, and then install first the sheet steel which he had backed the panel door with, then the cork which now lined the entire cavity. Consequently, a tap on the closed wood panel produced only a solid sound, alleviating Elser's fears of discovery in the same way he had narrowly avoided with the excessively zealous Gestapo officer from Berlin.

Elser turned the key in the padlock, opened the two door flaps, stepped up on to the cobbles and resecured the doors, before walking through the archway on to the street. He pulled his coat tightly about him as meagre protection against the chill wind and rain, and seized the handle of his case firmly, suddenly aware of its dangerous contents, no longer safe in his workroom, but now at risk – as he was – on his familiar route to the crowded beerhall.

With a roar of laughter, the four SA men thrust their way through a group of people at the entrance of the Burger-braukeller, jostling Georg Elser, then pushing him aside so he slammed against the stone-and-plaster wall. He used his body to cushion the case, grasping it with both arms.

Several people in the queue patiently filing into the huge and packed hall, who had been waiting for vacant places along with Elser, seemed to be pointing at him. He broke out in a cold sweat, then realized they were discussing something behind him, on the wall. He turned to see, poorly illuminated in the dim lights of the entrance hall, a large poster of Adolf Hitler, dressed without a helmet, but in full medieval knight's armour, seated on a horse, holding an upright lance. His expression was serious, his manner assured. The image conveyed strength and confidence: the visionary leader of great armies, proud and indestructible.

Elser stepped back quickly against the poster on the wall as more loud-mouthed SA men, ignoring the queue, bullied their way, despite weak protests, directly into the main hall, where songs were already being chorused with more cacophony than melody. He surveyed the full tables and benches and noted more brown shirts of the SA than he had ever seen before. His mouth was dry – perhaps, he began to think, it would be better tonight not to attempt anything at all. He could come back tomorrow . . .

Annalise saw him across the room, immediately came over and took him from the head of the queue, leading the way between the long trestle tables directly to a seat behind one of the pillars away from the main floor area. Gratefully, Elser slumped against the warm wood panelling and unbuttoned his wet coat. It was half an hour before Annalise could return to him with affectionate apologies, beer, bratwurst and sauerkraut. He hardly saw her the rest of the evening as she, with the other girls, rushed about serving throughout the hall, which was packed tight to overflowing with customers. As they began to thin out, Elser timed his goodbye to Annalise, promised a meeting with her the following day when she was free in the evening, and slipped into the shadows of the stairway leading above to the balcony and seldom-used upper toilet.

181

It was almost one o'clock before he was able to snap on his torch, wrap the light in the blue cotton scarf and explore his surroundings, where the rolled carpets had again been shifted around. The Burgerbraukeller was closed, dark and silent; only the wind and rain disturbed his thoughts as he crawled over to the main pillar and prepared to install the frame and explosive. He had wished for noise on previous nights during the installation of the steel and cork. It had been awkward and arduous. His hammer and chisel had seemed to resound louder than ever before, but the job had been done and the nights passed without incident. Even the watchman had only entered once for his bottle of beer.

Elser inserted the thin blade under the beading of the panel carefully, and the screw catch slid easily from the hollowed tube. He examined the cavity in the pillar. Another hinge had been necessary to support the weight of the thin steel sheet, which had been time consuming. So had inserting numerous shallow screws through the prepared holes and turning them to within a millimetre of the surface of the panel. The cork would muffle any sound of the ticking clocks and was thus equally necessary, and Elser justly congratulated his workmanship. His inherent perfectionism was leaving nothing to chance. He assembled the framework of his mechanism as quickly as the dulled light of his torch would allow. He bolted the metal arms together, secured them firmly with the nuts, which he tightened with a small spanner. Satisfied, he gently placed it against the carved hollow and slid it into the cork cushion. It fitted perfectly. Elser took the torch and, leaning close, made sure that he would have sufficient space to install the other components: clocks, detonators and explosive.

The last first. He reached down to his case and one by one inserted the dynamite sticks, each resting against the other, the bottom three on a rack of four metal bars. He clamped them in place with more metal bars, which he bolted against the main struts. He sat back on his heels and slowly pressed the panel shut. The wood-and-steel plate swung against the

182

beading of the pillar and, as Elser applied more pressure, with the sound of a click the panel was flush with the pillar. He tapped first the upper panel, then the centre of the door in the lower section that he had created. The steel sheet contained the vibration and returned no echo, no hollowness, no intimation of a cavity. The sounds were the same – solid. The pillar sounded and looked, unless closely examined, completely untouched. He breathed deeply – he'd done it.

The half-smile of achievement faded from his face as he watched the panel door, as if gently pressed from within by a hidden hand, slowly open of its own volition. For a moment he was stunned. The screw, the catch, the hollow metal tube, the metal frame, even the dynamite! What? Then he heard loud voices outside, keys jingling in the locks of the rear door and the watchman's barking dog. He froze. This was not the usual interruption of the old man in search of a beer. Younger, authoritative voices accompanied the watchman and his Alsatian as they entered and switched on the lower side lights. Elser was already scrabbling for his case. He pressed the panel door closed again, prayed as he applied his shoulder to it, then crawled to the carpets and concealment.

'What nonsense,' he heard from the watchman.

'It's like a grave!'

The Alsatian barked in agreement. Then one of the younger voices spoke up. 'We have had reports.' Elser's heart lurched. His worse fears were then confirmed. 'We have to follow up reports, old man. Orders.'

'Well, once in a while I might come in myself,' went on the watchman. 'Only for a beer. The nights are cold and my blood is thin.'

'We've been told people have heard noises . . . '

'Well,' began the watchman, 'I may be clumsy sometimes . . . and then there were the girls . . . '

'Girls?' said one of the other voices.

'Well . . . yes,' hesitated the old man.

'Did you make a report?'

'Well, no . . . ' admitted the watchman. 'I mean yes – to the proprietor.'

'Herr Payerl?'

'Yes.'

'Did he come to the station?' asked one voice quietly.

'No,' answered another. Silence held for a moment. Elser, behind the carpets on the balcony, thought he saw flashes of light from torches, then he heard, 'What's up there?'

The Alsatian began barking happily, before the watchman shut him up and replied, 'Storage mostly, and a toilet. Nothing.'

Georg Elser in his private darkness closed his eyes and lowered his head. Boots sounded, echoing to the roof as they crossed the floor, making for the stairs to the balcony.

'You don't have to bother,' muttered the watchman. 'It's my job,' he finished. Someone else coughed below as the heavy boots climbed the stairs.

'Not when we've had reports,' echoed a voice shouting a reply across the empty hall.

'Do you have permission – a warrant to search the place?' asked the watchman, quietly belligerent.

'We are police, you are an old man,' said a voice menacingly. 'Do we need more than your cooperation?'

'No,' murmured the watchman. The Alsatian barked. 'Schatzi!' exclaimed the old man, and hit the dog hard. The boots reached the balcony and suddenly there was silence. Elser could hear only his breathing – even the wind and rain outside seemed to have stopped. He moved frantically and squinted into the sliver of light penetrating the stacked carpets, but could see nothing more than the pillar in front of him. Then the regular tread of leather soles started again and the policeman passed by, pausing momentarily to touch the fabric of one of the carpets. Elser's gaze remained fixed, unable to see more than the panelled pillar. He concentrated on it, listening intently as the sound of boots faded then stopped at the small toilet. Below, the dog started barking but was again silenced by the watchman.

'Find anything?' shouted a voice. Elser gritted his teeth.

'I'm looking,' came the reply. 'But it stinks in here.'

There was laughter as Elser heard the chain pulled. He let out the breath he had been holding in an attempt to lessen his tension, then saw the impossible directly before him. Slowly the panel door swung open several inches, lost its momentum and was still. Elser almost screamed aloud, but already the policeman's steady tread was approaching as he retraced his way back to the stairs. The Alsatian started barking again, now insistent, as if it sensed something. A shadow passed in front of Elser, obliterating the pillar for a moment, then was gone, leaving him with the view of impending disaster as the boots continued down the balcony. If the policeman looked back . . . Elser began to pray as he had never done.

'Schatzi!' bellowed the watchman. The dog had broken away and was bounding towards the stairs. Halfway up, Schatzi smelt his familiar friend Elser, and barked happily. At the top of the stairway the policeman reached out to grasp the Alsatian, missed him with one hand, spun around and grabbed his collar with the other. Schatzi rose up, straining against the firm grip of the big man in uniform. Elser's fingernails dug into his palms, hearing the dog pulling away from the man. Then, feeling the superior strength, the Alsatian succumbed, dropped to all fours and growled disagreeably.

'Schatzi!' commanded the watchman. 'Come!'

Elser could not take his eyes from the open panel resting comfortably on its hinges, revealing to any inquisitive glance a crafted cavity, the mechanism and sufficient explosive to decimate the interior of the Bierkeller. The policeman's boots and the nimble feet of the Alsatian blended in Elser's ears as man dragged dog to his master below.

'Well?' Elser heard above Schatzi's whining.

'Nothing,' said the policeman, and relinquished the dog.

'I told you,' mumbled the watchman. 'It's like a grave here.'

Elser continued to stare at the panel in disbelief, ignoring the cold sweat beading on his brow. One section of lights was switched off, dimming his view of the pillar. The voices receded to the bar area.

'Would you like some beer?' asked the old man.

'Not allowed,' replied one of the policemen, 'on duty.'

The sound of a bottle-cap being removed, a pause as the contents were drunk in several gulps, then the clink of empty glass on the metal bar top were a prelude to the exit of the three men. With lights off, a moment later, the rear door slammed. Keys jangled in the locks and conversation faded into the night.

Georg Elser crawled out from behind the carpets, crossed to the pillar and fell against the open panel, slamming it shut. He lay in the same position for minutes on end, cheek pressed against the wood backed by steel plate, centimetres from ten sticks of dynamite. Only when the sweat had dried on his forehead did he sigh and murmur, 'God almighty!'

Georg Elser trudged through the grey streets shrouded in fine drizzle and gratefully reached Turkenstrasse. He stepped through the archway into the cobbled courtyard and crossed directly to the front door of 94. He paused, and perhaps instinct gave him an afterthought. He went back to the entrance of the cellar, released the padlock, deposited his case in his workroom, resecured the doors and, when he unlocked the door into the warm hallway, he was empty-handed. Shuffling down to the lounge area, Elser stopped for a moment to light one of his half-cigarettes, toying with the idea of a few minutes beside the roaring fire he could hear crackling in the grate. Rubbing his tired eyes, Elser wandered around the ornamental pilaster and newly placed urn with its spray of aspidistra leaves, then seeing the area empty but for the admonishing face of Hitler on the wall, made his way directly to the comfortable armchair, sank into it and closed his eyes. He did not fall asleep or even doze, but perhaps it was through a trance-like waking dream that he heard the words spoken and knew they were directed at him. The voice was authoritative and the question quietly incisive.

'Did you really think you could get away with it?'

It was a moment before Elser realized he was awake. He opened his eyes and turned to see the police officer who had previously been at the house looking for aliens, together with his two uniformed men, standing behind the landlady.

'Georg,' she whispered, 'what have you been doing?' He just glanced from one face to another, then feeling the butt-end between his fingers, flicked the extinguished cigarette into the flames roaring in the grate.

'Get up!' growled the officer. Elser stood shakily as the policeman formally questioned, 'Elser? Georg?'

He nodded slowly in answer.

'You know a woman named Annalise Palin?' Elser nodded.

'Where have you just come from?'

Elser said nothing, praying he could find a lie.

'Answer me!'

'The Burgerbraukeller,' mumbled Georg.

'For breakfast?' asked the officer.

'Yes.'

'We were there.' Elser's expression hardened as the officer approached him slowly. 'And you know a man named Dreschler?'

Elser swallowed before answering. 'Yes.'

'Good,' smiled the policeman grimly and snapped his fingers as a command to his two men. 'You are under arrest!'

'Why?' faltered Elser, as the burly men seized his arms.

'You know quite well!' replied the officer.

Elser was hurried out of the house, leaving the landlady biting her lips and in tears. In the street, a police car had drawn up. Elser was bundled inside and, with a siren carving its way through traffic, the fast vehicle took the prisoner into custody.

16

The elegantly dressed woman was ushered through the large double doors, past the guards and escorted along the corridor by a young man in a smartly cut uniform. Another door, an outer officer, then she was presented with a clicking of heels and left alone with the officer behind his desk, who remained standing out of politeness. His respect was now as forced as it had once been so overwhelmingly natural that it had become love.

'Good morning,' said the officer. 'Please sit down.'

'Where is he?'

'Marianne,' said Otto Meyer, 'please, sit.' She hesitated, then sat down abruptly and settled herself in the leather chair, already uncomfortable in the presence of the man to whom she had once been married.

Meyer lay back in his own seat, and deliberately took out and lit a cigar. 'Well?' he said.

'You heard the question. I want to see him.'

'Who?' murmured Meyer.

Tears of frustration sprang into Marianne's eyes. 'Please, Otto – Michael . . . '

Meyer's heart hardened towards his wife, and now hearing the Jew's name spoken in the same breath as his own, he lost all sympathy. 'Where are the children? Here?'

'No,' faltered their mother. 'In Munich.'

'Good. I leave tomorrow. I will see them.' He paused. 'Where are you staying?'

'You know where – where else? My father sends his regards.'

Meyer nodded. Marianne sobbed suddenly and bent her head. 'Help me, Otto.'

'When will the child be born?' asked Meyer quietly.

Marianne raised her face to stare at the Gestapo officer through her tears. 'It is dead.'

'*It*,' emphasized Meyer softly, 'should never have been alive.'

'You bastard!' exploded Marianne.

Meyer nodded. 'Then you understand.'

Marianne sucked air between her teeth. 'I want Michael. I want to help him . . . leave the country. I will pay anything.' She looked long at the man. 'What do you want from me, Otto? What must I do?'

'Nothing,' he replied quietly. They regarded each other for some time, Marianne searching the man's face, Meyer revealing nothing.

'There used to be something,' she murmured.

'It's gone,' he said.

'Are you sure?' she whispered.

'*I* am.'

'Otto, to me you were always . . . '

'Beg if you must,' he snapped, 'but don't lie.'

Her lips curled and she spat the words, 'I was taken by the "authorities", put into a hospital and deprived of my . . . offspring, and you ask me to *"beg"* for the father!'

Meyer's face set in an expression of disgust. '*Your* father was informed of your condition and took . . . the necessary steps.'

'And you did nothing?'

'Why?' Meyer smiled.

Marianne took out a handkerchief, blew her nose, wiped her eyes and composed herself. 'Is he . . . in a camp?' she asked eventually.

'I have no way of knowing,' answered Meyer.

'I love him, Otto. I want to know.'

'Ask your father.'

'He will tell me nothing.'

'Then what can I say?'

'You hated each other. What has happened?'

189

'Perhaps we found a common enemy we could exploit.'

'Hitler? He will kill us all.'

'You have courage. I will say that for you.' Meyer's gaze wandered around the large panelled room he had inherited as his office. 'The Führer is leading us all towards a greater Germany. A future undreamt of by the allies to whom we surrendered so ignominiously twenty years ago.'

'Twenty-one,' corrected Marianne.

Meyer smiled again. 'Yes,' he said, 'each year takes us deeper into an epoch the world will never forget.'

'What floats can sink,' said Marianne. 'Can't you see, Otto? You are committed to a circus encamped outside a town and it has only been assembled for a duration . . . '

'Duration?' questioned Meyer.

'Yes,' she confirmed. 'The town will wake in the morning. Germany will survive. But Nazism, Hitler, his henchmen, all the pretty flags, uniforms, imposed authority and fear will not be there after the show is over – and they will not have moved on, they will have been destroyed because we are adamant, imperious, unyielding, words my father used against the Kaiser years ago. We are a stubborn people. Courageous, foolhardy, idealistic yet we learn nothing. War, persecution and deprivation we impose on others and finally always on ourselves.'

'You always had a tongue.'

'And a mind! Have you lost yours?' Marianne's eyes glared accusingly. 'Look at you, a part of it all. What is the price of your uniform? Your conscience?'

Meyer's eyes had narrowed and his face became ominous as he reached out to press the button for Schneider. 'You have said enough.'

'I have only just started,' said Marianne defiantly.

Meyer stood up slowly, his eyes fixed on the woman. 'Enough!' he bellowed. A quiet fell between them as only the clock on the wall ticked away softly. Schneider entered, absorbed the scene before him immediately and from respect, remained silent.

Then Marianne found the clue in Meyer's eyes. 'He's dead, isn't he?' she whispered incredulously.

'Take her out.'

Schneider nodded at the command.

Marianne rose to her feet, her face white and filled with a growing hatred. 'Then so are you,' she hissed.

'Have a care,' growled Meyer.

Tears flowed from Marianne as she took in the large elegant office at a glance. Her voice remained clear and firm. 'God help you.'

A brisk knock heralded the adjutant, who paused, hesitant at the obvious emotion he saw in Meyer's ex-wife. 'Herr Obersturmbannführer . . . ' he began.

'She's going,' murmured Meyer, and came around the desk from politeness to offer his hand. Marianne waited until he was abreast of her then spat in his face and hit him across the cheek as hard as she could. Instantly Meyer's reflexes responded and the impact of his open-handed blow drove the woman to the floor.

No one moved, then Schneider bent to help her up. She brushed him away. 'Leave me,' she said hoarsely and stood up shaking. There was blood beneath her nose and bruising had already started on her jaw and thickening lips. The hate had gone from her cold eyes, now filled with sympathy. When she spoke it was with a slur as blood appeared in her mouth. 'Thank you,' she said harshly.

Meyer himself could now taste blood and reacted with disgust in his voice. 'Get this Jew's whore out of here!'

Schneider escorted the woman out. The adjutant stood uncomfortably. He coughed, deciding to come back later. Meyer continued to stare at the closed door.

The adjutant went out, already composing a report. It would have to be mentioned, of course, he reflected. Women were such a – liability.

Alone in his office, Meyer turned to face the window and, leaning forward on his desk, bowed his head. He knew he must now cauterize what emotion remained. There must be only the children, when he could see them, and the responsible job he had accepted. Nothing else.

Thundering over the rails, the Berlin express made its way south, through the fading day, towards Munich. For Schneider and Meyer, seated in the Führer's private carriage, talk was unnecessary; merely gazing out at the countryside flashing past filled their minds.

'How long?' murmured Meyer absently.

'One hour,' replied Schneider.

Meyer stood up in the swaying carriage and wandered the length of the room created within the welded steel frame. The sleeping area with a bath was at the end. Tables, chairs, even a sofa, were dispersed as if in the lounge of a house. Shortly, as the official directive indicated, an armoured anti-aircraft car and communications Pullman with teletype machine were to be added, with a dining car, guest accommodation, personnel carriers – a full command centre on wheels. Now the single special carriage was a last vestige of pre-war life.

With Germany committed to hostilities, security measures had been increased. Enemies were seen even under the bed. Meyer stepped through into the compartment where Hitler slept en route, and saw the pyjamas laid out by the ever alert valet, noticed the mild heating regulated perfectly, glanced at several pictures on the wall of the mountains over Obersalzberg, Alsatians and the woman Eva Braun. There was a bathroom containing washbasin, mirror, and shelf with toothbrush and paste in a tin. Hitler seemed to enjoy travel; he had certainly used every opportunity to exploit modern machinery, sometimes flying to as many as five cities in one night to make his campaign speeches. That was legend. Now, when he did not fly, the Führer's special carriage provided swift passage between the two Germanys of north and south.

Meyer stepped out and closed the door of the sleeping area – a bed big enough only for one, he remembered. He stopped beside Hitler's desk as Schneider joined him, peering out of the window at the fading dusk. The leather top was worn, the wood old, the numerous pens in a ceramic pot from Dresden. Schneider, turning from the condensation on the glass, stretched, yawned and almost placed himself in Hitler's chair.

'No, Wolf,' said Meyer.

For a moment Schneider didn't understand, then he nodded in agreement. 'Sorry, sir.'

'There are other seats.'

'Of course, sir.'

'A small thing, perhaps, but authority and respect are one and the same and depend on more than public show.'

Schneider snapped his heels together and nodded, acknowledging Meyer's precept. The older officer smiled, gesturing the length of the fast moving carriage.

'No matter, Wolf, what seat we're in, it's one train and we are all going in the same direction.'

It was dark when they arrived. A car was waiting and, on Meyer's instructions, the chauffeur drove them directly to his old house, where his two children were waiting to be taken for a late dinner with their father. It was a mere afterthought on the way to the restaurant that Meyer ordered the driver to stop at the several Gestapo offices which the SS shared with the police. Headquarters would wait until the following day, but with Hitler's public appearance in Munich fast approaching, Meyer had decided to appraise local reports of violence, group disturbances, and demonstrations, and check the problem districts. He said nothing to Schneider, whom the children liked and had insisted join them for dinner. He merely smiled and chatted with his beautiful daughter and exuberant son and tried to dispel the image of their mother. The Mercedes stopped outside the police station.

'Is Mr Rosenburg in there?' asked Gabbie.

Meyer, taken aback, glanced at Schneider, who twisted

193

around in the front seat, and raised his brows. Was it a child's intuition or had Marianne been telling them . . . ?

'I didn't like him,' murmured Peter.

'Has Mama gone away too?' asked Gabbie, suddenly on the verge of tears.

Meyer took a deep breath, but Schneider answered quickly for him. 'Only to Berlin – for a few days. We saw her.' He avoided Meyer's eyes and indicated the building to Peter. 'Do you want to come in for a moment with us?'

Peter's face lit up. 'Please!' He got out of the car together with Schneider and began babbling as they crossed the pavement to the entrance.

Meyer watched them a moment, then touched Gabbie's cheek. 'One minute,' he said.

'Are you coming home with us now?'

Meyer smiled sadly. 'I'll take you home after dinner.'

'You won't stay?'

Meyer looked at the imploring eyes and shook his head. 'Not now,' he said, kissed her forehead, climbed out of the car and checked his watch. 'This won't take long, Josef.' The chauffeur nodded.

17

'You are a lucky man,' the police officer told Georg Elser, who remained slumped on his cell bed. The sudden light from the open door was blinding and he blinked, disbelieving the invitation to leave his incarceration. The policeman gestured again, and slowly Elser got to his feet and shuffled out into the brightly lit corridor. The two men walked the length of its green painted walls, went up some steps and entered the first of several interrogation rooms Elser remembered from three days before.

The landlady was standing there, anxious and agitated until she saw Elser. With first a smile of relief, then an admonishing voice, she crossed to him quickly. 'I told them the truth, Georg,' she blustered. 'You didn't know – did you?'

Elser waited beside the desk while his records were presented and the brown envelope containing his personal possessions was upturned and emptied of a ring, the pocket watch, papers, a wallet, even the small black leather sheath and padding taken from the stub of his little finger.

'Three days is long enough, I said,' went on the woman brusquely. 'I paid the Herr Officer . . . ' She paused, and realized her mistake. The policeman's face had hardened. Exchanged favours, or at least the promises to be kept, were supposed to be a shared and certainly unspoken secret. 'I mean, Herr Dreschler should never have asked you the market price for . . . ' Again the woman had been indiscreet. ' . . . well, restricted war supplies cannot just be paid for and carted away. He knows that, and you are a man who needs materials to work with, but obviously it is wrong of him to give you – let you buy – even a discount is not . . . '

'Stolen articles,' broke in the officer, 'which you acquired. This lady has intervened for you, as indeed has Dreschler, who has his own problems . . . '

'Indeed he has,' said the woman. 'He certainly has, now!' She folded her arms across her bosom as Elser identified his belongings. He was distracted for a moment by the arrival of two uniformed officers and a young boy at the door, but continued to pocket his possessions as the policeman beside him snapped to attention, seeing Schneider, Meyer and his son Peter step into the large room. The two Gestapo uniforms with the Hitler Youth demanded respect from the plain police officer. He flushed, recognizing the two arrivals and remembering the money he had accepted from the landlady; now even more urgently he wanted Elser to go.

Meyer nodded. 'Stand down. This is not official. I merely want a look at recent files.' He led the way to the records cabinets just behind the half-glass partition. Schneider opened the middle drawer and searched for listings of past weeks. Elser's file remained on the desk top and would have gone unnoticed, had not Meyer's eyes wandered to the manila folder.

'Well, if the formalities are completed . . . ' said the landlady, hesitating. The policeman nodded and indicated the door. The woman smiled as Elser signed the release form and, gathering the last of his possessions, shuffled towards freedom. Meyer crossed to the desk as Elser, at the doorway, juggling keys and money awkwardly before pocketing them, dropped his key-ring together with some loose change on to the floor.

'Come on!' shouted the landlady, already outside in the darkness. Elser bent painfully to pick up the key-ring and coins. His knees had begun to hurt and he felt moisture as if the skin had broken. At the desk, some metres away, beneath the electric light bulb in its bakelite shade, Meyer took the manila file and cursorily examined the contents, listening absently to Schneider explaining the files to Peter as he extracted what was required – the reports on recent offenders. Reading on, Meyer's eyes hardened as he saw the single word heading a paragraph describing a past history.

'Dachau?' he murmured, and looked up. Elser was just pocketing the last of his coins.

'You!' barked Meyer. Elser straightened and turned around slowly.

'Well, come on!' shouted the landlady impatiently outside. 'You're free now!'

Grasping the folder, Meyer slowly approached Elser. He stood less than a metre away and studied the man's features. 'Have we met before?' he asked quietly.

Elser shook his head, seeing Meyer's quizzical frown.

'I know your face.'

Elser said nothing, but swallowed mightily. Meyer only interpreted this as the natural nerves of a civilian confronted with authority.

'From where . . . ?' murmured the Gestapo officer.

Elser remained silent, but the landlady shouted, 'Herr Elser!' He glanced outside then saw that the other officer was approaching ominously.

'Elser,' mouthed Meyer softly, 'what do you do?'

Elser coughed. Meyer waited patiently. 'Make things. Mend things,' muttered Elser.

The landlady climbed the short stone stairs outside and seemed to burst in the entrance, angry at the delay of her 'charge', but her mouth fell open as she saw Elser being questioned.

'What things?' asked Meyer. Elser only shrugged and sought desperately for inspiration, when the officer whispered, 'Recently . . . ', his eyes fixed on the man, piecing together from his memory the lost information that would give him . . . 'The Burgerbraukeller!' he said suddenly. Elser gritted his teeth, now in the hands of fate.

'He is such a clever man, Herr Officer,' interposed the landlady. Meyer looked at the deteriorating flesh, expanding figure and unfashionable but well cared for clothes, and reacted only to the patronizing tone and applied smile.

'Is he?' answered Meyer with amusement. 'And who are you?'

'His . . . landlady,' stated the woman proudly, and saw him open the manila folder – Elser's file. He read for a moment, then frowned.

'Civil disobedience. Corrective instruction.' He looked up again into Elser's eyes, sensing something more, as if he knew the man, but intuition gave him no further clues. 'You learnt your lessons, I hope?'

Elser nodded slowly. Meyer was reluctant to finish, looking for some excuse to continue what was quickly becoming an interrogation. Then he saw Elser's little finger and the black padded sheath he had again strapped on.

'Accident?' he asked. Elser nodded. Meyer was still disturbed, his gaze wandered to the police officer, his assistants fidgeting uncomfortably, Schneider hardly containing laughter at the pathetic loyalty of the woman to the dark-haired little man with regular features and a Swabian demeanour. Meyer's son Peter came to his side and remained respectfully silent. Dinner, Meyer remembered. He glanced again at Scheider, who read his thoughts.

'It's almost nine o'clock, sir,' he reminded him. Meyer nodded and handed his assistant the manila folder containing Elser's record.

'Yes,' he said, 'it's late.' He grasped Peter's shoulders and turned him around. 'Hungry, boy?'

'Yes,' replied Peter.

'Good.' He smiled.

The landlady looked at Elser, then coughed politely. Elser could feel quite distinctly now the fabric of his trousers sticking to his knees. Blood, he knew, but dared not look. He just gazed at the Gestapo officer blankly. But Meyer had already almost forgotten them both. Hunches could not always be right. An insignificant little man and a woman he was obviously involved with – dinner with his children was more important. Interrupting his last thoughts of the couple, he made a small gesture.

198

'Go,' he said.

Georg Elser and his saviour, Ilse Guber, gratefully stumbled out of the police station into the cold night air of Munich.

'Well, here he is! We have him back!'

The motley crowd assembled in the lounge area of Turkenstrasse 94 murmured a welcome as the landlady ushered Georg Elser into the room towards the fire roaring in the grate. It had begun raining on the way home and they were both wet, having walked the short distance from the tram stop. Elser had gritted his teeth as he fell behind the woman's brisk walk. The warm lounge was welcoming and he could see snacks laid out and numerous small schnapps glasses beside the plates on the centre table. Herzog greeted him with a pumping handshake and wide grin. He held up his watch, indicating the working parts beneath the silver casing.

'Still going, you see! Very good!' Then he came close and whispered conspiratorily, 'Stolen goods, eh?' Elser nodded ruefully. 'Steel is a war supply, too,' went on the old man, 'and cork. You know – ' He paused. 'Did you know?'

'But he didn't, Herr Herzog,' interrupted the landlady, who had overheard.

'What did you use it for?' asked Herzog curiously.

Elser looked into the clear eyes of the old man and shrugged. 'I'm making something.'

'Is it secret?' whispered the old man again, now grinning. Elser nodded. 'An invention?' hissed Herzog. Elser nodded again. 'Will it make money? Will it sell? Those are questions you must ask yourself, young man. Will it affect our lives in any small way? Yes, you must ask that of yourself. When I was in business . . . '

'Schnapps, gentlemen,' said the landlady loudly, and led the two men over to the others, who were at last sampling the food and drink they'd been eyeing for several hours. 'They didn't feed you, did they?' she said, with a shake of her head. 'Come on, everyone.' All faces turned to Elser and glasses were raised. The woman lifted her own to make the toast.

Elser was bewildered by this show of, if not affection, then some kind of acceptance.

The landlady smiled at him and gestured to the portrait of Adolf Hitler on the wall. 'To all clever men,' she said, then turned to Elser, and everyone drank schnapps. Herzog nudged Elser, who followed the others and downed his glass in one. More drink followed. Another bottle was brought from the kitchen, and a third. The radio was switched on by one of the old men, who could only drink milk and had become irritable at the growing atmosphere of which he was not a part. Grumbling, he leant against the speaker, listening to a speech from some distant city, punctuated by applause and cheers. Even at half-volume on the dial, it was drowned by the laughter of his immediate neighbours, his fellow lodgers who, for this single moment in time, had allowed their faces to light up with remembrances, stories and anecdotes of their various pasts.

Elser began to laugh at the impressions Herzog was performing to accompany a story of a lost love, a herd of goats and a village railway station. By the time he had finished, the normally sombre residue of Weimar's lower classes were roaring appreciation at the old man's loud imitation of the train leaving, together with the girl's exhortations to her goats not to miss her and the guard's lecherous anticipation of the journey to come, having abducted the maiden, 'who lost more than her goats that day!' finished Herzog. The telling was better than the content, but the schnapps helped and the convivial atmosphere was heightened. Elser, with tears in his eyes, convulsed with humour, bent to sit on a vacant chair next to the now ravaged table of half-empty plates.

'Careful!' bellowed Herzog, now in full flight. 'The leg needs work!' Too late, Elser rested his weight and the chair gave way, throwing him to the floor. This was better than the story to the flushed faces, and even louder peals of laughter began. Elser lay on the carpet, sprawled in front of the fire, sobbing from his diaphragm as if he would never stop. Only when the landlady knelt beside him in full view of everyone, was there a sudden silence.

The radio droned on in the background, murmuring started amongst the older women, then someone shouted 'Sieg Heil!' and old Herzog lowered himself beside the two bodies on the floor. 'Me next,' he said, grasped the landlady's face and kissed her full on the lips. Laughter exploded again from all in the group except Elser.

'The Burgerbraukeller,' he murmured, but the words were lost to the noise in the room.

When Elser entered the beer hall, clutching his case, it was already late and the crowds were thinning out. It was warm and bright, contrasting with the dank cold outside, and he soon found a vacant table and, sliding on to a bench, placed his case beneath it. There were many SA uniforms evident amongst the civilians, but Elser hardly noticed. He had ignored warnings from the group at Turkenstrasse that he had had too much to drink and, disregarding their advice, stumbled out into the night from his workroom cellar on to the familiar route.

Annalise saw him from the kitchen door and almost dropped the steins of beer she was carrying. She rushed over to him, searching quickly for damage. He grinned up at her as if there was no mystery.

'Georg, where have you been? I didn't know what to say . . . The police were here . . . and . . . ' Glancing around, she sat down beside him. He leant towards her, misjudged the distance, and kissed her awkwardly on the cheek. She drew back.

'Have you been away?' She examined him and saw that his normally pale skin had heightened with colour. 'Sick? A fever?'

Elser shook his head. 'I'm back now,' he slurred. Annalise's eyes narrowed. 'Switzerland,' he went on, then lowered his voice. 'You must come with me.'

'I will,' she answered slowly.

'Sauerkraut . . . sausages and beer,' said Elser.

'Have you been drinking already?'

'Only schnapps,' nodded Elser. 'A party at the house, but I didn't eat.'

'Well,' she hesitated, 'it's late . . . I don't think . . . '

'I'm not drunk you know,' he interrupted, and he actually believed it. 'Tomorrow we will go out to that little restaurant . . . '

'There's a dance, Georg, till late – I can't. Another night, the day after perhaps . . . ?'

'A dance?' asked Elser flatly.

'Always on the sixth. It's the last one before the party gathering.' She smiled.

'I didn't know,' said Elser, and hiccuped.

Annalise pointed above his head at the poster clearly stating the date and time. He turned around slowly and peered up at the information.

'You live in another world, my dreaming gypsy,' she said softly as Elser, having read the poster, grunted and looked at her unsteadily. She kissed him as he reached for his pocket watch. It was already ten thirty. The zither player, with two violinists, continued to play wearily.

'Shall I come tonight?' she whispered.

Elser shook his head. 'Tomorrow.'

'But the dance . . . ?'

'I'll come to the dance.'

'And wait?'

'And wait,' said Elser.

Annalise's eyes lit up, but her pleasure was disturbed by Payerl's loud voice. She leapt up and smiled, then curtsied 'Anything else, sir?'

*   *   *

After an argument with the chef in the kitchen, Annalise was able to serve Elser cold meat and potatoes, which he wolfed down with chilled beer. It improved his condition until the strong Löwenbräu went to work, by which time he had paid, slipped into the shadows of the stairway and climbed quickly to the balcony area. He heard the far toilet flush, then a loud curse, and saw a man emerge buttoning his trousers, who grunted as he passed Elser. It was too gloomy for recognition and the man was half drunk, as indeed was Elser.

'It'll fall one day,' the man said, and was gone.

Elser missed the reference to the loose cistern and, glancing through the balustrade to ensure he could no longer be seen, he slid behind the stacked carpets and tables, leant against the familiar cold outer wall and closed his eyes.

In tears, Annalise lay back on the kitchen tiles beside the window and watched the other girls finish their clearing. Payerl was contesting the following day's menu, shouting loudly about war shortages at the chef. The chef's plump assistant was staring across at the pretty waitress, who was in obvious distress, and grinning to himself at the possibilities. He might even walk her home tonight, he thought. It was dark and wet and dangerous for a girl alone in the black-out.

Inside her, Annalise could feel the changes which had begun to confuse her, creating a sense of joy, together with insecurities, suspicion and fear for the future. Waves of despair came when Elser was gone, and she felt vulnerable and alone.

'Stop snivelling and finish your work!' snapped Payerl harshly, blowing cheap cigar smoke in her face.

Biting her tongue, she turned away and by midnight was dressed for the street. She stood just inside the back door with the last of the staff, behind the black-out curtain, and watched as the lights were turned off one by one. Then they all stepped out into the rain. The door was locked and each of them went off to their lodgings. Annalise avoided the advances of the plump chef, electing to walk by herself with a secret companion – her cherished hopes which seemed always, like Elser, to fade into the night as she entered the hostel. In the narrow dormitory bed there was at least the blessed oblivion of sleep and dreams of the pass to Switzerland and a new world. She had no doubts of that – if Elser said he could do it, he would. She had come to believe in this quiet little man from Württemberg. Perhaps from love, possibly desperation – she had nothing else but Elser.

When Elser awoke, his head was swimming. He shook it, but even with the torch on found it difficult to focus. He crawled out on to the balcony and stood up. Immediately he had to reach out and grasp the rail and lean against the balustrade. He swore under his breath at the stupidity of drinking schnapps. The white fruit alcohol was strong and he had no head for spirits. Already it was 5 November. He looked at his pocket watch and swore again. Three thirty! Now it was the sixth! He knelt unsteadily in front of the pillar, prised open the door and studied the interior, bending close to the torchlight to examine the framework, the secured dynamite and space for the detonators and metal bar where he would screw the clocks.

He set to work. Unwrapping the detonators carefully, he slid them into place and attached clips that would hold all four tightly. He began to feel sick, but continued, knowing he must complete the job tonight. He'd run out of time. He put two cotton reels on to the thin metal axis made from hatpins, spun them to be sure they were free, then released the strands of wire he had attached, the rest of which was bound around the reel. He had calculated the length of the wire exactly and cut it to measure. The stabbing pains in his knees had begun to distract him, but he determined to ignore them. He must finish. Placing wooden wedges on the detonators, which he gingerly inserted into the explosive, he looped the four strands of wire from the two reels each to their own wedge through a metal eye screwed into the wood. He wrapped the wire into a knot and twisted it until he was sure it would pull the small wedge cleanly away from the detonator head at the set time.

The clocks would be difficult, he knew. The space was now restricted, and although he had stripped the mechanisms to their bare essentials, they remained bulky. At the appointed hour the wire wound around the hands' axis would become taut, and he knew there must be strength in the turning cogs to pull the last millimetre and loosen the wedges, which would be set finally between the detonator caps and the strikers that would plunge into the small charge and thus set off more than a chime of bells. After thirty minutes he was satisfied. The clocks fitted perfectly into the frame as he had ensured, many times over, in the quiet of his workroom. He set no hour yet, but wound the clocks until the key would turn no more, then withdrew them slowly. The first *tick-tock* seemed to echo into the great hall. Elser sat back and, shaking his head, swallowed bile and checked his pocket watch. Fifteen minutes to six.

Once set, the mechanism would do its deadly job. Made to mark the passage of time, the two clocks would now curtail an era as efficiently as the makers claimed. The English firm of Westminster Clocks would have much to answer for – and the world would thank them when the assassination had succeeded. For a moment Elser's pride surged. So it was over. At last. Something prompted him to place his hand on the door. He wanted to hear if the noise of ticking could be detected.

'Perfect,' he murmured, pushing the panel against the surrounding beading and pressing lightly for the catch to connect and hold. He pressed harder. A third time. His lips began to tremble. The panel would not close.

Buckets, mops, keys, voices and lights were the overture to the one-act comic opera, as Elser had come to call it, of the women cleaners, who alternatively swore, sang, hummed snatches of forgotten songs and barracked each other with either filthy jokes or intricate descriptions of sexual inadequacies in either passing trade or drunken husbands.

Holding the two clock mechanisms in his hands, staring at the pinpoints of light in his concealment, Georg Elser heard nothing of the noise that sixth November morning of the year 1939. His eyes were wide and full of tears. The panel door was closed, the mechanism and explosive hidden, but the heart of the framework, the clocks that would give it all a short life to kill, would not fit. He had somehow miscalculated by a fraction, and unless he could rectify his mistake it was certainly all over. Hitler would live.

18

Georg Elser stared at the ceiling in his room. Lying on the bed, his head on a hard pillow, he rediscovered old patterns formed by the light that penetrated the thin curtains. He knew them all. What sleep he could snatch during the day was always punctuated by waking fits of calm or panic when he examined his resolve and alternately made decisions to continue or abort his now almost completed scheme. He had avoided Dreschler since the incident with the 'war materials', but he knew the man was astute enough to talk his way out of anything. Borg, the carpenter, was still a business friend and provided some craft work in the afternoons. The landlady had proposed what amounted to a complete refurbishment of the entire house, and although Elser had shown some enthusiasm, he was reluctant to commit more time than was necessary to the woman and her dreams. Broken furniture, cracked bric-à-brac, cupboards, shelves, door frames and floorboards all demanded little artistry and gave no satisfaction other than work for rent. The patterns danced on the ceiling as clouds shifted outside.

Elser glanced at his pocket watch on the bedside table. It was gone midday, time to retreat to his cellar and try to discover what had gone wrong. He knew he must remove some of the outer casing of the two clocks – but as yet did not know how, without weakening them and therefore jeopardizing not only the efficiency of the mechanism, but the success of the whole plot. Then the woman and her trivia. With a sigh he swung himself out of the bed yet again.

Secure in his workroom, Elser measured the two clocks taken from his case, within the set width of the frame he had already installed, and found both of them to be some

207

millimetres larger than he had estimated originally. He swore to himself, knowing that the excess measurement was exactly that of the metal bar at the base of the frame. How had he inaccurately calculated something so simple . . . ? He swore again and quickly began to experiment with ways of removing some more of the clocks' outer casings, without damaging the finely interlocking cogs.

By four o'clock he had stripped down both Westminster timepieces. Familiar with the mechanism, he knew exactly what could be removed, but it was difficult until he released the fine screws and took off the washers against which the nuts bit hard. Now against the casing itself – although the immediate cogs were almost touching – the clock functioned perfectly. He made a decision, watching the movement smoothly tracing time – it would work and, most importantly, fit.

He lit the luxury of a whole cigarette and leaned back on the bench, staring around the room slowly. Soon it would be at an end, all of this would be gone. He had almost forgotten why he had embarked upon such a business as he had undertaken. Why him? Why become an assassin, as he would certainly be branded? Elser drew on his cigarette. People only wanted to live. Now they were being manipulated. Sold lies. Peace guaranteed some future. War gave none. Georg Elser recognized himself as merely an ordinary man, wanting only something to look forward to – some horizon to be crossed. Life was gamble enough without armed conflict. Hitler had stirred the minds of so many to be prepared to fight for survival. The truth was that he could only offer death.

Georg Elser smiled to himself as smoke curled around the lamp in his rented cellar of Turkenstrasse 94 that afternoon of 6 November 1939. His logic may not have been perfect, but his motives were of the highest order, and if his device would now work, as he had painstakingly prepared it, only a miracle would save Hitler.

*   *   *

With the tables pulled back from the centre of the floor of the Bierkeller, enough space had been created to provide a dance area, and by the time Georg Elser arrived it was packed. Safely ensconced against the wall behind the pillar, Elser was first served by Annalise, then invited by her to dance. He reluctantly agreed, having put the case, which now contained only the two Westminster clocks, under his bench.

Leaving his coat to mark an occupied place, he was led by the pretty young waitress into the throng. It was less like dancing and more like communal jostling. But Annalise seemed to enjoy it. The noise, music, coarse laughter, shouts, screams and sweat, together with the physical discomfort of aggressive bodies thrusting against each other, fuelled by beer, began to sicken Elser, and even the shining eyes of the woman in his arms could not distract him from his secret preoccupation.

'What is it, Georg?' smiled Annalise.

Elser saw the concern in her eyes and suddenly felt more isolated than ever. Even amongst so many people, or perhaps because of them, he could no longer truly be part of his surroundings. The largely unthinking, pleasure-seeking, sensual self-indulgence of these crowds made him realize that he was not an ordinary man any longer. Without setting out deliberately to achieve it, he had become different, but only he knew it.

Feeling the frightening loneliness that had crept into his life, unwanted but impossible to dispel, he reached out and seized Annalise's face between his hands. Gently he relaxed the pressure, seeing shock in her expression, and he kissed her on the lips, appreciating her instant response. He felt her body pressing against his and sensed her longing to be with him, alone and making love, when they could exchange that rare gift which all lovers have, until it sours, of wanting with great desire to give more than to receive. They squeezed from the dance floor and Annalise, having seen distantly the admonishing stare of Herr Payerl, led Elser back to his seat.

He immediately checked his case beneath the bench, and

watched the young waitress thread her way between the tables, back to the kitchen. Elser, in the shadow, looked out at the continuing dance, the people moving more wildly, frothing steins constantly being emptied. The atmosphere was growing coarse and the music was far from enchanting. He glanced at the stairway, where numerous SA men were sprawled drinking, laughing and pointing at fellow members in brown shirts scattered around the great hall. It had to be tonight, he thought. It was so nearly done, and with the clocks in place they would be free. He would persuade Annalise to leave. It must be tonight. Tomorrow, as she had told him, the place would be occupied, perhaps for most of the night, by SA men whose job it was to provide security on the night of the eighth, when Hitler spoke. It must be tonight.

Elser glanced at his white knuckles grasping the stein of beer in his hand so tightly, and then looked up, a deep, unsettling sensation within him. Although his expression hardened, there was compassion in his eyes as he stared out at all the unsuspecting faces in the crowded hall. Faces that might be in the Burgerbraukeller on the night of the eighth. His gaze went up to the ceiling above the main pillar, then to the moving dancers below. There would be sacrifices, there would be others killed. Although he had known it all along, seeing the rough enjoyment in this hearty assembly, he suddenly wanted to abort the whole thing. It might be years before the panel was discovered – and the clocks? He could throw them in the river. Innocent victims, by what right did he . . . ?

He cut off his thoughts sharply. It was too late to turn back. He had already made his decision and commitment. Some would die, but millions would live – and that would be justice enough and, at least, ease his conscience. With some luck, Hitler's entire hierarchy would be surrounding him and, Elser thought, with some satisfaction, he might get the lot of them.

The dance came to an end at midnight. The music stopped and people began to file out noisily on to the streets, where they were reminded that a war was on and they should go back to their homes quietly. Elser was staring across at the stairway to the balcony area, which was still occupied by SA men, when Annalise sat down beside him, dressed to leave, and Elser knew he was finished.

She laughed and touched his cheek, 'Oh, my long-faced Ziga,' she whispered, and kissed him.

Across the room, where the musicians were still packing up, the zither player, seeing the young couple, began to play 'Kom Ziga'. Annalise laughed and began to sing the song, waving happily to the man, who waved back with a grin and played on.

'They let me off early,' she whispered. 'Can we go?' Elser said nothing. 'Georg, what is it?' she asked. 'Tell me.'

But Georg Elser had already seen them and could hear, as all those who remained in the Bierkeller could not ignore, the sound of marching feet. A troop of SA men marched through the entrance, down the centre of the Bierkeller and stopped. On command, they fell out of column and started roughly shouting and manhandling all those that lingered. Elser and Annalise were no exception and, as the Burgerbraukeller doors slammed shut behind them, Elser distinctly heard the bolts and bars securing the place until dawn. For a moment Elser was unable to believe what had happened. He remained atop the short flight of steps, bewildered, clutching his case, pulling his coat tighter against the gusting wind and fine rain.

'Georg,' murmured Annalise, and kissed him tenderly. Her warm lips reminded him there were other worlds than the one into which he had climbed night after night; and perhaps there were other solutions, but what there was not, was time. Elser felt Annalise's hand seeking his, and together they walked into the night towards Turkenstrasse 94, exactly as sirens began to sound. Both of them glanced up automatically into the darkness, where a fine drizzle blotted out even the stars. Only searchlights illuminated huge black clouds, but found no enemy intruders.

Annalise started to run, but Elser stopped her.

'If they want us, they'll get us.'

'But, Georg, I'm frightened.'

'So am I.'

'Please, Georg, let's find the shelter.'

'Don't panic.' He looked up again and almost spoke to himself, but she heard the words, 'When they come, we'll hear them.'

'It's only just begun,' said Elser. The sirens stopped.

'What?' whispered Annalise.

'The war.'

Outside his lodgings, moulded by the distant searchlights, was the shape of a dark police car, its driver asleep. Elser registered this but said nothing to Annalise as they ducked quickly through the archway, hoping not to be detected. He found the lock and opened the door. With finger to his lips, warning Annalise, they stepped softly along the corridor, seeing the glow from a fire in the lounge. Pausing midst the leaping shadows, Elser looked in and smiled to himself. Several empty bottles on the centre table told part of a story, and two bodies on the carpet, half-clothed and writhing in an attempt at ecstasy, revealed the rest.

It would be safe tonight, he reflected to himself and took Annalise directly to his room, where they undressed and explored each other – at first furtively, then with haste and urgency, as if an alarm would sound and they would be torn apart. But it was not to be that night. Annalise became worried when she gently touched Elser's legs and found the damaged knees, but he said he had merely fallen, and confidently assured the beautiful naked young woman in his arms, until their lovemaking became sensuous, creating an erotic languor between them, a timelessness that exists between those lovers who banish all else and are aware only of each other and the moment.

'Oh, Georg,' Annalise whispered, 'I do love you. Please tell me that we will always be together.'

Elser sighed and lay beside her, staring at the ceiling. He

212

found no dancing patterns – only darkness. He wanted to believe the words he answered, but something in his heart told him they were not true. 'Yes,' he said, 'we will always be together.'

Suddenly Annalise raised herself and turned to him, finding his lips, then seeking his eyes. Elser picked out in her face something he had not seen before and could not be sure he saw now. But there was an intensity in her voice which was unmistakable, a sureness, a new strength that was more than a lover's. Perhaps it came from the mother to be. 'We will, Georg,' she said quietly. 'We will always be together . . . '

'In our hearts?' he smiled.

'Wherever you are, I shall be. Wherever I am, you will be with me.'

'Wherever?' he questioned.

'Anywhere,' she answered, and kissed him with passion. They held each other tightly, as lovers do, and for those seconds believed nothing could come between them, that the great forces of destiny would bless them and fate would direct their path into a future of eternal happiness. Annalise's tears were silent now. Elser knew they were there. A waitress and a mere artisan, what chance did they have? And now a child.

'He will be a boy,' she whispered. Elser said nothing. 'And *I* will call him . . . '

'*We* will call him . . . ' he said softly. Then Annalise pressed close and clung to him in an attempt to dispel her fears, committing her body and soul to this man who had already decided his final course of action.

Dawn light was showing through the curtains by the time they were dressed and ready to leave. Elser went ahead, then beckoned her to follow, and they walked quietly down the corridor, past the lounge area where the fire had become ashes. An overturned bottle, empty glasses and a woman's blouse were the only evidence of the landlady's night dalliance. Outside, the police car was gone. Perhaps the woman had found what she was looking for – an occasional lover who would enter her dreams as he entered her bed; if the officer found it a fair exchange he would come back. Elser wished her well; it was no longer his concern, and he was going.

He walked Annalise to the Bierkeller, where he suffered the morning chill, enjoyed the early sun and remained outside at one of the tables until she had changed and brought him a steaming coffee.

'They're inside, everywhere,' she said. Elser nodded. He could see several SA men outside, cursing and shouting at each other as they hung swastika flags. One of them jeered at Annalise, and Elser looked up. A half-hearted challenge was thrown at him, which brought laughter from men on the roof.

'Ignore them,' she said, but saw anger in his eyes.

'Everyone says that, as if they'll go away.'

'Well, what can you do?' she asked. Elser only smiled.

When Elser left, Annalise began her day's work, knowing it would be more awkward because of these Nazi bully-boys. From experience she knew that they created trouble, and she was already wishing the next few days over. With the Führer back in Berlin and most of the Brownshirts gone, apart from regular customers, who were better behaved, working life would become almost tolerable.

Inside the Bierkeller the walls and pillars were festooned with Nazi bunting. Large flags, drapes, rearranged tables and chairs, the podium in place – it was all familiar. Hitler was coming.

Georg Elser had begun to find walking for any length of time difficult. His knees were suppurating and as he had never trusted doctors, he had begun to make occasional visits to the pharmacy. He was given ointment and lotion to apply, but they generally caused him more pain for little effect.

It was for that reason that he sought relief, more than anything else, in St Stephen the Martyr, where he slumped gratefully into one of the pews at the back. He was unwilling to return to his lodgings because he knew the landlady would be demanding more work from him. He needed to apply his mind to the last part of his task ahead. Inserting the clocks would be easy, attaching the wires a little more complicated, setting the time, necessary – but getting into the Bierkeller and up to the gallery now seemed almost impossible.

'Do you wish to pray?' asked a voice. Elser looked up. The Reverend Father was standing there with his practised smile. 'Then kneel, my son,' he said. Elser bowed his head and began to move and his knees gave warning signals. 'I can't,' he mumbled. The Reverend Father's face hardened as he recognized the trouble-maker. 'You were here before,' he stated. Elser said nothing. 'I remember you. You had certain opinions, made suggestions, I think.' Elser said nothing. 'This is a church and here is God. You will respect that,' said the man, drawing his robes about him. 'If you wish to pray, kneel. If you do not, leave.'

Elser again looked up at the man and this time his gaze was disconcerting. The Reverend Father widened his eyes in ineffective retaliation.

'Kneel!' he commanded softly. Elser slid from the pew on to the hard cushion. The pain shot through his body as the broken skin, become taut, erupted against the bone. Elser's face showed no emotion, but what colour there was drained away. The Reverend Father released his cassock with a smile of satisfaction.

'Help me,' whispered Elser. But the man was already striding down the aisle towards a polished brass crucifix on his altar.

19

The Burgerbraukeller closed at midnight on the seventh of November 1939. It had been predominantly full of SA men and those civilians who were friends of the party. A detail of Brownshirts were left behind to occupy the premises during the night, with strict instructions to remain alert and leave the beer in barrels and bottles. These men had saluted their officer and promised to obey, knowing that every rule can be broken.

Outside, several guards had been placed and were to patrol the building. They would be relieved at intervals. They were told, although this was a normal precaution, now that Germany was at war, the Führer had many enemies. Initially this caused the men, huddled in greatcoats with rifles and helmets, to respond to any sound as though it were a potential enemy. But the increasing rain and the cold night affected their enthusiasm as it does any guard's, even those of the Master Race.

By two o'clock a moon was trying to appear between scudding clouds, but the rain remained unceasing. Two of the guards managed to light cigarettes, sheltered from the downpour by the coping of the roof. They pressed close amongst the many large beer barrels stacked up at the rear of the building, cursed, grunted a brief conversation and parted. Having heard their companions inside laughing over cards and already drinking, they knew that dawn, that night, would be slow coming.

The bodies in the dormitory beds were still. Two of the girls snored; one continually broke wind and another moaned in her sleep. Annalise slipped from beneath her covers and knelt at the window. She pulled back the black-out curtain just enough to look out. There were bars outside, and through them she thought she could see the glow of a moon amongst the clouds. She was confused that Georg had not even shown himself during the evening. She understood that he might have been uncomfortable in the presence of so many Nazi Brownshirts, but she had wanted him there because she had begun to miss him more and more. She was learning the other side of love – the emptiness and loneliness.

'Kom Ziga,' she whispered to herself. 'Kom Ziga.'

Her hands traced the fullness of her naked stomach and lay in her lap, seeking some response from the growing child within. Her fingers slid between her thighs and she remembered the previous night and the lovemaking. They discovered the moistness as she thought of Georg and began to move, slowly. One hand slid back to her breasts, outlining their contours and hardening nipples. Some of the girls could only do this, she knew – she'd heard them, moaning with their fantasies as others, still awake, giggled until they too felt their sexual deprivation. It was another reason why they were jealous of her with Georg, and after nights when she did not return, there was gossip, which she tried hard to ignore. She began to feel the blood coursing through her veins as her hands and fingers heightened the pleasure, but her body had not forgotten Georg, and the moon appeared through clouds in the night sky like a kindly face, to remind her of patience and the greater fulfilment that had become her privilege.

She bent her head and clasped her hands together, feeling the cheap gold ring on her finger, realizing she had so much more than those around – not only Georg, but now his child. Tears of happiness appeared in her eyes and she reached out, drawing a heart in the condensation on the window, inscribing their initials within it. She blew a kiss to the moon, which watched her climb back into bed before disappearing amongst the black rain clouds.

*   *   *

Georg Elser reached up for the top of the wall, which was slippery in the falling rain. He levered his body to the rounded bricks, remained poised, peering into the darkness, where he could see nothing. With gritted teeth, he dropped down into the garden of the Burgerbraukeller. He had estimated the distance during the day but, not knowing where the guards were, the run across to the stacked barrels was a gamble which he had to take. He stumbled twice, his knees refusing to obey, and when he fell into shadow, only the smell of stale beer told him he had achieved temporary sanctuary. It was difficult to hear any sound above the steady downpour. He hoped the guards would be sheltering from the rain, and heard the expected noises of the SA men inside the building with growing trepidation. If he was caught now there would be no excuse. In each of his side pockets he carried the two Westminster clock mechanisms wrapped in oilskin. He looked up, the rain spattering his face, and found the small window of the toilet in the balcony area. He hesitated, feeling the weight of the clocks in his pockets. Laughter roared from within the building and prompted him to move. He climbed on to the first barrel, wary of the wet wood, pushing against the wall for support, extended both arms and found the lip of the barrel above, and pulled hard. With his muscles quivering, he slid on to the flat top and lay there listening for sounds in the night. Somewhere a dog howled; a train passed distantly with a familiar clatter as it negotiated the complicated points system in the goods yard; then he heard voices and pressed his face to the beer-soaked barrel.

Two guards wandered past below, complaining of the cold and the filthy night, hoping to be relieved sooner than was scheduled. Elser waited until he could hear only the rain again, then painfully brought his knees beneath his body and stood up, shaking. He was now a considerable height above the ground. He stretched and the barrel swayed. The sill of

218

the window was above his reach and the decision he must make was not easy. He would have only the one chance. He crouched to test his balance. The empty barrel, though heavy, was not firmly placed. He bent his head and waited patiently. Then it came, the other train. There might be a noise, to give him a chance, however small.

He looked up, ignoring the increasing pain in his knees, and with all the energy he could muster, leapt for the sill. His fingers grasped the concrete ledge, slithered for a split second, then held the weight of his body exactly as the barrel from which he had sprung wobbled and fell on its side. The rattling train echoed between the nearby buildings and the noises merged – the train continuing even as the barrel rolled against the wall and wedged itself amongst the others. Elser did not have to look. Now there was no way back.

Clinging to the sill, he felt his arms being torn from their sockets. His face screwed up with the strain of holding on. Rain fell into his eyes as he tried to pull himself up. His shoes scrabbled against the wall, trying to find even the smallest foothold on the brick, but there was nothing, only the smooth and slippery rear wall of the building. Then he heard louder noises from inside. Feet running on the stairs. Boots approaching along the balconied gallery. He swore to himself, tried to readjust his grip, slipped and grasped again. A light went on directly above his head and two SA men were in the toilet, only the width of the opaque glass away from him. They began to laugh and make jokes at the smell of old urine as, unbuttoning their trousers, each of the men bet the other they could put more into the enamel bowl than they had drunk.

Georg Elser's face, staring up at his illuminated fingers on the sill, became contorted. It couldn't finish like this, surely, he thought, not after all he had done? As the two men in the toilet began to compare the length of their sexual organs their laughter became louder, which brought a shout from below. One of the patrolling guards, hearing the noise, had looked up, recognizing his friends' voices, seeing only the faint light through the pouring rain. Elser, not for the first time, prayed to be invisible. The guard shouted something Elser did not catch. One of the two men inside opened the top of the small window and shouted out in a high voice, imitating a woman. Elser hung limply, conserving his strength, begging that there would be no torch, praying that the light would remain dim.

Below, the guard wandered off, laughing, wiping the rain from his eyes. In the toilet one of the SA men pulled the chain and shouted in alarm as the cistern moved. Elser heard the toilet flush, the window closed and again secured, then the light went off and the men ran along the balcony to the stairs, where they shouted to their companions and rejoined the card game.

'Our Father,' began Elser, 'which art in Heaven . . . ' he gritted his teeth and applied all the power he had remaining. He got first one elbow on the sill, then the other, slid his hands until they were side by side in the centre of the sill and pressed with all his might, levering his body until first one knee touched the edge then the other was over and resting on the narrow concrete ledge. His face forced against the cold glass of the window, he balanced, removing one hand at a time, supported only on his knees, where the pain was becoming memorable but he knew must be ignored if he was to survive the night, as he would certainly not survive the fall or the guard.

One hand pushed against the bricks above the window, locking his body in the small space. His other hand, with urgent fingers, reached into his top pocket and found the small diamond he had taken from his own watch and secured to a short steel blade. He inscribed a circle at the centre of the upper window. A second and then third time he followed the scar on the glass, pocketed the diamond-tipped blade, then, holding his breath, tapped the bottom of the circle. It seemed to turn on a hidden axis and immediately Elser slipped his fingers beneath it, catching the almost perfect circle of glass safely in his hand. Carefully he placed it beside him on the sill then reached in, found the arm of the frame, released it and opened the window above his head. Now grasping the metal, he stood up, toes on the sill and leaned forward, pulling himself in.

Directly before him was the cistern; there was a space between it and the roof of the toilet. He had no alternative but to partially support himself on it as he raised his legs. Inching forward, his chest was pressing against the cast metal and he could quite distinctly hear water filling up, then the cistern moved on its supports. Plaster flaked from the walls and Elser froze, trying to readjust his balance, but he was still applying too much weight.

Again the cistern moved, and now it was brick that began to crumble to the floor as he could hear clearly, above the laughter from the SA men below, one of the clocks in his pocket caught against the window frame. Painfully he had to slide to one side, almost on his groin, to give himself access for his legs.

Yet again the cistern moved, and Elser realized that cautiousness was no longer worthwhile. He scrambled in as fast as he was able, turning his knees and dropping his feet to the inside sill. They found the basin, the toilet seat and, finally, the floor. He was actually facing the cistern when it gave way completely and he caught it in his arms, pressing a shoulder beneath it to support the heavy weight. Laughter from the card game below drowned out the sound, even as the window with the inscribed circle dropped with a small clang against its frame.

Elser tried to move, and staggered beneath the weight of the cistern. Below, he could hear men shouting that they too wanted to go to the toilet and he heard two of them running across the Bierkeller floor. Only jeering cries describing the smell above stopped them, and they were content then to thread their way back through the tables, past the kitchen, to the other urinal.

Again, summoning what energy remained in his body, Elser lodged the cistern on one shoulder, reached out for the first support, which was hanging loose, ripped it from the wall and thrust the pointed end back into the hole. He did the same with the second support and held his breath as he released the weight on to the two metal arms. Immediately, he pushed the arms hard and they bit deeper into the loose brick. He lay back against the wall and saw that the cast metal was temporarily secured.

His mind raced. Now the barrel was fallen outside, it would be a dangerous drop even if he could hide until morning. Then, with so many guards, how would he remain undiscovered? The alternative would be to hide and leave as usual – but how, if the place was crawling with guards? He sucked air nervously and decided to complete his job before solving the problem.

Firstly he cantilevered the arm of the top window against its frame in case he needed a quick exit, merely for the chance of escape. He explored his body, head back, eyes closed, arms hanging limply. He was already exhausted – and wet. He would have to hug the walls to the stacked carpets, then reverse his coat before he knelt on the floor, to avoid leaving what his hunters would see as spoor, which might trap him.

Cautiously he stepped out of the toilet, slipped off his shoes and in stockinged feet made his way through deep shadow to the stored carpets and tables. He crouched and surveyed his surroundings. He could hear the card game in progress, the SA men becoming noisier with beer and the excitement of increasing stakes. Elser removed both clocks wrapped in their oilcloths and placed them on his coat, which was folded in on itself so that only the lining was showing. Pushing it before him, he crept towards the pillar.

He noted gratefully that all the lights were not on; only in the area around the kitchen was there any illumination, but it was sufficient to allow him to see the panel and where he must insert the thin steel blade to release the catch. He knelt on the lining of his coat, levered the panel open then quickly unwrapped the first Westminster clock. He reached the cavity and felt for the exact space where he must insert the mechanism. Gingerly he put it into place, connected the wire to the axis then reached for the second clock. This, too, he slid into the frame, where it fitted perfectly. Now from his back pocket he took the key, found the octagonal hole in the first and second mechanism and wound the springs until they were tight. He set the time of the first and the second after he had connected the final wire, which led over the cotton reels to the wedges separating the strikers and the detonators set into sufficient dynamite to tear the pillar apart. Elser bit his lips and only now did he realize it was set. He reached in, spread two fingers and pressed the two plungers. Immediately both clocks began ticking. A roar of laughter exploded from below as a hand of cards was lost and won. Elser was shaking. He pushed the panel closed and it shut flush with the beading. He put his ear to the pillar and could hear nothing. He closed his eyes with relief.

At nine twenty the following night, half-way through Adolf Hitler's speech, his bomb would go off and destroy not only bricks, mortar and concrete, but with luck, the future of the Third Reich. For one moment, as the tension seemed to ebb from his body, Elser congratulated himself. He'd done it.

In the toilet, both support arms of the cistern snapped. The heavy weight, now full of water, fell heavily on to the toilet seat, bringing with it bricks and plaster from the wall. The vibration even disturbed the cantilevered window, which fell to its frame, smashing the glass exactly as the cut circle outside slipped from the sill and fell, splintering on the barrels below. Elser, dumbfounded at the noise, was frozen to the spot and took almost a second, which seemed like an hour to his sluggish reflexes, before he moved. Dragging the oilcloth and his coat, he scuttled towards the tables and the carpets, plunging amongst them as the entire SA group of men below, shouting an alarm, thundered up the stairs and ran the length of the balcony gallery to the toilet.

The first men burst open the door to see the cistern pouring water. Immediately the group began to laugh. One grasped the single toilet roll and, squeezing it, stuffed it into the broken pipe. Shouts from outside and barking dogs brought two faces to the shattered window, which was assumed to have been damaged by the falling metal.

'Cistern!' shouted one of the SA men. There were grunts from below, someone made a remark, a joke was attempted and Georg Elser, curled in the darkness, heard the SA group wander back along the balcony area, down the stairs and return to their cards and beer. How he could get out in the morning, he felt sure, would be a problem that would solve itself. Surely fate owed him something?

As he sank into blissful sleep he thought he could hear the voice of Annalise softly singing 'Kom Ziga, Kom Ziga.' And now he knew he would come to her. It was over. They were free.

20

At eight o'clock in the morning, the Gestapo headquarters in Munich was already a hive of activity, there was excitement throughout the building in anticipation of the Führer's imminent arrival. Security operations were in full swing, relevant streets checked and cleared for the Führer's car and entourage. That night the Bierkeller, the following day, the march to the Feld Herren Hall. All these preparations necessitated minute planning and coordination amongst the different units concerned with the Führer's welfare. SA, SS, local police and even 'the old comrades' of Christian Weber's who had been given the ultimate privilege to provide protection for Adolf Hitler within the Burgerbraukeller.

This had caused some amusement amongst the Gestapo staff, who, as Meyer commented, had the slightly more difficult task of guarding the Führer everywhere else in the world, but not in a beerhall full of brown-shirted friends.

In his private office, Meyer was lost in thought, and only the sound of a tapping pen, as he absently counted the seconds, interrupted the moment of silence between him and Schneider. They had been studying an official report sent from Berlin. The tapping stopped, Meyer looked at Schneider.

'A gypsy?'

Schneider nodded in reply.

'An astrologer?'

Schneider nodded again in answer. 'It is an official report,' he said.

'Himmler believes this . . . information?' asked Meyer sarcastically.

'*He* paid the astrologer,' shrugged Schneider.

Meyer glanced again at the report and raised his eyebrows.

'Then I suppose that is sufficient reason for us to take this . . .' he wafted his hand over the sheet of paper, ' . . . seriously. Officially!' Meyer stood up, turned behind his chair and stepped to the window, gazing out. He looked up as a formation of Messerschmitts passed overhead, a rehearsal for the Luftwaffe's contribution the following day to impress the public. Meyer glanced back at Schneider. 'Do you believe it?'

Schneider shrugged again, non-committally. 'Caesar had a seer.'

'And the ides of March,' Meyer grunted.

'I'm sorry, sir?'

Meyer ignored his assistant's question and again looked out into the dull morning. 'What is this gypsy going to do, do you think?'

'Well, it was just a warning, sir. Apparently this man . . . this astrologer . . . "saw" something.'

'What, Schneider?'

'The report doesn't specify, sir.'

Meyer spun around to face Schneider, clasping his hands behind his back. 'Helpful, isn't it?'

Schneider saw the irritation in his superior officer's eyes, and respect brought him to his feet.

'Where, Schneider, are we going to find a *"gypsy"*?'

Schneider knew it was an impossible question. The helpless look on his face was unmistakable to Meyer.

'In a concentration camp, perhaps?'

Schneider smiled. 'Then he would be no problem, sir.'

'Are we to assume that this gypsy of the Reichsführer's astrologer has intentions other than to sell clothes-pegs to the Hausfraus of Munich?'

Schneider merely coughed.

'Shall we say that this imaginative diversion from Himmler himself is, as we are told, a warning that we have an unknown assassin in our midst?'

Schneider coughed again, nervously. 'The report doesn't say, sir.'

'Then we should assume he is unknown, Schneider, yes?'

The younger man did not like the gleam in Meyer's eye, but nodded in answer. In a tone between sarcasm and sympathy Meyer continued, 'Schneider, all assassins must be unknown. If they were not, their failure would deny them their title.'

'Of course, sir.'

'How is he to kill the Führer?'

'The report doesn't . . . '

'Where is it to happen?'

'Well, the astrologer . . . '

'Here, in Munich?'

'Perhaps we should . . . '

'The Burgerbraukeller?' snapped Meyer.

'Well, tonight, sir, is a very . . . ' Schneider stopped himself.

Meyer nodded as if agreeing that nothing could be said. 'Confusing, isn't it?' he said softly. The telephone rang loudly. Schneider began to move, but Meyer picked it up and listened to the information given to him briefly. 'Thank you,' he said and replaced the receiver. He turned to look again out of the window. The Messerschmitts were returning on their flight path. He grunted and sighed with exasperation. 'He's cancelled.'

Schneider was disbelieving. 'What?'

Meyer continued to stare up at the grey clouds, already assessing the implications.

'Hitler is not coming, this year,' he said.

It was almost nine o'clock before Georg Elser felt confident enough to crawl out from behind the carpets and tables for the last time. Keeping close to the wall, he was at the very top of the stairs before he was spotted by several SA men in the crowded beerhall below. One of them shouted and Elser slowly descended the stairs. His shoes were still wet and his coat damp. His knees almost gave way before he reached the bottom of the steps.

'What are you doing here?' asked one of the Brownshirts roughly, pulling him from the stairway.

'I came for coffee.'

'Not today, little man.'

'How did you get in here?' asked one of the other men, and glanced up to the balcony area.

'It doesn't matter how he got in,' said the first SA man. 'He's going out through this door.'

Stumbling, Elser was pushed to the entrance and only had time to note that there were no waitresses as yet in the building, whose interior was now exactly as he had seen in films and photographs, with swastika flags, emblems, insignia – everything prepared for the Führer's speech.

He managed not to fall on to his knees when he was thrown out, and endured the parting remarks of the bully-boys as he shuffled off down the street. He knew where he was going. First to Dreschler's, who had survived interrogation, paid off the right people and delivered a message to Elser that he could pick up his requested favour. Then, if his pretty girl wasn't working, he'd give her a surprise. There was a growing sense of elation in him. He even began laughing to himself. The overwhelming sense of joy and relief, he wanted to share – to give to Annalise.

The dormitory in the hostel was not yet completely empty. One girl, who couldn't find work, still slept. The others had gone to their various jobs. Only Annalise, who had enjoyed the luxury of a bath, remained. She was dressing beside the windows, whose curtains were pulled back to reveal the dull day outside. She was not due in the Burgerbraukeller until eleven o'clock and she was enjoying the unusual hours of freedom. For almost a minute, she did not see the face that appeared beyond the bars on the other side of the glass, and only after she had dried herself and put on new underwear, did she hear a tapping on the window. Through the heart she had drawn in the condensation on the pane in the night, she

228

saw the smiling eyes of Georg Elser. Quickly she lifted the window until it pressed against the security catches. She knelt down and peered through the small gap between window and frame.

Elser grinned. 'Hello.'

Annalise could not speak at first. The happiness in her face was obvious, as were the tears of joy in her eyes.

'I came visiting,' said Elser.

'I start late today,' laughed Annalise. Elser assumed a serious expression and took from his inside jacket pocket the freshly sealed white envelope. Annalise's eyes opened wide as he handed it to her through the small space.

'A pass,' he said.

'For me?' whispered Annalise, taking the envelope as if it contained precious stones, and indeed it would prove to be worth far more.

'Switzerland,' whispered Elser. 'You must pack.'

'Georg, I can't, you know that, not today.'

'I'm leaving,' said Georg pointedly, 'today. Soon.'

For a moment Annalise was stunned. She could see by the expression on her lover's face that he meant it. She tried to press closer, her fingers squeezing the metal bars as she reached towards him. Unwanted tears formed in her eyes. 'Georg . . . Why? If you love me . . . '

Elser sagged, arms spread on the bars of the window, forehead pressing on the cold metal. He was exhausted, and in the face of this emotion, impotent. There was almost nothing left inside him. 'If you love . . . Germany, you would understand.'

Annalise's fingers released the bar and her hand touched his unkempt hair. His eyes fastened upon hers, imploring her to understand without words. Annalise, appreciating the vulnerability, smiled and spoke softly. 'Three more days – that's all. I get a bonus on the eleventh for the Armistice, Remembrance Day. It will help . . . us.'

Elser looked away and saw more than the gloomy garden, grey earth and broken wall at the rear of the hostel. He was looking back into another time, another life – his youth. 'Armistice,' he murmured. 'When what was called the Great War ended, I was still a child . . . and a fool. Even then I wanted to fight. For my country. I actually believed what I was told. We were right . . . God was on our side . . . And . . . ' He began to laugh at the thought. 'He . . . God, failed *us* because . . . we lost.' He reached up a hand, squeezed Annalise's fingers gently and drew them to his lips. 'Can you imagine God failing . . . anyone?'

'Georg,' whispered Annalise.

He pressed close against the bars, eyes glistening now, and spoke with passion. 'If it is his will . . . it *will* happen.'

Annalise was confused. 'What, Georg?'

He ignored her question and continued. 'Our leaders failed *us* then, as they have failed us now.'

Annalise bit her lips, perplexed at the intensity she had not seen before. For a moment his eyes almost seemed those of a fanatic. 'Hitler,' he spoke the word ominously, 'promised peace. He has given us war.'

'Georg,' pleaded Annalise, 'we are only ordinary people . . . He is the Führer, he is guiding Germany.'

'To what?' snapped Elser.

'Victory,' said the young woman hesitantly.

'Germany was told that once before,' said Elser.

Annalise, in a conciliatory voice, interrupted quickly, 'Georg, someone must make the decisions. We, the people, have chosen him . . . he is a *great* man . . . '

'It is the ordinary people who make a *country* "great".' Elser paused, censoring his words. 'And we . . . *I*,' he emphasized, 'did not choose war.'

Annalise hung her head. 'Georg, nobody wants war,' she finished weakly.

Elser grasped her hand tightly. 'He does. This "great man" – and he must be stopped . . . now!'

'How?' asked Annalise, and stared into the stranger's eyes she saw before her, in the face of the man she so much loved.

'I'll walk you back,' said Elser. 'To work.'

'Back?' questioned Annalise.

'The Burgerbraukeller,' said Elser quickly.

'Why do you say back,' said Annalise. 'Were you there already?'

Elser lowered his eyes, realizing he had revealed what was unintended.

'Oh, Georg, were you there for me?' She raised his chin with her hand and they tried to kiss between the bars, which was difficult and awkward, and they both began laughing. She gripped his fingers and pulled his hand between the window and its frame, through the small gap. She placed his hand on her stomach.

'Feel,' she whispered. 'I think it's moving.'

Elser withdrew his hand slowly, and watched Annalise finish dressing. He appreciated her every movement as he saw her don the attractive work clothes, finally lacing her dirndl at the front, which emphasised her breasts and narrowed her waist. She slipped into her heeled shoes, which gave form to her long slender legs. He waited for the window to be closed and secured, as if he were a prisoner having been given the dubious privilege of sexual titillation without fulfilment.

When she left the dormitory, just before he turned to run across the grey wet mud of the neglected garden, he saw the fading heart and the initials, picked out by the strengthening sunlight of the brightening day. The child-like gesture done on the window, perhaps in the middle of the night, reached deep into his soul and the responsibility of her obvious love suddenly became an added burden to the secret he carried alone. On impulse, he inscribed a swastika across the heart and made a silent prayer that they would both survive what might be imminently about to happen.

Only after he had scaled the back wall and felt the warm flesh beneath the clothes he pressed into his arms, in front of the hostel, where Annalise's lips eagerly found his, did he know that what they had was true. As his imagination had found, within the energy, discipline and motivation to create a machine of death, so reality had disturbed his placid

231

exterior – and, discovering his touchstone, reluctantly he had conceded, love.

Annalise, although appreciative of Elser's excessive emotion this morning, above all others, was almost overwhelmed by the intensity of his physical presence as she had been unsettled by his burning eyes as they walked hand in hand to the small coffee-house near Rosenheimerplatz. They made a strange couple, seated at a window table looking out through the condensation on the glass – she, a natural, almost guileless beauty, dressed presentably for work and he, unshaven, bedraggled, in a crumpled suit with tousled hair, like a street navvy who had been unable to find shelter in a storm. But his clear blue eyes and what they contained were enough for Annalise. She saw, finally, quite unmistakably, love – and the two of them sipped hot, steaming coffee and just gazed at each other over the rim of their large cups and were content just to be together, silently exchanging as much as two people ever can.

Then Elser reached for his pocket watch. 'The train leaves at ten thirty.'

'Georg, please . . . '

'We get out at Constance, you have the pass . . . I will meet you . . . on the other side.'

'I can't,' she whispered. 'Not today.'

'You must tell them you're leaving this morning, then pack.' He looked at his watch. 'It's only nine o'clock. I'll meet you at the station. We'll go to the border together.'

Annalise shook her head in frustration; why would he not understand? 'It's important to me, Georg. Tonight. The Führer.'

Elser clasped her hands. 'Tonight we'll be in Switzerland.'

Annalise sighed sympathetically, appraising the earnestness on the man's face. 'How can I expect you to understand, Georg? You are a gypsy. I will leave, but I have my pride. When I go I must do it properly. Three more days. Is it so much to ask?'

'You won't come with me?' he murmured.

Annalise took out money to pay for their coffees and stood up. 'Oh, my Ziga,' she said, 'I would go with you to heaven or hell, if you asked me, but please, Georg . . . *just* three more days.'

Elser stood up. 'I'll walk you to the Bierkeller,' he said.

At nine thirty on the morning of 8 November 1939, Georg Elser was smoking a half-cigarette, surveying the cleared workroom, which was tidier than when he had arrived and no longer bore any trace of his presence. The two lamps continued to flicker, throwing their familiar shadows. Turkenstrasse was merely an address he had remembered – a place he had once stayed, returned to and used. The residents would hardly know he was no longer there, when he was gone. Most of them were merely passing away the time before death, a hopeless life without ambition, some with limited experience, full of prejudices, bigotry and malice. He would leave them to the gossip that fuelled their very existence and the woman who was overseer, whose only problem was the Nazi block warden, who had recently been introduced to the several houses fronting the small courtyard as an adviser on any problems that might arise, but had begun quickly to recruit a coterie of obvious spies. Elser blew smoke between the two flames, then turned off one of the wicks. His few bags were packed. His case contained only his tools, no longer the two Westminster clock mechanisms. He could do nothing more, now. If it was the will of God and fate smiled, he would at least have made a contribution to history. His knees were a testament to that, but they would heal. It was time to leave.

'Herr Elser!'

Elser recognized the voice and glanced towards the stairs as the landlady negotiated the wooden steps gingerly. He had paid her what money he could afford, and told her of an offer elsewhere that would give him work on a more permanent basis. The woman examined the room swiftly, then her eyes rested on him. Despite the hour of the morning, she sipped schnapps from the glass in her hand and gestured, as if to an audience filling the cellar.

'But why?' she asked.

'I have a job,' said Elser, 'I told you.'

'But where?'

Elser hesitated. 'Switzerland,' he said, and regretted the word the moment he had spoken.

The landlady sat down on the stairs slowly. 'We will miss you.'

Elser said nothing.

'You owe me money.'

Elser nodded.

'So,' smiled the woman, 'you will come back?'

'Thank you,' murmured Elser. He stood up and reached for his bags. Seeing this, the woman's sense of loss hardened her heart. Her voice became harsh.

'Don't forget your debt to me.'

Elser shook his head and held out his hand. The woman put down her glass and took his hand in hers, examining it in the dim light. She lowered her cheek to his extended fingers. 'Such clever hands,' she murmured, and Elser felt the tears on his flesh. Gently he persuaded her to her feet, guided her out up to the cobbles, returned for his bags, then locked the two door flaps.

By the time he had strapped his bags to the bicycle the woman had encouraged most of her lodgers out of the house into the courtyard. Only Herzog waved as Elser paused beneath the archway leading on to the street. The others stared as if they had been conditioned to show and feel nothing. Life had been hard for them all and they knew that people came and went in their lives as if they had never been. They had been born victims and were trapped in an existence not of their own choosing. They had learned to suffer and endure. How could they do anything? That was the way it was. Nothing could be changed.

They began to file back into the warm house immediately Georg Elser had gone.

*　　*　　*

Outside the Burgerbraukeller, Georg Elser paced up and down. He paused occasionally, looking towards the kitchen entrance. He referred to his pocket watch twice. It was difficult to tell the time in the weak light, but he knew already he had a problem. He had asked one of the other girls to speak to Annalise, but only now was she coming out of the door, surrounded by the light, releasing the increasing noise of the larger than usual morning crowd, which burst from within. Elser stared at her. She smiled and looked him up and down. There was almost relief in her face when she spoke. She knew he would wait.

'Where are your bags?'

'At the station. I cycled back for you,' said Elser.

Her face fell and she glanced towards the wall, where she saw Elser's bicycle propped, awkwardly by the gate. Singing began in the hall. Nervously Annalise looked over her shoulder then back at Elser.

'Please . . . ' she pleaded, 'you know I can't. Not today.' Still on the kitchen steps, she reached out her hand as if with a single touch she would be able to convince him that her decision was the only one she could make.

Elser was merely confused; there were no more words he could use to persuade her without revealing the whole plot. He had trusted his ability to make decisions for them both.

'You must come with me,' he said, and grasped her arm, pulling her to him. He seized her tightly and ignored the shock in her eyes. The kiss between them reminded both of dalliant pleasures in the past, but it was insufficient to lure Annalise from her duty and sense of responsibility.

'Georg, if you love me, *you* will stay . . . only three days. Georg, please!'

Elser hung his head. 'You don't understand . . . ' he began.

'What?' asked Annalise coolly.

He looked up and could find no words but the simple ones. 'I love you. You must come.'

The pretty young waitress shook her head. 'You're being selfish, Georg. Three days only. What can they matter?'

'Please!' begged Georg.

'Annalise!' called Herr Payerl from within the kitchen. Martial music began as the band practised for the evening. Loud cheering sounded out in appreciation from the brown-shirted SA men already in the hall.

'I must go!' said Annalise, pulling away.

'No,' stated Elser simply.

Annalise's bewilderment turned to irritation. She spun on her heel and was about to return to the kitchen, when Elser seized her roughly and dragged her back into the darkness. Her first reaction was to scream as Elser, pressing her to him, could only hiss with exasperation into her ear. 'You *must* come with me!'

She sagged in his arms. 'Georg, what are you doing?'

He dragged her back to her feet. 'You *must* come!' he shouted, and grasped her firmly by the shoulders.

Annalise felt his fingers digging into her flesh in a way she had never before experienced, and screamed, 'Let *go* of me!!'

Elser tried to kiss her again, but now she thrust him away exactly as a shout, followed by others, came from the open kitchen door. Then bodies emerged. Large SA men, followed by Payerl, separated Elser and Annalise. Elser, reaching out for the woman, was thrown to the ground by the burly proprietor. Annalise winced as the SA men pulled her away from what was about to happen. They grinned in anticipation.

'No!' she cried. But one of the men clasped a hand to her mouth and took her back into the kitchen.

'Annalise!' shouted Elser, trying to stand. Payerl, finally being given his opportunity, kicked Elser hard, missed the man's chin and caught him beneath the shoulder, which turned him in mid-air so that he fell heavily on to his back.

'Go!' shouted the stout proprietor. He glanced behind to

236

see Annalise limp in the SA man's grasp, his hands still over her mouth, her eyes now flooded with tears. He grinned and looked back at Elser in the grass and mud.

'I *said go!*' he bellowed.

Now, two of the SA men moved quickly. One pushed Elser as he stood upright. The other gave him a hefty kick which caught him on the thigh so that he sprawled again on the ground.

'And don't come back here!' exclaimed Payerl. 'I've never liked you and you're no longer welcome!'

Elser crawled several metres, then found his feet and stared back at the leering group outside the kitchen door. Frustration turned to welling anger. There were too many to fight and fists were not his way.

Red-faced with physical exertion, Payerl pointed to the gate and screamed, *'Go!'*

Elser hesitated only a moment longer and stumbled towards his bicycle, the rear exit and his freedom. Once at the station he could collect his bags, board a train for Constance and never return. It was anger that filled his eyes with tears as he cycled to the Bahnhof, but by the time he arrived there was a hardness in his soul as there was compassion in his heart for the young woman with the guileless nature who had found her place there. Georg Elser had come to terms with the fact that there must be victims, but had never even considered the idea that one of them might be Annalise.

In his mind's eye he could see the huge beerhall filling with the Nazi Brownshirts, but only he could hear the steady ticking of the mechanism in what he had long since privately referred to as 'Hitler's pillar.'

When Georg Elser reached Munich's railway station, he fought through the many passengers to find his train. Several locomotives already departing and numerous other trains awaiting their passengers, made him confused. Smoke, steam, whistles, cries, among the many crowded platforms as people who were lost frantically sought each other, merged in his mind, becoming a dull roar, making decisions difficult.

He wheeled his bicycle to the queue, waited until he was able to buy a ticket from the counter, then pressed through the bustling throng towards a sign which indicated 'train for Constance'. When he arrived with no pass across the border, he knew it might be difficult and he would have to disembark and find his own way, which he was confident of doing. He could meet Annalise the other side. If Dreschler had done his work well, and Elser could only trust him that he had, she would have no problem. He showed his ticket at the barrier and wheeled his bicycle to the baggage van, where it was taken on board by a guard and his assistant. Elser signed a receipt for it, then stepped back amongst the hurrying crowds. He looked at his pocket watch – perhaps there was time. A loud whistle sounded nearby and made him jump and move quickly. If he was going to telephone, it had to be now.

He walked rapidly back to the barrier and eventually found the telephone – occupied. He waited. A fat Hausfrau was babbling on and she began to scream with laughter. Elser checked his pocket watch again; it was only a few minutes before the train was due to leave. He tapped on the glass of the booth. The woman ignored him at first, then indicated he should go away, or worse. Another loud warning whistle sounded. People all about him began running in panic. Elser glanced towards the barrier and knew the train's departure was imminent. He began wandering along the station wall and kept close to make headway against the flow of passengers from a train newly arrived at one of the platforms. And there, to the right of the barrier, he saw another telephone booth. There was a large poster of Adolf Hitler pasted on the glass. The folding doors were open. Elser leapt in, took up the receiver and began to dial the number he had memorized, which was the kitchen to the Burgerbraukeller. He bit his lip impatiently, waiting for the tone, but there was

238

none. The phone had been disconnected. Examining the box, he saw that the lead had been pulled out.

A final whistle blast prompted instant action. He jumped out of the box, ran through the barrier and leapt on to the train as it gathered momentum down the platform – destination the border town of Constance. The wooden seats were uncomfortable and the train rattled along as if the driver's home was on the lake and he wanted to be in his own dining room that evening for supper.

Elser peered out of the window into the chill morning. Within the crowded compartments, luggage, bags, boxes and almost every conceivable object that could be carried, it seemed to Elser, were stacked and packed into every space. The large peasants sitting opposite Elser smiled in re-assurance at his anxious expression. They seemed to have the air of carnivores from a Grimms' fairy tale. People were talking to each other animatedly, but the rattling and roaring of the train speeding south-west created a cocoon that absorbed all other noise. Elser had trusted his personal belongings, tool-box and zither, along with the bicycle, to the guard, but his case he kept between his feet. Nervously he reached for his pocket watch and managed to make out the time. It was approaching eleven. He looked up at the woman opposite, who was foraging for food in an open bag between them. Accidently she knocked against the case; it fell open to reveal a white-faced puppet, which sprawled on the floor. Elser bent to pick it up, but small hands had already taken the strings and were holding the clown on its feet. He turned to see a child, who had darted across the compartment and seized the toy, expertly dancing the arms and legs on strings. Elser grinned. The child remained stony-faced, as if manipulating the figure was a job not to be taken lightly, then large hands emerged, words were spat out at the child as if it was a dog and a firm grasp whisked it away. The puppet crumpled back to the floor. The large female opposite Elser leant forward, apologizing.

'I'm sorry, I didn't mean it!' she shouted above the noise of the train. Her husband loomed forward to join her, and the two large lined faces formed expressions of apology as spatula hands made gestures, accompanying further words that were lost to Elser, who merely nodded in acceptance.

'Forgive us!' shouted the male peasant. Elser smiled, quickly took up the puppet and replaced it in the case, which he locked carefully. He sat back in the uncomfortable upright position forced on them all by the wooden seats and looked again out at the passing countryside. The train entered a tunnel and in the half-light, reflected in the window, Elser saw the old woman lean back and cross herself. Some impulse made him follow suit, to the woman's satisfaction.

'Forgive me,' he whispered, and closed his eyes, to see only the innocent face of Annalise staring at him with a forlorn expression. Gritting his teeth, he began mumbling to himself. Eight hours to the border. He must ring her when the train arrived – he *must* get her out. And it would be already dark when he reached Constance.

21

Even through the large windows of Munich's airport lounge, the final acceleration of the Junkers 52 Tri-motor passenger aircraft could be heard loudly as the pilot gunned the engines before turning a wing and coming to a halt at the end of the runway. Immediately uniformed figures surrounded the plane. The door was opened on its corrugated metal side, and passengers began to emerge. Lights remained on the length of the landing strip, and inside and outside the airport buildings. What had started as mist earlier was fast becoming fog and thickening.

Schneider glanced at Meyer, who nodded at the silent rebuff.

'So I was wrong,' he murmured. 'He's here.'

Hitler stepped out of the aircraft and saluted. There was a roar of 'Sieg Heil' from the assembled guard of honour, then Hitler and his immediate entourage were ushered into the main building. Meyer watched as two other aircraft loomed out of the growing murk, their lights merging with those on the runway, and as they taxied towards the reception complex he realized that here was now the very core of the Third Reich. All the leaders of the various departments, brought by a tradition that Hitler had established and already assumed would last for a thousand years. Police, Brownshirts and the ever-vigilant SS, black-uniformed or in plain clothes, and some even disguised as airport workmen, surrounded the dignitaries as they were escorted through open doors into a spacious foyer, then out to the many waiting cars. One by one the Mercedes limousines whisked these very important people away towards the Burgerbraukeller across Rosenheimerplatz.

Schneider turned to his chief as they stood side by side on a small balcony overlooking the foyer, watching what had been carefully prepared and planned in detail. The crowds of well-wishers had been kept carefully at a distance; security was at the maximum. The bustle and rush of movement, paeons of salutation, cheers and cries from the crowd, all added to the minor spectacle.

'Even God would be pleased,' murmured Schneider.

Both men were proud of the efficiency and organization they represented. Both men knew their jobs and perhaps their lives depended on it. Meyer turned and looked out into the growing dusk, where the sun was almost lost in the murky grey fog. 'It's thickening,' he said, and sighed with exasperation. 'He'll never get off tonight.'

'He must be in Berlin tomorrow, sir. If I remind you, even the march to the Feld Herren Hall will take place without him.'

Meyer nodded. 'Yes, I read the report. I wonder why it's so urgent he returns so quickly? Surely the Chancellory could exist for a day without him?'

'Decisions of state, no doubt, sir.'

'I wonder where we're going next?' murmured Meyer.

'I'm sorry, sir?'

'West?' said Meyer, and his expression puzzled Schneider.

'Against Britain and France?' whispered the young officer.

Meyer nodded. 'We are at war with them, Wolf.'

'But nothing's happened, sir.'

'Yet,' said Meyer softly.

'Do you think it's imminent, sir?'

'What?'

'War with the western allies.'

'Declarations have been made . . . a stalemate never lasts for ever.'

'But surely they will come to their senses, sir? Make some kind of compromise? Even the English are calling it a "phoney" war . . . '

'They may call it what they will, but when Hitler moves it will not remain a *drôle du guerre* for long.'

'But they have seen what we have done in Poland, sir.'

Meyer smiled. 'Mark me, Wolf, that is only a beginning.'

A roar went up from below in the foyer as more Nazi dignitaries filed out to their waiting cars. Meyer's back was to the spectacle; he remained staring out at the fog. As if reading his thoughts, Schneider said quietly, 'The last express leaves for Berlin at 9.31 tonight, sir.'

Meyer's fists smacked into his palms behind his back. The decision was made. 'Then he must be on it. This airport will be closed in an hour. Make the arrangements for the Führer's special carriage to be connected to all the service leads. It should be coupled at the rear. Alert guards on all stations north that a special visitor is travelling. We will inform all the necessary parties that he is flying out. Only select names are to be informed of his real movements. I will assume the authority for this.'

'Yes, sir,' said Schneider. 'But the speech . . . ? If he begins soon after eight and, as is normal, two hours . . . '

'He must cut it short!' snapped Meyer.

'But, sir, he has come a long way and it might be difficult to persuade . . . '

'Use your imagination, then. Be inventive, Schneider.' Meyer pulled his fingers tightly into his black gloves and strode to the top of the stairs. Below, the Gestapo car awaited them outside the small terminal. Seeing Schneider lingering, Meyer barked, 'Come! I do not want to be late. He must start on time!'

Lying against the cold tiles of the scullery wall, Annalise no longer attempted to hide her tears. The day had been long and she had become distraught. Only the two young boys and maid had even acknowledged her presence when she tried to find privacy away from the bustle of the kitchen. Now, they ignored her.

Payerl suddenly thrust open the door. 'I've been looking for you everywhere!' he shouted. Then, with disgust, spat on the floor, unmoved by her sobbing. 'Work or leave!' Grabbing her awkwardly by the shoulders, he stared into her face, and immediately his attitude softened as he felt an unmistakable attraction, which he had always tried to conceal with a bluff exterior. 'Which?' he hissed. 'Choose now. Don't expect to find anything else; work doesn't come easy for the likes of you.'

Annalise was defiant. She began to take off her apron.

Payerl seized her arms in a tight grip and raised her from her feet, pulling her body towards him. 'You sluts are all the same! You think you can play a man with a smile and words of encouragement which you never mean! I know, I've seen enough of you come and go, and you're no different from the others.' He stared into her pale eyes, gritting his teeth in an attempt to control both anger and desire. 'If you had known me when I was younger, you wouldn't have dismissed me so lightly.'

Annalise was at first confused, then an inner confidence softened her face and brought a smile of pity to her eyes.

'So you leave!' he hissed. 'But when *I* say. Tonight you will work or get nothing!'

'He wants me to go,' murmured Annalise.

Payerl sneered, casting an eye to her naked bosom, wet with tears. 'He'll be back – for what he can get. You've been generous with the wrong people. I've watched you, and what has it got you? A cold bed in a filthy hostel. When you first came here I thought . . . ' He paused and his hands slid over the crisp cotton puffed shoulders of her dress, to rest lightly on the warm flesh of her neck. He distinctly felt the blood pulsing in her veins, and could control the frustration of past years no longer. He pulled her lips to his and kissed her with passion, which surprised even himself. She tried to drag herself away, tasting the stale tobacco on his thick, greying moustache, feeling the heat from his flushed, bloated cheeks, smelling the rancid sweat of a decomposing body. But he thrust his tongue deeper into her mouth – so she bit him.

With a scream, Payerl threw her against the tiled wall and sucked the blood from his tongue. Breathing heavily he stared across at the beautiful young woman whose hair had become dishevelled, but whose eyes remained self-possessed.

'You bitch!' he spat. He raised a fist and advanced towards her. The two boys and the scullery maid had hastily ducked out when Payerl arrived, so now the two of them, proprietor and waitress, were alone. That had given confidence to the burly man's advances, as it now provided the boldness to strike her. The swing door moved again, barely an arm's length reach from the pretty waitress, and Payerl glanced over his shoulder. Gestapo officer Otto Meyer stood in the doorway.

'Crying, Annalise?' he said softly. She dropped her head and began sobbing. Meyer crossed the small scullery, extended a gloved hand, and lifted her chin. 'Why?' he whispered, ignoring the large man beside her.

Payerl began babbling. 'Her boyfriend – he's gone off, Herr Obersturmbannführer . . . she's wasted herself on him. And now, look.' He pointed at her. 'Work!' he growled. 'Cry later!' Nervously he stepped back from Meyer and, seeing Schneider enter the scullery room, bowed to both officers and slipped out of the swing door back into the increasing hubbub of the kitchen.

Meyer smiled at Annalise. 'Gone?' he questioned sympathetically. She nodded. 'Not too far, I hope?' he said. She turned to face the wall, weeping into her hands. Schneider looked on, amused, but Meyer's natural feelings prompted him to reach out and, gently touching Annalise's hips, he turned her back smoothly to face him. She looked into Meyer's eyes as if he could solve her problem. Any fear of his uniform was dispelled by the power of emotion and her sense of loss. Her seeming innocence touched Meyer, and it was a genuine question when he asked, 'Does he love you?'

Annalise nodded.

In the beerhall itself, the military music had become

strident, stimulating the increasing atmosphere of excitement. Meyer acknowledged this, but something about the girl, some hunch, gave him patience to continue. Schneider began to explore the room, as an excuse to remain with his superior officer.

'And you love him . . . ? Obviously,' said Meyer.

'I asked him to stay,' sobbed Annalise. 'Only three more days . . . I get a bonus on the Armistice day. But he said . . .' Tears began to well up and her anguish attracted even Schneider, who also now recognized her but did not remember her name, as Meyer had.

'He'll be back, pretty thing,' said the young officer. Payerl, from the kitchen, shouted loudly, 'Annalise!'

She sniffed, began wiping tears with her handkerchief, curtsied quickly and pushed through the swing door into the kitchen and her duties for the night.

Schneider grinned at Meyer. 'If he doesn't come back, sir, with your permission . . . Frankly, I think she's . . .'

'Pregnant,' said Meyer quietly. Schneider was surprised, but continued to watch his commanding officer with growing fascination. Meyer was staring at the wall, seemingly oblivious of all the noise surrounding him, the important arrival, imminent events which would be part of history. His mind was racing, exploring, seeking clues.

'What kind of man?' murmured Meyer.

Schneider coughed. 'Not our business, sir.'

22

The Burgerbraukeller was almost filled to capacity by seven thirty, predominantly with Brownshirts or invited party members. Some civilians and numerous police uniforms were scattered amongst them. The Gestapo were hardly in evidence – the distinctive black uniform, with its swastika emblazoned on a red armband, was worn only by Otto Meyer and Wolf Schneider as, unobtrusively in their minds, they wandered about the building amongst the crowded tables and Meyer greeted several faces that he knew.

Outside the Bierkeller, the black uniforms were everywhere, awaiting Hitler's arrival at the Brauhaus which had been the Nazi party headquarters at the beginning of the struggle for real power in Germany. Old comrades, SA men who had started with Hitler on his road to dictator, enjoyed the privilege of maintaining the Führer's security in the hall, and circulated amongst their friends where, as Meyer noticed, they were already drinking far too much. He surveyed the noisy Bierkeller from the shadows, leaning against the wall beneath the gallery, with a vantage point directly across at the podium, lectern, microphones, and Hitler's pillar, where he would speak.

Schneider made his way across and stood beside his chief with a smile on his face.

'I have devised something, sir,' said Schneider and snapped his fingers to a waiting policeman, who arrived, came to attention and showed Meyer the cards Schneider had prepared. Clearly written on one was 'Thirty minutes', on another, 'Twenty minutes' and on a third, 'Five minutes'.

'They will be shown at the correct intervals, sir, so the Führer may conclude his speech in both his and our time.'

Meyer nodded. 'Good idea.'

'To allow fifteen minutes for the journey to the station, sir.'

Meyer turned to the policeman, who came to attention, clicked his heels and went back into the crowd and across to the podium, where he had been given a seat directly in front of the lectern so that Hitler would be able to see the cards, discreetly shown at the correct intervals.

'Perhaps,' murmured Meyer, 'this time, he will stick to the point.'

'I'm sorry, sir?' said Schneider, deliberately misunderstanding.

Meyer glanced at the young officer and smiled. 'Nothing, Wolf.' He remembered that criticism of the leadership was neither taught nor allowed in the new officers' schools. It was deemed unhealthy and even dangerous. For Meyer, loyalty could only be maintained, and would therefore always remain unaffected by criticism, which was natural and healthy for any political system to survive. If there was one failure in the Nazi aims, it was in the attempt to rid this all too human trait from the people. As an intelligent man, Meyer accepted that especially in war-time measures to control the population must be increased, but to deny them the right of an opinion and public discussion of what were personal observations, might well lead to a nation who paid lip service through fear, but whose hearts had been lost. What of the people who smiled and cheered? What of all this almost three thousand strong audience? Hitler's will had brought them so far – how long could he hold them, banish doubt, sway opposition, without applying to his own people those very ruthless measures he advocated for their enemies? And if that time came, thought Meyer, what would his part be and where would his loyalties lie then?

A roar went up from the assembly which was almost deafening. Meyer looked towards the entrance and checked his watch. It was a false alarm, but an indication of what was to come when Hitler finally arrived. The morale of everyone was at an all-time high. The atmosphere in the hall was one of euphoric anticipation. Germany had gone to war, once again under a new flag, beaten the enemy in an astonishingly short campaign and established a large area of occupied territory, regaining honour and proving to the world that Hitler was no idle boaster, and a force to be feared. Meyer saw von Eberstein and Weber arguing at the table nearby and, followed by Schneider, strolled across with an amused glint in his eye. The harsh features of Munich's police chief were focused on the more generous contours of Christian Weber's flushed expression. Appropriately, the one was drinking schnapps, the other beer in a large stein.

'I accept no responsibility,' snapped von Eberstein.

Weber only grinned and gulped from his glass. Meyer clicked his heels politely as von Eberstein acknowledged his presence. 'The security arrangements.' He wafted a hand at the SA man. 'Weber's authority exceeds even my own.'

'And, indeed, mine,' said Meyer quietly. 'I have none, here.' Von Eberstein lit a cigarette quickly and looked Meyer up and down.

'You've done well, Otto. Your father would have been proud.'

'Thank you,' said Meyer.

'The question of responsibility has arisen, Meyer. It is the Führer's explicit orders, I like to think it's merely a request, that the "old fighters" of the Party are to protect him,' - his gaze took in the entire room - 'here in this beerhall! But why? From what?'

Meyer nodded and glanced at Weber with instant dislike. 'Such a difficult task,' he said, then smiled coldly at von Eberstein. 'We have the easier one of guarding the Führer when he steps out into the world.'

Weber slammed down his stein of beer. 'This, Meyer, *is* his world. Look around you. We made it and we gave it to him!'

Meyer looked stonily for a moment at Weber, nodded his goodbye to von Eberstein, then stepped away from the table exactly as another roar came from the crowd, this time to herald the first Nazi dignitaries, Dietrich, Kriebel, Rosenberg, Frank, Streicher, Bouhler, even Goebbels, Ribbentrop and finally Himmler himself, who gave no acknowledgement that he had even seen Meyer across the room and, amidst the cheering went directly to his allotted seat around the podium.

'It will be time soon, sir,' whispered Schneider. Meyer shrugged and leaned closer so that the young officer could hear. 'It's not our problem, Wolf.'

'No, sir.'

'Just be sure he finishes and we can get him outside in time for the train. The carriage has been prepared?'

Schneider nodded, 'Yes, sir. It will be connected very shortly when the express Pullmans are assembled.'

'Good,' he said, and checked his watch. As the noise began to die down within the beerhall, he heard another roar, this time from outside. Mentally he checked the positions of his men and was confident that they would keep the crowds at bay when Hitler walked from his car, crossed to the entrance of the Bierkeller and stepped into the arms of his beloved comrades.

The band at the back of the hall struck up the Baden Weiler march and suddenly everyone was on their feet, roaring 'Sieg Heil – Heil Hitler!' The great man had arrived.

Meyer was impassive, surveying the room again and again for any sign, any clue, any threat of violent behaviour towards the Führer. There was nothing, only a great wave of devotion that was almost palpable, and he could feel it, inexplicably, throughout his body – it was the quality in the crowd that Hitler was renowned for utilizing, manipulating for his own ends.

The Führer had many personalities, as Meyer knew, but what emerged when he was confronted with this atmosphere, for which any actor would have sold his soul, was something which always astonished Meyer, even though he had become familiar with it – the controlled gestures and staring eyes, the almost demonic presence of this man who absorbed the world, feeding from the minds of others as if a parasite. He would start slowly, estimating the power he was absorbing, and then build with force and conviction until he could persuade anyone to do anything. It was a pattern Meyer had come to know and never ceased to wonder at, despite his personal knowledge of the man.

The Führer threaded his way through the crowds, which parted respectfully but with the noisy exuberance he seemed to relish, and when Hitler stepped up on to the podium, the sustained cheering lasted fully seven minutes. The microphones had been pre-set and tested with typical expertise by the numerous technicians who were assembled to one side, and had already started transmission to all of Germany on the radio.

Arms spread on the lectern, leaning forward with an expression of growing seriousness, the Führer waited patiently for the noise to die down. Meyer tapped Schneider, and the two of them made their way quickly along the back wall and pushed through the kitchen door to join the staff who were gathered about. Even the zither player, who had been sitting on a cupboard, slipped to the floor and stood at half attention. Seeing the two black uniforms, Payerl bowed, and there was a moment's silence as if everyone held their breath. The beerhall had gone quiet in anticipation of Hitler's first words. Meyer glanced up at the clock on the kitchen wall, the only noise interrupting the absolute silence, ticking away the seconds. He checked his pocket watch by it; it was absolutely correct – perfect time. Ten minutes past eight.

Georg Elser wheeled his bicycle across the cobbled square and propped it alongside several others outside the café. He bent painfully to take off his bicycle clips. It had been a long train journey to Friedrichshafen, but the steamer connection he had taken across the lake had cleared his head, as it had saved him time. The small station stops along the north shore always added several hours to travel and he had become impatient to be over the border and, more importantly, in

251

Switzerland, safe. He stepped inside the café, where the room was crowded but strangely silent. He found a seat just inside the door, against the window, and glanced around the room. All the faces were staring towards the bar, where the large, unshaven proprietor served beer as he stepped back from the radio which he had just adjusted. For the moment there was crackling, then again the room was completely quiet with anticipation.

Elser glanced at his pocket watch exactly as the guttural voice began hesitantly to talk about beginnings which were already in the past. He looked up at the clock upon the wall above the many bottles behind the bar. Hitler had started late, which was even better than he could have hoped. Nervously the pretty young waitress, who had recognized the attractive stranger with anxious eyes, made her way through the quiet customers and bent close to whisper in Elser's ear.

'Hello,' she said. 'Coffee?'

Elser smiled.

'And you'd like cream?'

Elser nodded, seeing pleasure in the girl's face.

'Are you passing through again?'

'Yes.'

'Going far?'

Elser broke a cigarette in half, took out a match, lit it and inhaled, watching the girl smooth down the skirt of her dirndl, catching herself in a reflection on the window. Even the dimmed light complimented her clear features, as she knew. She seemed reluctant to turn away, and Elser touched her arm. She leant close again, and Elser asked her quietly. 'Have you a telephone here?'

The waitress looked around as though searching for one, but actually looking to see if there was a quick way to the back room, past the customers grouped around the radio at the bar listening to the increasing resonance of the voice, occasionally muffled by static.

'We can go behind them,' she hissed. 'I'll show you.'

He stood up and followed her past several empty tables at

252

the rear to a door into a short corridor, where one electric light indicated the entrance to a small lounge. She took a phone from a small table and handed it to him.

'You must ask for the operator. They will tell you the charge. And, please,' she pleaded, 'be quick, my father won't like it.'

Elser smiled, and the girl blushed at thoughts that flooded into her mind. She remembered him very well. He didn't look much from a distance, but the eyes and teeth and something else about him had lingered.

'What's your name?' she asked.

'Georg.'

'Gerda,' she said. 'You were here before.'

'Once,' said Elser.

'I remember.'

No words were said between them as Elser gently took the telephone, listening to the invective on the radio from the café.

'Are you going back to Switzerland?'

'How do you reach the operator?' said Elser, ignoring her.

The girl pouted and dialled for him. He listened until there was a voice at the other end of the receiver.

'Would you like your coffee here?'

Elser nodded.

'I'll bring it,' she said, ran her hands over her hips and stepped out into the corridor. Elser gave the number and waited. It was almost two minutes before he heard a ringing tone. Grinding out the cigarette butt in an ashtray, he leant against the cupboard full of porcelain and clasped the receiver to his ear, gripping it with knuckles showing white. Six times it rang, then a voice answered, hissing on the other end. It was Payerl.

'I want to speak to Annalise, please.' Like an echo, Elser could distinctly hear Hitler's voice from the kitchen of the Burgerbraukeller as clearly as it came from the wireless in the café. With an oath, Payerl slammed down the phone.

253

Otto Meyer watched curiously as Payerl replaced the receiver of the kitchen phone. Roars of 'Sieg Heil' from the appreciative audience thundered through the building, so loud that some of the waitresses put their hands to their ears. Hitler had obviously taken one of the deliberate pauses for which he was famous, as he gradually sucked in the minds of his willing listeners in preparation for the core of his text. By the time he presented his simple logic with wide appeal, there would be no dissension. Meyer could hear the process of gradual hypnosis taking place and, even familiar as it was, it had a chilling allure. Payerl moved from the phone and hissed to several of the staff who were commenting on the speech that they be instantly silent. Meyer caught the burly man's florid features and patronizing smile as he nodded back.

'Who was it?' mouthed Meyer, with curiosity, over the noise.

Payerl merely shrugged and pointed to Annalise. 'For her,' he said.

Meyer suddenly felt cold – instinct was dictating to his intelligence, something was happening. Schneider was oblivious of everything but the enveloping aura from the Führer in the beerhall. Meyer stared at the young waitress, huddled against the tiled wall, alone near the scullery door, again in tears. In the beerhall the sounds died down as Hitler waited for silence. Stepping softly, Meyer crossed to Annalise and lifted her chin with a gloved hand, gazing into her face with a hard expression as if she might know something.

Hitler began again, quickening his pace, selling platitudes, describing what was known, creating an idealistic world without substance, invoking history as a witness and possibly excuse for events to come and actions in the future that would be forced upon the new lenient, almighty Germany. As he reached a phrase which meant that all transgressors would be punished, which produced an immediate roar from the packed crowds, many of whom leapt up from the tables, Meyer detected the plaintive but urgent sound of the telephone once again. Immediately he strode across to it, pushed Payerl aside and slowly lifted the receiver to listen. He said nothing in answer to the questions asked, merely turned to face Annalise Palin and beckoned. She crossed the room and put the receiver to her ear. She recognized the voice instantly.

'Georg.'

Meyer looked at Schneider and snapped his fingers a second time at the young officer, who crossed briskly to Meyer.

'Another phone – fast!'

'What is it?' whispered Annalise, putting a finger to her ear as the noise in the beerhall continued, now seemingly with every other sentence Hitler uttered.

'You must do as I say,' she heard. 'Go back to the hostel. Leave now. Take the night train to Constance. Use the pass and cross the border. I will meet you. You will be safe. Everything will be well. I promise. Nothing else matters. Put down the phone and leave.'

Annalise shook her head in confusion. 'Georg, I can't.'

'Now!' came the voice quietly.

'Please, Georg,' whispered the girl, her eyes full of tears, staring up at Meyer as three thousand voices began chanting, 'Heil Hitler. Sieg Heil!' from the Bierkeller. Then she heard a click on the line as if someone else had taken up another phone.

'What are you saying, Georg?' she shouted above the noise. 'Where are you?'

Meyer snapped his fingers at Payerl. 'Who is he?'

'Her boyfriend,' murmured the proprietor.

'Name?'

'Georg,' shrugged Payerl, ' . . . Elser.'

Meyer frowned, then realized the implications of the name. 'Elser,' he hissed, and took a deep breath to control welling anger directed only at himself. How could he have

255

been such a fool? He had known all along there was something, and now here it was. He reached out and took the phone gently from Annalise, then firmly directed her towards the wall. She struggled for one moment, but realized she was trapped and became still. Meyer put the receiver to his ear. The noise in the beerhall drowned all else, then suddenly died, as if at a gesture from the Führer.

'Elser,' said Meyer.

'Yes,' came a voice.

'Where are you?' asked Meyer. For one second he thought there would be an answer – but then the phone went dead. He slammed the receiver into its cradle, grasped Annalise's arm and, as Hitler began his invective again, led the girl quickly through the swing door into the scullery. Annalise's eyes were wide and frightened.

Meyer, controlling his voice to speak softly, asked, 'How long have you known him?'

'Not yet a year, sir.'

'Where is he from?'

'Württemberg.'

'And . . . ?'

'Here, sir, Munich.'

'Where does he live?'

'Near, sir. Turkenstrasse 94, but he is . . . '

'Before?'

'Well . . . Bodensee, somewhere . . . '

'Where, exactly?'

'I don't know, sir,' sobbed Annalise, and tears began to fall, making rivulets on her cheeks. Meyer's face was only inches from hers, and even if his voice remained soft, she could see his eyes full of anger.

'Where?!'

'In Switzerland, sir, somewhere.'

Meyer let out a sigh of astonishment. It was as if he was listening to the impossible, as if he had been staring at a puzzle for so long without a solution and was now being given the key.

'What does he do?' he asked. 'What work?'

'He's only . . . a . . . an artisan.'

'An artisan,' said Meyer, seeking some significance.

'Yes, sir . . . he makes things.'

'Makes things?' Meyer repeated again, and now he knew.

'Mends things, sir,' she whispered.

The audience roared again loudly from the Bierkeller; there was the sound of much applause.

'Makes things, mends things,' whispered Meyer to himself, remembering the face at the police station, recalling the little man one morning at a table in the Burgerbraukeller, seated alone.

'Yes, sir, and he . . . plays the zither.'

'A zither player.'

'Yes, sir,' nodded Annalise. There was even significance in this, Meyer knew from sheer instinct, and yet could not find it.

'Where – is – he – now?'

'Constance, sir . . . at the border.'

Meyer closed his eyes as the applause in the beerhall dwindled. Georg Elser was the man's name. Now he knew the face and remembered the eyes from the police station; and that morning at the Burgerbraukeller, he had noticed the man wearing a sheath to cover the stump of his little finger. One other place he had seen that – the torn flesh of a hand in an inn at Königsbron, clutching the remains of a zither. If destiny had brought Hitler to power, then fate had given him this gift of . . .

'Georg Elser,' he muttered.

'Yes, sir,' sobbed Annalise.

Meyer exploded, 'Scheisser!!'

Seizing the young waitress, he dragged her with him to the swing door where everyone in the kitchen, having heard the obscenity, was staring. Silence had fallen in the Bierkeller as Hitler's eyes ranged over his audience. Meyer's eyes remained fixed on Schneider's face across the kitchen as he explored all the possibilities of instant action. He glanced up

257

at the clock, which had begun ticking away the minutes towards the hour of nine.

'Do you think we can clear the hall, Schneider?' snapped Meyer.

'No, sir,' answered Schneider, astonished. Meyer looked around wildly, seeking inspiration and finding none. 'The speech, sir,' said Schneider quickly. 'It would be impossible to stop it. The wireless throughout Germany . . . The entire nation is listening.'

Meyer looked into the girl's eyes as if he could read something. If the man was at the border, there could no longer be a threat, could there?

'What is it, sir?' asked Schneider. There was only Turkenstrasse, thought Meyer. He would have to start from there – and immediately. 'Take over, Schneider,' he ordered. 'Immediately the Führer's finished I want this hall cleared!'

'But why, sir?'

'I want a thorough search.'

'For what, sir?'

'Anything suspicious. Something . . . '

'Sir, you are not making yourself clear. I don't under-stand.' Turkenstrasse 94, thought Meyer. There was *something* – he knew it, he could feel it with everything in his blood that had made him a policeman. He had been chosen for his present duties because he had proved to be exceptional and his abilities had been trusted, as he now trusted this instinct. 'I want all the borders alerted for Georg Elser. He might have a work pass. He must be stopped.'

Annalise stared wide-eyed at the Gestapo officer and tried to pull away. She began sobbing hysterically. Meyer slapped her. He had already decided to go out through the garden; the girl would lead him to the lodgings.

'Sir, may I say . . . ' began Schneider.

An ovation began in the hall, followed by applause, drowning the words of protest from the young officer. Meyer bellowed above the noise, 'Do exactly as I say. That is an order!' He pushed Annalise out of the back door and escorted

258

her briskly through the garden to the front of the building, where his car was waiting.

'Turkenstrasse 94,' he said.

'Where is that, sir?' asked the driver.

'She'll tell us,' answered Meyer. He thrust her into the back seat, slammed the door of the car, which nosed through the crowds then accelerated down the road, closely followed by a second Mercedes containing four black-uniformed SS troopers armed with machine guns.

The two cars stopped as Annalise pointed to the entrance of Elser's lodgings. Meyer stepped out and, followed by the helmeted SS guards, he entered the courtyard through the archway, crossed to the door and rapped hard. A light showed between the ill-fitting black-out curtains and, after knocking a second time, Meyer saw a face appear at the small window in the door.

A bolt was thrown, a lock turned and a moment later, there in front of Meyer, stood the blowsy figure of Elser's landlady, Ilse Guber.

'Yes?' she whispered.

'You have a lodger here by the name of Georg Elser?'

'He's gone.'

Meyer nodded and stepped back. At the unspoken command three of the SS guards plunged into the building, one of them pinioning the woman against the wall. The other two ran down the corridor and entered the lounge, where their presence caused shouts of alarm from the assembled group. Only old Herzog stared defiantly at the black uniforms. Meyer entered slowly, casting an eye about him as he walked to the lounge area at the fire in the grate, the mantelpiece with bric-à-brac, Hitler's portrait, the wireless, the swastika flag, the clock against the wall. Flames leapt in the grate, coal and wood crackled, the clock ticked and, as one of the old men turned off the radio, everyone held their breath, frightened at the intrusion. Meyer took in the room, examining faces. The landlady hovered in front of a guard.

'Which is his room?' asked Meyer.

She pointed with a shaking hand. Meyer continued down the corridor, opened the door and saw that the room was empty, awaiting the next occupant. He closed the door and turned to see that some of the lodgers had followed him.

'He lived here?'

The landlady nodded. Old Herzog stepped forward and grinned. 'But he worked in the cellar.'

Meyer's eyes narrowed. 'Show me,' he said.

The padlocks were released, the door flaps opened and two of Meyer's men descended the steps quickly, found the lamps and lit the wicks. When he stepped into the damp workroom Meyer's mind was racing. He had certainly found something, his blood told him that. Instinct and experience had combined over the years to give him a 'feel', a sense of the unusual. An artisan who made things, mended things . . . a zither player with his own workroom . . .

'Convenient,' he murmured.

'He spent hours down here,' said Herzog from the top of the steps.

'Shut up!' snapped one of the guards.

'Let him speak,' said Meyer. 'Bring him down here.'

The landlady followed the old man until they were both standing beside the bench.

'Hours, you say?' questioned Meyer.

'Inventing,' nodded Herzog confidentially.

'What?' asked Meyer.

Herzog shook his head. 'He never told me.' Then his voice dropped to a whisper, 'I think it was something special.'

Meyer stared into the eyes of the old man, then looked at the landlady. The lamps cast grotesque moving shadows across their faces, animating expressions frozen in fear. Only the old man continued to volunteer information nervously. 'Hour after hour,' he said. 'Into the night, sometimes. All night, even. Why, I've seen him on many mornings, unshaven, looking terrible, as if he hadn't slept. Dedicated . . . A good workman. Do you know, he mended my watch, which never kept good time?' He took it out of his

260

pocket. 'And now,' he held it up, 'it hasn't even lost a second.'

Meyer glanced at the white face, which showed eleven minutes to the hour of nine.

'And furniture,' said the landlady softly, then coughed.

'Furniture?' murmured Meyer.

'Yes, he did a very good job on many of the pieces I needed repairing.'

'He even built a cabinet for us in the lounge,' interrupted Herzog, now oblivious of the uniform and merely talking to a new face. 'You should see it. The craftwork is excellent. I was in business, you understand, and therefore I appreciate such things.'

Meyer nodded. 'Clocks and furniture,' he said aloud, seeking something else.

'Then it was so much better,' said the landlady, 'than working in the quarry.'

The single word alerted Meyer immediately, and only then did he realize that this dishevelled woman was the one he had seen in the police station, who had successfully pleaded for Elser's release.

'He had such fine hands, you see, Herr Officer. Not delicate, but sensitive. Clever hands,' she finished, and then she too recognized the face beneath the black peaked cap from the many uniforms she saw daily; it was the Gestapo officer she had encountered when she had gone to extricate Elser from his 'awkward' situation.

'He worked in the quarry?' asked Meyer flatly.

Herzog began laughing. 'He'd come home all hours, dirt and grime sticking to him.' He shook his head. 'It wasn't for the likes of him, not hard labour. He was a craftsman.' He held up his pocket watch again, 'An expert, here's the proof.'

'What did he do at the quarry?' asked Meyer softly.

The landlady looked at old Herzog, who giggled. 'He blew it up.'

Meyer closed his eyes. 'Arrest them all!' he said.

261

23

Georg Elser thanked the pretty waitress in the lounge of the small café at the border town of Constance. He paid her for the telephone call and drank the coffee she brought him. He went back into the main room; moving discreetly, he watched the rapt audience of customers who continued to give all their attention to Hitler's voice on the wireless. Only as he left did several faces look up with mild curiosity that someone should be leaving, missing the Führer's words commemorating the historical event and describing with grandiose eloquence a visionary's version of a future that would be available to every man, woman and child in Germany.

Elser put on his bicycle clips, but the pain in his knees changed his mind, and he began wheeling the bicycle across the cobbled square. The only eyes on him were those of the waitress, who looked longingly through the window until he merged with the shadows and disappeared into the darkness, leaving the square once again empty, illuminated only by the dim border lights. She looked at the clock on the wall as Hitler's voice ranted with threats against the western allies. It was almost nine o'clock.

Creaking bicycle wheels marked Georg Elser's route into the night as he made his way behind the border post. The sloping grass led towards a copse, at the bottom of which was a stream. Once across this, if he successfully avoided the border patrols, which normally consisted of two guards wandering over a fixed area, then he would be in Switzerland. If, as a result of the war, there was increased security, then that would be a problem he would have to face when he came to it, and if he was caught by the Swiss authorities and interred, he had already prepared himself to tell the truth. In a coat pocket were a postcard of the Bierkeller, some brick chippings, wire, and a detonator, which he had de-activated, but would prove with the other items, certainly with forensic evidence from the Munich beerhall and his description of the bomb, that he had killed Hitler. After that it would be for the Swiss and the allies to decide what to do with him. If he had created such an annihilating checkmate so early on in the game, the chances were he would be declared a hero and the present stalemate of war would be negotiated into peace.

He stopped and listened. The wireless in the border post was turned up loud and Hitler's voice was drowned by an ovation, seemingly in full agreement with his advocation of further aggression and intimidating promises of violence. Against his better sense, Elser turned the handlebars and began to wheel his bicycle nearer to the building, which was lit by the dim outside light. He stopped again, remaining in deep shadow. It was only thirty metres to Switzerland, and it must be less than twenty minutes to the explosion. The sense of elation inside him gave him a strange confidence. Now he knew it would happen. It would be the will of God. He would listen for only a few more minutes, then once across the border it might be possible to hear the silence that would result when the bomb went off, cutting communications instantly with the Burgerbraukeller.

There was still Annalise. He was sure she would come to him that night; she would look at her pass, realize what it meant, go back to the hostel, pack her things, take the train and cross the border, where he would meet her on the other side in the Swiss station. He was prepared to wait several days and even phone on the morrow if she was foolish enough to remain. The only security he had in his mind was that if she was there she would be in the kitchen with the other staff, where the walls were thick. Only those in the hall itself would be in danger. He closed his eyes tight, offering a silent prayer for those about to die.

'You!' said a voice. Georg Elser squinted into two torch beams and could see the unmistakable glint of gun metal on the muzzles of two rifles. The helmets of the guards were German. 'And where are you going, little man?' said one. The other guard thrust a cartridge into the breach and slammed down the bolt of his Mauser. Elser raised his hands slowly, high above his head, relinquishing his grip on the bicycle. It fell on to the wet grass between him and the German border patrol. He had been caught.

Meyer's driver flashed lights at the crowd, which parted to allow the car access to the pavement immediately in front of the Bierkeller.

'Watch the girl!' snapped Meyer, and stepped out of the dark Mercedes. He went through the first doors and paused, remaining in shadow, his eyes surveying the dense seated crowds stimulated by Hitler's invective and awaiting any signal to roar their response yet again. Meyer watched Schneider's man quickly place a card on the podium in front of the speaker, indicating that the Führer should wind up his speech. He checked his watch, having noticed the cars outside for Hitler and his entourage moving into position through the growing fog. Everything was planned. The security screen was as tight as ever. No one was allowed access to the beerhall, and if Elser was indeed in Constance and indeed a potential instrument of death, which at that moment Meyer acknowledged was mere supposition, how could there be a problem here? The staff were in the kitchen, and there was no threat from them.

He quickly gave instructions that the crowd outside be moved back twenty metres. There was always the possibility of a high-powered rifle, which was, in fact, Meyer's greatest fear, but there were sufficient SS men outside to spot even the intimation of trouble. Meyer checked his watch again; it was now gone nine. He began to relax. They'd get Elser, of that he was sure, but knew he'd be happier when Hitler was out of the building and he was convinced that no longer could anything go wrong.

Behind the panel set flush with the beading of the pillar directly above Hitler's podium, where the balcony area was packed with SA men and bodies leant over the balustrade and faces peered in awe that they were so near to the Führer of greater Germany, Elser's device activated. As he had pre-set, the wires were becoming taut and had begun to exert pressure on the wedges, separating the strikers from the detonator caps. The many hours which had passed when the clocks had been unable to chime, had released the mech-anism for the strikers to hit hard where there was no longer a bell, only the wood that separated them from igniting the explosive, and now those wedges were being drawn away by the tightening wires. A whirring noise had started, adding to the regular ticking, as pressure exerted on the turning axis of the clocks' hands began to interfere with the mechanism and disrupt the second hand, set within its own circle on the face of each clock.

A roar went up in the Bierkeller as Hitler re-emphasized Germany's conquest and now proven military might. As the Führer absorbed the ovation with silent pleasure, a last card was placed on his podium which said five minutes. He wafted an arm and created order and quiet expectation. Meyer had been making his way around the back of the hall, where he found Schneider behind the police chief's group. He beckoned to the police chief, who discreetly excused himself from the table as Hitler began a summing up, and in a moment was open-mouthed at Meyer's whispered sug-gestion.

'Impossible,' he said.

'I repeat,' snapped Meyer, 'I want you to clear the place the very moment the Führer steps out!'

The SA man, Weber, curious at the whispered confronta-tion behind him in the shadows, also left the table and joined the two men, listening to Meyer's urgent request. 'Clear the place?' he murmured. 'You try.'

'Von Eberstein,' said Meyer, appealing to the police chief, who shrugged.

'It is a question of responsibility.'

Weber nodded and grinned. 'And I will not accept that responsibility.'

'You are a fool,' said Meyer.

Weber shook his head. 'There's nothing here, look around you. What can anyone do here? There are no weapons aimed at the Führer. In this place they are only for his enemies. Here is where it all began, and we are the heart of the National Socialist Party. No one would dare do anything here. Nothing will happen. Go into the kitchen and get yourself a beer.'

His voice was drowned by Hitler's, resounding in the great hall as it echoed from the walls of so many homes throughout Germany. Weber made to return to his table, but Meyer seized his arm.

'Weber!' he began, but his voice was lost as everyone in the beerhall stood up, cheered, bellowed 'Sieg Heil' and applauded so loudly Meyer thought the roof would come down.

'I will not accept responsibility,' mouthed Weber.

'Then I will!' exploded Meyer. Hitler, with a stoic expression surveying his loyal followers, had concluded his speech. Weber, surprised that it was unusually early, raised an arm for the band at the back of the hall to begin. Instantly the military music seemed to incite the Brownshirts to even greater efforts and the ovation actually increased. Meyer checked his watch – it was coming up to nine eight; they had to get him out. He pulled Schneider close and shouted in his ear, 'Remember, do exactly what I have instructed!'

Schneider nodded, still bewildered but prepared to obey an order from his commanding officer.

Meyer pushed through the crowd along the back of the wall and made for the entrance through which Hitler would soon pass out of the building. Already the Führer was leaving, talking to several faces he knew. At least he had stepped down from the podium, and the other Nazi dignitaries, Goebbels, Hess and the crowd that had been immediately around the speaker, were making their way towards him. Meyer gave orders to his men outside, six of whom ran into the beerhall and began pressing the Brownshirts back from the entrance area.

Meyer stepped outside and saw the first cars arriving. He checked his watch. He had to get Hitler out by nine thirteen, nine fourteen at the latest, just to be able to make the schedule with the express. He had calculated the distance to the Bahnhof from the Burgerbraukeller and in this fog . . . He looked across the other side of the road, where he could just make out his own car and the waitress seated tearfully in the back. She could wait until later; he would deal with her when he had dealt with the immediate problem of these Brownshirts. Anything could still happen, and his eyes roved over the crowd. Pressed back by his men, they were cheering as the leaders of the country got into their cars one by one and were whisked away into the murky darkness. Then the Führer stepped out and a roar went up, which he acknowledged gracefully. He shook hands with Meyer, who snapped to attention, and in the next moment, to Meyer's relief, Hitler was in his car and on the way to Munich's railway station, where the waiting special carriage was coupled to the rear of the northbound express.

Meyer checked his watch and swore – the cars were running late; it was almost nine fifteen, but the improvised arrangements had gone according to plan, Schneider's 'cards' had worked discreetly and it was with pleasure and pride that Meyer reminded himself that what had been his responsibility had been executed precisely, according to his orders. He would thank Schneider and compliment him; then he remembered that the young officer had been asked to clear the hall and would need help. He stepped through the entrance and saw Schneider on the podium, at the micro-

267

phone, adjusting the pitch, being applauded by the SA men as Weber, quite clearly, was inciting the band to play louder. The Brownshirts, as Meyer could see, were becoming belligerent and uncooperative.

'Gentlemen!' shouted Schneider into the microphone, 'I want you to clear the hall immediately!'

Meyer hesitated. He could do no more than Schneider was attempting at this very moment, and to push through the crowds would be difficult and unnecessary if Schneider succeeded in making them move. He turned to look out into the fog, where some dim lights showed and he could see the girl's face. Now there was this other problem – Elser and his Annalise.

It was only a suspicion, but for a moment he had felt sure he had stumbled across something. This insignificant little man he had almost forgotten and his attractive girl, this pretty waitress who seemed, as she probably actually was, so innocent. Meyer had never liked coincidence; it disturbed him. There was something strange – all Meyer's instincts told him that – but the threat was over, Hitler was gone. The little man could do nothing with the carriage at the Bahnhof. It had been a last-minute decision to put Hitler on the train, and the special carriage was always under guard. The old man in Elser's lodgings had said he 'blew up a quarry', but he would certainly not be able to do the same with the express which would shortly be moving out of the platform of Munich's station and, mused Meyer, he'd certainly accomplished nothing here.

He turned to stare through the open doors into the lit beerhall full of Brownshirts. They were bellowing to Schneider on the podium their disapproval of his suggestion to leave immediately and, thought Meyer, perhaps they were right. What would he do if the hall was clear? What was he looking for? He glanced at his watch; it was nine nineteen. The crowd outside remained, expecting other dignitaries to appear. Meyer saw his men coping with them admirably. Several cars awaited some of the police and SA leaders, but in the main, the occasion was over. Yet something continued to disturb Meyer. He had discovered too much about this little man. The craftsman, the perfectionist, the time he had spent not only with his girl, but here. He looked about him and again through the short, tunnel-like entrance into the throng, most of whom had now taken up the Horst Wessel song, almost drowning out the band. The little man from Württemberg called Georg Elser: what significance could he possibly have?

Meyer smiled to himself, realizing that perhaps once again he was being over zealous. He heard Schneider inside, in a last desperate attempt to have his order obeyed, shout into the microphone 'Now!' Meyer shook his head. He would talk to the girl, find and interrogate the man, but only out of professionalism. There would be plenty of time. He had thought there was something and, being proven wrong, he dismissed Georg Elser in his mind and discounted the case built up against him. The facts spoke for themselves. The evening had passed without incident and what had happened?

'Nothing,' Meyer whispered.

Behind the panel in the pillar of the Bierkeller which supported so many tons of steel and concrete, within the cavity Georg Elser, the little man from Württemberg, had created, the second hands on both clocks traced the last seconds to nine twenty. The taut wires pulled at the wedges. Fifty-eight. The wedges slipped away. Fifty-nine. The strikers slammed into the detonator caps. Sixty. The detonators ignited the explosive.

Alone in the corner of the large room at the back of the customs and police post in Constance, Georg Elser sat patiently waiting for an officer he had been told would see him. At a desk across the room, one of his captors was making out a report, and the scratching pen was the only other sound apart from the ticking clock above the man's head. Elser looked up and saw it was nine twenty precisely. He closed his eyes.

Silhouetted for a split second against the flash of white and yellow in the entrance of the Burgerbraukeller, Meyer was then hurled across the road, thrown on to his car and spread-eagled against its side. Stunned, he crumpled on to the road, hearing – mingled with a mighty thunderclap that still resounded in his head – a strange roaring sound as if from an approaching express train. The noises of grinding steel, collapsing masonry and falling concrete gave way to animal-like cries of pain, screams of shock and shouts of fear within the beerhall. All about him, outside, there was both alarm and confusion. He heard running feet, then hands were grasping him and talking, asking questions. He looked up, disorientated, wondering what had happened, to see the faces of two of his men. The dream-like quality of the moment began to fade, to be replaced by harsh reality and horrifying sounds of the maimed and injured.

Meyer got to his feet, staggered a moment, then stumbled towards the entrance of the beerhall. He heard from somewhere a steady flow of oaths seemingly directed against every living thing, and only as he ran up the steps and hesitated before plunging into the great hall, did he realize the words were coming from his own mouth.

'Schneider!' he bellowed, and then saw the full extent of the damage done to the interior of the Burgerbraukeller, which froze him where he stood. The centre of the roof had collapsed. The pillar behind the podium where Hitler had been speaking had disintegrated. The gallery and balconies had fallen, together with the steel, concrete, bricks and mortar, directly on to the central area, where minutes before the entire hierarchy of the Third Reich had been assembled. It would have been astonishing had it not been so appalling. The smoke and dust, swaying lights and still falling debris from parts of the sagging ceiling, which had been torn apart and was now open to the night sky, obscured a clear view of the source of the bomb. Even fog had begun to sink into the great hall, but Meyer was already calculating from the angle of the beams and the position of the fallen rubble where the bomb might have been placed. Then the screams of the maimed and injured again flooded into his mind and he became conscious of bodies – prone, squirming, staggering and stumbling about. Perhaps the middle ages had had a special insight in their descriptions of Hell, he thought. They'd got it right. This was it.

Meyer paused only a second longer, hearing the welcome sirens of approaching fire engines and ambulances. He saw a number of his men from the guard outside, their black uniforms contrasting harshly within the now dulled interior, making their way amongst the victims. He knew, as a witness to this catastrophe, these first impressions would never leave him, but his professionalism dictated action beyond emotion, and he heard himself barking out orders rapidly. The gravely injured were left to the ambulance teams, who rushed in wearing white coats and immediately started to tend their charges. The wounded who could move were helped to one side, for fear the central structure would collapse further. The dead who could be identified were respectfully put on stretchers and their bodies placed together at one side of the entrance to the Bierkeller. Then, as the firemen arrived, the more unpleasant business of extracting the trapped victims, both the dead and the horribly maimed, from the tons of steel and concrete accumulated by the explosion began with a cold attitude Meyer could only admire. People were being sick, crying, hysterical. Nurses arrived. Two field telephones were brought in by army personnel, and suddenly there were Wehrmacht soldiers everywhere. The Brownshirts, few of them unscathed, most of them bloodied, had grouped themselves against the walls of the building. Meyer's men began escorting them out, roughly handling all those that lingered either from curiosity or incapacity.

Meyer watched the firemen dragging at the rubble and realized that if a miracle had saved Hitler, there would be none for Schneider. His heart hardened as he felt a twinge of emotion which he could not afford if he was to solve the immediate problem. Weber and von Eberstein were nowhere to be seen. Most of the high-ranking SA officers had either already gone or scuttled from the building seconds after the explosion, fearing it to be only the first of several. Their distance from the pillar had obviously provided them with some advantage.

Amidst the slow order being created from chaos and confusion, Meyer stared at the collapsed structure, then turned and looked at the opposite pillar; if a bomb had been placed, it would have been at ground level or in the upper panelling. He turned back and stared up at the gaping hole in the roof, where he could now feel fine drizzle entering with the fog. Only the weather had saved Hitler and, in fact, as he realized, preserved his own job. Call it luck or fate, thought Meyer, Hitler was alive, and he would not have been had he finished his speech, as initially planned. Obviously God knew more than man and had other plans for the Führer.

For a moment Meyer observed the bustling action around him, appreciating the increasing efficiency of the emergency services. It was only as Schneider's mutilated body was dragged from the huge pile of debris that tears of anger formed in Meyer's eyes. He watched the firemen bring the body down into the crater, then heave it on to the broken floorboards, where two ambulance men knelt and gently placed the body on a stretcher, even though it was obviously beyond saving and, perhaps, recognition, to anyone except Schneider's commanding officer.

The anger welled in Meyer as he saw the two men lift the stretcher to their waists and then stand awkwardly from their knees. The first man turned and the body was taken to be placed with the others. He had gone from this hell either to another, or, if there was one, whatever heaven was supposed to be. Something remained in Meyer's mind and he looked back to where Schneider had been lifted on to the stretcher. The two men on their knees had found it awkward, even painful, on the hard floor. He spun around and looked at the pillar above him, which remained as it had been constructed. He remembered having examined the very pillar that had been blown apart that night and realized that the most effective position for a bomb would have been on the gallery level, concealed behind the panelling, set above the floor into the brick, close against the steel supports. He did not have to sink to his knees; he knew how uncomfortable the position of praying was even for a short time. But what would happen to a man who would have to spend many hours in that position to create, God knew how, a device that had been undetected and deadly accurate. The man's knees would give him away, Meyer realized, and tried to imagine one hour, then more, even with padding, working with difficulty – and it would have to have been at night. As a child, he had once knelt regularly in church. He would never forget the stabbing pains that taut skin over raw bone had given him.

Despite himself, Meyer's respect for this assassin mounted. It was almost unbelievable, but all around him was proof it was a fact. Meyer shook his head in wonder. 'So near,' he murmured to himself.

One of the field telephones, ringing shrill and loud, cut through the shouts, murmurs, cries, continuing screams and running feet within the Bierkeller. He turned to see a Wehrmacht officer kneel and pick up the receiver then speak briefly, and as Meyer listened to the man babbling before replacing the receiver, the name came to him, which had literally been blown from his mind – Georg Elser. He began to move. If he was wrong it could now be proved, at least in his mind. He seized the phone; the army operator answered. He gave instructions, replaced the receiver and waited impatiently, watching some semblance of order being created by the emergency services. It was almost five minutes before the phone rang again.

'Constance, sir. The customs and police building.'

'Thank you,' said Meyer. There was a pause.

'Yes?'

'Obersturmbannführer Meyer, from Munich.' He was on one knee; it was uncomfortable so he shifted his weight.

'Yes, sir, what can I do for you?'

'I wish to check orders already dispatched, that a man of Swabian origin by the name of Georg Elser must be arrested on identification. I want patrols sent into the town and extra guards alerted should he try to cross . . . '

'But, sir,' came the voice, 'I believe there is a man of that name already apprehended. He is waiting to see our commanding officer.'

For a moment Meyer could not speak.

'Sir, I can't hear you.'

'I am here,' murmured Meyer. 'Where is he exactly?'

'In the detention room, sir, awaiting interrogation.'

'Give me the officer in command,' said Meyer.

'Yes, sir. Can you wait?'

'Yes,' said Meyer. He looked up quickly as some loose rafters, dislodged by the firemen, fell heavily to the floor, bringing with them plaster and tiles, which broke and shattered on the once polished wood.

'Obersturmbannführer Meyer?'

'Yes.'

'What can I do, sir? Is it about the prisoner? You are interested, I understand?'

'Do one thing,' said Meyer, 'and if it seems ridiculous I will make it an order.'

'Of course, sir . . . ' began the officer in the customs post at Constance.

'Roll up his trousers,' interrupted Meyer, 'and look at the condition of his knees.'

'I beg your pardon, sir?'

'That is an order,' said Meyer.

'But I . . . ' began the officer at the other end of the telephone.

'An order!' shouted Meyer. 'Report!'

There was a silence on the line. 'Will you wait, Herr Obersturmbannführer?'

'I will wait,' answered Meyer, and now sank to both knees, cradling the telephone in both hands. It was fully three minutes before another sound came with a crackle on the line. 'Yes,' answered Meyer.

'His knees, sir . . . ' began the officer. 'The skin is heavily damaged.'

'Did he say anything?'

'No, sir.' The officer paused, hearing nothing from Munich. 'But the flesh, sir, is broken. It had been wrapped but the dressings were soaked with blood and pus.'

'They were suppurating,' said Meyer quietly.

'If that is the word, sir.'

'It is,' said Meyer. 'He is to be detained indefinitely.'

'Yes, sir.'

'I will be with you before dawn.' Meyer put down the phone – and now he knew he was right. Instinct gave him a familiar rush of euphoria, which dissipated as the pain he felt in his knees reminded him to move. He stood up awkwardly and, even in the midst of this tragedy, was now able to smile. The girl was unimportant now – where could she go?

'I have him!' hissed Meyer.

24

Several of the windows were shattered in the Mercedes and the driver was unconscious. Annalise, crouching in the rear, had only been stunned by the force of the blast and was able to watch Meyer being helped to his feet before he entered the Burgerbraukeller. Scrambling for the door, she had found the handle and stepped out, as all around her the panic increased. She was already walking quickly away as sirens and bells heralded the fire engines and ambulances which emerged out of the fog, making for the entrance of the beerhall. Soon the noises of confusion were behind her and she was moving through familiar streets in the dark. Something terrible had happened, she knew, but exactly what she could only guess at. It had sounded like a bomb, and she could not even bring herself to imagine the horror and damage it must have created amongst the crowds inside.

All she had discovered in her fear, sitting in the Gestapo car, was that nothing mattered but Georg. The officer had not been rough with her but the many questions had caused confusion in her mind, and the mere fact that Georg had telephoned was enough to spur her into action. As she walked even faster she repeated his words over and over, to leave, to take the train, cross the border at Constance and meet him on the other side. He had given her the pass to Switzerland. She had saved enough money, and now, turning the ring on her finger, which was the only link with the man she loved, she had no further questions and was determined to do as he had asked.

The idea that Georg had something to do with the explosion did not enter her head, although the officer in black uniform appeared to think he was guilty of some misconduct.

She had known him long enough, and he only made things and mended things. What had happened was probably a political incident, and she was only grateful not to have been inside the building. How could Georg have known anything? How could anyone think he could be connected with such a terrible act? After all, he was already in Constance. And if she had followed his advice, she would have been with him instead of hurrying back to the hostel.

She entered the dreary and dimly lit corridor, which smelt instantly of everything she wanted to escape from. Opening the door to her dormitory, she found it already half-occupied. Candles and battery torches provided the girls with additional light, but the blue bulbs, compulsory since the outbreak of war, together with the black-out curtains, made it difficult to find her things beneath the bed and in the small locker. The suitcase had only been used once before, on the holiday she had taken with Georg, beside the lake, in the summer. Even though only of average proportions, it would hold all she possessed in the world. She began packing quickly, knowing that the last train for Constance was leaving soon and determined that even if she could not find a tram, she would run the entire way to the Bahnhof. More than ever, in the surroundings she had grown to hate so much, the idea of life without Georg was impossible. She ignored the comments of the other girls, which increased as she pressed the catches on her case.

'Leaving, Annalise?'

'What's she doing?'

'Going in.'

'Where?'

'Oh, doctor . . . I was a virgin . . . '

'She was a what?'

'Never!'

'She's a whore. Why else would she work in such a place. She's been selling herself for Reichsmarks since she started.'

'But she's only a waitress.'

'She's going to be a mother.'

'Oh, doctor . . . '

'How much is it going to cost you?'

'What's going to cost her?'

'It won't be cheap.'

'What?'

'Abortions are painful, Annalise, remember the pleasure when you feel the pain.'

The pretty waitress spun around, case in hand, ready to leave. 'Shut up!' Her voice created immediate silence. Even beneath the blue bulbs, candlelight and torches, her eyes seemed to glow. 'You've never been anything – none of you – and you never will amount to more than a sack of potatoes in some drunk's bed! I have listened to your spite and resentment, your jealousy of anything worthwhile. You only want to destroy what you can't have. God help you all!'

'Where are you going, Annalise?' whined one of the girls. Hesitant laughter started, then faded as the pretty waitress stepped to the door and paused.

'To find,' she said, 'and enjoy, what none of you will ever know.' Someone spat, other girls began catcalls, but Annalise slammed the door and was already moving, praying that she would first find a tram, then endure the long train ride to the lake on the border and, finally, know the pleasure beyond imagination of falling into the arms of the man she had come to love, desperately.

She stumbled out of the hostel and made her way through the thickening fog. Her feet found the tramlines and she began to run, ignoring the weight of the case clasped firmly in her hand. The ring on her finger, pressed against the handle, cut into her flesh and the pain stimulated her to think of Georg, which gave an increasing impetus. If she did nothing else, she swore to herself, she would see him before the dawn.

The lights of the approaching tram gave her only an instant before the warning clanging of its bell indicated that it was about to stop. She stepped to one side, and a moment later was seated with a paid ticket for Munich station.

Curious faces peered towards her, but she ignored them all. Finally she had found the courage to leave. At last she was going to something better, and anything would have been, than the future she had been destined for.

She closed her eyes and quite clearly saw the countryside across the lake, which she and Georg, in each other's arms, had talked about months before. If he loved her as she did him – and she believed he did – there would be no more problems. He had telephoned, even while she'd been working. He needed her, and she had been a fool to think that she could be without him even for a day, without the sure knowledge that she would see him again. And now she carried his child. As she placed her hands on her stomach, the tram bells started clanging. A shout sounded loudly and the tram stopped. Outside in the swirling fog was Munich station. She ran into the great entrance hall, crossed to the ticket office and passed through the barrier to board the night train for Constance, even as the engine up front whistled shrilly, the noise reverberating against the glass and steel roof of the Bahnhof.

She squeezed herself on to one of the wooden benches in third class amongst numerous peasants from the border region already eating sausages, black bread and sauerkraut in large jars they passed amongst themselves. Following a huge blast of smoke and steam as the locomotive jerked its load forward, the carriages began to gain momentum and the train threaded its way through the many points systems of the terminus to find the steel rails that would take the passengers crowded aboard south-west to their destination, where they would arrive before dawn. Ill-concealed interest surrounded Annalise from the passengers chewing on their food like animals. Annalise turned her face to the window and leant her cheek against the cold glass. More than eight hours to Constance.

'Oh, Georg,' she whispered to herself. 'Please be there. Please wait for me.' As she saw tears appear in her reflection under the blue light, she squeezed her eyes tight and silently began to pray.

The door to the large detention room in the customs and police building at Constance was opened brusquely as the commanding officer stepped in, followed by several of his men. One of the guards who had apprehended Georg Elser sprang to attention behind the desk. At the far end of the room, Elser, seated on a bench, having been allowed to roll down his trousers, merely stared anxiously towards the uniformed official. His confidence had begun to evaporate, leaving him with the increasingly gnawing suspicion something had gone wrong, although how he could not guess. Perhaps the bomb had failed to go off. Surely they could not associate anything with him, yet? he thought. When the officer examined his knees, his heart had lurched. Only when the man had gone had Elser been able to explore all the possibilities. Yes, something had gone wrong – but what? He watched the officer and his men approach slowly. Whatever, if the bomb had exploded, Hitler was dead – and that fact would furnish him with the courage to endure whatever lay ahead. He swallowed. No matter what. The officer stopped and looked at the little man on the bench. The other policemen stood either side of their commander, awaiting orders.

'Get up,' said the officer. Elser had been sitting too long and, as he attempted to rise, he felt the stabbing pain through his stiffening muscles. He stumbled forward. The officer lashed out, catching Elser's face with a heavy blow, knocking him to one side.

'Pick him up!' ordered the officer. The policeman pulled Elser to his feet. 'So you wanted to go into Switzerland?'

Elser looked into the officer's leering face, but did not answer. A second blow knocked the little man from Württemberg to the floor. Unbidden, the two policemen lifted Elser once again, now with blood showing around his mouth and nose.

'Bring him to the desk,' said the officer, and led the way as

Elser was dragged across the room. 'Empty his pockets!'

The two policemen obeyed the order and Elser's alibi to the Swiss authorities was clearly laid out under the strong light on the leather top of the desk, beside the paper describing his attempt to avoid detection. The police officer ignored the more subtle clues of wire, brick chippings, even the detonator, and merely looked at the black and white photograph on the postcard of the Burgerbraukeller in Munich. He turned his head to Elser, and smiled coldly.

'Souvenir?'

Elser nodded. The officer hit him. Elser sagged and sighed with the pain, but still, as yet, did not cry out.

'What have you been doing?'

Elser shook his head.

'Everyone is looking for you – an SS Obersturmbannführer telephoned me personally, from Munich. You are a famous man, it seems.' He paused and repeated, 'What have you been doing?'

Elser raised his head to speak, but could only spit blood. The officer signalled. 'Sit him down!'

Elser was thrust on to a chair. He shook his head and tried to focus on the officer, who glanced at the clock on the wall and perched on the edge of the desk. He lit a cigarette, then offered one to Elser, who reached out for it and put it in between his bloody lips. The officer leant forward and lit it, using the same match for his own before inhaling deeply.

'There are rumours from Munich of an "incident". What would you know about it?'

Elser merely sucked smoke into his lungs, unable to speak.

'And by coincidence,' said the officer, 'you have here a postcard of a beerhall.'

Elser's tongue thickened in his mouth, but his eyes found the clock on the wall.

'A bomb has exploded,' murmured the officer. Elser coughed, and his head fell forward. He started sobbing, which turned to laughter. Blood, mucous and tears could not stifle the sheer relief of that information. So he had succeeded, after all, he thought to himself, and began to gird his body for the troubles ahead. Now they could do with him as they wished.

At an unspoken command, the two policemen behind Elser sprang into action, one lifting his head, tearing at his hair, the other hitting his face with efficient and hard blows from both fists, smashing into the man's face, knocking the cigarette across the room. As Elser slumped from the chair, ignoring the pain and welling bruises, he could only think of the cigarette, and the policemen watched him crawl towards it. When it was almost in his grasp the officer took one pace and ground the tobacco into the floorboards. Elser looked up at the officer, who stared down at the pathetic face.

'You're going to receive a very important visitor.'

Elser's mouth fell open and blood seeped from his teeth and tongue as it coursed through his nose and from a cut under his right eye. The officer placed his boot beneath Elser's chin, then thrust at his chest so that Elser fell back heavily. The two policemen, expecting further orders, watched their commander pull down the cuffs of his shirt beneath the uniform. It was a gesture which they had grown accustomed to associate with the dismissal of a victim.

'Clean him up!' said the officer, his lips curling. 'We'll get no thanks anyway. Let the Gestapo have all the glory, as usual.'

The cuckoo clock in the small inn north of Lake Constance whirred for a split second, then the painted bird sprang out of its doors, and some device within the mechanism, concealed beneath the cabinet in the shape of a Swiss chalet, activated what sounded to Otto Meyer like a mocking comment on attempts to telephone the border post. Eleven times the cuckoo sang out, then popped back in its Swiss chalet, whose doors abruptly closed. Only then was there an answer from the telephone, and Meyer pressed the receiver to his ear; his back was to the wall and he was staring around the half-filled bar, where most of the customers, who were either absolutely silent or merely whispering to each other, tried to ignore the presence of the Gestapo officer. Having given his name, infuriatingly Meyer had been asked to wait. At last there was a respectful reply, to which he answered harshly, 'Before dawn!' then slammed down the phone.

He surveyed the bar once more and nodded to the proprietor, whose wife had arrived and was clinging to him as if he were to be taken away. With relief the old couple bowed to Meyer, who turned on his heels and stepped out of the door, quickly making his way towards the headlights of the Mercedes. He had forced his driver to go faster than he wished to travel in the thickening fog; he was still feeling the effects of the explosion, and had understandably shown his nervousness, but Meyer had urged him on. He slid into the back seat and slammed the door.

'Drive on!' he snapped, and the Mercedes accelerated into the murky night.

The loud voice, shouting the length of the carriage, woke Annalise with a start. The ticket inspector, stepping over cases and baskets in the aisle, repeated 'Constance. We are arriving in Constance.' Annalise stirred, rising uncomfortably after so many hours cramped in her seat. She stood up in the still swaying train and reached for her case in the rack above. Already others were on their feet and it was amidst a press of people that she finally stepped down on to the platform.

It was still dark, dawn light had yet to show. For a moment she was bewildered, not knowing what to do. Then she saw the huge locomotive emerging from the other side of the station building, where even in the dim arc lights she could see quite clearly first the swastika flag, then on the other side of the boiler, the white cross on the red background, which she knew meant Switzerland. She shuffled amidst the crowd towards the station barrier. Some had merely come home to

Constance, where they lived. Others were transferring to the train which was preparing to cross the frontier. Numerous guards were in evidence, examining passes. Annalise's heart began to pound as she joined the queue. The smoke and steam, swirling fog beneath the lights, shouting, arguments, whistles from the trains, loud voices of police and customs, merged in her mind. It all seemed to represent Germany – everything in the nightmare she was leaving behind.

She clasped her coat tightly, pressing the white envelope between her palm and fingers, until the police official seemed to tear it from her hands. As he examined the document within, then the woman's face, he began to read carefully, and as he lingered there were loud voices behind, impatient to be on board the connecting train. The gesture the man made gave Annalise freedom – she was allowed to pass through to buy her ticket to Zurich.

The guard blew a whistle loud and long and almost caused a stampede amongst the milling crowds. It was only minutes, which to Annalise seemed like a lifetime, before she clambered aboard the Swiss carriage and found a seat against the window someone had pulled down so that it was fully open. She was shaking, with both excitement and fear. If Elser was waiting on the other side, where she had been told the train would stop briefly to pick up passengers over the border before continuing to its destination in Zurich, her every dream would have come true.

The longing in her body, the blood coursing in her veins as she watched the moving throng below on the platform, appeared to be answered in her womb, and although she knew it was too early, she felt that the child, growing within her, was willing, as much as its mother, that the father would be there, waiting.

Annalise's head fell forward as the noises around her increased and the people pressed into seats all about her. She began crying uncontrollably and could only whisper his name, 'Georg, Georg, Georg . . .'

25

'Please.'

The two guards in the large detention room of the customs post ignored the voice and continued chewing.

'Please.'

One of the guards looked up.

Georg Elser attempted twice to get up from the bench. Finally he succeeded, swaying, and pointed. 'Could I . . . ?' he coughed and wiped blood from his mouth.

The two guards exchanged a glance. They had eaten sausages and black bread and shared a beer. The empty bottle was placed beneath a chair, in case the officer came in. One of them picked his teeth, the other belched. They'd been whiling away the hours and had become bored.

'Could I go . . . ?' Elser began again and coughed once more. Feeling the pain from his beating and the weakness in his knees, he gritted his teeth.

One of the guards winked at the other. 'I think he's going to shit his pants.' The two men laughed. Elser waited patiently. The guard who had belched stood up and stretched, then reached down for the empty bottle, crossed the room and opened the door. Outside it was still foggy. He shouted, and two guards, wearing helmets, with slung rifles, appeared. The man thrust the empty bottle into Elser's hand.

'Go with them,' he said roughly. 'They will show you. And get rid of that.' He indicated the bottle. Elser stepped down and nearly fell.

'Make him walk!' said the man to the two guards with rifles. Elser hesitated.

'Well, go on!'

Painfully, Elser began to move.

'Over there!' came a voice beneath one of the helmets.

Elser saw a small hut, twenty metres away, with a sign above the door declaring it to be a toilet. He began walking, slowly, watched without compassion by the two duty guards. One of them readjusted the strap of his rifle and glanced back at his comrade standing in the doorway. The man pointed to his knees and began to laugh. Light from the building guided Elser to the first railway track, which he stepped over but, catching his foot, he fell heavily on to the other steel rails. There was laughter from the guards, and someone shouted, 'Get up!'

Preserving the bottle in his hand as if it were valuable, Elser stood up, feeling the gravel beneath his feet, and carefully picked his way across the other pair of steel rails, before shuffling towards the hut. When he reached it, breathing heavily, he gratefully leant against the wooden side. They'd made him kneel from sheer cruelty once the officer had left the room. For half an hour he'd not been allowed to stand, then when he did, he'd needed help. He was still concussed from the blows he'd received, and felt that if this was only the beginning, it would be better to die. He looked at the bottle in his hand and threw it into the shadows behind the hut. He heard it shatter, and then heard a whistle – the sound of a train, an engine, a locomotive, perhaps taking people away. Lying against the hut, staring across the railway line at the amused guards talking amongst themselves outside the border post between Germany and Switzerland, that long-drawn-out blast of steam was the sound of freedom.

He turned slowly and stepped into the darkness of the hut which smelt of urine, as reminiscent of the Bierkeller as the noise of the approaching train he had heard so many times during those nights, alone, creating from the pillar a housing for his device. Leaning forward he pressed his head against the wall above the enamel and, unbuttoning his trousers, began to relieve himself into the filthy trough. The Gestapo, the officer had said, and he shuddered at the thought. What would they do to him? How would he survive? Now he could taste salt on his lips as the first tears of self-pity flowed from his eyes. Then came the anguish he had managed to control all this time, just with the thought of Annalise – he spoke her name softly – it could all have been so good for them. What would happen to him was already out of his hands, but Annalise – he repeated her name and the word came in a sob.

The whistle sounded again – now much nearer – and he heard wheels on the steel rails, only then realizing that it was not in his mind, but outside. He leant back, buttoning his trousers and peered through the frosted glass of the small window to see a light moving through the fog and darkness. For a moment he could not make out what it was, then he saw the smoke and steam, two flags illuminated, both red – one with a white cross, the other with a black swastika in a white circle. His eyes widened. It was the early train for Zurich. He took a pace forward and fell awkwardly against the wall. He could see, across the tracks, the guards outside the border building, still talking, one of them lighting cigarettes for the others.

He stepped out of the toilet, remaining unsteadily on his feet, watching the locomotive coming nearer and gaining speed slowly. A shout of alarm went up, and Elser saw one of the guards pointing. He was confused – what had he done?

'Stay where you are!' bellowed the guard, unslinging his rifle.

Then the locomotive obscured his view and he realized the train had cut him off from the border guards. He began to laugh, and as if with a will of their own, his feet were suddenly moving. Ignoring all pain he began to run, but the train was gathering momentum as he reached it, so he increased speed, running parallel to the first carriages, knowing that his hand had only to reach up and grasp escape.

The kind face of the Swiss woman opposite Annalise Palin smiled, and she indicated, 'Switzerland.'

287

The pretty young waitress looked up.

'There,' said the woman, 'look!'

Annalise stared out, seeing only the darkness and fog, but there were lights in the distance – which was perhaps what the woman meant: no restrictions. A different world. Annalise knelt on her seat and leant out for a better view. Only then did she see the figure running beside the train and recognized him instantly.

'Georg!' she screamed. 'G-e-o-r-g!!'

Elser, now finding it difficult to keep up with the increasing speed of the train, heard the familiar voice and glanced over his shoulder. He stumbled, but continued running, now with his last energy, reaching up at anything he could grasp. A handle, a bar, anything . . . Already the carriage with the open window and the young woman leaning out was upon him. She was reaching down.

'Georg!' she screamed again.

People were pulling at her in the carriage, but she ignored them. Elser's fingers scratched the swiftly passing metal side of the carriage, seeking one solid object – a simple grip. With the last ounce of what energy remained in his body, he reached up in an attempt to seize the edge of the open window. It was only a split second in time, but his eyes, staring into the face of Annalise, were full of love as their fingers touched.

SS Obersturmbannführer Otto Meyer's Mercedes staff car slewed to a halt outside the border station at Constance. He stumbled from the car and was about to stride towards the main building, when he saw two of the guards ahead, with unslung rifles, running towards the first train of the morning which was already crossing the barrier on its way to Zurich. He shouted above the noise of the wheels on steel, and one of the guards turned to him. Even from twenty metres, Meyer could read panic in the man's face and he strode briskly towards him. Lights from the windows of the carriages began to flicker across the ground as they were turned up to full to pass over into neutral territory, where the black-out restrictions were no longer in force.

'What's going on?!' snapped Meyer.

'The prisoner, sir!' The guard hesitated. 'He's . . . on the other side!' He indicated the muzzle of his rifle.

Meyer's face became a mask of fury and he turned to the passing train as if he could see beyond it. Carriage lights continued to flicker across his face, faster by the second, and he willed Elser to be there. Suddenly the train was gone, leaving behind it only smoke, steam and disturbed fog, which swirled around the guards and Otto Meyer . . . and Georg Elser, who had pulled himself to his knees, having fallen heavily, and with head bent, was staring at the gravel on the other side of the tracks. Meyer ignored the shouts of jubilation from the guards and, respectfully, they became silent.

Meyer stepped forward, one boot on the steel rail. He stared at Georg Elser a long time before the kneeling man lifted his head to look back. Meyer did not recognize the expression; it was not one of a beaten man. There was a calmness in Elser's face, a peace that was disturbing. When confronted with his quarry, the hunter was surprised that there was no triumph in him, if anything only respect and a compassion he found difficult to explain. Otto Meyer leant forward and put out a hand to help Elser to his feet. Finding the man's grip, he lifted him slowly until he could stand.

'You missed him,' stated the Gestapo officer softly, 'by seven minutes.'

The information seemed to take away what little energy Elser had left in his body. He slumped forward and Meyer caught him in his arms. The two guards stepped closer, sensing a threat where there was none, brandishing rifles.

'Who is he, sir?' asked one of them curiously.

When Otto Meyer spoke it was hardly a murmur.

'No one,' he said.

Epilogue

Adolf Hitler's last birthday was on 20 April 1945. It was celebrated with some improvisation in a bunker beneath the Chancellory as the first artillery bombardment from the Russian forces closing in on the city of Berlin began to devastate what remained from the aerial bombings of the British and American armies.

For the Führer's remaining entourage it was a long way from first shots fired at the roof of a beerhall in Munich. The declared revolution had never taken place. Hitler had been incarcerated in Landsberg prison and two years later a book had emerged entitled *Mein Kampf* unveiling his intentions to conquer the world. If the struggle to power had been hard, the effort to maintain it had proved more difficult. In the minds of men, power develops a momentum of its own, and it takes courage to accept such responsibility when so many others can be affected at whim. The boy from a village in Austria had led the German-speaking peoples out of one chaos merely to create an order which had plunged it into an Armageddon.

Forced congratulations were extended to the hunched leader from those around him, and from others come to pay their respects in the extensive underground accommodation, as the whistling shells from heavy artillery thundered above in the streets of a once bustling metropolis.

By mid-morning, orders of the day had been issued; phantom battalions were to engage the enemy and hurl them back from the capital. Like a phoenix, the Third Reich was supposed to resurrect itself, but the roaring flames of the buildings and streets in the city were all-consuming and there would be no miracles for Adolf Hitler. He had gambled and lost. Already in private he had begun to look at his Luger pistol as a travelling companion to an unknown destination. The castle of sand which had stood, so mighty and seemingly indestructible, had been inundated by the tide of retribution, yet even as the walls crumbled and the fabric of the nation dissolved, in the very midst of this collapse of an already redundant society, issued orders were adhered to and carried out to the letter.

One of the two guards that arrived at the door of the long house in the Dachau concentration camp actually knocked before entering, a measure of respect to the little man within who was imprisoned in the political block and had therefore achieved certain privileges which had long since been established. Georg Elser was alone at an improvised workbench when he looked up and saw the two familiar faces. Many of the SS guards had come and gone over the years, but these two had stayed the longest, more than eighteen months, and had sometimes talked to him, smoking cigarettes, as if they were friends from boyhood days merely sitting on different sides of the fence.

Elser had once been moved to Sehsenhausen, but was returned to Dachau, where he tried to ignore what he had seen and heard, especially when the Jews were paraded every morning. He had now ceased to watch from the windows of his accommodation.

Why he had been accorded privileges had been a mystery to him initially, then the rumour was that when Hitler conquered Britain, he would utilize this little man from Württemberg as his witness, citing him as the instrument of a British plot against the Führer and, no doubt, therefore providing an excuse for what retribution he deemed fit. To corroborate this, two British officers called Best and Stephens, taken on the Dutch border during an incident at Venlo, and even a pastor named Niemöller, who was declared a staunch enemy, had argued the facts and doubted that Elser was merely as simple as his motives.

Elser had come to terms with having failed in his attempt at assassination; he accepted that, had it been God's will, he would have succeeded. All that he had done had been conceived and executed to perfection, even the Gestapo conceded this during their regular interrogation in his first year of trial and torture. He had even built the bomb again as proof that he had always worked alone. The story had remained consistent, and, despite attempts to persuade him to admit he was a British agent, by the winter of 1940, when the focus of Germany's attention had shifted to the east, he had been given some respite and was allowed to recover his health in the Dachau camp. When it was discovered how proficient he was with his hands, he made things and mended things – furniture, cabinets, anything to which he could turn his skilled hands. He did it willingly to occupy both the time and his mind. He even constructed a zither from matchsticks and glue.

It was unnecessary to ask the course of the war; it became obvious in the faces of the guards, anxiously staring at the sky during the day and amongst the clouds at night, when Elser, lying in his bunk, heard quite clearly the droning of hundreds of engines as the RAF passed overhead with their huge payloads of bombs. When Munich was the target, the sky was as bright as dawn, and when dawn came often it heralded more squadrons of high-flying American bombers. The interlacing vapour trails which he had begun to see so often were Germany's death knell, of that Georg Elser had no doubt.

But he passed the time as an artisan, as he had always done, as he had always been. A quiet man who applied himself to any task presented to him. He had long since ceased regretting the deaths he had caused in the great explosion. At first he had cried with compassion when the Gestapo deliberately showed him film of their bodies, and prayed for their souls. But time had created distance and he had become inured to anything but the survival of mind and body.

And Annalise . . . at least she had been given a chance. If he lived through it all perhaps he would be able to find her – one day in the new future that was imminent. And the child – perhaps he was a father. The fact that he had survived so long gave him confidence to hope he would see the war ended and then . . . He had given Annalise the address of the old man in Zurich. He would start there. Freedom through work, the motto over the gate of Dachau he had first seen so many years before, might prove true for him yet.

On 20 April 1945 when he smiled at the familiar guards who received orders merely to take him over to the mortuary where he was to repair some tables, Georg Elser had no idea that his destination that day would be the same as all men's. He ever left his packet of cigarettes, each one of which he had carefully cut in half, on the workbench beside the crafted zither which still invoked admiration from both guards and prisoners alike. His unassuming, quiet personality had made him popular, and there was an obvious friendliness between him and two guards as they escorted him across the compound, through fine drizzle.

He stopped between the guards as they reached the long house with a tall chimney. So far, so good. The mortuary had been rebuilt since Elser had first worked in it many years before, but the marble slabs were still in place and had become used more often. The guards had instructions to leave Elser at the door, but ushered him in to be met by the two Lithuanian inmates. The SS men snapped to attention seeing the uniform and insignia of an officer inside. The door was closed, the officer indicated the work to be done, and Elser put down his tools, quite unconcerned by anything but the broken tables placed to one side. He knelt to examine the damage and for a moment remembered similar furniture – the trestle tables stacked together with carpets against the wall of a balconied gallery in Munich's Burgerbraukeller – and he smiled for a moment at the thought of how near he had come and how different everything would have been if he had only . . . The bullet that entered the back of Georg Elser's neck snapped his spinal cord immediately and what was already a corpse fell forward heavily to the tiled floor. With little concern, no conscience and practised efficiency, the two Lithuanians picked up the light body of the little man and carried it to the long-handled metal stretcher, where it was dumped unceremoniously. The officer replaced the automatic pistol in its holster.

'Burn him,' he said.

He turned and walked back to the door, where he stepped outside into the fine drizzle. Duty was becoming tedious, but an order was an order, especially when it came from so high a source.

As the first Lithuanian opened the oven doors, the second looked up – he could hear the droning of the American planes once more approaching. Sirens began to wail in the distant city of Munich; soon it would all be over, as it was for this corpse.

The second Lithuanian turned the body over and looked into the face. He could already feel the heat of the roaring flames as he stared down at the eyes, which had an expression of wonder and bewilderment, and there was a sadness about the lips. The man grunted, then inserted a small metal bar roughly between the teeth and levered the mouth open. He turned the head first to one side, then the other, looking for gold fillings. There was nothing. He grunted again and from irritation smacked the side of the face heavily with the metal. Unlucky, he thought. This one wasn't new, he looked as if he'd been in camps for some time. Sallow skin told him that. Privileges at least had brought him better rations.

He looked at the hands, which were fine-fingered, and there gleamed a ring. Using the sharp end of the metal bar, he levered it, then, finding difficulty, broke the finger and pulled the ring off. He bit it. It wasn't good gold, but it would do. There was what looked like a woman's name inscribed on the inside, which he could not read, but it might scratch out. Some German bitch no doubt, he thought, and slipped the ring into his trousers. Taking the two long handles, he thrust the metal stretcher towards the oven. Guided by the first Lithuanian, it entered the flames. Both men watched, with a curiosity they never seemed to lose, as the contracting tissues

294

pulled the body upright where it seemed to sit amongst the flames. Then it sank back on to the metal, the flesh charring, the bone powdering.

'The orders came from high up,' said the first Lithuanian, 'Who was he?'

The second man, fingering the gold ring in his pocket, grinned. 'Who knows?' he said. 'And who cares?'

The two men slammed the oven doors shut.

A fire was roaring in the large grate of the hallway, as part of the final preparations made to receive the Führer at the Berghof in Obersalzberg above Berchtesgaden on the morning of 25 April 1945. SS Brigadeführer Otto Meyer, in full dress, now sporting a Knights Cross at his neck, had arrived to supervise everything.

The Luftwaffe were to fly Adolf Hitler, under the very noses of the Russians, out of Berlin and across Germany, where he would land at a small airfield that had been created near Bad Reichenhall. From there he would be driven a short distance to what had become more than a home.

In the minds of the world, the Berghof had come to represent all that was private about Germany's leader, the place to which he retired to conceive his great strategies. Many of his plans and concepts for the future had been created during the walks he took with aides and advisers, both civilian and military, along the forest paths. In the golden days of triumph and success there had been a definite aura about the complex. It had become a veritable fortress, and now with good reason it might serve as a final redoubt.

In recent years Hitler had only been able to retire to this place to lick his wounds. Too late he had discovered that the giants he had taken on with such confidence had seemingly inexhaustible power and energy and were destroying everything he had created and dreamed for Germany's next thousand years. Perhaps, thought Meyer, it was appropriate that the Führer might make an end of it here, not submerged beneath the armies of a country that must now be scarred into his heart – Russia. The USSR had bled the nation of Germany's finest troops, division after division had been consumed by Stalin's vast forces, then with the Allied invasion of Normandy it had all become merely a matter of time.

The heady days of victory, the indestructible, unbeaten Third Reich cutting a swathe into the world, seemed so far away to Meyer as, with greying hair and gaunt face above a leaner body, he crossed the large hallway, past the leaping flames of the fire and thankfully stepped out into the crisp air of the clear day. His boots crunched on the gravel as he made for the small parapet with its view beyond the mountains towards the borders of Germany and Austria, the small town below, the distant valleys, the far-off plain with roads meandering through villages, and the mountains all about, huge and eternal like protective guardians thrusting their snow-peaks into the magnificent day. It seemed absurd to Meyer that there could be war, as his lungs inhaled the crystal air, but the barracks, marching feet, moving vehicles, all the paraphernalia that now went with the Berghof – no longer just a small mountain home – soon almost painfully intruded the reality of the present situation.

As a boy Meyer had climbed these mountains; as a youth he had attempted to scale the highest peaks and now, as a man, he commanded a special section of security created to insulate Hitler from any danger. Here in these mountains, he was supposed to defend this man against all comers. Once, that might have been possible, but now, with the Allied army across the Rhine and already in Germany to the west and to the east, actually tightening the noose around Berlin, anything that took place here in Berchtesgaden would be merely a futile gesture, a small mark amidst the stain the Third Reich had left on the world's map.

Meyer took off his black peaked cap and began to laugh quietly to himself. He spun on his heel and stared up at the forests and meadows above. He had an hour before the 'official' lunch – and decided there was time enough to take a

296

walk. After all, one world was coming to end and there might not be another.

It took him twenty minutes to reach the first tree-line bordering the wide sloping meadow. The incline took a toll on ageing bones and lungs which had absorbed too many cigarettes over recent years. There was warmth in the sun and flowers amongst the grass. Again he plunged into the trees, upwards along the path overgrown during the winter, brushing aside fern and bracken, ducking beneath young branches of new leaves. The smell of pine around him began to affect his senses as, he had read, opium could. A wonderful and welcome euphoria began to grow in his soul and he looked ahead, beyond the forest shadows, out into the sunlit, lush grass of a huge meadow, as if expecting to see familiar faces.

He unbuttoned his jacket and paused for a moment to catch his breath. Regrets were useless, he knew that, but perhaps Marianne had been right; he should never have become part of all this. Easy with hindsight, but at the time it had all seemed glorious. Those early beginnings, his zealousness and, he remembered – yes, that little man in Munich, so long ago now, who had nearly put an end to it all there and then. He began to laugh loudly at the stupidity of history. If nothing else, he recognized that the lure of glory was a poor substitute for what was all about him. At that moment he felt part of nature in a way he had never before experienced, as if his body had already been interred and consumed by the very earth from which the spring flowers were blooming with the naive hope and expectation that they would last until summer. Standing in the middle of the great meadow, looking down at the now distant Berghof complex, he could hear only the faint chatter of birds and hum of insects in the grass which the wind rustled and undulated.

Brigadeführer Otto Meyer sighed for the other life that could have been, and appreciated that this moment might be the last he would know of tranquillity and peace.

The noise of the insects seemed to become louder until it was a regular droning. It began to echo all about the Gestapo

officer, increasing in volume, filling his mind. For a moment
he thought he was going mad; there was nothing else but this
sound. The droning became a roar as if a storm was
approaching, so Meyer looked up. They'd come – finally. He
could already hear the boom of anti-aircraft guns and saw
ineffectual puffs of smoke appearing amidst the huge aerial
armada. Suddenly there were bullets bursting all around
him. He fell to the ground. What seemed like a never-ending
stream of American fighters, which he identified as Mustangs, passed low overhead, their engines bellowing like some
primal horde of hunting beasts. A second pass by another
squadron came as Meyer clung to the earth, and within the
cacophony of aircraft engines he could detect that most of the
anti-aircraft guns surrounding the Berghof had been silenced
until there was only one regular crack as men at the last 88-
millimetre continued firing. Then, with more machine-gun
and cannon fire as the Mustangs banked out of the valley, it
too was silenced.

The pattern in the sky that the hundreds of Lancasters
made, high above, continued to fascinate Meyer as he lay on
his back, staring up at the silhouetted four-engined British
aircraft. They had been the scourge of Germany for so long at
night, and now in broad daylight they were directly over the
place where, it was rumoured throughout Europe, Hitler
would make his last stand.

Then the bombs came. Thousand-pound and four-
thousand-pound warheads, many primed for deep penetration into the concrete shelters below the Berghof, they rained
down, their whistling drowned out by first explosions as
gigantic geysers of bricks, mortar, earth, concrete, bodies and
vehicles rose amongst the pine trees.

Meyer stood up, no longer concerned with his own safety, in
awe of the scene before him. The noise of the detonating
bombs deafened him. He could feel the shock waves and was
twice thrown back to the ground but again stood up. He

became aware that tears were pouring from his eyes, which were narrowed against the searing heat. He clasped his hands about his head but could not tear his gaze away from the increasing devastation. He knew he was shouting but could not hear the words. Twigs, pine needles, cones, leaves, swirled in the air around him. Smoke and debris were rising beyond a hundred metres into the sky, underlit by multiple flashes as the hail of bombs continued to hit with deadly accuracy. Even in the cities when he had been caught by raids, he had seen nothing like this, sheltered safely below the ground, protected by tons of concrete in various bunkers that had become a refuge until the all-clear sounded. Only during the Great War had anything comparable ever come near in his experience, but this was horrifying in a way he had never expected. Fear had seized his body, which was shaking uncontrollably.

The high formation seemed to turn away and what he identified as Mosquitoes, fast twin-engined British fighter bombers, passed low, some directly through the smoke and flames, firing cannon and rockets. The last pass by the Mustang squadron machine-gunned everything in sight, then suddenly the Allied aircraft were gone, turning back over the mountains.

In a daze, Otto Meyer began to wander down the sloping meadow into the forest and finally slithered down onto the road directly above the Berghof. It was littered with debris, bodies, limbs, upturned vehicles, splinters of steel and huge sections of concrete torn out of the ground. A pall hung over everything. Skirting the many smoking craters, he picked his way amongst paving stones ripped from the earth, and only as his boots crunched on gravel did he see what was left of the building, where a fire had been roaring in the grate to welcome the Führer such a short time ago. Incredibly there were people moving, emerging from bunkers, that had miraculously survived. There had been no warning, even the fog canisters designed to cloud the area had been ineffective.

He shook his head; this was no longer war, merely a sport of .

annihilation. Only now did he hear sirens and the clanging bells of the few fire engines and ambulances Berchtesgaden possessed. He would stay, of course, and help as he could, from pure humanitarian reasons, but what could he do? There were no more illusions. He would go to Munich and, if it must all end, it would be there. His one wish was to see his home, perhaps for the last time.

It was more than a week before Meyer left Berchtesgaden. The news came at the beginning of May that the Allies were close and Hitler was dead. Strangely, Meyer felt a combination of relief and elation as he sat in the back of what was probably the last staff car to arrive back from Bad Reichenhall to the ruins of Munich. The city was devastated, and perhaps it was merely fate that took the car down Turkenstrasse, which had been bombed and gutted by the night raids of the British and the day sorties of the American Air Force. Meyer noticed that number 94 was boarded up. The entrance into the courtyard through the archway firmly sealed with planks and metal bars against possible intruders. The Mercedes continued, crossed an intersection and then passed in front of, what Meyer realized was, the Burgerbraukeller. Here damage was also apparent and the windows were shut, the main door closed. Meyer smiled to himself. It was irony, perhaps, that where it had all begun was now closed to the public. He leaned back in the rear seat of the car, recognizing the route as the Mercedes made its way towards what had once been his home. He held his breath as the driver nosed into the pretty street, where long ranks of trees were heavy with blossom. He stopped the car and got out slowly. Here nothing had changed, it was as it had always been. He began to walk along the familiar pavement towards the house where he had married and started a family. His black Gestapo uniform, once an indication of such power wielded throughout the Reich, was a harsh contrast to the subleties of nature and the delicacy of the buildings around him. The street had been created in another era and would now survive as a testament that there had once been a city before

Hitler, as there would be many things after him.

Meyer reached the gate, which still sagged from its post and needed oiling, then noticed that the hedges should be cut as the trees wanted trimming. There was a movement at the window and just for a moment he thought he could hear piano music. It was then that the two American Jeeps slewed into the road, and full of GIs, accelerated towards him. He heard a shout and could see guns raised. The first Jeep stopped abruptly and several of the American soldiers jumped out. An officer seemed to be shouting at them.

Meyer glanced again at the house and smiled. It was, after all, a perfect place to surrender. With his left hand he unclipped his holster and began to pull out his Luger, which he had intended to throw as far away as possible. The shouts of alarm he heard merged into a single crack, and the very sound seemed to hit his head and penetrate his mind with the force of a bullet. For a moment he was bewildered, then he felt something against his cheek – it was the cold stone of the gutter. He had been thrown backwards by the impact of the .45, turning in the air so that he lay face down. He tried to move but his body did not respond. He opened his mouth to speak and felt the first gush of blood over his tongue. Only as he heard voices did he realize what had happened.

'The Captain shot a Kraut.'

'What?'

'Where the hell is he?'

'Over there.'

'Get the car.'

Meyer heard his driver trying to accelerate away; there was a burst of machine-gun fire and the sound of breaking glass as the Mercedes collided with a tree.

'You got him!'

'Sure as shit!'

'Check him out!'

The Jeep accelerated past Meyer, whose eyes would not respond as he tried to follow the noise. He could only stare, watching the blood spread about his face, then he heard a woman's voice shout in alarm, and he recognized the sound of the creaking gate being opened.

'Hey, Fraulein! Do you speaka da Americano?'

'Shut up, Silberman!'

'Excuse me, ma'am . . . ' began the officer.

'Yes,' came the woman's voice calmly, 'I speak English.'

'This guy seemed to be trying to get in here. D'ya know him?' There was silence, Meyer could no longer feel anything and his vision was blurring. But there was no pain. If dying was this easy, he thought, who would ever have a conscience about killing? All the ingenuity of man and all the bombs – too complicated, he thought. The combined might of the RAF and American Air Forces had been unable to kill Hitler, as had the massed Allied armies. Every plot against him had failed, and even that little man from Württemberg, who had tried so hard and come so near, with such persistence. And it was so simple. Meyer could not smile, but the irony was in his mind. Someone should have shot the bastard at the beginning – with one bullet. It might have put him out of a job, but it would have saved the world a lot of trouble. Then his mind clouded and only a single word remained – 'Duty'. He tried to spit, but coughed blood.

The American officer turned over the SS Brigadeführer Otto Meyer's body with his boot, so that the last glimpse of life he had was looking up at the sky.

'Do you recognize him?' asked the officer. There was silence from the woman.

'I wonder who he is,' murmured the American.

'No one,' said Marianne harshly – and she was right. Otto Meyer was dead.

The young policeman was very proud of his new uniform. Working with the occupying American forces, he had begun learning English and, as he was determined to advance his career, another language would obviously help. The small amount of Russian he had picked up was no longer necessary as the Soviet armies were in a different sector of Germany. In Munich, if rumours were true, there was a more lax atmosphere, created by the gum chewing GIs, who knew the war was over and were affable and, in the main – apart from drunken brawls during leave – without resentment. There were the war trials, of course. When they started it might be different. Preparations in Nuremberg had been going on for quite some time – evidence gathered, witnesses found, international lawyers brought in, atrocities uncovered. What a way for it all to end, mused the young man. He had been in the Hitler Youth, then the army. Wounded in Russia, he had been invalided out, recuperated in the mountains and joined the police just after hostilities ceased. Again a new Germany had begun from the rubble of the old, and he was a part.

'Wachtmeister!' barked a voice. The young policeman, once an army officer, winced at his lowly rank, turned and snapped to attention as the fat Hauptmann approached stiffly, squeezing the last ounce of authority out of his buttons and insignia. He pointed across to the large building. Several people lingered outside, watching with curiosity as GIs drove up in trucks or Jeeps and came and went, some briskly, some sloppily.

'Move them on!' snapped the officer, referring to the small gathering. 'It's the Yanks' Red Cross Centre and we must ensure security outside, even if they do it within. Any of those people might have a grudge or . . .' he stopped himself. Why explain to the Wachtmeister? An order was sufficient. This was still Germany and rank was respected. Everyone obeyed an order. 'Now!'

The young policeman crossed the road to the old, converted beerhall and noticed that his presence was almost sufficient for most of the group to scuttle away. Only a woman with a child not more than seven stood silently watching the to-ing and fro-ing of the American uniforms.

'Move along,' said the Wachtmeister pleasantly. 'There's nothing for you here.'

The woman turned to him.

'I used to work here.'

She was attractive, with large eyes. The little boy, obviously her son, had a shock of black hair and a curiously mature expression. Wachtmeister Meyer noticed the tears appearing in the woman's eyes; some private tragedy no doubt. She was wearing a simple gold ring – perhaps she had lost her husband even as far back as the explosion he'd heard about in this once famous Burgerbraukeller. But such speculation was unprofessional, he had a job to do and became gentle but firm.

'Please . . . nothing for you here any more.' For a moment it seemed that Meyer looked into the woman's soul, as if he recognized her, and some strange impulse prompted him to ask the name of the boy, as he ruffled his hair.

'Peter,' answered the woman. Meyer smiled at the coincidence.

'And you?' he murmured as the couple turned to go.

'Annalise,' she answered.

'Nice name,' said Peter Meyer.

'And you?' asked the boy with Swabian bluntness.

'The same as yours,' came the reply. Annalise tugged at the reluctant hand as the boy stared up at the policeman.

'What's your daddy called?'

'Was . . . ' said Meyer, subdued by both the knowledge of his father's death and the cold eyes of the child. 'Otto.'

'Mine,' said the boy proudly, '*is* called Georg. Georg Elser.' For a moment the name seemed familiar to the young policeman.

'We're looking for him,' said the attractive woman quietly.

'I hope you're lucky,' responded Meyer.

'We'll be together,' smiled the woman confidently, 'soon.'

The young man was still searching his mind, but the war had dulled his memory, so he just smiled again and watched the mother and son walk away down the street. Only as they turned the distant corner did he remember, and his words came in a rush, 'Wait a minute!' he shouted and hesitated. But his voice was drowned by the clock in the square, chiming the hour. When it stopped, it was too late, they were gone.

304